The Scarlet Papers

Matthew Richardson studied English at Durham University and Merton College, Oxford. After a brief spell as a freelance journalist, he began working as a researcher and speechwriter in Westminster, and has also written speeches for senior figures in the private sector. He is the author of *My Name is Nobody* and *The Insider*.

The Scarlet Papers

MATTHEW RICHARDSON

MICHAEL JOSEPH

PENGUIN MICHAEL JOSEPH

UK | USA | Canada | Ireland | Australia
India | New Zealand | South Africa

Penguin Michael Joseph is part of the Penguin Random House group of companies
whose addresses can be found at global.penguinrandomhouse.com

First published by Penguin Michael Joseph, 2023
001
Copyright © Matthew Richardson, 2023

The moral right of the author has been asserted

Set in 14/16pt Palatino
Typeset by Jouve (UK), Milton Keynes
Printed and bound in Great Britain by Clays Ltd, Elcograf S.p.A.

The authorized representative in the EEA is Penguin Random House Ireland,
Morrison Chambers, 32 Nassau Street, Dublin D02 YH68

A CIP catalogue record for this book is available from the British Library

HB ISBN: 978–0–718–18345–5
OM ISBN: 978–0–718–18346–2

'Like one
Who having into truth, by telling of it,
Made such a sinner of his memory,
To credit his own lie'

William Shakespeare, *The Tempest*

PART ONE

1

It all started with the card.

Max looked at it again as the taxi neared Holland Park. It had been waiting in his office, sent through the internal university postal system and deposited among the usual confetti of flyers and coursework. It was one of those old-fashioned calling cards, like a prop from a period drama. The instructions were handwritten in light blue ink and were stylishly formed but brutally clear.

> *Tomorrow 11AM. Take a cab and pay in cash. Tell no one. Dry-clean thoroughly. Scarlet King. (PS ATLAS)*

If it had been any other card, on any other day, he would have binned it. But the name had stopped him. He looked at it now and almost mouthed the three syllables.

Scarlet King.

Yes, that wasn't a name dismissed lightly.

The taxi stopped abruptly, dodging a passing cyclist. The cabbie cursed, stabbing the radio off and leaning back. 'All right here, mate?'

'Thanks,' said Max. He took a crumpled twenty-pound note from his pocket and handed it over. 'Keep the change.'

'Ta.'

The cab pulled out and was soon snarled by

late-morning traffic. Max walked on and tried to focus, his head still elsewhere. Scarlet King was a legendary, almost mythical name in the intelligence community. Once upon a time, she'd been the top Russian expert at MI6 and even lined up to be the first female Chief. There was no public photograph available of her – which hadn't stopped numerous tabloids and broadsheets trying – and her name never appeared in government records. She was that tantalizing thing for all intelligence historians: a real-life ghost.

Why, of all people, would Scarlet King want to see him? Why today?

There was no mistake about the envelope either: 'Dr Max Archer, Associate Professor of Intelligence History, London School of Economics'. The address was written in a different hand from the card, black rather than blue. The card had arrived yesterday. Hence the fruitless last twenty-four hours trying to make sense of it all. Max had consulted library books and reference tomes and old papers to try and catch a glimpse of Scarlet's name: the post-war years, the mole-hunts of the sixties and seventies, Gorbachev and Thatcher, the fall of the Berlin Wall. But there was nothing.

Max picked up his pace, debating again whether this was some kind of trap. He'd heard all the scare stories. Who hadn't? The Russians and the Chinese were known to target academic conferences. The ritual was always the same: the complimentary wine, the fuzzy head, the blackmail footage and the threats to post it on YouTube, all horribly compromising and career-ending. But that was for physicists, geneticists and other high-value academics on the wish-list of Beijing and Moscow. What could the MSS or the SVR want with a forty-two-year-old intelligence historian?

No, he was almost sure this wasn't a trap. He pushed his nerves away, tried to focus.

Max took out the card again and paused over that penultimate line: *Dry-clean thoroughly*. It was spy speak for counter-surveillance, shrugging off a watcher. He'd spent a further hour in his office yesterday with a hard-copy map of West London trying to plot the route and feeling mildly ridiculous, a mid-career academic pretending to be a spook.

Now there was nothing for it. He decided to try the simplest method first. He bent down and pretended to tie his shoelace, allowing him vital seconds to map out who was around him. One elderly woman with a small dog. Two young men jogging with earbuds in. There was a traffic warden and, to complete the set, a young woman pushing a pram. Could one of them be a tail? The idea was ridiculous and yet somehow eerily plausible. Especially when Scarlet King was involved. Spies didn't advertise themselves. All of them could be threats, or none. Max finished retying the lace and then resumed walking. He spent the next few minutes glancing into shop windows, doubling back, turning suddenly into side streets and then – the final piece of showmanship – idling in a local newsagent and checking each person following him in, feeling even more ridiculous than before. By the time he arrived at the destination, he calculated that it had taken him nine and a half minutes for a walk that should have lasted two.

For once in his life, he was even slightly ahead of schedule.

He reached the address and saw the house. It was one of those stately London mansions now converted into flats, with its classical symmetry, fluted pillars and a sense of Edwardian glamour gone to seed, urgently in need of a repaint and a clean. He found the flat number on the right and pressed the silver buzzer.

The intercom crackled and echoed fuzzily: 'Hello?'

A woman's voice. Younger than he expected. Not Scarlet herself, then. A helper perhaps or a care worker. Max realized his palms were sweating. His throat felt like glue. He tried to shake off the nerves again and keep his head straight.

He thought back to that final flourish on the card: *(PS ATLAS)*. Over the last twelve hours, he'd skimmed every intelligence book – including his own – to see if it was the codename of some long-forgotten Cold War operation. Was Scarlet King teasing him with a clue of some kind, the legendary spymaster flaunting her tradecraft, or was this tailored to him specifically?

But he'd found nothing. He remembered one of his old academic mentors, a whiskery veteran who'd served on the frontline with SOE during the war.

Clever people make stupid spies.

Breathe, man.

'Mr Atlas,' he said, at last, praying it was correct. 'I believe you're expecting me.'

There was a moment of emptiness, the aftermath of a dog yapping nearby, and then a loud click as the door opened. 'Second floor,' said the voice. The intercom crackled into silence.

Max Archer checked around him for a final time, then pushed the front door open and took the stairs. When he arrived on the second floor, the flat door straight ahead was open. A petite woman of indeterminate age – thirtyish, perhaps, though with an older, weathered air about her – stood in the doorway. She had shoulder-length jet-black hair and thick-rimmed glasses, like a sixties revival band, Max thought, and then wondered if he was going mad.

He considered his errand. A strange flat, an obscure calling card, a woman he'd never met – this was insane, surely. He thought about running. He could ditch the card and forget all about this invitation. He could be back in his office in no time.

'Were you followed?' said the woman now.

Max walked inside, his feet moving faster than his head, and heard the flat door close behind him. 'No,' he said. 'I'm clean.'

'Good.' The woman attended to the door, sliding a bolt across the top and then setting an alarm with a passcode. She saw Max's surprise. 'Ms King is vigilant about her personal security. We can't be too careful.'

Max felt the first prickle of adrenaline. He could see it all now: the exclusive access to undiscovered secret papers, the eight-way book auction for the tell-all biography, the mini-series deal, an armful of literary prizes and then – twenty years in the making – the elevation to a full professorship. Spy history was all about scoops and access. It was the closest academia ever came to showbusiness. This could be his only chance.

'If you'll follow me, please.'

He took a deep breath and dried his palms against his trousers.

Showtime.

Despite possessing three degrees, Max Archer had been too busy looking for pavement artists to spot the A4 watchers on the top floor of the stuccoed house opposite. Few ever did notice A4 branch, which was just as intended. The man and woman, both mid-forties and casually dressed, finished uploading the photos of the target entering Number 12 and began cross-referencing his facial features against MI5's internal database.

By the time Max Archer was refusing tea or coffee inside the flat, the A4 team had found the Department for International History website at the London School of Economics. The faculty page was at least five years old and the photo showed a slimmer version of the target. But it was undeniably the same man: around six two, sandy-blond hair, a ruffled handsomeness, high forehead and a scruffily donnish dress sense. The nose, eyes and jawline showed a 92 percent match.

The faculty biography read:

Dr Max Archer
Associate Professor of Intelligence History
(BA MPhil Cantab, PhD Harvard)

Dr Archer is the author of *Double Agents: A History* (Viking) and *The Honourable Traitor: An Unauthorized Biography of Kim Philby* (Hodder & Stoughton). He is a regular contributor to the national press and served as historical consultant to the BBC documentary *The Cambridge Five*.

The two watchers confirmed the target name with Thames House and then prepared to vacate the property.

The time was 11.03 a.m.

Operation Tempest was officially in motion.

2

The first odd thing was the flat itself. They continued further down the corridor and Max noticed the modish decoration – the art on the walls, the mod cons in the kitchen. No, this was the flat of someone younger, not a woman in her nineties. He'd spent enough hours looking after his elderly father to know that the scent and spirit of old age lingered. He wondered if this was the woman's flat and Scarlet merely used it as some kind of safe house. Or whether Scarlet was landlord instead of tenant. Perhaps, once again, he was over-thinking things. After all, he knew next to nothing about Scarlet King. Was this woman her daughter? Did she have grandchildren? Husband, partner, or multiples of each? Spies haunted the shadows, enigmas even to their friends and family. Anything was possible.

They reached a sitting room at the end of the flat. The woman checked behind her, almost on instinct, then knocked lightly and opened the door. The sleeve of her sweater fell slightly to reveal a deep scar etched across the underside of her left arm, tracking from wrist to elbow. Max noted it and entered the room. His theory was confirmed now. There was a large flat-screen, iPads and laptops strewn around, the detritus of the twenty-first century. Then a small, elderly figure sitting in the middle of it all. Scarlet King looked like an anomaly in a high-backed chair by the coffee table, a leftover from a previous century.

'Scarlet,' said the woman, raising her voice only slightly. 'Mr Atlas has arrived.'

Max smiled as neutrally as he could. He looked at Scarlet and was surprised by how bird-like she was. There was a copy of *The Times* on her lap, still open at the crossword, and a pair of reading glasses perched sternly on her nose. Her skin was browned and crinkled, her hair a silvery-white thatch that was brushed backwards with immaculate symmetry and held in place thanks to an old-fashioned hair clip.

'I'll leave you to it,' said the woman. 'Call me if you need anything.'

Max wondered if the last remark was addressed to him. He thought about the scar on the woman's arm again and the various blades capable of slicing the skin like that. It didn't look like self-harm. That was a combat wound, surely, proper hand-to-hand fighting. Or perhaps he'd just watched too many Bond movies. He saw Scarlet nod and noticed the small bell placed beside the teacup and saucer on the table. Perhaps this was like an audience with the Queen: once she wearied of a guest, the signal was given. He had to make the seconds count.

'Sit down, please,' said Scarlet, indicating the armchair opposite. Her voice was stronger than he predicted, almost younger than the body it came out of. She smiled now. It was a spymaster's smile, Max knew, having seen copycat versions in all the former spooks he'd met. The smile charmed while exploiting. It had a venomous sincerity, like a weapon, teasing out secrets. Few were ever fully immune.

'It's an honour to meet you,' said Max, already regretting the oily forelock-tugging tone, but unable to take the words back. 'I was intrigued to get your card.'

He took the armchair opposite and was about to introduce himself fully – the whole '*Dr* Archer, LSE' routine – but stopped himself at the last minute. Scarlet reached down to the coffee table and picked up a single folded piece of paper. She adjusted her reading glasses and scanned the sheet again. Then, as if it were the most casual thing in the world, she said, 'You're about to get divorced, is that right?'

For a minute, Max was too stunned to respond. As his brain began functioning again, he wondered if he'd misheard. He smiled sheepishly and said, 'I'm sorry?'

Scarlet scanned the page with a clinical detachment. 'I see your wife is a senior partner at Simmons & Simmons and you're separating after twenty-one years of marriage. Now, tell me, why is that?'

Max was speechless. He looked to the door, then tried to listen for any nearby sound, wondering if this was some kind of practical joke. One of his colleagues, perhaps. For a moment, he considered how difficult would it be to hire an elderly actor, rent out a vacant apartment in Holland Park and then plant the card in his office. Gallows humour, yes, but academics were known for their vinegary, even acidic stunts. They would have caught all those counter-surveillance measures from the taxi. The shoe-tying, the zig-zagging route, laughing themselves hoarse at his self-delusion. The spy historian desperate for a scoop. He felt sick. Someone had put him up to this. The bastards.

'I'm sorry. But I don't understand.'

'Clearly,' said Scarlet. 'No children, either, which is interesting. Was that you or her? I would have said a conscious decision – two career-minded people – but your wife was one of four. Close to her siblings, too. Which means it's more likely to be biological.'

'What is this?' Max's voice was louder now. 'Who put you up to this?'

'My final guess is that it was an unhappy accident. She was too busy, your career was stalling, life happened while you were making other plans, then biology didn't oblige. Though I don't think that's the reason you're divorcing.'

She was serious. Max could see that now. He cursed himself for being so naïve. Scarlet King had served at the top of MI6. She'd spent her life finding the weak points of others. This wasn't a practical joke foisted on him by narrow-minded academic colleagues. This was a full-on spy interrogation.

'We tried early on,' said Max, at last, trying to keep his voice steady. It was time to either play along or storm out. And he needed this. For the sake of his bank balance, his academic prestige, his future life direction – boy, did he need this break. 'But it wasn't to be. We buried our sorrows in our respective careers and, well, life took its course.'

13

'Financial difficulties too, I see?'

Max knew he had to stay calm. This was a test. She was quizzing him like a potential asset. She wanted to know the measure of him, see how quick his temper was, how well he withstood pressure. 'A few cashflow issues, but only temporary.'

'She got the house and you're in a studio flat courtesy of an old friend.'

'You've been watching me?' said Max, an edge creeping into his voice.

Scarlet smiled again. 'I like to know who I'm dealing with.' She considered the piece of paper for a final time, then placed it back on the coffee table. Max desperately wanted to see what was written there. How did she know so much about his life? How could she know about his finances, Emma and the house? What else did she know? Was she inside his phone, laptop and work folders too?

'So, tell me,' she continued. 'Is that why you're really here? A quick buck, the tell-all book, middle finger to the ex-wife and school fees for the Archer family mark two?'

'No,' said Max, feeling almost undressed by these questions. It was as if she could peer through his pretensions, see into his soul. 'Well, not entirely.'

'Why are you here then? Do you often respond to odd calling cards from complete strangers telling you to arrive at equally odd locations?'

'No,' said Max. 'I came here because I've spent my professional life trying to understand what went on during the Cold War.'

'Ah, I see.' She looked like one of those old

Cambridge tutors unable to disguise their disappointment at the wrong answer; or, even worse, the mundane one.

Max tried to do better on the second go. 'Intelligence history isn't like other types of history,' he said. 'We don't have archives and secondary sources. All we have are eyewitnesses. You're the ultimate witness. Everyone else of your generation within SIS is dead. You know secrets that will die with you. I came here today because I want to ensure those secrets – those memories – don't die.'

She seemed more impressed now, a subtle liveliness around her eyes. 'But spies can never be relied on for the truth,' she said. 'You know that as well as I do. We spin lies for a living. Spies, my dear, are the ultimate unreliable narrators.'

Max could feel instinct taking over now. These were arguments he'd rehearsed with himself, pitches stored away for just this moment. 'Not always.'

'No?'

'Not in my experience. Death is the greatest truth serum ever devised.'

'How so?'

'Politicians have statues. Soldiers have memorials. Spies die unremembered.'

'Is that your answer?'

'Spies, you see, are just as vain as the rest of us,' said Max. 'They want a legacy, something their children can remember them by. That's why you asked me here. That's always why.'

There was a thoughtful pause, then Scarlet said, 'If I'm going to be open with you, Dr Archer,

I believe you owe me the same courtesy. So I'll ask again. Your lack of children might be one reason for your failed marriage. But I don't believe it's *the* reason. Why, then?'

From then on, Max would wonder how Scarlet managed it. She had that ability to spot lies without a symptom, a near faultless nose for half-truths and wriggly evasions. Others had perfect pitch or could memorize objects at a single glance. Scarlet King could read people. She had distance and empathy – a truly lethal combination.

'Is there always a single reason?'

'Tell me your secrets and I might tell you some of mine. Lie to me again and I won't. Quid pro quo.'

Max thought about attempting a small white lie, but he was an amateur here against a professional. She would spot the tell before the words left his mouth. He never did have much of a poker face. It was why he was still marooned in a lecture theatre rather than knee-deep in fieldwork. He sighed, and felt curiously emotional, as if he might spill all his darkest secrets to a total stranger.

'Why are you really here, Max?'

He composed himself. Then, at last, he forced the words out and said, 'My wife's getting remarried as soon as the divorce is through.'

Scarlet nodded contentedly. And, for a moment, Max wondered if she already knew. This was another test. 'She cheated on you?'

'Yes.'

'Is that all?'

Max hated her in that moment. She was like some of the therapists he had known decades ago, needling away until the most placid patient exploded. One more step, that's all. 'My ex-wife and her new man want to hold their wedding in October,' he said. 'Hence the quick divorce.'

'Why October?'

Later, Max would realize this was the moment Scarlet broke him. The last stage of recruitment, the point of no return. He had joined the long list of assets undone by this small, fragile, wispy figure armed with nothing more dangerous than words. It was a secret he had withheld from his own father and friends; a truth he'd so far refused to acknowledge even to himself.

His life, his marriage, his future.

Max swallowed painfully. 'My wife is getting remarried in October because their new baby's due in August,' he said. 'She finally got the family she always wanted.'

3

It was like an initiation. After that, there was a peculiar kind of intimacy between them. Scarlet knew his worst fears. The high-flying academic, the hotshot marriage, the ritzy book launches and North London semi – all of it was cover, an alias of epic proportions. Max Archer was childless, middle-aged and still correcting spellings in undergraduate essays while earning less than most of his former students. There were school newspapers that sold more copies than his last book, paper rounds with higher advances than he could now command. Scarlet King had stripped away the surface.

Max heard the old joke his father liked to trot out. He'd waited for a big break for so long that he'd gone broke instead. Now he had to watch another man take his place. He could already imagine Emma beaming from the latest round robin, her gap-toothed son or daughter dressed like the cast of *The Railway Children* at their obscenely expensive prep school, with news that Husband No. 2 was taking early retirement from the City and devoting himself to charity work. Even the faculty nicknames from those stuck-in-the-mud academics would get worse: 007, Dr Evil, Austin Powers. Spy history was fun at twenty; mildly embarrassing at forty-five; downright tragic at sixty.

It was then that it happened. Max glanced round

the room again, convinced the entire adventure had been a dreadful mistake, when Scarlet reached down to her left and withdrew a large sheaf of paper from a Gladstone bag beside the armchair. The papers had a yellowed, tea-stained quality to them and billowed out uncontrollably, almost incapable of staying still.

Scarlet stared at Max, and then said, 'A deal's a deal, Dr Archer. You've told me your secret, now it's time to tell you mine.' She handed the papers across to him. 'Why don't you take a look at these?'

Max took the papers. Scarlet nodded for him to examine them. He was used to handling sensitive archival documents with gloves, careful to avoid sweat or moisture corroding the pages. He rubbed his palms against his trouser legs, then gently turned the pages.

The first thing he saw was that all the pages were scans of a notebook, the sort of handouts he gave to students during seminars when introducing them to archival documents. The script was hurried and practical, written in a sloping hand and dark blue ink. In places it was faded and in others the ink had been refreshed. Most of all, however, he saw the dates scattered at the top of the second page: '1946'. This was a diary or memoir of some kind, then.

He turned back and looked at the very first paragraph. He started reading:

It was on her fifth day at the Vienna Station that Scarlet King saw the target for the first time. They had decamped to the bunker, as always, the

19

sound-proofed secure room with its funny wall-padding and dry-as-dust acoustics. Archie Grenville lit a cigarette and failed to offer her one.

'Memorize this face,' Archie said, sliding across a single photograph.

Scarlet would always remember the moment when she first saw Otto Spengler's face . . .

Max looked up at Scarlet, failing to hide his confusion.

'This sounds like the story of an operation.'

'Well observed.'

'A novel?'

'No. A memoir.'

Max looked back at the page. 'In the third person? She not I.'

'I'm a spy, Dr Archer. Spies never use the first person. Consider it a form of cover. If it's good enough for Mr Rushdie, it's good enough for me.'

Max was familiar with the reference. The novelist Salman Rushdie had famously written a memoir called *Joseph Anton* using the third person; the name was his alias while in hiding from an Iranian fatwa and under strict police protection. David Cornwell, once a low-level MI6 officer, hid behind the pseudonym John le Carré. The former MP Rupert Allason wrote juicy real-life spy books under the name Nigel West. Yes, there was precedent.

He tried another angle. 'SIS officers aren't allowed to write diaries, memoirs or any kind of autobiography.'

'No.'

'The very existence of these papers breaks the Official Secrets Act in every possible way. You could get jail time for this.'

'Possibly,' she said, almost matter-of-factly, as if the thought had already been debated.

'How possibly?'

'The lawyers would have to prove that the "she" in question was me. That would involve SIS revealing all the operations I worked on. Scarlet King could be a dramatic creation. As I said, the third person is a form of cover.'

Max almost laughed. It was known in media circles as the 'Lorraine Kelly defence'. The Scottish TV presenter had successfully avoided paying HMRC back-taxes by claiming that 'Lorraine Kelly' was an on-screen persona and therefore not related directly to herself as a private individual. It was certainly a novel way of getting round the Official Secrets Act.

'By handling the material, of course,' she said, 'you also become complicit. How do you fancy your chances inside?'

Max was suddenly conscious again of fingerprints and the lack of gloves. His prints – or 'dabs', as his colleagues in the Criminology department liked to call them – were all over the papers now, impossible to completely erase. Trace evidence would be in this flat, too, and it was possible he'd been picked up on CCTV during the approach. Yes, more than possible. He was already compromised.

'Where's the original?'

'The notebook is stored far away from here under

lock and key. That is a scanned copy of the first section.'

'There's more than one section?'

'I've lived a long life, Dr Archer. My story has many sections.'

'Do you have any idea how dangerous this could be?'

'Yes,' she said. 'By your research record, I think you do too. Why else do you think I chose you?'

Max looked at her. Of course. Nothing about this meeting – from the calling card to this house – had been accidental. Everything had been planned with a spymaster's precision, including the target profile. Max's PhD had been on the fate of spies who went public. The thesis was still available online; no doubt Scarlet knew it by heart. It examined the case of Richard Tomlinson, a former SIS officer, sent to Belmarsh in the nineties for breaching the Official Secrets Act and attempting to publish an autobiography. But Tomlinson was a junior errand boy. Scarlet King was espionage royalty. No one of her seniority had ever gone public before.

'This is madness.'

'On the contrary. It's the sanest thing to do at my age. Logic at its most elegantly rational.'

'You're prepared to go to prison?'

'I'm prepared to die, Dr Archer. Death is far more frightening than prison.'

Max was still holding the papers. He knew he should put them down, limit the contamination. But he was too shocked to think. 'Was this memoir written at the time or after the fact?'

'Does it matter?'

'If I'm going to be part of a criminal act against Her Majesty's Government, then I like to know what I'm dealing with. How do I even know it's genuine?'

'You don't.'

'Why now?'

'I'm in my nineties. Now seems as good a time as any. Russia is once again our greatest adversary. The world needs my help again. Everyone could learn some lessons from the Cold War. And I am the ultimate cold warrior.'

Now the focus was turned back on her. Max almost enjoyed the role reversal. He pressed home his temporary advantage. 'No. That's not it.'

'You sound worryingly sure.'

'I am. Spies are human beings. You're not doing this for others. The risk is too high.'

'No. Why, then?'

'The three Ls. It's what I teach my students. Lust, Lucre, Loathing.'

'I see. So, in your thesis, which is it? I'm rather past my sell-by date for lust. Loathing seems plausible, if rather pointless at my grand old age.'

'Lucre, then. Your funds have run dry. This is a chance to help the grandkids get a foot on the property ladder. You bank the big advance and pop your clogs, then I'm left facing prosecution with nothing to show for it. The perfect crime.'

'Is that really what you think of me?'

'You're a spy,' said Max. 'Once a spy, always a spy. I barely know the first thing about you. I don't know what to think.'

'True,' said Scarlet. She took off her reading glasses and polished them against her cardigan, waiting until they were spotless. 'Welcome to the secret world. Do you roll the dice or do you walk away? Is this gold dust or chickenfeed?' She put her glasses back on and smiled. 'The choice, Dr Archer, is entirely down to you.'

4

The weather was filthy and showed no sign of brightening. Saul Northcliffe tried to duck another greyish gob of rain as he scuttled along the slick pavements, wending his way through a crowd of tourists sheltering under a group umbrella.

It was funny how quickly the view changed. Parliament Square looked regal and golden, the Palace of Westminster rising up like some mythic fortress guarding the ancient seat of power. Whitehall itself was classical and almost Roman in its nobility, a symmetrical parade of fine buildings that hummed silently, the nerve centre of a mid-ranking global power. Yet only a few minutes away was Millbank and the dirty churn of the Thames. It was a world of litter and concrete: the buildings all looked menacing, the bus stops scrawled with graffiti, and the two bastions of British intelligence – MI6 and MI5 – duelled glumly across the riverbank.

SIS's lair, Saul always thought, looked like a reject design from a bad eighties Bond film. Thames House, the Security Service's headquarters, should by rights have been the watering hole of some misbegotten government agency or quango, the realm of Ofcom or the Environment Agency, a bureaucratic wilderness of open-plan offices and the soulless clack of keyboards.

No, Thames House was hardly the stuff of the

movies. Saul could still see himself in the industrial soot and grime of his childhood, a regional escapee dreaming of the secret service with its promise of beaches, cocktails, tailored suits and liquid lunches in clubland. Irony, was that the technical term? His stomach growled and he took out a half-eaten cereal bar from his pocket, munching on it wearily. He ducked right for the private entrance to Thames House and thought he could hear fate chuckling at him. That line came to him again: *as flies to wanton boys are we to th' gods / They kill us for their sport*. He checked his personal mobile and saw a WhatsApp message from his wife reminding him to pick up some spaghetti on the way home. He docked his mobile, went through security, and then took the lift to the sixth floor.

Five more years. That was the figure in his mind, as he stepped out and headed towards his office. At least he had an office. He'd listened to the horror stories from GCHQ where even the Director now was expected to slum it in open-plan and put their hand up for the tea round. Five years and then he would have his pension. He could forget the sweaty commute and keep his brain working with the odd consultancy job with half the work and twice the pay. Now, though, he forced himself to bury the thoughts; the days in captivity seemed to lengthen every time he dreamed of freedom.

He'd hoped for a quiet hour to get through some admin. But Saul saw one of the fast trackers hovering nervously outside his office door. She looked young enough to still be in school, about the same age as his eldest daughter. Casual, too, as everyone in this place seemed to be now. All scuffed sneakers with the laces tailing, slouchy jumpers and a creative array of personal ornaments. Saul could still remember the Head of Personnel upbraiding him during his first week for failing to polish his shoes properly. Perhaps his wife and daughters were right: he really was becoming a bore.

Now to remember her name, a more perilous exercise than it used to be. Once upon a time a junior intelligence officer would answer to anything when a Deputy Director addressed them. Saul had spent three long years in the eighties being addressed as Paul. He delved deep now. Shoulder-length blond hair, medium height. Charlotte, at a guess, or was it Vicky?

'Ah, there you are,' said Saul, switching his smile to full wattage, as if he'd been waiting for this moment all day. Gender-neutral, not name-specific, perfect. 'How are you?'

Charlotte, yes. He was sure that was it.

'There's a stomach bug going around,' she said. 'I've avoided it so far. Fingers firmly crossed.'

That was another thing with the newbies. Back in his day, Saul still called some of the senior managers sir. Now they treated you like a guidance counsellor or therapist. 'Good to know,' he said. 'Let's hope so.'

Saul unlocked his office and ushered Charlotte inside. Thinking about it, of course, that was another thing he wouldn't miss. The Security Service currently employed over four thousand people, piling in each morning from all corners of Greater London and the commuter towns. There was never a day when some bug, cold or other ailment wasn't circulating rapidly through the hallway. Five years. 1,825 days. Then liberation.

Saul shook the rain from his coat and hung it up. The office was cramped and box-like. There wasn't even a decent window in case some foreign intelligence service tried to sneak a look at his computer screen with a long-lens camera. He referred to it as the cave, though even caves felt more homely. There was an ever-present staleness – a combination of mouldy takeaways and dust – that no amount of air freshener ever quite erased.

'What do you have for me?' said Saul, as he settled in behind his desk and whirred his computer to life. Thirty-two unread emails, including one from the Director-General. He deleted the overtures from HR and the round robins from the social secretaries – the MI5 staff choir, film club and athletics society – and then opened the first email from the DG.

'We have some further developments on Operation Tempest,' said Charlotte, producing a manila file and placing it on his desk. 'A Branch got some good close-ups of a target visiting the premises under surveillance. They've identified him as an academic from the London School of Economics.'

The missive from the DG concerned a media problem. *The Times* was set to publish an article tomorrow criticizing the intelligence services for failing to stop a recent terror attack. The DG had responded robustly to the editor and copied in the DDGs and comms. Saul imagined the newspaper editor in his far larger office, fresh from a three-course lunch with a cabinet minister, tinkering with tomorrow's leader column before being chauffeured to dinner then back to the mews house in South West London. He cursed the world and then clicked off the message.

'Remind me?' he said, picking up the briefing file. 'Operation Tempest was an SIS referral, yes?'

Charlotte nodded. 'Vauxhall Cross think a former Sovbloc Controller might be responsible for the recent leaks regarding UK policy against Moscow. They asked us to keep an eye on things in case it escalates. We started some low-level watcher engagement several weeks ago.'

Saul saw the photo of Scarlet King and then the surveillance photos and the print-out of Max Archer's profile. Ah, yes, Operation Tempest. Various unflattering pieces, though suspiciously well-briefed, had appeared in the *Guardian* alleging intelligence failures surrounding the death of Russian nationals on UK soil. The unnamed source had disclosed classified details about the original Cold War operations. Scarlet King was a possible source. Not just a veteran, but a certified legend of the secret world. The most prominent woman in the history of MI6. Saul remembered the face all too well.

So they want us to do their dirty work, he thought. Technically, British legislation stopped SIS undertaking intelligence operations on the UK mainland or British Overseas Territories. They gladly shunted all such tasks on to Thames House or GCHQ. In reality, it allowed the SIS prima donnas to do the glamorous wining and dining on the embassy circuit while Five was lumbered with the uglier legwork.

Saul looked through a summary of Max Archer's publications. 'Is there any sign that Scarlet might have known Dr Archer prior to this?'

'No. I've gone back through all the files. I can't find any trace. This appears to be the first time they've ever met.'

'What about Archer's books? Are they credible?'

'I've skim-read both on Kindle. It looks like he was trying to start a career as a media don. He knows his stuff and specializes in Cold War history. Not bad, as they go.'

Saul finished browsing the file. All verifiable information went into the file. The sort that could be footnoted and double-sourced. Non-verifiable information – single-sourced rumours, chatter from sources, street-level gossip and innuendo – was delivered verbally. The intelligence community had been badly scarred over the WMD fiasco. Nothing went in print for a politician unless it was iron-clad.

'What about chatter?'

'I checked with HR and looked through some old recruitment files. I found two things. First, Max Archer's father served as a NOC under journalistic cover throughout the Cold War, mainly in central Europe. Second, Max Archer applied to join MI6 after graduating from Cambridge and was considered for IONEC.'

The Intelligence Officers' New Entry Course. The six-month training ritual for all new MI6 officers at

Fort Monckton in Gosport. They were schooled in tradecraft, psy-ops, secret writing, basic weaponry and the elusive art of charming, recruiting and running an asset in denied areas.

'Why was he rejected?'

'The files are patchy and non-digitized. But from the recruiter reports it seems Archer was considered too individual and creative. The application was vetoed personally by the chair of the recruitment board. It was also the early noughties, just after 9/11. The Service was trying to diversify and recruit officers with fluent Arabic who could work in the Middle East.'

'A dad in the business and a Cambridge education,' said Saul. 'Not much of a poster-boy for diversity.'

'That too.'

'What's your assessment of the situation?'

Charlotte appeared more nervous now, as if she'd rehearsed the answer, eager to get it right. 'I've gone through Dr Archer's list of recent op-eds. He's not the sort of person you brief if you just want a few stories in the broadsheets. Anyway, if Scarlet is behind the recent leaks, she has her own contacts. Dr Archer must be for something different.'

'How is Scarlet King doing financially?'

'She owns a flat in Chelsea and has substantial investments.'

'She's not hunting for money then. Anything else?'

'I tried to get Scarlet King's full service record from Vauxhall Cross, but they wouldn't budge. All we have is the redacted version. They won't even provide it to strap three or above. I mentioned this had DDG approval.'

Typical SIS. It had been a century now, but they still viewed the Security Service as over-promoted policemen, there to do their housekeeping without the necessary information. Saul sat back and steepled his hands, swivelling gently in his office chair. He thought back to the *Times* article forwarded by the DG. Yet again, MI5 seemed to be the whipping boy for all the nation's ills. Saul was sick of it: the broadsheets, the River House, the cosy establishment club. Yes, there would be a certain satisfaction in turning the spotlight on the other side of the river for once. Catching a former MI6 officer spilling their story to a civilian and leaking to the media. Rather too satisfying to pass by.

He had an idea.

'We're going to move Operation Tempest to the next level,' he said, feeling newly invigorated. 'Get everything ready for a SIGINT request to the Home Office. We need to know why Scarlet King is cosying up to Max Archer and what they intend to do together. This needs priority access. If we don't go now, it could be too late.'

'What should I tell Vauxhall Cross?'

Saul smiled. 'This is a Security Service operation,' he said. 'Tell them nothing.'

The SIGINT request was sent that afternoon via secure channels from Thames House to 2 Marsham Street, the glassy headquarters of the Home Office, marked urgent. Twenty minutes later, the Director of National Security, Jo Harris, had drawn up the paperwork and was heading across Westminster to New Palace Yard, the entry-point for all vehicles to the Palace of Westminster. She was waved through by the armed members of Parliamentary and Diplomatic Protection guarding the main gates. Within the hour, she was waiting in the parliamentary office of the Home Secretary behind the Speaker's Chair in the Old Palace.

The Rt Hon Lucas Harper MP, Secretary of State for the Home Department, returned from a bruising two-hour session in the Commons chamber, trying to defend another cock-up from border patrol. He smiled on seeing Jo and gratefully accepted his favourite pick-me-up: weapons-grade black coffee with some extra-thick cream stirred in, the ingredients always kept on-hand.

Lucas took a seat and loosened his tie. He said, 'You know, when the PM asked me to do this job, I actually thought it was a promotion.'

Jo smiled. 'At least you get the bullet-proof car.'

'Just a shame about the political death sentence.' He took a long gulp of the coffee. 'Please tell me you're not the bearer of more bad news. What have our compadres at the Security Service done this time? Left the nuclear codes on a train?'

'Alas, no.' She pushed the documentation across the table towards him. 'They want your authorization on a SIGINT request against a British national. They believe the target could be collaborating with a former SIS operative named Scarlet King.'

Lucas glanced up sharply at the name. '*The* Scarlet King?'

'Yes.'

'The former Sovbloc Controller who handled the Mitrokhin Archive and knows more state secrets than most former Prime Ministers.'

'Quite.'

'What are they asking for?'

'Renewal on the King permission and one new request. An academic from the LSE, apparently. Thames House think they could be planning something.'

Lucas reviewed the documentation. 'And you're positive I'm not going to be accused of letting the Stasi loose on an innocent British don?'

'The Security Service clearly thinks the risk is high,' said Jo. 'They need your authorization within the hour.'

'You didn't answer my question.'

'It was a political question. I can only give a civil service answer.'

Lucas had the pen in his hand, poised over the document. 'The spooks will keep it tasteful though, yes? No over-reach or personal probing.'

'They'll take every necessary precaution, Minister.'

Lucas yawned wearily, then signed the document. He closed the folder and slid it back. 'The risk is high all the same,' he said, glancing at his watch. 'Don't let them muck this up. Scarlet King and the grey lobby after me is all I bloody need.'

There was a knock on the door and one of the private secretaries walked in juggling briefing folders. Lucas's personal protection detail waited to ferry him to his next meeting.

'I'll keep you updated,' said Jo.

There was a flicker of anxiety again in Lucas's expression, then it was gone. 'Thank you.'

The group departed with the usual whirl of activity. Jo packed up her things and then headed back to Marsham Street. By 4.30 p.m. MI5 received the authorization.

Operation Tempest moved to its second phase.

5

Max returned to the office in a daze. The International History department based near Lincoln's Inn Fields was an anomaly at the best of times. Outside was the smooth veneer of corporate London – the tasteful townhouse headquarters of PR firms, boutique law outfits, the fund managers with their anonymous names and tieless employees. On his daily commute Max could almost believe he was part of it. That he'd taken a different turn after that careers fair at Cambridge and become a banker, analyst or spin-doctor. Instead, as he entered the building, he inhaled the familiar smell of all universities: an institutional mustiness peppered with over-loud deodorant, not quite as bad as school but not far off. It was terminally adolescent, somehow, and mildly unwashed.

Not to mention the Soviet-style decoration. There was the all-pervasive colour that could only be catalogued as 'suicide vanilla' and the underfloor texture that was neither carpet nor stone, merely an adhesive speckly concoction that seemed unique to British establishments of higher education. He'd barely thought of tradecraft on the journey back. The odd zigzag, perhaps, stepping on and off a bus or two, but his mind was fried. He'd walked inside that flat in Holland Park with visions of a publishing sensation. He left with omens of lifelong incarceration. He couldn't even afford a decent lawyer. He'd be reliant on legal aid, some cut-price junior with zero knowledge of the intelligence world who would huff and puff and persuade him to plead guilty.

'Ah, Maximillian.'

The voice was low, gravelly, like an old edition of *Desert Island Discs*. And the sartorial choices only enhanced the image: a polka-dotted red bow tie, a chalk-stripe suit and a pair of scuffed Hush Puppies. Max turned reluctantly and saw Sir Vernon Kessler, Head of the International History department, approaching down the corridor. It was as if someone had taken the brief 'eccentric history don' and constructed it rather too literally. Despite the establishment acoustics, Sir Vernon – or Professor Sir Vernon, as he preferred to style himself – had graduated from youthful Marxism to middle-aged socialism and was now a Bollinger Bolshevik of the first order, famed for his extensive wine cellar and marrying into old money. His eldest son was in his last year at St Paul's.

'Vernon.'

'Tut tut. Why am I hearing complaints about cancelled seminars?'

Max knew he should have prepared a better answer. It was the spy's first rule: always attend to the basics. 'Emergency dentist appointment. The only time they could fit me in. Total pain, I know, but there we go.'

Kessler was closer now, emitting a faint odour of claret. 'Health matters are for personal time, Max, as you well know. I'm not paying you to skive off the job.'

Max wondered how long Vernon's liquid lunch had been today. He usually favoured one of the grander hotels, entertaining a visiting scholar and so able to put the whole thing on expenses. 'Lesson learned, Vernon.'

'Next thing it'll be all over Twitter. Then we'll have the parents up in arms. Before you know it, the Vice-Chancellor will be breathing down our necks. Rumours spread and suddenly the next board meeting is like heading into the Somme.'

'It won't happen again.'

'Isn't one of your students related to the Deputy Editor of the *Mail*?'

'*Telegraph*, I think. And Assistant to the Deputy Editor.'

'Exactly. We can't be too careful. You do know the internal promotions board casts a keen eye over student assessment marks?'

Right then, right here, Max wanted to confess to the whole thing and tell him about Scarlet King and the card. But Vernon had contacts high up in the MoD. Plus, the department would suspend Max for even entertaining the idea. Breaking the Official Secrets Act, handling illegal documents, bringing the full wrath of the Home Office on their heads – no, there was only one way that discussion would end.

'I'll rearrange the two seminars and add extra office hours to catch up,' he said.

'That's what I like to hear. How's the new book going?'

Max felt his spirits slump further. The question had haunted him for too many years to remember. His last book had been published five years ago, the half-decade since consumed by a failed marriage and childlessness. Max had endless files on his laptop marked 'Book 3'. Each began with a spurt of enthusiasm and then puttered out.

'It's ticking along,' he said, eager to get to his office. 'I might have a paper to show you shortly.'

'Good.' Vernon looked uneasy now. 'Look, I was sorry to catch wind about the whole marriage business. I was always fond of your good lady wife. Pity you couldn't keep hold of her, hey. Let me know if there's anything I can do.'

Yes, thought Max, there is one thing: you can die. Die now and free up the Head of Department position. Or retire with immediate effect and nominate me as your successor. But he merely smiled. 'Thank you, Vernon.'

'Well, mustn't stand chuntering. Things to do.'

Max saw Vernon shuffle off and looked at his mobile again. There was another hostile email from Emma about the fact he still hadn't signed some final bit of paperwork. He deleted it, then headed gratefully to his office and locked the door. He glanced at the ceiling as if there might be cameras there and wondered if he was being too paranoid. Then he remembered what Scarlet King had told him. He checked the door was locked, turned off his mobile and made sure his PC and iPad were off. No digital eyes at all. He was clean.

Finally, Max unzipped his rucksack and took out the sheaf of papers. He thought of the original notebook still in Scarlet's possession and wondered where she'd stashed it. A further meeting with Scarlet had been arranged – along with suitably convoluted tradecraft – and Max was to give his definite answer then.

He smoothed the pages with his palm. Then he thought about the deleted email from Emma, feeling that familiar pain claw at his belly. Perhaps history happened by accident. If they'd been able to have children, if he hadn't buried himself in work, if Emma hadn't toiled every weekend of their married life, if his resentment at a stalled career hadn't festered until he became someone different. But counterfactuals were useless. History was just hindsight after the facts. What was that Alan Bennett line? *History is just one bloody thing after another.* It was often hard to disagree.

Max checked the time and then prepared himself. He looked down at the papers and prayed for some anomaly. The wrong date, a misplaced timeline, any of the usual signs that a document like this was a blatant forgery. That, surely, was the easiest route out of this. The spy world, like special forces, was riddled with convincing liars. He'd interviewed people who proudly claimed they worked behind enemy lines or parachuted into occupied France – the tale replete with nuggety detail and idiosyncratic nuance – before a basic check exploded the entire tale. Perhaps this was an elaborate hoax.

Max Archer breathed deeply. Then he started reading.

*

MI5's A Branch were nicknamed 'the Watchers' and lived by one golden rule: don't get caught. A4, a sub-section of the Watchers, specialized in black bag jobs, including planting listening devices in embassies and concealed inside diplomatic vehicles. The team were often recruited direct from the military – preferably either Royal Marine Commandos, Paras or special forces – and favoured regular soldiers to the officer class.

A4's primary skill was visual assimilation, an optical trick that stopped witnesses ever remembering specific details. Their favoured disguise was the building team, plumbing crew, removal outfit or smart-meter installers tramping shamelessly through private property.

The rest of Thames House kept their identities secret from the outside world. A Branch kept secrets even from their own.

The target profile for the second phase of Operation Tempest was drawn up and the bugging op divided into three stages. The first team staked out the studio flat in Fulham, which the target was currently renting at a below-market price courtesy of an old university friend. The team entered the property by the rear entrance disguised as plumbers and picked the lock for Flat 15 within a minute. The rest was routine. Small dots originally developed at Hanslope Park in Buckinghamshire, the technical hub for all three major services, were installed in the ceiling lights of the bedroom, kitchen and living space. Some for audio, some for visuals. The bathroom was fitted with bugs in the mirror, showerhead and towel rail. Sound quality was checked as was signal strength. CCTV later showed the five-strong A4 team exiting the rear entrance after nine minutes. No face was ever subsequently identified.

The second team staked out the department building at Lincoln's Inn Fields and clocked the target leaving his office at 22:06. Posing as night-shift cleaners, the A4 team had the small office covered within three minutes. They also planted spyware in the office PC, a bug on the landline receiver and two further devices by the bookcase. To ensure blanket coverage, they fitted devices in the Senior Common Room and staff toilets.

The final destination was by far the trickiest. The target profile showed that a Mr Oliver Archer, born 1937 and once upon a time serving under non-official cover for SIS as part of the news agency Reuters, was currently resident at Trinity Care Home outside Lambeth. The target was believed to visit his father twice a month. The care home had over a hundred residents and was staffed 24/7.

After much discussion, the A4 team received permission to pose as council workers carrying out a flash inspection. But that was as simple as it got. The complications piled up: a death in the home overnight, residents confined to their rooms and the presence of two real council workers on another errand.

On Saul's order, the physical op was pulled and replaced by the back-up option of direct cyber action instead. From the minute the receptionist clicked on a link regarding health and safety proto-col, every PC and device within Trinity Care Home was weaponized. Not perfect, far from it in fact, but usable for now. They would be able to monitor when Dr Max Archer visited the home and install HUMINT sources as required.

It was only much later that any of the devices were found in situ by a cleaner, but they received little mention in either the broadsheet or tabloid press. They were soon disposed of by a visiting team, again dressed in council uniforms. The cleaner in question – an Estonian male in his mid-twenties – later received a letter from the Home Office confirming that his application for permanent residence had been accepted and inviting him to apply for a passport, no strings attached.

Neither the cleaner nor the council team were ever seen on the premises again.

The Scarlet Papers
1946

1946
The Target

It was on her fifth day at the Vienna Station that Scarlet King saw the target for the first time. They had decamped to the bunker, as always, the sound-proofed secure room with its funny wall-padding and dry-as-dust acoustics. Archie Grenville lit a cigarette and failed to offer her one.

'Memorize this face,' Archie said, sliding across a single photograph.

Scarlet would always remember the moment when she first saw Otto Spengler's face. The photo showed a youngish man in his thirties with a brush of thinning hair and meaty cheeks. His eyes, though, seemed intelligent and piercing, quite distinct from the bulldog scowl around his mouth. There was something contradictory about him even then, a poet's soul in a gladiator's body.

'Dr Otto Spengler,' said Archie. 'The primary target for Operation Hercules. Dr Spengler is the golden boy of German science, one of the best bio-chemists in the world. He has a first-class academic trail and numerous prizes. He disappeared from sight in 1941 for undisclosed war work. According to our latest intelligence, however, he's currently hiding in Vienna using the alias "Richard von Braun".'

Archie glared at her, as he did with all the under-lings, with that headmasterly frown. He was tall and prematurely stooped, like an oak tree. Yes, Scarlet could quite see what the others had meant by the old soldier description. His hair was greased back and his suit needed mending. He had a weak voice, almost reedy, and he coughed away nerves, reaching for a soiled handkerchief and blowing loudly. His official title was Deputy Head of Station; but he seemed to run things here, the NCO bellowing gruffly at the troops. Deference, surely, was the best way to play him.

'A Nazi?'

'A German. Not always the same thing. Your job is to turn Dr Spengler and get him to work for us.'

'What's his background?'

'Top of his year at Friedrich Wilhelm University in Berlin where he studied under three Nobel laureates and completed a doctorate within two years. His services are currently being sought by both the Soviets and the Americans. For now, only *we* know about his alias. That gives us a minuscule advantage which must be fully exploited.'

'What about his current whereabouts?'

Archie slid across two further photos showing Dr Otto Spengler leaving a small, run-down flat complex and then entering a café. 'His downfall is a Teutonic regard for routine,' he said. 'Dr Spengler lunches at the Café Landtmann on a daily basis at about 1.30 p.m., which means he believes his cover is strong enough to see off any unwelcome advances.'

She stared at the three photos again, contrasting them all, noticing how the young scowler from the first had morphed into the emaciated figure in the second and third. Otto Spengler seemed to have aged decades in only a few years. He had a wispy moustache and floppier hair. His face was hollowed out. The beady eyes were all that remained.

'What did he do during the war?'

'Whatever he did, it's well above your clearance levels, Miss King. Your studies at Oxford were in Modern Languages, I hear?'

'Yes.'

'Use your scientific ignorance to lure him in. Your task is to establish an observation post and work up an assessment of the asset. I want a full log of his movements, habits, friends, political views, anything you can find to build up a background profile.'

'And after that?'

'Once I've reviewed your assessment, then you will prepare for "the bump".'

Scarlet thought of her training at Arisaig House. She could hear the Groundskeeper drilling them in those tradecraft sessions as they were schooled in the declensions and vocabulary of this new secret world. The 'bump' was jargon for an engineered recruitment meeting between a case officer and a potential asset. It would be her first attempt at serious tradecraft in the field.

'What are we recruiting him as? A long-term asset or some kind of fellow traveller?'

Archie sighed, as if dealing with an uppity child. He glanced at his pocket watch then at a small cluster of damp in the ceiling, dreaming of the reality he'd left behind. For a moment, Scarlet could imagine Archie as a minor public-school headmaster or prosperous tenant farmer; yes, or perhaps something vaguely mathematical. He would be married to a stout and solid woman, perhaps a sprinkling of squarish children. Like so many, his past had been erased by war, now bluffing his way through with mock-soldierly contempt.

'None of the above,' he said now. 'The time for complex agent networks is over. We've missed the boat by some distance. The Americans and Russians got there before us. You are to invite Otto Spengler to the Epsilon safe house within the next five days for extraction by T-Force. Do that, and I'll send you back to Broadway with medals and commendations.'

Archie slid across the last photo showing a small safe house flat on the outskirts of the city alongside a map. Even the safe houses had codenames: Alpha, Beta, Gamma, Delta, Epsilon.

Scarlet glanced at the photo and the map. 'He'll suspect something. I need longer.'

'Broadway want us to move Dr Spengler to Britain. They badly need his knowledge of chemical and biological warfare. If we wait any longer, he'll be snatched. Five days is all you have.'

'I see.'

Archie pressed both palms against the edge of the table. 'Otto Spengler is our way back into the game. You're new, green and far from my first choice for this mission. It's this or masterminding the tea trolley at Broadway. Are we clear?'

'I'll find a way.'

'Good.'

And, despite everything, Scarlet almost liked

Archibald Grenville in that moment. Somehow he reminded her of her father, a man she hadn't seen for so long. There was a flicker of vulnerability tucked just beneath the surface.

They were about to leave the bunker and return to the din of the main office when Archie paused at the door. 'Yesterday we were fighting these people. Now we're trying to get them to work with us. Makes no more sense to me than you. Either way, we're all just following orders.'

He left the bunker and Scarlet watched him march away with that rigid soldierly stride. She picked up the photos and stared at the target again.

Dr Otto Spengler. Her new joe.

1946
The Bump

Another day, another alias. The briefing file was complete. The authorization given. Today she was no longer Scarlet King. No, this morning – or was it afternoon? – she was an Austrian journalist, 'Isabel Charlemont', with a native fluency and a fledgling journalism career. There were so many lies they almost became true.

As she prepared for the bump, Scarlet dispensed with all those outward signs of Englishness. Gone was any sense of stodge or artlessness. She must appear more continental, less frowsy and angular. The secret war, the scientific struggle, depended on that. Spying was a performance and the costume, the voice, the initial entrance were as vital as the lines themselves.

It was just after midday when she arrived outside Café Landtmann and found her usual spot opposite. This served as the improvised observation point. She had already clocked the target's rhythms. Today, in particular, she looked for any kind of watcher detail. Pedestrians circling backwards, loiterers hiding behind newspapers, women with buggies or old men dressed as road sweepers or officials. An hour or more drifted by until her brain and eyes became tired under the relentless concentration. So far, she spotted nothing to suggest the operation was compromised. She noted all the human scenery and vowed to check again on the way out.

It was 1.34 p.m., to be exact – slightly later than yesterday – when the figure from the photo burst into three dimensions. Scarlet was well enough hidden on the opposite side of the road to avoid being seen. Each day he surprised her. He was bigger than the photo suggested. He looked squat and almost tubular in the photos; he was lanky and somehow thinly perpendicular in real life, a hangdog droop to his stride pattern.

Dr Spengler walked like a man still learning how to use his legs, as if the limbs might detach at any moment. He wore a threadbare coat and his spectacles looked misty. His collar was smeared with blood – from shaving, presumably – and, like most people in the city, there was a general air of dishevelment. He didn't look rich but, as per the previous days, seemed to be accepted warmly by the waiters and shown to his usual small two-seater table in the corner. Scarlet wondered how he afforded it. His file suggested a moderately well-off Berlin banking family. Perhaps he had enough stashed away to sustain life as a fugitive. He kept his jacket on and took out a book. He didn't make eye contact with other diners, content with being alone.

Unlike the other days, Scarlet knew she had to move. Watching was one skill but pitching an asset – the bump itself – was quite another. The training from Arisaig began to flood back. Every successful 'bump' was meticulously choreographed. The recruit must never suspect any intelligence links or secondary motive. The target was not

'Dr Spengler', but Otto now, a single man in his middle thirties sheltering behind a fake name and facing an indeterminate life on the run. Spies didn't have to feel sympathy, only empathy. She had to put herself in his shoes.

She was up, clearing her mind of debris, fully inhabiting her role. She crossed the street and nonchalantly entered the café now and smiled at the maître d', indicating towards the single table opposite Otto. Other diners glanced up and stared, but Otto was patiently absorbed by his book. The book was scuffed and, as she took her seat, Scarlet couldn't make out the title. The waiter came and she ordered. As she waited, Scarlet reached into her own bag and removed a copy of *On the Origin of Species* by Charles Darwin. She flaunted it, propping the hardback up with a salt shaker, and took out a small compact mirror, waiting until those misty, spectacled eyes gravitated towards her.

Then, finally, it happened. 'Are you enjoying your reading, madam?' he said now.

Scarlet didn't react instantly. His voice was deep, almost velvety. Despite the ungainly mannerisms, he had that self-possession of an older man entering his prime. His German was bombastic and precise.

Now she turned, as if seeing him for the first time, almost surprised by his intervention. 'Yes, thank you.' She smiled, but almost inadvertently, merely to be polite. 'And yours?'

He smiled for the first time now, slightly shy and bashful. He held up his book and she saw a German translation. It was tattered, careworn.

'Shakespeare. *Hamlet*. It is the only book I always carry with me.'

'Ah, I see, you are a scholar then?'

'I happen to be so, yes. But not of Shakespeare. That is why I carry it around. I am a scientist by training. And you?'

'No, no, I am not a scholar. I am a journalist. But not of science.'

'Then we are both improving ourselves.'

'Or rather attempting to, yes.'

Silence lingered again and her order arrived: the Viennese Melange. As the waiter left, Otto said: 'Is learning science your only hobby, madam?'

Scarlet smiled again. 'No, well, it's music really. Music is a hobby. Science is an assignment, though I can hardly claim to understand most of it. I fear I will have to forgo the story this time. Though I'm told by those who know that music and science have rather a lot in common.'

Otto had an intense, almost otherworldly gaze. He didn't look away. His stare was scientific, like an analytical study of a natural object. Yes, play into his academic vanity. Rouse that spirit of intellectual gallantry, as if he alone could help her. Spying was about human nature and the foibles of others. This man had foibles aplenty.

Otto didn't take the bait immediately. Instead, he said: 'And who, may I ask, is your favourite composer?'

Steady, now, not too quick or he'll get suspicious. Feed it in casually, even a little bored. 'I'm afraid that is quite an impossible question to answer.'

'Of course. But if you were absolutely forced to

pick one. If, say, your life or those of others depended on it.'

She glanced at him as he said it, seeing only those bold, unblinking eyes, and wondered again how real that statement was. She had heard about the camps, those skeletal figures in their striped uniforms. She heard Archie's careful evasions at the station about this man's past. Best not to think of that now. She buried the thought. 'Wagner would be by far the safest choice, I suppose.'

'Indeed. But not your real choice, I imagine? Who would be an unsafe choice? A riskier passion, perhaps?'

'Beethoven, then.'

'Ah, yes, far more romantic in every way. A true son of Vienna.'

She worried she'd already gone too far. Would he recoil, close his book and bid her farewell? Beethoven was another detail from the target's file. Otto had been lauded for a recital at school; he played the violin at university in Berlin. The fact was tailored precisely for the asset. Scarlet couldn't show doubt. Not now, not this far in. 'You disagree?'

Otto's face relaxed into a smile, enchanted by a memory. 'On the contrary. I'd do anything to hear the Fifth Symphony again. Anything at all. Nothing seems quite as bad, does it, when you have things like that to go home to.'

The recruitment game was all about pacing: pounce too quickly and the entire operation would be blown; move too slowly and momentum leaked away. Scarlet could already imagine the contempt on Archie's face if she failed, the harsh end-of-term

56

report back to Broadway. Those days in the wilderness of Arisaig House – brutalizing, soul-sapping days – would have been for nothing.

Scarlet went with her instinct and decided it was almost time. But not quite yet. This was a seduction, and the formalities must be respected. Otto had already forgotten about his food. He soon became chattier, almost garrulous. He had clearly been denied serious company for too long. She played along for another ten minutes. It was only at the end that she mentioned it, as if the thought had just occurred.

She was paying her bill and getting ready to leave. She pushed her cup away and wiped a spot on the tabletop. Then she said, 'If you love Beethoven, of course, you're quite welcome to listen to my collection. I have a recording of his Fifth Symphony which is tolerable, if not ideal. I could also do with an expert guide to Mr Darwin here. You mentioned that you are a scientist, yes?'

There was a gleam of interest in his eyes. 'I'd be happy to help, madam. I should like that very much indeed.'

'Good then. My flat can be found here.'

She gave him the address for the safe house and suggested an appropriate day and time. Then she smiled and exited the café. This was arguably the most treacherous part. Not the bump, but the exfil. She stayed completely in character through the dry-cleaning run. Ensuring that a second set of eyes weren't trailing her, never breaking the fourth wall. If a watcher team were lurking, they would try and catch her returning to the station.

There was a man in a soiled mackintosh who seemed to keep time with her step. She veered towards crowds and used the distraction to alter her profile. It was too dangerous to go back to Archie just yet. Her instructions were to lie low for a day or two and conduct further counter-surveillance runs over the coming days. Above all else, she must be clean. Everything depended on that. There were too many enemies now: Otto, yes, and the runaway Germans, plus the Americans and Soviets. Too many pairs of eyes. This city crawled with them.

Scarlet reached the safe house by nightfall. The small two-bedroom flat was cluttered and squalid, an authentically bohemian base for a freelance journalist. The boxy little second bedroom was for admin and housekeeping. She took out the short-wave radio and a one-time pad and sent the required message to Archie confirming the bump was successful and the meet was now on.

Once done, she felt adrenaline falling out of her, like energy puddling on the floor. She changed, ate and read the newspaper. And then, like all spies, she waited.

1946
The American

The new orders came through the next morning. She was to remain absent from the station until the meet took place. The old soldier in Archie prioritized immaculate operational work. It was too dangerous for her to return in case she was spotted entering or leaving the building. Already, though, Scarlet felt entombed in the four walls of the safe house. She escaped for occasional errands, the sort of things a freelance journalist might plausibly do in a city like Vienna. But there were too many men in crumpled trilbies who moonlighted as friend and foe. This city was a bazaar of grifters, hawkers, conmen, spooks and fugitives. She had already spent too much time alone.

On the second night of isolation, Scarlet gathered her things and took a circuitous route through the city. Only one bar in Vienna was on the BIOS approved list, a pre-war haunt newly restored in the city centre and frequented by members of the diplomatic corps. Just the place for a freelance journalist to visit, surely. She had a duty to live her cover, especially if anyone was watching the flat. A monastic routine would fool no one.

The bar was already humming when she arrived, filled with drunken English chatter and demob-happy vibes. There were no BIOS officers she recognized, which was a small mercy. She found a seat at the bar and ordered and – vigilant for Archie and his lookalikes – she only saw the man to her left when it was too late. Not Archie, thankfully. But a younger man in his twenties with a classless smile and preppy arrogance.

'Bad day?' he said, draining the last of his glass.

American, then. She prayed he was of the secular kind, a clerk from the State Department, perhaps. She would give anything for dull, kind men.

'It's really that obvious?'

'Come on. You're young, you're still alive and this is Vienna. The city of dreams. Honestly, how bad can it be?'

'That depends how drunk you are.'

'Let's go with moderately. No, scrap that. I'd say pleasantly.'

'How much is pleasantly drunk?'

'Drunk enough to feel happy. Sober enough to still feel at all.'

'I see. Perhaps I should try it sometime.'

'Perhaps you should.' He raised his glass to the bartender and signalled for another. Then he said, 'Caspar Madison. State Department. Pleasure to meet you.'

'Sarah,' she said, remembering in time to use the right alias. Here she would switch back to being 'Sarah Webber' rather than 'Isabel Charlemont'. 'Foreign Office.'

'How about that. We're practically brothers and sisters in arms.'

She was tired now, her expression giving her away. 'I suppose so.'

'Unless, no, don't tell me. You're really one of them, aren't you?'

'A woman?'

'No, a "friend". What is it you Brits call it? The Office. The Firm. All that John Buchan baloney.'

It was a mistake. She knew that almost instantly. She should get up and walk out and never return. And yet the sound of another human voice was too intoxicating. He was thoroughly drunk already. How much could he possibly remember?

She kept her face calm. 'I'm a secretary to the Deputy Ambassador. Not quite as glamorous, I fear.'

'Please. This town is buzzing with them. Humanity's second oldest profession. Relax, your secret's safe with me.'

'I don't have a secret.'

'Which is just what a spy would say.'

'I'm afraid I wouldn't know.'

He smiled, tapped his nose in a comical version of secrecy. 'How long have you been here?'

'Already longer than I'd like. A few weeks. I used to be on secretarial duty for the Permanent Under-Secretary in London.'

Caspar looked impressed. 'Well, trust me, the old place grows on you. Or you adapt to it. The Madison clan may not be the brains of the outfit, but we sure know how to have a good time.' The barman poured another measure of whisky and Caspar drained it in one go. 'That's more like it.'

'The Webbers, I'm afraid, are renowned for early nights. Sadly, I can't stay out too late. Strict curfew.'

'Who's watching? Parents, teachers? Nanny?'

'His Majesty's Government?'

'Trust me, His Majesty will understand. I bet the old guy likes a night on the town as much as anyone. Especially in Vienna.'

'You're not a royalist?'

'I'm an American. We fought wars over that kind of thing.'

'Nights on the town?'

'Calling old men His Majesty.'

'Ah, I see.'

It seemed to start without a clear beginning. Caspar ordered more drinks and – after weaker protestations – Scarlet accepted one of them, then another, slowly surrendering to the next few hours.

The bar closed soon after and they wandered the streets together. Oxford had been haunted by the rumblings of war. Her time with SOE at Baker Street by the fighting of it. This was the first glimpse – momentary, but real – of a life beyond duty and service. Scarlet closed her eyes, inhaled the dusky air, and tried to pinpoint this feeling. It was something gloriously akin to freedom. Almost like being young.

Later, she calculated that it was early morning, a shiver of light just breaking, when Caspar first mentioned the word. They were still strolling the city streets, surveying the chaos of it all, tiring now.

'It's all about science, you see.' The words were slurred so science became like a bastardized version of 'silence'. 'Paperclip. Why call an operation after a paperclip? A stapler, fine, even a typewriter. But the humble paperclip? I'm scientifically illiterate. It's true. My college teacher confirmed it. And yet here I am. Head honcho on Operation Paperclip.'

'How impressive.' Scarlet was able to hold her liquor. She looked at him now. Caspar Madison was handsome in that All-American way. He looked like a figure from an F. Scott Fitzgerald novel, as if he should be wandering round East Egg or West Egg or whichever Egg it was. 'What is Operation Paperclip exactly?'

'Roll up a bunch of Nazi scientists and send them to the good old US of A. We wash the blood off their hands, give them a nice condo in the suburbs and put them to work at NASA. I almost envy the bastards.'

'Only ex-Nazis?'

'If they're any good, they usually are. If these guys were good enough for the Nazis, then they're good enough for us, right? It's a sewer out here. Even Truman's getting cold feet. Did I tell you my uncle works at the White House?'

'If you know nothing about science, then why are you here?'

'I just told you. I have an uncle who works at the White House.'

'What's the real reason?'

'You don't want to know.'

'What if I do?'

Caspar smiled, his spittle-soaked lips contorted awkwardly. Then he said, 'To see in the great revolution, of course. I have a Russian soul, you know. Those people know what greatness is. The West is all so cheap. All money and no soul. The Russians won the damn war for both our countries. A blood sacrifice that must be repaid.'

'You're drunk. Not pleasantly, but stupidly.'

'That's an affirmative, ma'am. I'm young and have a brain. Who isn't a Red?'

'I think politics is for people with too much time on their hands.'

'You're an agnostic.'

'I think you need some rest.'

They walked on and Caspar gave mumbled directions. Scarlet tucked away the information about Operation Paperclip. They reached his embassy accommodation. She watched him stumble inside. The safe house was within walking distance and she felt more than slightly afraid in the eerie darkness of the city. She walked briskly, weaving her way round back alleys and side streets. When she reached the safe house the hair she'd planted earlier was still in the doorway.

She washed and ate. Her head throbbed and she gradually sobered up, debating whether to file a report on the meeting. Caspar Madison, State Department employee, possible communist sympathizer, involved in Operation Paperclip. She began the message and then stopped. She thought of that heady sense of liberation and scrunched up the piece of paper.

No, tonight was secret. And for her eyes only.

1946
Operation Hercules

She woke to the summons the next day. The secure message ordered her back to the station by 0700. Her head throbbed. Her mouth was parched. Getting out of bed was agony.

'Ah, Miss Webber.'

Archie Grenville was waiting for her by the door when she arrived. He looked even more sergeant major-ish than usual. His moustache bristled. His posture was ramrod straight. She felt the dread of it even before he started.

He held up a manila file. 'Tell me. Are you certifiably stupid or merely incompetent? Or, perhaps, a unique blend of the two?'

Scarlet kept her voice quiet, level. She had debated how to play it, settling on denial. 'I'm sorry?'

Archie took out a photo from the file and held it at her eyeline. She tried not to react. It showed the Gatsby-esque figure from the bar: Caspar Madison.

'Do you know this man?'

'Yes.'

'Would you mind telling me how?'

'I saw him in a bar. He said he was working at the State Department. I don't know him, but I do know of him.'

'Semantics.' Archie shook his head. 'And like a damn little fool you believed him, I suppose.'

65

'I didn't have enough information to make a proper assessment. In the spirit of Anglo-US relations, I was cordial. Would you rather I blanked him?'

'Don't be clever.'

'I'm sorry. How stupid would you like me to be?'

'A comedian and a harlot. A rare array of talents.' Archie removed a second photo from the file and handed it to her. His frown looked positively volcanic now.

She stared at the second photo. It showed Caspar Madison with his arm around her shoulder as they reached his accommodation. She felt a sudden spike of shame – hot, clammy – and then an equally furious indignation.

'You were following me!'

'This is what happens when Broadway sends a girl to do a man's job.'

'He was drunk. I was helping him back to the US embassy.'

'A likely tale.'

'It's true.'

'That man isn't State Department. He's OSS! Madison, first name Caspar. Harvard scholar, Princeton PhD. Here in Vienna to steal Otto Spengler from right under our bloody noses. All thanks to you.'

The rest of the station was eerily silent now. She could see the others craning their necks to watch. Those crusty old-timers would be delighted at such a public spectacle, running the latest recruit out of their patch.

'I swear,' said Scarlet. 'I told him nothing about Spengler or Hercules.'

'By the visual evidence, you were probably too drunk to remember.'

'No. I'm certain. *He* was the one who was indiscreet.'

'Caspar Madison is the OSS's great hope. Wild Bill Donovan hand-picked him from Princeton. Madison was playing you from the very start. Did you spend the night with him?'

'I don't like that insinuation.'

'It's a blessing for you, Miss Webber, that your likes or dislikes are immaterial. Answer the question.'

'Of course not.'

'Lie to me now and your career is over.'

'I'm not lying.'

'Just as you weren't lying when you failed to report your contact?'

'The operation is still intact. I said nothing about Spengler. I saw Madison was drunk, and I used the chance to pick up some background information about the American operation. They're codenaming it Paperclip. Apparently, Truman is getting cold feet about the class of Nazi they're recruiting. Madison's uncle picked that up directly from his work at the White House.'

Archie seemed to have exhausted his anger. He scratched at his hands, fury turned to torpor. 'Well, if you're wrong, the Yanks could ruin everything. Months of work chucked away. All because someone couldn't keep her hands to herself and her trapdoor shut.'

'Spengler is coming to the Epsilon safe house tomorrow night. The meeting is still on.'

'The operation – possibly. You? Not a chance. I'll

call Broadway and have you on the first flight back.'

Scarlet could see the rest play out: the disgraced return, the clerical work, a slow slide into irrelevance. 'No.'

'I beg your pardon?'

'Otto Spengler expects to see me tomorrow night at the flat. He's coming to listen to my record collection. If I'm not there, the entire operation falls apart.'

Archie considered. The audience behind him had resumed their work. It was just the two of them sparring now. 'Very well. I suppose one more day won't hurt. Broadway will have to deal with you on your return.'

'Return?'

'Yes. It's your job to accompany the target on the boat trip back.'

'As punishment?'

'Perhaps.' Archie sniffed, as if mildly embarrassed about the next part. 'We also believe Dr Spengler is susceptible to female charm. He's unmarried and spent his twenties in a laboratory. You may be the only one who can coax something out of him. From your performance of the other night, it seems something of an inspired choice.'

'I'm an intelligence officer, Captain Grenville,' she said. 'A professional.'

Archie smiled mournfully. 'This is war, Miss Webber.' He turned and began walking away, already dismissing her. 'For now, you're what I say you are.'

1946
The Cabin

She had always secretly loved the sea. Others spent the return voyage crouched over metal buckets, violently evacuating their insides. There was barely an hour when the sound of retching wasn't heard somewhere on board. But Scarlet sat contentedly in her cabin and looked out at the blue-black wash of ocean around them, the largeness of it putting everything into perspective. They were ants, all of them, swept away in seconds. All the petty concerns of the last few days seemed trivial in the face of nature.

There was a firm, insistent knock on the cabin door. 'Ma'am, he's ready.'

'Thank you.'

Scarlet got down from the bed and slid into proper shoes again. She combed her hair, made herself look presentable, and then eased the cabin door open and locked it carefully behind her. As she walked unsteadily towards the prisoner's cabin at the other end of the lower deck, she could still feel the events of the last week repeat like a play in her mind, an endless circle in wake or sleep.

Act One: waiting for Otto in the safe house, welcoming him warmly, even flirtatiously, and taking his coat. She buries the nerves, focuses on the task. Everything appears normal. That form of double-think again, knowing one thing and saying another.

Act Two, then. Scarlet still in the kitchen, carefully pouring the sedative into Otto's drink. Emerging with two glasses, handing him the glass on the left, and then taking a seat as the stirring sounds of the Fifth Symphony play. She watches Otto as he stands transfixed, the music visibly moving him. Like the sound of long ago, beauty breaking through barbarity. And, at last, he sips.

Then the final act. She waits in the kitchen. The dosage is calculated exactly, designed to take effect quickly. She continues with the pretence of a meal, laboriously setting out cutlery and stirring things in pans. The music in the sitting room filters aimlessly through the flat. She sees him begin to sweat, then the tiredness sets in. The music swells to a crescendo as his legs buckle and the horrible realization dawns. She retreats to the kitchen again, shutting the door as he crawls towards it, his nails scraping against the paintwork. Then, when the scratching stops, Scarlet opens the kitchen door again and checks his pulse.

Finally, she turns off the music, which acts as the signal. Within seconds, the safe house door fills with armed members of the T-Force strike unit, snapping into place with restless efficiency. Otto is transferred to a body-bag. They carry him out of the apartment. They lift him down the stairs with heavy, almost primal grunts.

And, then, the epilogue. Archie pouring them both a drink and the rest of the work: cleaning the safe house, ridding it of any trace, sanitizing surfaces, ensuring the last few hours never happened.

They are cleaners, truly, plumbers, odd-job specialists, working anonymously. The customers in Whitehall – the Foreign Office, Downing Street – see only the fruits of their labour, never the moment of creation. They are ghosts.

Scarlet reached the prisoner's cabin now. A young naval man stood guard, barely out of basic training. He nodded at Scarlet and then opened the cabin door. The death certificate for Dr Otto Spengler had already been issued. Prisoner 8793, as he was thereafter known, had been processed at BAOR HQ in Bad Oeynhausen. On arrival in Britain, he would be taken straight to Spedan Towers in Hampstead, the BIOS office for the debriefing and interrogation of high-profile Nazi prisoners.

Scarlet had already burned most of her cover documents and would soon dispense fully with the Vienna alias. The only item she kept was an address, a piece of notepaper from Caspar Madison. But that was for later. Much later.

She could smell the room before she saw it. The cabin was humid and foul with the lingering odour of vomit and stale sweat. She walked over to the window and eased it open, letting in a blast of icy ocean air.

Otto lay on the bed with a thick blanket curled around his body. He was sitting up against a bank of pillows and his otherworldly stare had returned. He adjusted his glasses and then said in a haltering voice, 'So it's you.'

Scarlet sat down on the trunk opposite the bed. She thought of Arisaig again, those sessions learning the basics of interrogation. Already it seemed like a lifetime ago. She decided to speak in German, putting him at some sort of ease.

'Your death notice was issued to the international press before we departed,' she said. 'From this moment on you no longer officially exist. We are your only hope now.'

'And who has killed me?' he said. 'Your German is good. But no German would kidnap me. The Americans? The Soviets? Perhaps the children of Israel?'

'I work for the British government. We are taking you to the British mainland for further interrogation.'

Otto nodded. 'I see. Not a journalist, then, but a spy.'

'If you co-operate with our inquiries, we can help you start a new life.' Yes, this part would be gentle, like coaxing a child. 'That's what I'm here to discuss.'

A small, defeated smile crept around Otto's lips. 'You win a war to defend freedom, due process and human rights. And then you kidnap men and fake their deaths with no due process and justify it by those same freedoms. One has to admire the British talent for moral hypocrisy if nothing else.'

Scarlet felt unnerved by Otto now. She had expected him to be broken, the shy exterior giving way and the reality emerging. But he appeared as gentle as he did in the café. There was no raised voice or threats. He was calm, still highly rational. His voice sounded curious rather than defeated. There was no sign of the monster yet.

'I'm merely doing my job.'

'Of course. I was merely doing mine. You under-stand, that, don't you?'

'No one is looking for you. No one can get you back home. Co-operation is your only realistic chance of any sort of freedom now.' Scarlet rose from the trunk and made for the door. 'We'll arrive in England in a matter of hours. You have until then to decide how difficult you want to make things.'

Silence. Scarlet knocked on the door. The naval guard fussed with the key and unlocked the cabin.

Otto shuffled in the bed, then called out. 'Wait! What is your real name? If I'm going to tell you my secrets, surely I deserve to know one of yours.'

Scarlet stood in the doorway and looked back at the bed. Otto seemed newly vulnerable, somehow, a cadaverous figure swallowed by the sheets. Young, too, wrenched from any family and caged here amid the sickness and the squalor. All because of her. Scarlet flinched at the thought.

'Scarlet,' she said, already regretting her honesty. 'My name is Scarlet.'

1946
Aunt Maria

Two days later Scarlet visited the small SIS technical office in Whitehall Court, hidden away alongside the National Liberal Club. She returned her diplomatic passport in the name of 'Sarah Webber'. She was almost sad to see this fictional creation die, a better version of her own life: still Lady Margaret Hall, her old Oxford college, then work with the Foreign Office, then BIOS. Still unmarried, still the same age. Her life but in new form.

Broadway granted her one weekend of leave to visit family and friends. She decided to travel down to Oxford. She felt a flutter of surprise seeing Aunt Maria at the station. She was ration-book thin now, her hair grown greyer and wilder. The prickly spray of it scratched as they hugged.

Aunt Maria – not a real aunt, but a guardian and friend – seemed more bohemian than ever. The house in Jericho was cluttered with books, dust covering every surface. Maurice, Aunt Maria's mathematician husband, was even more untidy, a 'monument to man's animal nature', as Aunt Maria always put it. Scarlet had an urge to clean the place, establish order and rhythm. She was more at home now with the discipline instilled at Arisaig. The house was small but somehow lifeless and cold, a wintry rationalism pervading each room.

'So?' said Aunt Maria that evening as they

settled in her study by the fire. Both of them sipped at hot toddies, a Jericho favourite. 'Your first assignment was a success?'

Scarlet nodded, safely home now. 'Yes, I think it was.'

'Where?'

'Vienna.'

'Ah, yes, just as we planned then. I think this calls for a celebration.'

'We should be careful,' Scarlet warned. 'This one's high-level. You never know who might be watching.'

'True, true. But, my dear, you must tell me everything.'

Despite the oath of silence, nothing could be secret from Aunt Maria. That was always the deal. The story of Operation Hercules had to be carefully curated, filtering out the noise and distractions. Aunt Maria was a tenured Professor of Russian History. She missed nothing. As Scarlet narrated the tale, she saw Aunt Maria's face react, one of the reasons she was a handler rather than in the field herself. There was still that classical beauty in her long neck and the effortless geometry of her face; a design buried beneath the academic disorder. It was that old White Russian heritage, the past still branded on the present.

There was supper after the initial debriefing with Maurice's usual bluish anecdotes, then more drinks in front of the fire. Scarlet reached the boat journey and Otto's demeanour and the strangeness of him. Aunt Maria didn't take notes but logged the details in her head. She would wait until Scarlet left before using her radio in the attic to make contact with the Centre.

That night Scarlet saw the second bedroom was still decorated as before. This was where she had spent her teenage years. She cleared more books away and snuggled under the thin sheets. She thought of all the stories now, the layers of myth, trying to sift the fiction for fact: her parents long since dead in Africa; the orphan finding a home in Oxford with an eccentric professorial guardian and her mathematician husband; the work with SOE, the interview in Carlton Gardens; now a picnic of selves.

Scarlet closed her eyes and temporarily banished all thoughts of Otto Spengler, Caspar Madison and the lawless streets of Vienna. The house had a monastic hush. She slept soundly.

1946
Section IX

Everything seemed like a disappointment after that. The headquarters of the Secret Intelligence Service, for one, was far less impressive than she had imagined. She turned left and walked through the final stretch of St James's and up to Broadway. The grey expanse of the building loomed. It was almost exactly twelve months since that first interview at 3 Carlton Gardens when she'd been quietly recruited from Baker Street. Now, after the probation, it was time to be welcomed properly into the fold.

She went through some elementary security inside and was greeted by a bustling secretarial figure staring at her watch. As they headed up to the fifth floor, Scarlet took in the surroundings. War still seemed to hang over it all, from the beige-coloured walls to the terrible blackout-style curtains. The rest was a circus of suits and smoke. Typewriters crackled through the dingy hallways. Occasional secretaries clacked noisily across the hard floor. Being holed up in an embassy wasn't much fun, nor the gloomier confines of a station or safe house. But here was simply administration, divorced from the adrenaline of the field. Scarlet almost regretted coming here at all.

They reached the fifth floor where the décor seemed to marginally improve. The rumours about this floor were boundless, even to a recent trainee. Sir Stewart Menzies, the Chief himself, was said to have a grace-and-favour flat with a direct link to his office. He wrote in green ink, never used his name in any official correspondence – merely signing the initial 'C' – and had a secure phone with a direct connection to the Prime Minister at Downing Street. As they continued down the hushed corridors, nerves crept up her spine. She was due to be upbraided, surely, or demoted. Despite her debriefing success with Otto at Spedan Towers, her midnight stroll with Caspar Madison was coming back to haunt her. Hampstead couldn't atone for the sins of Vienna. That much was obvious.

She expected to see her usual contact, but it was a different man who greeted her this time. He was younger, though similar in many ways. His hair was slicked back, and he was jocular rather than military. He invited her into his office and casually wafted her into the seat opposite. He sat with his feet perched on the desktop and she had the distinct feeling that he was squatting here, a schoolboy inhabiting the role of a housemaster. He had a slight twinkle in his eye, rebellious and half-amused.

He found a sheaf of paper on the desk and held it aloft. He scanned it once, then said, 'Well, Miss King, your report on Dr Spengler certainly makes for compelling reading material. Something of a hit around these parts, I can tell you. You got him to open up in some quite remarkable ways.'

Scarlet couldn't decide if this was praise before the fall. 'Thank you.'

The man opened the report and glanced at a

highlighted passage. 'You conclude your assessment by stating that Dr Spengler is an academic rather than an ideologue. So, in your view, we can trust him, then? No pining for the good old days? No odd salutes or oaths to a fallen Führer?'

Scarlet took a moment to collect her thoughts. Then she said, 'I think it all depends on the level of sensitivity.'

'The Treasury's decided to invest more into our Salisbury facility at Porton Down. We need some brainpower to help us get up to speed with the Americans. We think Dr Spengler might be put to good use there. He's about the only serious hope we have.'

'Classification level?'

'Strap three.'

'I see.'

During the interrogation at Spedan Towers, she had sat opposite Otto for days, weeks even. They had shared meals together, walks, traded confidences, developing the peculiar intimacy between an interrogator and a subject. She knew him better than anyone else in this place.

'I stand by my assessment. His scientific knowledge is streets ahead of ours. We can use him. It sounds like we can't afford not to.'

The young man nodded. 'The Chief has glanced over the report too. You've met him, I take it? Rather a fan of yours. He concurs.'

'I'm glad.'

'In fact, the Chief in all his wisdom has decided on a new assignment for you. He's reallocating you to Section IX for a spell. Your natural aptitude for interrogations has been noticed. You outwitted the Americans and the Soviets in Vienna. Now it's time to outwit them on the world stage. How does that sound?'

Section IX was Russian counterintelligence. The high priests of SIS, the most secretive warriors in the new war. The true elite.

'What about Captain Grenville?'

The man smiled. 'The Old Soldier's had a good run. Time to put his feet up, don't you think? The Chief wants to ease him out of frontline operational duties with full battle honours.'

'He didn't say anything about my time in Vienna?'

'Were you expecting him to?'

'No.' Scarlet felt relieved. Archie must have given her the benefit of the doubt, looking beyond the security lapse with Madison. She felt silently grateful. 'And who exactly will I be reporting to?'

The younger man stood up now. He had one hand in his pocket and the other fiddling with his tie. It was an old-school tie. Westminster, she thought, a stone's throw from here. She was so used to the parade of head office figures without names, rank or titles that it was almost a surprise when he said, 'Me, as it happens. The Head of Section IX.'

He extended a hand. She shook it and felt the grip lingering slightly too long. His eyes fixed on her. He had a loose-limbed charm about him, drawing people in.

'Philby.' He smiled again. 'Everyone around here calls me Kim.'

PART TWO

6

Max put the papers down and glanced at the time. Hours seemed to have evaporated. Suddenly it was dark outside and the evening had run away with itself. He became aware of his surroundings again, checking the door and listening for footsteps. Every historian spent their lives wading through archives hoping to find a golden nugget, one fragment that could change everything. He looked at the collection of scanned pages with that sloping penmanship and allowed himself to wonder. Could it really be? Was this the moment he would write about in his memoirs – after the knighthood and full professorship, naturally – when things changed? The opening scene of his autobiography.

It was a fine, sultry evening and I was marking coursework in my dingy office. Many journalists have asked me since when I knew – or, indeed, if I knew – that I was sitting on the greatest memoir ever written about the Cold War . . .

The wonder lasted for several minutes before reason caught up. No, it was ridiculous. How gullible could he be? This was packaged for the market. He could almost see the screen rights being sold now with Judi Dench or Maggie Smith or some other grande dame of the British screen attached to play the lead. It would be like all spy books with the tiniest smattering of truth and a large dollop of exaggeration, even downright fantasy. Max had read every 'explosive' and 'true-life' spy memoir and never failed to spot at least five glaring factual errors in the prologue.

He got up now and hurriedly scanned his shelves. Googling this was out of the question and Wikipedia likewise, both smearing a fat digital fingerprint for everyone to see. Instead, Max eased out a bulky hardback volume that ran to over a thousand pages. It was one of those unfathomable reference works pumped out by university presses thanks to the inhuman toil of graduate students and PhD researchers. This one read: *Western Intelligence During the Cold War (1946–1991): An A–Z Companion* (Salford University Press). It was about fifteen years out of date now, but it covered the basics. Max had received a free contributor copy having spent every weekend for a year chasing £50 payments for entries on his pet themes: double agents, Kim Philby and – slightly more esoteric – the spying careers of the great inter-war novelists like Graham Greene and Somerset Maugham. Eventually the press in question had gone bankrupt and the payments never arrived. The free copy was compensation.

He flicked through until he found the first entry. He almost mouthed the words along as he read:

MADISON, Caspar: Former employee of the Office for Strategic Services (OSS) and one-time Director of Analysis at the Central Intelligence Agency (CIA) and long-time Soviet double agent.

Madison is currently serving a life sentence for espionage without the possibility of parole at the Federal Correctional Institution in Terre Haut, Indiana. He is estimated to have betrayed over eighty Soviet intelligence officers working as CIA assets. Many are believed to have been executed. *Time* magazine has called him the 'most effective Soviet double agent of the Cold War'. Prior to serving in the Directorate of Analysis, Madison completed operational postings with OSS/CIA in Vienna, Rome, Madrid and Moscow.

Max flicked on to another entry. The mention of 'Vienna' was, as all spy memoirs were, shorn of many specifics. But it meant Scarlet's memoir could be possible. He scrolled down the 'P's now until he saw:

PAPERCLIP (1945–1959): Operation Paperclip was a covert operation carried out by the US government to secure the services of high-ranking German scientists, engineers and technology experts. The operation involved over 1,600 Germans, many former high-ranking Nazis, who were relocated to the United States after the war. Led by the Joint Intelligence Objectives Agency (JIOA), Operation Paperclip involved famous scientific names like Arthur Rudolph and Wernher von Braun, as well as controversial figures like the double agent Caspar Madison.

Max became more frantic now. His brain was a jumble of acronyms and random dates, filtering each part of the memoir to try and find the clue which damned it. He checked the 'A's now and all those mentions of training:

ARISAIG: Arisaig House in Scotland is a country estate once used by the Special Operations Executive as a training base during the Second World War and subsequently by the intelligence services for basic training. It transferred from government hands to the private sector in the 1990s and is now run as a luxury hotel.

The pace picked up even further. It was the fault of all academics to ignore their own blind-spots. Max went back to the 'P's, checking his own entry to be sure he hadn't overlooked anything:

PHILBY, Kim (1912–1988): Former British intelligence officer, newspaper journalist and long-time Soviet double agent, part of the Cambridge Five. Following his education at Westminster School and Trinity College, Cambridge, Philby worked as a newspaper correspondent for the *The Times* during the Spanish Civil War and joined the Secret Intelligence Service in 1940. In 1944, Philby was appointed Head of Section IX in charge of Russian counterintelligence before being appointed First Secretary in Britain's Washington embassy in 1949.

Despite himself, Max could find nothing wrong with the dates so far. That, of course, didn't mean the account was true. Scarlet could have found a reference book like this and weaved together the threads of fiction with enough fact to make it plausible. Even so.

Max had one last idea. He replaced the reference book on the shelf and then scanned along until he found another similarly bulky tome, this time less well-thumbed. He guided it down from the shelf and wiped a layer of dust from the cover. This volume read: *The Dreaming Spires: Oxford Who's Who*. This, admittedly, was an even wonkier volume, long since out of print. Max had picked it up in a second-hand bookshop. This exercise was considerably harder than the last. All he had to go on was a first name.

In the end, it took almost an hour before he found the appropriate entry, a painstaking process of manually thumbing through each page:

KAZAKOVA, Maria (Prof.): Formerly Regius Professor of Russian Literature and Fellow of New College, Oxford. Professor Kazakova joined the Oxford faculty in 1932 and is the author of numerous works on Tolstoy, Dostoevsky and Pushkin. Following her election as Regius Professor, she also served as Pro-Vice Chancellor for Humanities from 1952–71. She is Emeritus Fellow of New College and continues to write regularly for *The Times Literary Supplement* and *Literary Review*. She is currently working on a new biography of Chekhov.

Max checked the copyright page and saw the printing was from 1992. She would surely be dead by now. But the most likely candidate for 'Aunt Maria', the Oxford don who Scarlet went to stay with, had definitely existed and was a prominent member of the academic establishment. Scarlet 1. Max 0.

Max replaced the book on the shelf and then gathered his things. He turned his mobile back on and left it inside the office. Then he secured the papers in his inside jacket pocket and slipped out of the department by a back entrance. As he lost himself in the crowds outside, he began plotting the next stage. The first thing he did was take out as much cash as he could from a variety of different ATMs. His card could be flagged, but the cash afterwards could not. Secondly, he purchased three burner phones in cash from a variety of small tourist shops. Finally, he found a specialist hardware shop in Fitzrovia where he purchased a further two items for a total of £120 cash. A newsagent nearby was still open and, thanks to a calendar reminder, he bought a card for his father's eighty-fifth birthday.

By the time he was caught on CCTV entering Green Park Tube Station, Max Archer had the rudiments of a plan in place. The cameras monitoring all incomings and outgoings spotted him scanning his wallet and proceeding towards the escalator. What they didn't see was the minutes before he entered the station itself. A small yellow chalkmark had been left on a lamp post further down Piccadilly, an old-school signal site.

As he found a seat on the Tube and assessed his fellow passengers, Max knew a second meeting was now on.

7

The signal site had a specific meaning: yellow chalk on the Piccadilly lamp post meant one thing; white chalk on another lamp post in Haymarket quite another. The instructions had been finalized during Max's first meeting with Scarlet. Back then, he had been mildly scornful of such scrupulous tradecraft. Now he was almost grateful.

The next day Max headed back down Piccadilly and entered Hatchards bookshop. He proceeded towards the lower-ground floor and the biography section. Tucked away was a single paperback edition of his biography of Kim Philby, still resolutely unpurchased. Less a book, he often thought, than a monument to four years of fruitless effort. It seemed to embody every wrong turn in his life. The endnotes alone took twelve months. Other people married, moved house and had children in that time. God only took seven days to create the world. That barely covered the footnotes for page one.

The instructions from Scarlet were clear. He picked the book up, flicked through until he found the note hidden inside, and then deftly pocketed the note and replaced the book on the shelf. He spent the next ten minutes pretending to browse, then left the shop and found a table at the nearest branch of Pret, making sure he was away from the main window and with no sightline behind him. He unfurled the note and saw the same writing as the earlier calling card.

St James's Park, today. 2PM. Moscow Rules.

Max scrunched up the note and then placed it into his coffee cup, watching as the ink melted away. Moscow Rules meant the highest form of dry-cleaning, the sort of counter-surveillance usually undertaken in the most hostile operations. Max found nothing absurd about it this time. The sample pages were hidden inside his jacket pocket. He was about to meet a seasoned spook for the second time to discuss breaking the Official Secrets Act. And there was every chance he could help publish a memoir that would change intelligence history forever.

As Max left Pret, he could almost imagine standing in Court 1 of the Old Bailey, some fossilized grandee in the judge's chair, exhausting the last of his excuses. One meeting could be put down to a mistake, Dr Archer. Two meetings looked like a deliberate act. Hell, there was even a specific term for this – Samson Syndrome.

It was the spy's equivalent of the mid-life crisis. The most famous case was the MI5 officer Michael Bettaney who was convicted of spying for the KGB in the eighties. The cause? Not buying a train ticket. Because he was caught fare-dodging, Bettaney knew he would fail his next security review; failing the review would lead to his dismissal from the Service; his dismissal would rid him of precious income and access to classified material; knowing his fate, Bettaney tried in desperation to earn some extra cash by selling British secrets to the Russian embassy before he was sacked. He was convicted under section 1 of the Official Secrets Act and sentenced to twenty-three years in prison. A train ticket in those days would probably have been a tenner.

No, Samson Syndrome was neither logical nor pretty.

Anxiety suffocated Max's insides now. Was he making the same mistake? Handling a sample of Scarlet's memoir was bad, yes. But it was survivable. He could claim ignorance, say he thought he could trust a distinguished former member of the Firm. Samson Syndrome was a stupid way to get caught, a lesser sin spiralling into mortal danger. And yet that drumbeat of anticipation wouldn't leave him. He could see Emma, his soon-to-be ex-wife, standing in the kitchen with that superior look she often adopted three glasses in, a slight raising of a dimpled chin.

You're a coward, Max. That's all there is to it. You'd rather hide behind a laptop and write about other people's lives than live life yourself.

The worst insults were the ones that doubled up as facts. He could still remember sitting in his student digs at Cambridge on that fateful morning twenty years ago. Every second was still vivid somehow. The college pigeonhole, the letter with the Foreign Office crest, running to his room. Soon – like so many former students – he would pack his bag, leave the ancient courts and lawns behind and enrol at Fort Monckton in Gosport, the training centre for new MI6 recruits. Head of Station by thirty, Controller by forty, Chief by fifty. The honours would follow: Knighthood, Peerage, perhaps even a return to Cambridge as Master of one of the smarter colleges. He sat down on his lumpy college bed and carefully opened the envelope before glancing over the words. And then he stopped.

He must have read it four times. Then once again just to be sure. There had been a mistake. They had posted the wrong letter. In that single moment, as clear now as then, Max Archer's entire future was cruelly extinguished. The next twenty years shattered by a mere four sentences:

Dear Mr Archer,

I regret to inform you that you have not been chosen to proceed to the final round of selection.

We thank you for your participation thus far. We would also remind you of your legal obligations under the Official Secrets Act 1989 not to reveal the contents of this letter to anyone, or the details of the selection process.

Our very best of luck for your future endeavours.

Yours,
Foreign and Commonwealth Office Co-Ordinating Staff

Was it possible for a feeling to last for two decades? Max felt it as bitterly now as he had then, perhaps even more so. He had missed the deadlines for all other graduate schemes and failed to build up any experience during the student holidays. He scrambled together a PhD proposal and tried to escape his troubles on the other side of the Atlantic at Harvard. That escape had somehow turned into a lifetime.

Soon the application to MI6 became a seminar anecdote, embellished in the telling. It was after one of those seminars that he met Emma. She was a Kennedy Scholar, bright and unfiltered, passionate about working in human rights and changing the world, an army brat who'd lived in more places than he'd ever been. She found him delightfully polite; he saw her as exotic and untamed. They had married too young before life rudely intervened.

Max's alternative career plan – tenure at thirty, professor at forty, the next Simon Schama by fifty – kept being delayed. The War on Terror dominated the headlines, Arabic was a must-have, and Russian specialists were part of a bygone age. Emma soon swapped her Treasury gig for a City law job. Max grew angry, Emma became successful – first slowly, then almost giddily. He began banging on about human rights while she lectured him on the merits of the free market. All building up to that make-or-break night, the bloodletting in the kitchen after which nothing was ever the same, their personalities twisted by events.

You're a coward, Max. That's all there is to it.

Max stopped in Piccadilly Circus and looked at the garish billboards to his left. He saw the swarm of people all around him. He felt the crush of humanity and heard that line of T.S. Eliot.

I had not thought death had undone so many.

Death, yes. It loomed in front of him every time he woke up. Another twenty years of marking essays, reciting old lectures, counting down the hours, nudging closer to the inevitable. Another sap with dreams who let them evaporate and trudged bitterly through the rest of his existence. Flush with anecdotes, a consummate nearly man. He saw that letter in his hands again. The creak and clutter of his old college room. Frozen in time.

The intelligence services had shafted him. Perhaps it was time to finally repay the favour.

Max checked his watch and calculated the distance to St James's Park.

He could still make it.

8

The first problem was finding the entrance. Saul Northcliffe reached Mayfair and got the cab to drop him on Hertford Street and spent the next ten minutes searching for a way into the private members' club. He patrolled the area once and still couldn't find any sign of Number 5. Finally, he tried what looked like a back entrance and found it was the carefully hidden main thoroughfare designed for those in the know. Next time he would insist on a pint and a kebab. This place had been the journalist's idea.

These sorts of meet-and-greets normally took place in the Travellers or one of the Pall Mall haunts with their drained décor and air of faded glory. But Felicity Goodhart had just won the Orwell Prize and Journalist of the Year at the British Journalism Awards. Membership of 5 Hertford Street – Mayfair's most exclusive club, or so Saul had read on Google during the car journey – was her due reward.

Usually allergic to all media types, Saul made an exception for Felicity. They had trained together before she transferred to SIS and he stayed put in the Security Service. While Saul dutifully slogged his way up, becoming a master of competency reviews, Felicity left Vauxhall Cross for Fleet Street in the late nineties, landing a plum role as Security Correspondent at *The Times*. She was now

Security Editor of the *FT* with a weekly column and a ubiquitous presence dispensing her wisdom on all things spook-related. She earned four times his salary, Saul knew, and one of her books – a true-life account of a joint MI6–SAS op in Afghanistan – was about to be made into a film. According to his car-bound Google research, the project had 'A list talent attached'. Though whether literally or metaphorically wasn't entirely clear.

Saul checked the Operation Tempest Update on his secure phone. Max Archer had returned to his flat and watched *Newsnight* and then the first half hour of *North by Northwest* before going to bed. Saul checked on another request regarding Hanslope and tech-ops – an insurance bugging device, nothing more – then pocketed the phone and headed through. The restaurant was heaving with notable faces: one senior cabinet minister rumoured to be on the way out in the next reshuffle; one junior Minister of State definitely on the way up; two captains of industry, one of whom was almost certainly on the CIA's payroll, and a rock star Saul vaguely recalled from the seventies, geopolitical allegiance as yet unknown.

'Well, this is certainly a surprise,' said Felicity as they analysed the menus. 'Few things have ever tempted Saul Northcliffe out of his lair. Things must really be bad.'

In his youth, Saul had cultivated an air of no-nonsense simplicity. The label had stuck and, despite his subsequent efforts, he found himself condemned to play the role. 'Give me a chippy dinner and a nice mug of builder's tea and I'm happy as Larry.'

'You sound like an extra from *The Likely Lads*.'

'Being underestimated is a useful skill for a spy. And much harder than it looks.'

'Well, you can drop the act. I know you like a decent bottle of vino and Bach's Cello Suites just as much as the rest of us. I even heard rumours that Saul from Stoke was considering a move into the private sector. Expense accounts, five-star hotels, complimentary season tickets.'

'We want to sell up and buy somewhere nice in the country. Some more funds for the refurb wouldn't go amiss.'

'I'm assuming you didn't emerge from the shadows to tell me about your taste in interior decoration?'

'Not exactly.'

They ordered and Saul was persuaded into a lunchtime glass of wine, much against his better judgement. He cycled through his cover as fast as he could. Felicity had a scoop she was sitting on regarding MI5 involvement in a leak inquiry at the heart of Downing Street. He quietly ushered her away from that story. In exchange, he offered her an exclusive: MI5 were about to launch an operation against a large multinational believed to be laundering money for organized crime, including Colombian drug cartels. The entire thing could be hers.

'Ha, well, no cigar, I'm afraid. Downing Street is infinitely sexier,' said Felicity. 'I can't just drop the story. It has spies, politicians, even an amusing anecdote about the PM's cat. It's front page.'

'Everyone has that story. That story is old news. Plus, the tabloids will do it better and you know it. No one has what I'm offering you. It's serious, international, and perfect for your readers.'

Felicity pretended to consider, then dabbed her lips with a napkin. She munched slowly on some bread. 'We'll have to find a compromise.'

'Oh yes?'

'I can agree to look the other way on the Downing Street story if – and I mean *if* – I get a full embed with the takedown. Exclusive photos, senior source quotes, the lot. I want to see the CEO being frog-marched out in his pyjamas.'

Saul took a sip of wine. 'I'm sure something can be arranged. No book or movie rights this time.'

'You always were a killjoy, Saul.'

They talked on about families, holidays and, as ever, the declining state of the country. Then, as the puddings were cleared and the coffees arrived, Saul made his move. Almost as an after-thought he said, 'An old name came my way the other day. Scarlet King. She might be dead now, probably long gone, but it brought back memories of our training. Did you ever come across her?'

Felicity looked immediately intrigued. 'In what context?'

'Oh, you know, just chitchat. Watercooler stuff. I thought you might have known her during your time across the river.'

'She was Controller Sovbloc. There was no one in the building then who didn't know her. Surely you can get her file from SIS.'

'The best bits are never in the file,' said Saul. 'We both know that.'

Felicity poured a dash of milk into her coffee and stirred. 'I've met some terrifying spies in my time,' she said, 'but none have ever come close to her. She was one of the old-school, trust me. Secrets weren't just for work; they were her entire philosophy of life. Scarlet King was more ruthless than the men and could be twice as charming, if she wanted to be. She turned down the chance to be Chief, did you know that? The only person who didn't want the green pen and the throne room.'

'Any idea why?'

'Sovbloc wasn't what it is nowadays. Everything's so damn transparent. Back then, even when I joined, it contained traces of the good old days. No one trusted anyone, even in their own department. The ghosts of Philby and the Cambridge Five had never quite been expunged. With Scarlet you were always guilty until proved innocent. I soon chucked it in and sought refuge with the Camel Drivers.'

Camel Drivers was SIS speak for Middle East experts. That was always the great rivalry within Vauxhall Cross. For the Cold War the Russia hands were dominant. After 9/11, the Camel Drivers were called back. Now, with the focus again turning to Moscow, Sovbloc was reasserting itself.

'I know she oversaw the Mitrokhin Archive. What else did she have her fingers in?'

Felicity laughed. 'What *didn't* she, Saul? SIS Chiefs back then saw the job as a licence to drink Scotch with whichever cabinet minister or Permanent

Secretary would have them. Scarlet was the one who did all the proper work. She had a sideline in counter-espionage and counter-penetration. That gave her the freedom to roam across any operation she fancied. She was an empire-builder. Napoleon and Alexander the Great had nothing on her.'

Saul sighed. He had prayed for another answer. Some spies were dutiful hacks but nothing more. They clocked in and clocked out, the world barely noticing their retirement. Others had a mission, hogging attention and stealing bandwidth, always causing trouble. Scarlet King was clearly the latter. It confirmed what he most feared.

He decided to be blunter. 'What else, though? What was the gossip, the rumours, the petty nicknames? What are the scandals your lot kept in-house?'

'You want me to tell tales?'

'If there are tales to tell.'

'Believe me, Saul, that woman is a riddle wrapped in an enigma. I think she was a mystery even to herself.'

9

Scarlet was sitting by a fountain in a secluded part of St James's Park. True to form, Max thought, she had a chosen a park bench, as if acting out a scene from a fifties spy thriller. She was reading a creased paperback and, as Max approached, he saw the title: *From Russia with Love* by Ian Fleming. He wondered if the joke was meant for him or if Scarlet thought there might be watchers on her. Targets in the secret world often enlivened things by needling their pursuers. It was all part of the great game.

There was no sign of the woman with the scar today, so Max took a seat and waited for Scarlet to respond. She looked different, her face slightly smudged with make-up and bronzer. She continued reading, as if failing to notice him there, before finally saying, 'How long do you have?'

It was always the first question a handler asked an asset, the practical realities of spying so much more mundane than the movie version. Assets didn't usually get caught by grand, heroic gestures. It was the small things that undid them: unexplained absences from work, erratic behaviour at home, seemingly pointless travel or diversions. Max bridled at Scarlet's tone. He was an associate professor, a critically acclaimed if commercially unloved writer ('cult status' was his current euphemism of choice). He wasn't her damn asset.

'Twenty minutes,' he said, knowing he couldn't risk another verbal assault from Professor Kessler. One more missed seminar and the formal complaints process would kick into gear.

'Did you read the sample pages?'

'Yes.'

'I'd like them returned.'

Max reached down into his rucksack. He'd bought a copy of the *Guardian* for this exact purpose and had already slid the sample pages inside. He took it out and pretended to glance over the front page.

'Were you followed?'

'Not that I was aware.'

'You're an academic. You probably wouldn't see them anyway.'

Max resisted returning fire, feeling mildly ridiculous again. The newspaper, the concealment, the park bench. This wasn't courage, surely, it was a mid-life crisis. Next, he'd be pawning his possessions and buying a second-hand sports car on credit. Or hooking up with one of his post-grad students and moving to Malibu.

Max put the paper down and slid it across to the middle of the park bench. He was tired of this. 'I don't believe you,' he said.

There was a flicker of reaction to his right. 'I beg your pardon?'

'You heard me. I don't believe it. You, the sample pages, any of it. You claim to be Scarlet King. There's no known photograph of Scarlet King anywhere in existence. How do I know you're not an imposter?

Some old lady who fancies trying to rustle up a few quid with forged memories and a tall tale?'

'You don't think the memoir is authentic?'

'It's impossible to tell without getting full access to the original document. Scanned sample pages aren't enough. It's the sort of thing that could be pieced together from a careful reading of the secondary sources. Clever? Yes. Assiduous? Most certainly. But genuine? I think not.'

Scarlet finally stopped reading now. She folded a page, closed the book and glanced at Max. 'Which parts didn't you believe?'

'All of it. I know nothing about you. As far as I'm concerned, you could be using my credentials as an intelligence historian to help you carry out a publishing fraud. You reel me in with hand-written notes and whispers about the Official Secrets Act and then use my position to add credibility to the whole scheme. I approach publishers, you pocket the advance, then you exit stage left. I carry the can and have my reputation ruined. You're like one of those Walter Mitty SAS types who claims they were part of Bravo Two Zero when really they were making tea in Hereford. Sorry, but I'm not playing this game any more.'

Max got up and started walking away. He was a few steps clear of the bench when Scarlet flickered into life behind him and said, 'Wait.'

Max stopped. He turned and looked at Scarlet. 'Why?'

'What if I told you there was another traitor? Someone even better than Philby, Blunt, Burgess,

Maclean and Cairncross. Someone who was never caught.'

There was a different cast to her now. She seemed more serious, less obviously theatrical, as if the time for spy games was over.

'Old news,' he said. 'I can't sell that, even if I wanted to. People have been hunting for a sixth man for forty years. Even if we found them, who cares? The Cold War's done. No, sorry, you'll have to do better than that.'

'I was the first British intelligence officer to meet Caspar Madison. What you read in the sample is just the start.'

Max had done more research overnight in the flat. British rather than American double agents were his specialism and he wanted to be sure of all the details. But there was no denying it. Caspar Madison was one of the most infamous traitors in the history of American intelligence, part of an unholy trinity with Robert Hanssen and Aldrich Ames. He'd become Head of the Directorate of Analysis at Langley while shopping his best secrets to the Soviet Union. A scoop on Caspar Madison would give the book transatlantic potential, foreign rights, maybe even Hollywood, one of the streamers reaching into their deep pockets. It was like lighter fuel underneath the entire project. But he couldn't let Scarlet know that. At least not yet.

'It could mean anything,' said Max. 'The scene you describe could be the first and last time you ever talked to Caspar Madison. Intelligence historians aren't even sure he was working for the

104

Soviets by that point anyway. We only have concrete evidence from the early sixties onwards.'

Scarlet smiled. 'That's a risk you'll have to take. I was the one who first met Vasili Mitrokhin when he tried to sell his KGB archive to the West. I was the only one in the West who read his papers and discovered all those other traitors still trying to escape their crimes. Norwood, Foot, the lot.'

Max could feel his resolve slackening. 'It's still not enough,' he said. 'The best bits of the Mitrokhin Archive were published by Mitrokhin and Christopher Andrew at Cambridge in the nineties. The original papers are still kept at Churchill College. The cat's already out of the bag on that one. I need something *new*.'

Scarlet was relishing the battle. 'You're right, yes. I suppose my memoir is worthless to you. I take it you fact-checked the sample pages?'

'As far as I was able to.'

'Did you spot any errors?'

'I've spent the last twenty years researching SIS operations during the post-war period. I've never heard of a British operation codenamed Hercules to recruit former Nazis to the UK mainland. Operation Paperclip on the US side is well known. There's nothing I've ever seen to suggest MI6 tried the same thing themselves.'

'I see,' said Scarlet, bowing her head. 'From reading your books I thought you were a cleverer man than that. I can see I was mistaken.'

'I'm sorry?'

'*Think*, Dr Archer. We were better than the Americans at that time. The mark of a successful intelligence operation is that the public generally *don't* know about it. I thought that much was blindingly obvious.'

Max felt the insult like a body-blow. Yes, this was the old case officer in her. He didn't have his marriage. He had no bloodline of his own. All he had left was his brainpower. Take that away and what else was there?

'Even assuming the first sample was true,' he said, trying to recover, 'that's still not enough to make me risk my career and reputation and potentially even my freedom. Self-publish it. Flog the pages round literary agents and good luck to you. But I'm not going to jail – or being extradited to the US – for old war stories about Caspar Madison, Mitrokhin or post-war Nazi scientists.'

Max turned back and walked away more determinedly now. He fastened his coat, flicked his collar up against the breeze, sure he'd made the right decision. He was nearly at the end of the small secluded area when he heard a sterner voice behind him. No longer an old lady but steelier, harder, someone who didn't suffer fools gladly.

'How about the last undiscovered double agent of the Cold War?'

Max turned for a second time. 'And who would that be?'

Scarlet looked at him fully now. 'Me.'

10

Saul tried to keep calm, fidgeting with his coffee cup. He could see he was on to something. Thirty years in the business had taught him to smell new intelligence like a scent. He kept his questions brief, prodding Felicity towards indiscretion. A memory stirred too. But that was in the past. He needed a second opinion, someone to confirm his own suspicions had been correct all those decades ago.

'The first thing you have to remember, Saul, is that Scarlet King had been in Section IX under Philby.'

He played the innocent now. 'Were they close?'

'In a way. Scarlet was a spook through and through, not part of clubland. She never married and had no family. Strictly speaking, I'm not sure anyone was ever close to her, as things go.'

'And after Section IX?'

'From what I remember, she was posted to Moscow Station sometime in the early sixties when Philby went into exile.'

'Sixty-four, then?'

'That sounds about right. After the Philby affair, of course, the gossip brigade went into overdrive. There was always a rumour of another British traitor within SIS who helped him escape.'

The Wilderness of Mirrors. Yes, Saul had

sometimes sympathized. Suspicion was a viral phenomenon, prone to contagion.

'Blunt and Cairncross. The Five?'

'Blunt was MI5, and Cairncross was Bletchley. No, this was about another double inside SIS. The Sixth Man. Possibly not even part of the Cambridge Five. Someone who slipped through the net.'

Saul fussed with his napkin, kneading it tighter and tighter in his palm. He felt his spine tingle slightly, his windpipe compress. 'What was the rumour?'

Felicity smiled. 'That it wasn't a sixth man at all, but a sixth woman. Better than all the blokes. Invisible, underappreciated, there without being seen.'

'You think Scarlet King was the Sixth Woman?'

'Hardly,' said Felicity. 'Everyone had a rumour that followed them around in those days. I never saw any evidence. It was just locker-room chatter. Everyone had some story from the past that made them seem like a mole. Roger Hollis, Dick White, the whole gang. We just wanted to make sure a woman was in the mix as well.'

'Equal-opportunity traitors.'

'Possibly.'

'I see.'

'It's ancient history though, Saul. You're not seriously interested, are you?'

Saul did his best to look underwhelmed. 'We currently face nine terror threats, two potential bioweapon cases and three banks laundering Iranian nuclear funds. We have better things to do than concern ourselves with Cold War spies.'

'As a taxpayer, and a journalist, I should damn

well hope so. Though finding the Sixth Woman, the last of the great Cold War spooks, would be quite the coup. Like that poor Japanese fellow still fighting the Second World War in 1975 or whatever it was.'

A coup? No, thought Saul, it would be more than that. Britain's highest-ranking Russia hand secretly working as a Soviet double throughout the entire Cold War. That wasn't just news. That was history.

The bill was soon paid and they both departed. Saul found another cab on Hertford Street and headed back to Thames House. No wonder SIS were refusing to share any files on Scarlet King. If the rumour was even half-substantiated it would embolden calls for intelligence reform. SIS had long since lost ground to GCHQ over budgets and personnel. A scandal this juicy could finish them off for good.

Back at Thames House, Saul called Charlotte out of a meeting and told her to bring the latest 'string', office jargon for SIGINT intercepts. He debated whether to take this straight to the Director-General but decided against it for now. He sifted through the other work on his desk and put most of it on ice.

Operation Tempest had just become a top priority.

11

It took a moment for Max to understand what he'd just heard. It sounded like a joke, at first, before Scarlet's fixed expression made the words horribly real. Without quite knowing it, Max was walking back, resuming his place on the park bench, conscious again of who might be within earshot.

'Why on earth should I believe you?' he said.

'Because this could be your redemption, Dr Archer. Your meal ticket to a full professorship, a new place of your own, breaking away from the pack of other academics with their leather elbow patches and second-hand cars. Your wife thought you were a disappointment, and this will show her what she's missing.'

Max couldn't deny the appeal of it. Professor Christopher Andrew, perhaps the most famous intelligence historian in the world, had been his hero at Cambridge, both an academic mentor and a career inspiration. Professor Andrew's profile had gone nuclear thanks to various well-timed scoops: first his book with Oleg Gordievsky, the famed Russian defector, in the eighties; then his two-volume collaboration with Vasili Mitrokhin, the former librarian of the KGB, in the nineties; and, most recently, Andrew's official history of MI5, the first historian allowed to glimpse the holy of holies and work with MI5's classified archive.

Set against that, of course, was the cautionary example of Hugh Trevor-Roper, another titan of the academic world and a former spook, felled by his misidentification of the Hitler diaries in the eighties. His reputation never recovered.

'Why tell me, though?' he said. 'For all you know I could walk into the nearest police station.'

'On what evidence? I'm an old lady. I can play that part very convincingly. Plus, I don't have you down as a rat. Doggedly loyal, one of your many failings. No, I have no worries there.'

'How could you possibly know?'

'Because you're desperate, Dr Archer, and desperate men grab any opportunity they can. Entangling yourself in a police investigation wouldn't be a good move for either of us.'

'You said it yourself. Spies lie for a living. How do I know this isn't another lie?'

'You don't,' said Scarlet. 'It all comes down to a question of trust. You know from our first meeting that I didn't pick you lightly. I dug deep, researched your profile, vetted you like I would any new joe. You know from your own studies that I was Sovbloc Controller. I'm not a crank like Peter Wright or a fantasist like David Shayler. Why would I out myself as a Soviet double unless it happened to be the truth?'

'Because you're too old to live with the consequences but you fancy cashing in before you go. What other option does a retired spook have?'

'If I wanted money, I would have cosied up to all the billionaires who fled Russia and bought up Mayfair in the noughties. I could've had

111

Berezovsky and his pals in my pocket and increased my bank balance by many millions in return. Their lives were in danger. They would have showered a former Sovbloc Controller with incalculable riches. And yet I didn't. I kept my paws out of their trough. No, I'm sorry, but this has never been about money for me.'

Max conceded the point. He had consulted occasionally for the private security industry and knew the main players. Scarlet seemed to be one of the only former SIS high-ups who hadn't cashed in during the boom years when Moscow money was laundered through the City. It's why the Americans christened the capital 'Londongrad'.

'How did you pass developed vetting?' he asked.

'Because I was the one doing the vetting. I knew every trick in the book.'

'Why go public now? If it's not money, what then? You've escaped capture for an entire career. Why not take the victory and die in peace?'

Scarlet breathed deeply, sniffing at the cold air. 'You'll have to read the memoir.'

'That's not an answer.'

'It's the only one I'm prepared to give.'

'When were you recruited?'

'See my previous answer.'

'What was your codename?'

'I was in place for forty years, Dr Archer. I had various codenames.'

'Are you still active? Once a Soviet double, always a double. Why didn't you relocate to Moscow when you left the Service or when the wall came down?'

'You know why. I was more use to them still in

place. I had the contacts, the network. Getting the first plane to Moscow would have burned my cover and my access. It would have undone all my good work. I would never let that happen.'

'Why, then?' said Max. It was the question he kept coming back to. 'Is it ideological? Did you want the West to collapse and the revolution to succeed? Why devote your entire life to a ruthless regime that killed millions of its own citizens while enjoying all the benefits of life on the other side?'

'You've migrated from factual questions to philosophical ones. I take it you will help me, then?'

'I didn't say that.'

'Oh, Dr Archer, people rarely say what they truly mean. It's one of the first lessons of spycraft.'

'What happened to Otto Spengler?'

'You'll have to read on.'

'And your relationship with Kim Philby?'

'See my previous answer.'

Max turned away, trying to deal with his frustration. 'I'll need full and unfiltered access to the original notebook. I'll have to test the pages and the writing itself, while of course reading the contents in full. Only then can I tell you whether or not I believe a single thing you're telling me.'

'Fine.'

'Really?'

'Of course. That kind of access naturally comes with certain conditions.'

'Such as?'

'The process will have to be done entirely off-the-books. No emails, phones, WhatsApp, anything digital at all. It will also need to be done quickly.

We have to assume that news of the memoir will leak and that the intelligence services will do everything in their power to stop publication. The clock is already ticking. This happens soon or it doesn't happen at all.'

'The memoir extracts I read won't be publishable on their own. They'll need context.'

'Why do you think I picked you, dear doctor?'

'It took me four years to write the Philby biography. I couldn't possibly write a book of a similar length in weeks. The very idea is nonsensical.'

'You don't need to. Give it an introduction, set out the context, and then let my material speak for itself. Just like Christopher Andrew and dear old Mitrokhin. This isn't a biography. This is an academic introduction at most with the occasional editorial footnote. The job of weeks if not days.'

'It's impossible. The fact-checking alone would take months to do properly. I have a full-time job.'

'You give two sixty-minute lectures a week and run two seminar sessions. Office hours are Tuesday and Thursday from two o' clock until four. Apart from that, you research. I'm spoon-feeding you all the information. All you have to do is give it some flavour. This is treasure falling directly into your lap, Max. My advice is to take it.'

Max tried not to show his unease at how casually she recited his teaching timetable. It reminded him of those rows with Emma; the arch way she raised her eyebrows and asked – supposedly without a hint of malice – quite what it was he *did* all day. He often wanted to ask the same. How did it take sixteen hours a day to shuffle pieces of paper?

114

She would storm out; he would drink in front of the telly. Thus a marriage collapsed.

'An outline, perhaps, even footnoting some sample chapters. That's all I could possibly do at such short notice.'

'No.' Scarlet's voice was peppery again, refusing to be ignored. 'This has to be ready to go. Proposals and samples give them time to shut us down. We have one chance to strike and we need to make use of it.'

Reluctantly, Max knew she was right, even if the 'we' seemed premature. His previous books – so innocuous they had barely merited reviews even within the academic journals – had been pounced on by lawyers from the Ministry of Defence and the Joint Intelligence Committee. It had taken months of wrangling to finally protect the publisher from being sued into oblivion. If the money on legal fees had gone into marketing spend instead, then – maybe, just maybe – more than three people and a dog might have read the books themselves.

'Do you have the notebook with you? The original, I mean, not the sample.'

Scarlet laughed. 'I've just told you that the memoir is a faithful account of my life as a double agent. Do you really think I carry the original around with me for every mugger and petty criminal to find?'

'When will I get access?'

'When you ask me politely.'

Max sighed. This woman was infuriating. It was as if she had found every pressure point in his body and was targeting them all at the same time. 'You want me to be complicit,' he said.

'You're not as stupid as you look.'

'Thank you.'

By asking to see the notebook, Max knew, he would erode his last line of defence. It would show clear criminal intent to break the Official Secrets Act. He couldn't claim it was a mistake or that he didn't know what was in the notebook. He was stepping over a line, crossing the Rubicon, and he felt strangely numb at the prospect.

'Are you recording this conversation?' he said, suddenly aware this could be fed back to a hard drive somewhere.

'That sounds like a personal question.'

'And I'd like a personal answer.'

'I'm still waiting. Think of it like God and forgiveness. Ask and it shall be given.'

Up ahead, Max could see the woman with the scar from the flat in Holland Park joining them now on the edge of the secluded area. Her appearance was slightly altered again. She had ditched the glasses and added extensions to her hair. She wore thicker-soled shoes which gave an inch to her height, and the dress sense was different, less studenty and more formal. That scar on her arm still haunted him. He always wondered what real physical pain must be like. Writing about it was one thing; living with the aftermath of it quite another.

He had to see this objectively. Was it the break of a lifetime or a dangerous trap to be avoided? Could the woman beside him really be an undiscovered Cold War mole or merely an elderly crank with a craving for publicity? It all came down to judgement. He saw himself walking away for good. He could picture the rest: another lecture, another seminar, the years crawling by until Professor Kessler's retirement do, everything mapped out and prescribed, the end as terminally dull as the beginning.

You're a coward, Max. That's all there is to it.

'Please may I see the original notebook,' he said, at last, the first word catching in his throat.

'Ah, well, I'll have to think about it.' Scarlet got up and steadied herself on the grass. She peered at him with a teacherly stare. 'And, from this point on, remember one thing, Dr Archer. I gave you all the clues when we first met. You already have everything you need to solve the puzzle of my life. It's just a question of seeing what's in front of you. The very best of luck.'

Max felt baffled, trying to untangle the latest riddle, as he watched Scarlet King hobble away towards her helper. Perhaps she had escaped from a home or a hospital. He would see a nurse approaching them any moment now, the entire scene swamped by flashing blue lights and paramedics taking this poor deluded woman for treatment.

He sat for another ten minutes and digested what he'd heard. Then, when the coast was clear, he zipped up his jacket and left.

Saul Northcliffe reviewed the latest string from Operation Tempest and felt his optimism vanish. There still wasn't nearly enough to work with. They needed clear proof of intent to break the law. Instead, there was footage and transcripts of

Dr Max Archer's seminars, a comprehensive overview of his TV habits and lists of academic journal websites. Saul reached a lengthy email chain regarding 'Post-Imperial Interdisciplinary Hermeneutics and the Amnesiac Process of a New Cultural Semiotics: Initial Thoughts' before he lost the will to live and gave up. The day was nearly done. He packed up and decided to take some open-source reading material home.

The train back to Kingham was jammed, as usual. Saul's daily comfort was a large bag of fries from the Burger King at Paddington Station with a full-fat Coke, slurping the lot with guilty pleasure and then covering his tracks thanks to a pocketful of Trebor Extra Strong mints. Whoever said secrets had no place in a marriage had clearly always been a bachelor. He would arrive home and declare himself famished, clutching his midriff for extra authenticity. Then dutifully help his two daughters sprinkle the last of the pumpkin seeds on the ever-present salad.

Tonight, however, he'd left it too late. No seats were available on the train and he was forced to lean against the toilet compartment and avoid the serial sneezer. He had a Kindle, instead, suitably modified by the techs at Thames House to avoid any hacking disasters. He glanced at the two titles listed under 'Dr Max Archer'. The first – *Double Agents: A History* – was £20.99 even as an e-book, and over 600 pages in length. He settled instead on *The Honourable Traitor: An Unauthorized Biography of Kim Philby* which was only £1.99, a permanent cut-price Kindle deal.

They were only one stop away from Kingham

when Saul found himself reading the final paragraph of the fifth chapter. He read it once and then again, pausing for a moment while he highlighted the paragraph with his index finger:

Like his father, Kim Philby's greatest strength as a double agent was recognizing a simple truth: those hunting him were always looking for the grand gesture that would give him away. The perennial mistake of the spymasters on his tail was over-thinking. They were so consumed in a wilderness of mirrors that they failed to see the obvious clue. Philby, instead, carried out his treachery in plain sight. He looked with thinly disguised scorn at those Trinity dons who were, in the words of one student of the time, 'so clever they were stupid'. Whatever else people said of Kim Philby, he was never stupid.

As the train from London Paddington drew into Kingham Station, other passengers were surprised to see a plump figure wearing a rucksack and grey raincoat dash past them towards the car park. A BMW was similarly spotted hurtling down the quiet roads of Kingham village at 85 mph before turning off just before the churchyard.

At 8:32 p.m., Thames House logged a call from the secure emergency line codenamed PANAMA, one of the home systems set up for the five most senior figures in the Security Service. Four minutes later, an information request had been sent with an extract from Dr Max Archer's Outlook diary: 'THE GORING HOTEL – DAD 85TH DRINKS (8PM)'.

Saul Northcliffe authorized the dispatch of an A4 watcher team and then cursed his own stupidity. He walked into the kitchen and made his apologies, glancing warily at the green-coloured soup in front of him that had cooled in his absence.

Max Archer was savvy enough to avoid careless conversations on mobiles or sending book outlines by email. He wasn't foolish enough to invite Scarlet King to his office. But a boastful word with his father at the old man's party? That was a different matter entirely.

It was time to catch Dr Archer in the act.

12

The Goring Hotel was so well hidden it almost didn't exist. Max left Victoria Station and reached the turning, glancing up at the nearby spectre of Buckingham Palace. It was odd to be near such a famous spot and yet find an enclave which felt so quiet and rarefied. Apparently, the Goring was where the Queen and Queen Mother used to come for tea. Typical of his father, then, to have chosen it. Oliver always had considered himself a mere step away from royalty.

Max felt that old familial rivalry reassert itself. Then he took a breath and heard his mother, Lily, an ever-present voice in his head. A bust-up at Oliver's eighty-fifth wasn't the done thing, even though she had more cause to resent him than most. He still remembered that anecdote about how they met, wheeled out every Christmas and birthday: an embassy ball in Paris, Oliver the roguish foreign correspondent, Lily a doe-eyed exchange student with dreams of a French romance. Bergman to his Bogart. They danced, talked and then Oliver disappeared without a word. It was a pattern that would be repeated for the next thirty years.

Oliver roamed the world with his typewriter, recording wars and great political upheavals while

Lily taxied Max to football practice and went to parents' evenings alone. The definitive break had come in Max's second summer of university. Oliver's affair with an American foreign correspondent had been an open secret for almost a decade. Max could still remember seeing Lily at the kitchen table nursing two empty bottles of wine. Max refused the invitation to Oliver's second wedding. The day after, Lily was formally diagnosed with breast cancer. The end sounded like a Victorian melodrama. But, despite everything, Lily's dying wish had been for Max to reconcile with his father. And so here he was.

The second marriage, in line with all expectations, hadn't proved to last. There were no further children, thank goodness, and Oliver had amassed a small fortune thanks to an early investment in a friend's photo-sharing app. Max knew it was mercenary, hating himself for even entertaining the thought, but that fortune had to go somewhere when the old man died. Plus, it would be delayed justice for Lily. Though not if Oliver spent it all first.

Max was about to enter the hotel lobby when his phone pinged. He glanced at the email alert and saw 'BOOK THREE' in the subject line. He tried not to flinch and wearily thumbed the email open, feeling the usual sickness:

FROM: Antonia Wickham (R.B. Wickham Literary Agency)
TO: Dr Max Archer (LSE)
SUBJECT: BOOK THREE – EDITOR UPDATE

Max,

Hope you're well. Just wanted to give you a v quick Editor update ref LNM. Good news: apparently, she was spotted last week at Soho House. Which means she's still alive (hurrah!).

Meanwhile, a friend of a friend's godson is going in for work experience at C&G next month and might be able to do a bit of literary espionage – just your field! – on our behalf and see what's happened to the emails that haven't been replied to. I also had lunch with a former intern at C&G who remembers seeing your proposal on one of the assistant's desks, though unfortunately he couldn't remember which assistant or which desk.

I know it's not quite the breakthrough we were hoping for, but I think it's definitely a move in the right direction. Hopefully we'll get a response soon and we can progress this project.

Fingers crossed,
Antonia

Spies were often said to be born liars. But they had nothing on the media industry. 'LNM' was Max's nickname for his editor – Loch Ness Monster – a figure often rumoured to exist but rarely actually seen. C&G was the publishing imprint Chatham & Grey. He still remembered the night he got the first set of editorial notes on the Philby biography. Names and gender were a moveable feast. The editorial letter was addressed to 'Archie'. Kim Philby somehow became 'Kym'. The fact it was non-fiction seemed to have been missed completely. The rest appeared to have been copied and pasted from a different project entirely. The final note called for 'Kym' to 'become a kick-ass heroine for our times'. Max started with a glass of Scotch and finished with an empty bottle.

He tried to shake off the book-induced despair. He pocketed his phone, checked his appearance and then headed into the lobby. He'd forgotten quite how deliciously neat the Goring was. He was used to academic conferences in soulless concrete monstrosities dumped somewhere off the M25 with lobbies the size of several swimming pools and the interior décor to match. This felt more like a private club. He was allergic to formality, so dressing up like this was as far as he got. The shirt was almost new, and the chinos had no obvious ketchup stains. The shoes were polished and he'd avoided sweater-vests or tweed-and-leather combos, the sartorial giveaway of any academic.

Max heard his father before he saw him. He boomed, every syllable fired like a warning shot. Oliver was already regaling the faithful with his war stories: the affair with a Hungarian student in the fifties, the run-in with Castro's Cubans in the sixties, his spell as a freelancer on the *Washington Post* during Watergate, then the time he tried to get an interview with Osama bin Laden during the Soviet–Afghan war in the eighties; finally, the polished jewel of anecdotage, came his dealings with a young Vladimir Putin in St Petersburg after the collapse of the Soviet Union. Oliver was always threatening to write a memoir but never quite got round to it. The stories, nevertheless, were subtly embellished with each telling. All of them had a nod and a wink, Commander Bond still on Her Majesty's Service.

Max entered the glass-ceilinged part of the bar with views of the small garden beyond. There was something about seeing Oliver in the flesh. The cresting wave of lavish grey hair swooped back like a thirties film star; the terminally tanned skin, so far removed from Max's pasty Englishness. Oliver was congenitally thin, too, able to eat whatever he liked without any risk of middle-aged spread. He had a trademark twinkle to seduce everyone from low-level sources to Heads of State and wine waiters, a natural behind and in front of the camera.

Max, by contrast, was thinning on top, perman-ently tired-looking, fast losing a battle with his waistline and – according to one benighted screen test for a Channel 5 documentary – 'had a face tailor-made for radio'. He struggled to see how he shared the same genes as the man before him. It was Oliver's usual crowd, of course, a showy mix of Fleet Street's finest alongside a scattering of pol-iticians, other media and advertising types, the occasional hedge fund manager and the peacocks of the academic world.

Champagne was doing the rounds. He grabbed a glass, eagerly quaffing it in one go. He could see some of his father's friends glancing at him sym-pathetically, after the double take about the weight gain, as if he was a stray animal in need of veterin-ary attention. They must have heard about the impending divorce. The news would have been greeted with a sly smile and recycled comments that Emma was always too good for him – an unlikely match that had lasted longer than it should. He wished Lily was still alive. She had a gift for one-liners, the result of a childhood among Oxford academics. Life was empty without her.

'Max!'

Max turned and saw his father in the distance. There was someone else standing alongside him too. A tall, rounded figure in a shimmering black dress. Max blinked, rubbed his eyes, then blinked again, and wondered if it was too much champagne. The figure approached him now arm-in-arm with Oliver, every feature memorized, far happier than she had any right to be.

Max grabbed another flute of champagne and sunk it in one.

This evening was about to get immeasurably worse.

Bugging a crowded public space was far easier than a private residence. The A4 watcher team was small this time – one manning the exit on foot, two inside. Charlotte remained at Thames House, ready to relay the details to Saul.

A Branch never publicized their methods, even to other parts of the Security Service. But tech-ops had solutions to almost any logistical problem. Bugs and cameras could be converted into all forms of household object, from earrings to menus. The key was to ensure decent coverage in case the target decided to move during the course of the evening. The job was part handyman and part soothsayer, foreseeing all future possibilities.

The hotel database showed that the booking 'Archer Birthday' was reserved solely for the bar area. That limited things, though it was always wise to plan for alternatives just in case. Bugs were placed liberally throughout the bar area of the Goring Hotel and also within the gents' toilets and by the wash basins. Once the signal strength was confirmed, it was possible for tech-ops to begin cancelling the extraneous noise and focusing in on the target's audible range.

Sixteen minutes after entering the hotel, Charlotte confirmed to Saul that his last-minute request had been completed. At her small open-plan desk on the third floor of Thames House, Charlotte opened her evening takeaway, cancelled her gym session and put on a pair of headphones. The fireworks were about to start.

Max Archer's ex-wife had been invited.

13

'You don't have to look so surprised.'

Max was on to his third glass of champagne now and longed for something stronger. He was already tipping into that delightfully fuzzy realm that lay between sobriety and drunkenness.

Emma. The old sod had invited Emma.

'I'm not surprised at the invitation,' he said. 'I'm just surprised it was accepted.'

He should have anticipated this. Oliver and Emma always had a bizarre bond. Perhaps that was why Max pursued the relationship to begin with. Emma was just the sort of person Oliver approved of. Forensically bright, occasionally bohemian, an illustrious cellar of semi-aristocratic relatives. She was neither too artsy nor too suffocatingly corporate. That was then, of course. Max had given up trying to figure out who she was now. Was it possible to live side by side with someone for almost twenty years and know less about them at the end than at the beginning?

'I was nearby. Your dad texted me specially and said he wanted to make sure things were all right. You know how much he means to me.'

Max smiled weakly. There had been no special text or WhatsApp for him. Emma's own father had died tragically young. Oliver had always been some kind of paternal substitute.

'I've signed the papers, Ems. My lawyer says there's nothing more for me to do.'

'That's not why I'm here.'

Max saw a waiter carrying another tray brimming with fresh glasses. They were thin. Four surely wasn't too much. He reached for another but held off drinking it, exhibiting some degree of self-control. Emma held her pregnant belly, wincing slightly with a kick. Max knew he couldn't ignore it any longer. The bump was practically staring at him. Even that seemed to mock him.

'When's it due?' he said.

'Nine weeks.'

'Do you know which it is yet?'

'It's a baby, Max, not a Labrador.'

'I was aware of that fact.'

'Cristiano and I decided not to find out.'

'Preserve the element of mystery. Very sensible.'

Cristiano. It was the name of a footballer not a fund manager. Though, no doubt, this particular Cristiano would be a dab hand at the beautiful game as well. Along with lavish attention to bathtimes, child development, nutrition plans and all the other accoutrements of modern fatherhood. Oliver's idea of the paternal gesture was bribing him with fruit pastilles on their biannual cinema trips. The one time they ever played football together Oliver had slide-tackled him. The whole thing ended in A&E.

'How's work going?'

Yes, it was that singsong quality that floored him. Max had friends who'd recently separated, and it was like the highlights reel from *Scarface*. But that was when there were kids involved. Violent disputes about custody arrangements, school fees and the torn allegiance of family and friends. Emma seemed to approach this entire subject with a preternatural sense of calm, as if they were simply two housemates who'd decided to move on. There had been few tears, precious little argument, just a sense of horrible inevitability. Emma had no close family, Max merely had Oliver. She had spent two decades chained to a desk. He'd researched other people's lives rather than bothering to live his own. Neither had much change from two decades of investment.

'Good, very good,' he said. 'Excellent, in fact.'

Emma smiled, even reaching out and brushing his shoulder. 'You deserve a break, Max. We all do.'

'And you?'

'I got the news last night, as it happens. They're making me a senior partner in California. The Bay Area. The engine room of Silicon Valley.'

Max wasn't sure if it was the champagne or the empty stomach. But he wondered if he could keep anything down. Emma wasn't just moving on. No, she was recreating herself. The days of drizzly old England with that deadbeat first husband would soon become a comic anecdote like misguided student drug use or teenage drunkenness.

'California? Ems, that –'

'Well, it was always a bit of a dream. But the chance came up unexpectedly. Cris is always over there anyway, and it just seemed *right*, you know.'

So that's why she was here. Tonight wasn't to support Oliver, not at all; it was to say goodbye.

130

Max felt that thudding realization again. Emma was heading off to the life she'd always wanted, with a new supporting cast and new storylines. He was doomed to repeat the same tired hamster-wheel, barely changed since his student days. Somehow the dream of adult life had always seemed just that – a dream that never turned into reality.

He gulped down the fourth flute of champagne and snatched at another one now. He could see the flicker of concern in Emma's eyes, which only spurred him on.

'Max, seriously, you're sure you're okay?'

'Me?' He took another deep gulp. 'Yes, yes. Fantastic, in fact. It's finally happening, Ems. Everything we used to talk about. You're going to the Bay Area with a kid on the way. I'm finally getting my big break. It's all coming together. The stars are finally aligning.'

At that very moment, Oliver sidled up to them and thumped Max hard on the back, sending a mouthful of champagne flying.

'So,' Oliver said, several decibels louder than necessary, 'she's told you the news about the land of dreams. Wonderful stuff.'

Max scowled at his father. He wiped the champagne stain on his trousers. 'You knew, then?'

Sensing a family disagreement, Emma quickly interceded. 'Actually, Max was just telling me about this big break of his. Apparently, it's finally happened. Whatever *it* is.'

It was Oliver's turn to frown now. Then the smile returned, wreathing his full, almost feminine lips.

'Forty-two years in the making. I bloody well hope so. Don't tell me. You've finally got a full professorship and a proper job?'

Max winced. 'Not quite yet, but this break will get me there.'

'They're finally paying you more than the receptionist?'

Careful, Max. Easy now. 'They won't need to once I get the advance on this next project. Six figures and counting. Trust me.'

Oliver was grinning sarcastically now, still searching for the exposed flesh, any sense of vulnerability. 'You've seen sense and decided to thrash out a novel? Just like I've been telling you to all these years. Six figures? The advance will be in roubles, will it? Or, no, the Zimbabwean dollar.'

The champagne, the empty stomach, Emma's pregnant belly, Oliver's laugh – all the pressure points collided until Max felt caution desert him. He didn't care any more. He was tired of all this. The whole bloody thing.

Emma was talking to Oliver now, as if Max no longer existed. 'You know I was always encouraging him with his creative writing. I think he has real talent.'

'As the old adage goes,' said Oliver. 'Those who can't spy, write. Those who can't write, write thrillers.'

There was another gale of laughter. Max saw Emma stifle a smile. Oliver thumped him on the back again. Before he knew it, Max heard the words tumble out without conscious thought or effort.

'I've got a new source actually,' he said, loud

enough to surf above the laughter. 'The last undiscovered Cold War double agent. I have exclusive access to her memoir, making it the first contemporaneous account of a real-life traitor working at the top of Western intelligence. I've verified the material and there's currently a secret bidding war on both sides of the Atlantic, not to mention some *very* serious interest from Hollywood. I'm finalizing the typescript as we speak. It's vulgar to talk figures, I know. But, Ems, let's just say I've been ogling that four-bed in Kensington we always talked about. Before I got here, my agent confirmed that bidding has now crossed the seven-figure mark. They're saying this could be bigger than Mitrokhin.'

Oliver looked put out now. 'Dollars?'

'Sterling.'

'Max, old thing, you've clearly had too much to drink.'

'I'm serious.'

'It sounds like a decent idea for a novel though. Not a bestseller, but a so-so beach read. You could always look at self-publishing. Apparently everyone's doing it now. Or a blog.'

'I've read the memoir,' said Max. 'Frankly, it's better than a novel. She was in Vienna hunting Nazis just after the war. She was intimate with Philby in Section IX. She was even a confidante of Caspar Madison, which means the Americans are lapping it up as we speak. They want me to fly out to Hollywood next month. You know, we should have a coffee or something. Or dinner while I'm in town?'

Emma had that wasp-stung look about her now. 'You really are serious?'

'Deadly.'

Oliver couldn't let this go. 'For heaven's sake, Max, this bloody woman must be ancient. She'd surely be long dead by now. I know maths was never your strongest card, but –'

'Not necessarily. If she was in her twenties in 1946, she'd only be in her nineties now.'

'It's a good thing old age doesn't affect your mental abilities then. No, wait –'

'The memoir is authentic.'

'But why the hell would someone like that come to you?'

'She'd read my work on double agents and my biography of Philby. I'm one of the few intelligence experts in Britain who can verify the details. She needs me to give the project credibility.'

Oliver laughed humourlessly. 'Sounds like a classic stitch-up to me, Max. Take it from an old timer. I'd steer well clear. You can't even be sure she's who she says she is. I worked with these people. Born liars, the lot of them. They're leading you up the garden path.'

'I did my homework. I've confirmed her identity. If you don't believe me, the details of the book deal should be released prior to publication. A seven-figure advance for the greatest true-spy story of the Cold War and the first memoir from a living double agent. That should get a few headlines. Hey, perhaps you could do a story on it. Something to keep you busy in retirement.'

Emma switched into her lawyerly mode now.

'Oliver's right, Max. Speaking as a lawyer now – and as a *friend* – you don't want to find yourself on the wrong side of this. My firm deals with this kind of thing all the time. Our side coming after you is one thing. The Americans, on the other hand, is a thousand times worse.'

'I thought you were in corporate law?'

'I'm just thinking of *you*, Max. I don't want to be arranging visits to a super-max federal prison.'

Max waved the concern away. 'Look, I don't care about the law. The Official Secrets Act deserves to be broken. We're the ones who pay for the intelligence services. The public deserves to know the truth. I'm not going to be gagged or muzzled by the state. Last time I checked this was still a free country.'

'Thank you, Cicero,' quipped Oliver. 'What's the name of this super-secret source, then? Deep Throat?'

'My source used to be Sovbloc Controller at SIS when the Berlin Wall came down. She was once lined up to be the first female Chief.'

'That's what they all say. And I'm the Wizard of Oz. Trust me, dear boy, she's pulling your leg. She's probably some two-bit actress looking for a fat payday. Look what happened with the Hitler diaries. Even Trevor-Roper fell for that one. If it sounds too good to be true, it always is.'

'Listen to him, Max.' Emma, again. 'This isn't student papers and academic conferences. This is the *real* world. You could get yourself into some serious trouble.'

Oliver smiled. 'Heed the advice of your good

lady wife, Maximillian. If you'd done a bit more of that, she might not be fleeing to the other side of the Atlantic. I bet you this so-called "source" hasn't even told you her name. You know, this is why academics should stay in their lane. Leave the heavy lifting to the proper journalists like me. People who've been trained.'

Max felt the champagne glass dig into his finger. He was gripping the top so tight it was almost drawing blood.

He turned to face Oliver, watching carefully for a reaction. Then he took a nonchalant sip to finish and said, 'Her name is Scarlet King.'

14

It was a lie, yes, but only a small white lie. It made life bearable. Even if it could be his downfall. After all, every decent politician had a secret life. It practically came with the job description.

For a blissful hour each night, Lucas Harper could veg out on the sofa free of the relentless grind of human and political misery. The only decisions that seemed to reach his desk now were the ones no one else wanted to make. He'd begun in politics as an idealist. Ministerial office had turned him into a blunt pragmatist. The Home Office had reduced that – one shard of human misery at a time – to permanent and stomach-clenching depression. The chorus of human suffering was truly something to behold.

His televisual habits, however, remained secret. He had his own private Netflix and Amazon accounts and was careful to log off before his three kids seized control of the TV remote and poured scorn on their father's post-work viewing habits. Each night his wife left him for a bath while he was studiously engrossed in *Newsnight*. Even so, he had nightmares about the smart TV being hacked by the Iranians or the Chinese. Great careers had been wrecked by less: *Maid in Manhattan, Sleepless in Seattle, Two Weeks Notice, The Rewrite, The Wedding Planner*. Which serious politician could honestly survive watching *Holidate* three times in a row?

Tonight's Netflix romcom was egregiously titled *Falling Inn Love* and was just as bad as it sounded. Lucas reluctantly checked his phone and the diary for tomorrow. A breakfast meeting with the Met Commissioner, a morning of meetings regarding a major NCA op to take down drug traffickers on the south coast, then an afternoon in the Commons on the new terrorism bill. The drudgery of it weighed on him. More brickbats, more abuse. He yawned and switched off the telly. Then the landline started ringing in his home office. It was the secure line, fully encrypted. Monitored round the clock by Thames House. Another damn emergency.

It was late. He'd been up since five-thirty and was about to repeat the whole charade in a few hours' time. He stifled another yawn and trudged through into the study. He picked up the receiver. 'Yep?'

'Home Secretary, sorry to disturb. It's Saul Northcliffe here.'

Lucas shook the late-night fug away. He tried to concentrate. Northcliffe was the second in command at Thames House mainly focused on special projects and the sensitive aspects of political liaison. He was sometimes present for Lucas's weekly intelligence briefings from the Director-General. A slightly crabby member of the old guard, immune to political charm offensives. 'What is it, Saul?'

'It's regarding the SIGINT operation you

authorized recently codenamed Tempest, Minister. Surveillance warrants on a former intelligence operative called Scarlet King and an academic by the name of Max Archer. You asked to be updated.'

Lucas felt that uptick of panic again. He longed to be back on the sofa, transported to another world. 'I thought you'd taken care of that,' he said. Even his voice needed rest. 'Shut her down. Stop her talking out of turn. Number 10 have given us licence to stamp as hard as we like on this one. Why can't we just send out a DSMA-Notice and be done with the bloody thing?'

'Alas, I'm afraid the string from the SIGINT op suggests we already may be past the point of no return on this one.'

There was a reason the Home Office was considered a ministerial graveyard. Few occupants ever survived more than a year or two. Lucas saw himself waiting outside the Cabinet Room and telling the Prime Minister and assorted special advisers why another disaster had occurred on his watch.

'You've lost me, Saul. How can that be possible?'

'We've been tracking the academic Scarlet King is working with. It seems the project may be even more advanced than we thought. The academic claims to have read the entire notebook and is helping prepare it for publication.'

Lucas was old enough to remember the Spycatcher affair in the eighties. He was already in Parliament during the David Kelly saga. Intelligence squabbles were not designed to be played out in public. The tabloids splashed on all the gory

details, while the broadsheets demanded accountability and resignation.

'How bad?'

'Our intel suggests the manuscript covers two
strap four items.'

Strap four was the highest possible classification. It concerned material that had a direct impact
upon British national security. 'Which are?'

'First, Scarlet King is threatening to out herself
as the last undiscovered Russian double agent of
the Cold War. Second, and equally inconvenient, it
appears she could blow the lid on the Hercules
programme.'

Lucas steadied himself against the desk. He felt
nauseous. 'That's not possible.'

'We thought so too.'

'If she's got away for this long, why on earth
would she out herself now?'

'It seems to earn a seven-figure publishing
advance and then die before we can mount a
prosecution.'

Lucas felt nervous even mentioning the next
part. On being appointed, each Home Secretary
was given a security briefing with MI5. It concerned all current operations and all 'legacy' cases,
a euphemism for state secrets under the aegis of
the Home Department which were known only to
the Prime Minister, Home Secretary and the senior
leadership of the Security Service. The Hercules
programme was the oldest and most classified of
all. Lucas could still remember being briefed on it
by the Director-General after the last reshuffle. The
name alone caused him sleepless nights.

'Surely we can stop anything about Hercules becoming public.'

'By traditional means, yes. But we can't stop it spreading on social media. If Scarlet King has enough to publish, there's very little we can do.'

'What about the academic? Do you have enough to bring him in?'

'Possibly. But I've spoken with the Director of Public Prosecutions. We don't have enough to authorize charge. Her sense was a fumbled arrest could do more harm than good at this stage. I have to say I agree.'

'What about Scarlet King? Why can't you arrest her?'

There was a pause on the line. Then Saul North-cliffe said, 'Candidly?'

'Yes.'

'She'll have anticipated it. She's been in the game too long. Bringing her in won't stop the memoir being published. But it will stop us being able to follow the trail.'

'It sounds like you're giving me no options.'

'Not quite.'

Lucas tried to calm himself. This was the problem with spooks. They were so damn spidery. Everything was slow, sotto voce, like trying to nail paint to a wall. 'Well?'

'I do have one suggestion, Minister. But, for it to work, we'll have to move fast.'

15

The party was still in full throttle when Max left. The new email had arrived six minutes earlier, pinging into the top of his faculty inbox:

From: parkbench1946@outlook.com
To: m.archer@lse.ac.uk
Subject: RTB (Stamford Bridge)

Max thought it was spam at first. There was no body to the message, just a subject line. He was about to delete it when his attention snagged on the sender's email handle: 'parkbench1946'. He thought of the meeting with Scarlet. The location, the date. Then he looked at the subject line: 'RTB (Stamford Bridge)'. RTB was spy speak for 'Return to Base', an emergency signal in the field for all operatives to get back to the relative safety of embassy territory. 'Stamford Bridge', meanwhile, was the home of Chelsea Football Club. Which meant two things: first, it was urgent; second, Scarlet knew about his actions in St James's Park.

Max made his excuses and, drunker than he thought, stumbled out into Belgravia. It was too risky to keep the email in his inbox. He was about to swipe across and delete the email – once from the inbox, the second from trash – when he saw the message was no longer even there. Of course.

The same method that MI5 and SIS used in their recruitment process. The email was self-deleting.

Max continued walking and wondered if he'd imagined that subject line. Emma had already gone, spirited away by Cristiano's driver, the small detail casually dropped for maximum effect. Who was he kidding? Emma was far better off, in both an economic and spiritual sense. That was the problem with marrying young. The woman in that Harvard library bore little relation to the person who'd just left in the back of a grey Mercedes, now safely tucked up in a Belgravia mews house.

The first twenty years of life, he was starting to realize, were all external. Spots, grease, hormones – the bumpy ride to adulthood. The next twenty were all internal, far more difficult to catch. The shop window didn't change – a few more wrinkles, perhaps, receding hairlines, a squashier midriff – but the real action was hidden. All the student rebels he'd known were now plump-faced reactionaries. The young fogeys, by contrast, were socks-and-sandals rebels earnestly hunting a lost youth. Metamorphosis, wasn't that the word? All of us shapeshifters, eternally mutating.

Max staggered past a nearby shop window and saw his own side-on reflection. He'd changed too. His old self was three stone lighter, even slightly dressy, brimming with optimism about the years ahead and still carrying something of Oliver's charm and Lily's intellect. Now what? His roguish side had gone for starters. The dress sense had worsened. Self-respect had flipped into pomposity. He used to be fun. But, at some nameless point, the jokes had turned sour. He could do a fine line in sarcasm now, scything others down to his level. This new, middle-aged incarnation was like a different self. The one that drove Emma away.

He tried to remember how many glasses of champagne he'd had and guessed around nine or ten. He fished in his pocket for the burner mobile he'd bought before the second meeting with Scarlet. The screen crawled with updates. He saw himself at the hardware store near Haymarket buying the tracker device in cash. Dropping it into Scarlet's handbag as they sat on the park bench in St James's. It had been his one genuine act of tradecraft, trying to suss out if Scarlet King was genuine, or merely some kind of false flag. He wanted to see where she returned to after the meeting.

Max sucked in a lungful of night-time air and tried to focus. The watch already felt heavy on his wrist. It was nice, though, far more than he could ever afford. The one unexpected bonus of tonight's proceedings. It had been just at the end of the party, as Max was crossing the lobby, that Oliver had buttonholed him, a slightly apologetic look in his eyes and a small black pouch in his right hand.

'I almost forgot,' he said. 'I had this little piece repaired recently and I wanted to pass it on. Something of a family heirloom on your mother's side. Rolex 3525 Oyster chronograph. Stainless steel. Ordered in '43 to Stalag Luft III in Lower Silesia. You'll doubtless know the rest of the story.'

Max remembered standing in the foyer and staring at the velvety black pouch and imagining the contents inside. It was a timeless family anecdote, even better than his parents' first meeting. Lily's father, Max's grandfather, had been interned as a prisoner of war in Lower Silesia in 1943 during the Second World War when serving with the RAF. Stalag Luft III was the POW camp later made famous by the Great Escape. Rolexes were all the rage among RAF officers and there were always rumours that this watch had been used to help time the movements of prison guards during the Great Escape itself. Flight Lieutenant Maurice Anderson, Lily's father, was one of the few spared execution. He dined out on the story ever after. The watch had been inherited by Lily and, after her death, Oliver. Now it was being passed on. Max had thought of Lily and felt a sudden terrible stab of sadness.

'Thank you.'

Oliver was soon called away. Max had made a quick exit. But the watch's history seemed to seep into his skin now. He was his grandfather's heir, capable of similar feats of bravery. He would guard it carefully, hand it down to his own children. No, one thing was for sure. This particular heirloom would never leave his wrist.

Max looked at the tracking app on the burner phone again. It showed Scarlet King had returned to an address just off the Chelsea Embankment on Beaufort Street. Present, not past. Concentrate. Don't over-think this. What did Lily used to say?

Instinct is everything.

Stamford Bridge. Return to Base. Scarlet was demanding a crash meeting.

Max found himself following the directions. He caught a cab near Victoria Station and watched blearily as they drove through Belgravia and towards Chelsea before turning left on to Beaufort Street. He paid in cash and got out feeling newly alive again. He could still see the look in Emma's eyes as he mentioned the memoir project. That was the only way to show her. To revive the old Max Archer. The man on the make, the young rising star, to seize his chance for the big break before it was lost forever.

Beaufort Street was lined with comely red-brick mansion blocks, all very tasteful and discreet. Max's stomach growled with hunger. He was getting drunker by the moment, pausing every few steps to try and keep himself upright. He would confront Scarlet and get the diary. He would work night-and-day, however long it took, to get it into a publishable state and write a learned introduction. It could happen soon. He could imagine Emma and Cristiano sitting down to breakfast in their Californian loft conversion and glancing haughtily at the *New York Times*: 'Double Agent's Memoir sold in seven-figure bidding war'. He would need a better profile photo, of course, perhaps dust down an older one. But that would show her. Emma, Oliver, Kessler – the whole damn lot of them.

Max reached the end of Beaufort Street and checked the tracking app against the building on his left. According to the app, Scarlet King had entered the building entrance and then a ground-floor flat. It was dark now and the entrance was illuminated by a patchy set of streetlights. Max found the entry-level door and saw the buzzers on his right. There was a lower-ground floor level and

Max tried to calculate how they would be numbered. He waited until another resident unlocked the door and left, too absorbed in her thick Beats headphones and a podcast to see him.

Max slipped inside before the door closed and into a bare-stone entrance hallway. There was a long stone staircase on his left. The ground-floor flats were down a corridor on the right. Max glanced at the tracker app. There were three ground-floor flats. Max expanded the tracker map to get a better view and decided it must be the end flat.

He was about to knock when there were more footsteps, voices too. He ducked out of sight, waiting as three twenty-somethings left the building in a whirl of gossip and laughter. He inched back out into the coppery light and approached the end flat. He was about to knock. Then, on impulse, he tried the door handle instead.

Max felt it give. The flat door was open. Later, with the aid of sobriety, he could see how wrong it all was. He would go over the exact sequence of events until every second was freeze-framed. But his brain was still fuzzed with champagne, his stomach churning emptily. Instead of a rational sense of fear, Max experienced a small bolt of elation. The door was open. Fate was on his side. The empty boast at the party. He would collect the diary tonight, contact his agent. The future – in all its redemptive glory – could be seized with both hands.

The first anomaly was the lack of light. Max glanced at his phone and saw the time was just after eleven. Scarlet was old. Did the elderly retire to bed earlier, like a reversion to childhood? Lily had, but she'd been ill. Oliver was the night owl of the family. Max followed suit, rarely asleep before one or two in the morning. Perhaps Scarlet was in bed. It was at that point, Max knew later, that he could still have walked away. Edged out, wiped the handle for prints, disappeared down Chelsea Embankment. The evidence trail against him – the witness testimony of the taxi driver, the CCTV positioned around the building, the trace evidence in the hallway – was damning. But survivable.

Instead, Max was seized by another desire, a mix of self-preservation and greed. Scarlet King was a trained hood. She had been Sovbloc Controller at SIS during some of the most dangerous moments of the Cold War. Moscow Rules – the most extreme form of tradecraft – was ingrained in all spies of her generation. Paranoia was part of her genetic make-up. Even at her advanced age, she would routinely check for any kind of bugs or devices which might compromise her. Max saw her finding the small tracking device he'd planted in her handbag. Was that why she wanted to meet, informing him their agreement was cancelled?

Max tried to orientate himself in the darkness, his eyes slowly adjusting. He tiptoed along the carpeted hallway and reached a small flight of stairs down into some kind of sitting area. Max clung on to a small banister, careful not to tumble headlong on to the floor. The emergency message broke all protocol. Crash meetings were rare, only ever used *in extremis*. For some reason, Scarlet needed to see him urgently.

There was a gargle of sound from the hallway, lights winking outside. Max waited, drink exaggerating his movements, until it was safe to continue. A TV in one corner. Two sofas. A coffee table.

And then he saw it.

The handbag Scarlet had been carrying that afternoon. Now perched on the sofa to his right. It was impossible to be certain of the colouring given the lack of ceiling light, but it looked almost identical. Max listened for any other sounds but heard nothing.

He reached down and carefully unzipped the handbag, trying to remember exactly where the tracking dot had fallen. It was the size of a polo mint, and he'd only had seconds to drop it into the handbag while Scarlet's gaze was elsewhere. Max searched within the bag, feeling a collection of tissues, a small compact mirror, even a paperback book – surely the novel Scarlet had been reading when he met her in St James's Park.

Then, finally, he felt a small metallic disc. It was cold and shiny. He prized it up between his right thumb and index finger until it was safely in his grip. Yes, this was it. It had done its job. Now it was time to make the evidence vanish.

Max pocketed the tracking dot and then swiped the app from the screen. There was still no sound from any of the other rooms. Max gave the place a final glance in case there was any sign of a safe or cabinet. He was tired now, his nerves fried. This was madness. Had he just imagined the email? He should turn and leave and pretend none of this had ever happened. He could pretend he was checking up on Scarlet's safety having found her door unlocked. That's what real spies did. They were storytellers.

Max was about to retrace his steps when he noticed a succession of marks on the carpet, a small drip-trail crawling into the main hallway. He followed them instinctively, fear tingling up his spine, until he reached a door off the right of the main hallway. The marks were more consistent here, smudging horribly against the carpet.

Max teased open the door and entered a small bedroom. The curtains were still open and the room was cast in a pale lemon-yellow light. The drip-trail increased here until there were stains all around the base of the bed. Max walked towards the bed. A figure stared up blankly at the ceiling.

He reached down, almost as if watching himself from above, then he took his hand away.

The first thing he saw was blood.

The Scarlet Papers
1964

1964
The Fourth Man

Control smiled, then coughed wheezily. His voice was thin. There were no introductions today, not even the customary drinks offer. According to rumour, he was ill. They were at his home, rather than Whitehall, as they always had been for all their off-the-books encounters. This was the last meeting.

'I hear they're sending you to Moscow,' he said, his fingers reaching for a pipe that was no longer there, strictly forbidden by the medical team.

'Yes.'

'Second Secretary cover as part of the Intelligence Branch. The only female intelligence officer deployed on an operational basis within SIS. Well, well. You have my sincere congratulations.'

Scarlet could read his real meaning by the inflection. She imagined the other hopefuls receiving the news that a woman had been plucked from relative obscurity and given the plum posting ahead of them. Some would offer their congratulations. Many would not. None of them would be sincere.

'Thank you.'

Control nodded, wincing at the movement. Yes, perhaps the rumours were true this time: he really was ill. Fatally, apparently. 'The situation, indeed, could hardly be more perilous. Especially after recent events involving your old comrade.'

It was all anyone within Broadway could talk about. The Third Man. Kim had finally gone through with it, bolting from Beirut. He was tucked up in Moscow with the rest of the rogues' gallery: Blake, Maclean, Burgess. Scarlet blamed Nick Elliott. Broadway, officially at least, had been silent, closing ranks. Betrayal felt curiously banal.

Control coughed again. 'There's something else you should know,' he said, meditatively almost, as if each word was precious. 'What I'm about to tell you must never go beyond the confines of this room. Are we perfectly clear on that? No one at Broadway must know I've told you this. Strictly our little secret.'

Scarlet didn't blink. Their usual terms. 'Of course.'

'We know that Philby associated with Burgess and Maclean at Cambridge. We also know of others who moonlighted at Five and Bletchley during the war. However, according to my sources, the high command has recently come across new information regarding the possibility of a fourth figure within the Firm who could pose a similar danger.'

Scarlet remained still. 'May I ask the source of this new information?'

Control nodded, studying her forensically. 'From what I gather, the source was recently exfiltrated from Moscow,' he said. 'That's why I asked you here. And that's why I'm telling you ahead of your new posting. This source is golden, apparently. I believe his codename is KAGO. Until recently, he was a senior officer within the KGB hierarchy.'

'And this source, KAGO, is sure about the

Fourth Man theory? There's no chance this is disinformation from Moscow to make us chase our tails?'

'It's a possibility that's been considered, of course it has. But apparently the current Chief is satisfied of his bona fides. No, KAGO is claiming that another Russian mole is still at large within the Service.'

'Does KAGO offer any concrete proof?'

'The source doesn't need to,' said Control. 'Apparently he's claiming that the Fourth Man tipped off Philby and encouraged him to flee to Russia. That's how Kim managed to elude our grasp in Beirut. That seems like evidence enough to me.'

She waited. There was a solemn silence as that fact was digested. Then she said, 'Why do you think I'm being sent to Moscow?'

'You'll have to ask your Chief.' Control was still lost in his own thoughts. He looked at her with a distracted air. 'But there are two things I need from you,' he said. 'Before it's too late. I can't impress enough the urgency of both.'

Scarlet nodded. 'What are they?'

'First, you must find out where the KGB are hiding Philby since his escape from Beirut. I want to know as much as you can find out about his circumstances and how they're using him. I suspect they'll be debriefing him intensely while the information in his possession still has some relevance.'

'Do you think there's a chance of turning him again?'

Control managed a smile now, his thin lips pinching together. 'Kim has a sybaritic side to him. We all know that. Cricket, English marmalade and *The Times* crossword. Like most of his tribe, he's a communist intellectually, but the theory is quite different from fact. The moment he realizes he's set to die in the greyness of the Soviet Union, I expect he'll slump into a profound depression. The Kremlin is eternally paranoid, anyway. Kim wants medals and attention, the sort of love he never got from that monster of a pa. I fear he may have walked straight into the arms of men far worse. No one is praised in Moscow, only suspected. Yes, I think there's a chance.'

Scarlet always saw Philby as Englishness incarnate, the clubman with his shabby-smart suits and amateurish grin. It was hard to imagine him patrolling Moscow, escorted through the loveless halls of the First Chief Directorate.

'And my second task?'

'The second task, I fear, is even trickier than the first. Given the new intelligence from the KAGO source, I want you to find any other KGB agents-in-place they have in Whitehall. I want the name of the Fourth Man. This is direct from the great man himself, you understand. We can't let our legacies be entirely dismantled.'

Scarlet knew Control's methods well enough by now. He had a snake-like aspect to him, a nose for cunning. She imagined the legions of other operatives he had seduced with claims that they – and they alone – could catch the Fourth Man. Despite the patrician formality, his genius as a spymaster was the hushed briefing, as if talking to a fellow member of the elect. He was the secret-keeper.

'Why me specifically?'

He was grave, more serious now. 'Because only you can do it, Scarlet. Only someone of your background. Find the Fourth Man. Bring me their name. Don't let history damn us all for one tragic oversight.'

'And after that? You will go through with what we originally discussed?'

He nodded. 'Of course, of course. After that, you can come in from the cold. You have my word on that.'

'And the Americans? Do we suspect them as well?'

'There's a new Chief of Station just been appointed. I believe you know him from the past. Madison, so I'm told. Mr Caspar Madison.'

She absorbed the news without reacting. 'We met briefly in Vienna when he was with OSS. Is he also a suspect?'

He held her gaze now. Earnest, almost fatherly. 'My dear, everyone is a suspect. At this point I'm afraid no one can be trusted.'

The meeting was over. He coughed again and then shooed her out with the usual lack of ceremony. She left the house and was chauffeured to the train station. She kept a close eye for any tail and then dry-cleaned herself on the route back to Broadway.

She wondered for a moment if Control ever intended to honour his promise or whether that was all part of the recruiter's trick. She imagined herself disappearing behind the Iron Curtain, providing the name of the Fourth Man, then left to the bloodiest of fates. She banished the thought and resumed her work. She could play him just like the other born-to-rule squires, deluded old men with third-rate minds.

Two weeks later, Scarlet boarded the flight to Moscow.

Three weeks after that, Control was dead.

1964
Moscow Rules

The letter was addressed to her personally. She found it in her pigeonhole at the embassy and recognized the messy hand: 'Miss S. King, Second Secretary, UK Foreign Service'. The front page was bland and formal, merely an American diplomat introducing himself and setting out his duties as the new First Secretary. It was only later that she saw the rest. That night she turned the paper over, delved into the small bottle of aspirin tablets on her nightstand – 'scorch' tablets, in the jargon – and the secret writing on the blank side came to life. There was the time and place for a meeting followed by the initials 'CM'.

She was almost lucky in some ways. Working in a denied area was perilous at the best of times. Moscow, though, was an open prison. Every move was shadowed. Diplomatic apartments were searched and left ransacked. They were hustled every time they left the nest of the embassy walls, the KGB hoods taunting them like spectres, or devils on the scent of a kill.

Tonight she took rudimentary precautions, nothing more. Others spent days losing a tail, whole afternoons of shortcuts, deviations, an absurd game of hide-and-seek where one error cost other people's lives. They lived in dread of the routine: the heavy thud at the door, the unmarked van, a black hood, then the dank cells of the Lubyanka and the relief of death itself, kneeling like an animal. Scarlet, though, was different. She was a woman and, therefore, not a spy. She was clerical, at best, her days filled with correspondence, her fingers scarred with staples and papercuts. Her footsteps left no imprint.

Amateurs chose famous places for a treff, landmarks that burnished novels or cinemas. The reality was drabber. Spies lived in the liminal places – cloakrooms, hallways, alleys, fields and cars. And tonight, as promised, the figure hovered in shadow, merely the outline of a long muffled coat and a hat silhouetted against the blackness.

She tried to remember how long it was since their last meeting. Yes, nearly twenty years. It felt more than a lifetime ago, the end of a different war rather than the middle of a new one. They had exchanged messages, of course, but at a distance. All she had were stories of his rise. There were pangs of jealousy, even; she was still a mere Second Secretary, barely granted a formal title within the Station. He was already Chief of Station, within sight of greatness.

The silhouette turned at her approach. The rudiments of his face became clearer. There was the same recognizable symmetry, though fuller now. His face had settled into itself. His hair was longer, and a forelock drooped below the rim of his hat. The boyish eyes remained, but the lightness was gone. The years seemed grooved into him, somehow, a story to each indentation.

Caspar.

1964
Mr Madison

They emerged on to another hidden street corner. It was oppressively dark, a stunning absence of natural light, and Scarlet tried to map the city in her mind. But Moscow was too labyrinthine. The American embassy boasted more staff and more money. They had better decoy routes as well. She followed him to a large, rather crumbly two-storey house. Caspar unlocked it and turned the lights on inside.

'One of our safe houses,' he said. 'That's the benefit of being CoS these days. I get a full run of the place.'

They took off their coats. Caspar poured drinks; Scarlet put on a record. It was almost like before. They sipped, talked of nothing, adjusting to each other's company. He said, 'I was thinking about our time in Vienna just the other day. Boy, I miss those days. Simpler times.'

'I would hardly call the end of a war simple.'

'A hot war's better than a cold one. At least everyone knows the score.'

She wanted to confess fully. How those days were sometimes all that sustained her. That those secrets taught her more about spying than any course or fieldwork. But, instead, she smiled disinterestedly and said, 'It all seems a very long time ago now.'

Madison nodded, silently accepting the rebuke. 'You're still in one piece, though, which must be good news. I wasn't sure either of us would last this long.'

She was back in Vienna again now, hearing those drunken boasts of a communist past and Operation Paperclip. There must have been other reckless moments since. Rumours suggested strong appetites for drink and women, often together. Some claimed he was made Chief of Station to avoid local difficulties at home.

'You're still on board with the project, though?' he said. His voice was lower now, oblique even. Ordinary conversation was too blunt and ugly on the ear. 'You're still fighting the good fight?'

Control, the old fool, was in her head again with those parting words. Caspar Madison could have an army of spooks hidden in the attic. Nothing could ever be taken literally, one of the logical paradoxes of espionage.

'Why the note?' she said, steering the conversation away from personal matters. 'The protocol is there to protect us.'

'Well, they're not wrong about that.'

'So?'

'Does the name Angleton mean anything to you? James Jesus Angleton.'

Yes, a name for the ages. She nodded. 'Langley's high priest of counterintelligence. He's obsessed, or so I'm told. Your very own mad monk. Rasputin himself.'

'Indeed.' Madison had even developed that older, slightly ponderous style. He was like a professor ripening for old age. 'I sent you the note because I want to give you a warning.'

That beat of fear again. With Kim's defection, the networks had been compromised. Escape was never far from her thoughts, a life lived by contingency plans: exit routes from Moscow, new identities, going underground. She was in a constant state of paranoia, hell even.

She steadied her voice. 'A personal warning or a professional one?'

'Possibly both. Before this posting I had a meeting with the Director. I know that Langley are seriously considering cutting intelligence ties with the British side. A clean break with all forms of intelligence sharing and SIGINT collaboration.'

'Perfectly impossible. The US–UK intelligence relationship has been in place ever since the war. It's the bedrock of the trans-Atlantic alliance. We still have diplomatic coverage in areas you can't access.'

'That's not how the Agency sees it. George Blake was one thing. The Cambridge group were another. Philby, on the other hand, could be the straw that breaks the camel's back. The guy was Head of Station in DC. A lot of serious people are asking how your guys let something like that happen.'

'You're serious.'

'Angleton has already begun a mole-hunt code-named HONTEOL. He's on the lookout for anyone else who could have consorted with Philby or is about to decamp to Moscow and buddy up with the Kremlin.'

'That sounds familiar.'

163

'Oh?'

'I heard gossip about a new source at Broadway codenamed KAGO. Apparently, he comes with news of other reds under the bed.'

Madison looked at her. She could see the divots in his face, a brow creased with worry. His voice was haunted. 'The source's name is Anatoly Golitsyn. He defected a few months ago. My handler confirmed it.'

'Is he dangerous?'

'Possibly.'

'What about Angleton?'

'Angleton's a maniac. He's on a divine mission to cut out anyone who might be tainted by association. He has an unlimited budget and almost no oversight. He's coming for us, Scarlet. He's coming for all of us.'

She stared straight back. 'And what happens then?'

Madison drained his glass. 'When they executed the Rosenbergs, they say smoke billowed from their skulls. The grand pooh-bahs won't be humiliated again. They want vengeance. And, by god, they're determined to get it.'

They were mildly drunk now. The fear and solitude overwhelming. They drank more. Scarlet kept meaning to leave. Caspar persuaded her to stay. Later, it was impossible to articulate quite what happened. For decades, she would interrogate the exact sequence of events. But it was fear, she decided. Fear made people do stupid things. Afterwards, in the spacious main bedroom with the cracks and pockmarks in the ceiling, they were silent together, hearing the rasps of the dirty Moscow evening and the rhythm of their lungs.

Caspar offered her a cigarette and lit it tenderly, cupping the flame and then smiling in that broad, primal way of his. For the first time, Scarlet felt almost normal. The half-life of a spy was replaced by something blissfully mundane. She forgot the watch in her jacket pocket and the outside world with its soiled, frenetic energy. The embassy was a ghost-town; each diplomat jailed in their rooms, only let out for clerical duties or administrative tasks. No, in Moscow, these few seconds were freedom.

The two of them smoked and remained silent. There was no regret. Eventually Caspar sighed and dressed. Scarlet left first. Caspar followed. They walked through the oily darkness of the city and imagined themselves as artists or bohemians, liberated from secrets. They reached the alleyway again.

Caspar stopped, his silhouette in shadow. 'Goodnight, Scarlet.'

She smiled chastely now and returned to the embassy with her usual care. She nodded to the guard outside and reached her room without being seen. That night she closed her eyes and slept easily. It was like the aftertaste of something.

Happiness, she decided.

1964
Broadway

The encrypted message arrived two weeks later, though it was hardly a surprise. The rumours of the mole-hunt at Broadway had reached epidemic proportions. All former associates of Mr Harold Philby in Section IX were being hauled back to London. In many ways she was surprised it took this long.

Scarlet knew as soon as she saw the read-out. It had the usual insignia of any missive from head office. But the words were cold and accusatory:

You are requested to return to Broadway immediately for an interview. Your section head has been informed. Do not repeat the contents of this message to any others inside the Station. DCIS

DCIS. The new Directorate of Counterintelligence and Security led by one of Broadway's rising stars, Maurice Oldfield. It was known by other SIS officers as the Star Chamber. They were the grand inquisitors employed by the new Chief to root out any other Soviet sympathizers or doubles within the ranks. The secret police.

She retreated to her room, pacing the worn carpet for hours. There was protocol for this, an exfiltration plan ready in hours. But the signal had to be sent tonight. The details were well-rehearsed: she would make a courtesy call to Aunt Maria in

Oxford and then use one of two possible paroles. 'I left my copy of *War and Peace*' would signal a long-term plan to gradually wind down her operational duties and disappear. 'I left my copy of *Anna Karenina*', however, put in motion a twelve-hour exfil, smuggled out of the embassy by a team disguised as cleaners.

Scarlet sat on the bed and read the message again. She thought of the exfil and Kim, condemned to an eternal Russian exile, a curiosity object paraded at KGB training days, always tarred with suspicion. Her mission – her purpose in life – would vanish. All the sacrifices since that first interview at Carlton Gardens almost twenty years ago would end in failure. And yet what was the alternative?

She calculated the time difference between Moscow and Oxford. Scarlet closed her eyes, breathed deeply. Then she made up her mind and left her room and walked down towards the secure bank of phones. She inserted the required passcode and dialled Aunt Maria's Oxford number from memory. It would be an unholy hour in Jericho. She prayed for an answer.

The line almost rang out before a voice crackled into life: 'Hello?'

'Aunt Maria,' she said. 'It's Scarlet.'

That, too, was another signal. 'It's me' was the usual greeting. 'It's Scarlet' denoted that the parole would be given. She heard Aunt Maria tense slightly, her voice newly formal.

'Scarlet, how good to hear from you. How are you?'

The conversation must seem normal. 'Fine, fine.

The weather's filthy this time of year. You got my card, I trust?'

'Yes, yes.' Aunt Maria was an old pro at this. 'Sorry, dear, I'm a tired old mess at the moment. I just finished my new monograph on Tolstoy. An unsightly slog. I'm sending it off to my editor next week. Heaven knows how they'll ruin this one.'

'When will it be published?'

'Next year, I hope. I've got some of the footnotes to correct first.'

They were light, breezy in fact, as if this were the most natural call in the world. 'Look, while I remember, I think I left my Tolstoy copy on the bedside table in the guest room when I stayed. I've been trying to find it for weeks.'

A suitable pause, the sound of confusion. 'Ah, let me see. I thought I saw something in there when I gave it a clean. Which one exactly?'

This was the moment. Everything depended on the next few words. Her fate, her life, her future. Aunt Maria breathed heavily on the line.

Scarlet made her final decision.

1964
Old Friends

Broadway barely seemed to have changed. The headquarters of the Secret Intelligence Service still looked greyly anonymous, befitting the craft, and even more in need of refurbishment. The flight back to London had been long and uncomfortable. Scarlet was put up at a Service house for the night, though she failed to get much sleep. The place teemed with bugs, no doubt, her every movement recorded. There was something voyeuristic about it. She wondered if the panel today would have reviewed the night's evidence like grubby old men.

The security checks were tighter than she remembered. This was the post-Philby paranoia, after all. Her bag was searched thoroughly by a uniformed officer, then she was patted down to check nothing was being smuggled in or out. Finally, she was let through and greeted by a new recruit she remembered from a visit to the Fort. Robertson, she thought, or perhaps Callaghan. The musty décor was still in place, but things seemed even grumpier now. The riotous clatter of typewriters and heels were replaced by nunnery silence. Every door was locked. Random checks were being conducted at the entrance and exit. The days of intelligence barons in their country tweeds carting off files for a long weekend were over.

Scarlet expected to be ferried to the fourth or fifth floor, the usual location for high-level interrogations. Instead, she was led to a new, mazy set of corridors on the basement level. There was a total lack of natural light. She was reminded of tales about the Cabinet war rooms underneath Whitehall and Churchill in his siren suit and the smell of body odour as unwashed generals talked about saving civilization.

'Not much longer now,' said her chaperone.

Scarlet had swallowed her doubts on the flight back, convinced in her bones that the first parole was the correct one. *War and Peace* rather than *Anna Karenina*. Steps could be put in place with the London KGB resident. Moscow alerted. The exfil – if it needed to happen – would be planned. An emergency escape from the embassy was too risky. There was every chance of a firefight, especially in the post-Kim climate. Now, though, as she walked the gloomy brick-lined basement corridors, fear smothered her. Daylight spelled freedom. This had the air of captivity.

There were a variety of suited figures walking past that she didn't recognize. This basement lair must be the headquarters of the new Directorate of Counterintelligence and Security. There was a scattering of women, too, most of them at desks with a fast, secretarial typing speed. The youngish man stopped at a room on his left. He knocked once and then received permission to enter.

Scarlet was a step behind. She felt nauseous. Why did Control have to die in disgrace at this very moment? She knew the measure of him. Others were a mystery.

'Ah, Miss King, glad you could join us. I trust the flight over was tolerable. Many apols for the short notice on this. Needs must, I'm afraid. You remember how things are here. Please, please, come in.'

Scarlet saw the two men in front of her and tried to hide her surprise. The first was slightly podgy, with a pair of owlish spectacles and a rather donnish presence. He extended a moist hand to shake and then readjusted his glasses. This was Maurice Oldfield, the head of the new Directorate of Counterintelligence and Security. One of the bright young things, tipped for the very top.

The second man smiled formally and said, 'Miss King. This is indeed a pleasant reunion. Do take a pew.'

Archie.

Scarlet cursed herself. All her assumptions about this interrogation were now redundant. Captain Grenville didn't seem to have aged much in the last twenty years. He still had that soldierly gruffness about him. His hair and moustache were greyer, perhaps, his back a little more stooped. But the scuffed suits and no-nonsense manner were identical. Archie was one of them. Oldfield would be the officer, Scarlet knew, charmingly detached. Archie was the Directorate's chief enforcer, the sergeant major with his parade-ground bark. He must be in his sixties now. He'd always seemed old.

'As you may have heard, Miss King,' said Oldfield, nodding for the aide to exit and shut the door, 'the Chief has decided to set up a new unit in charge of operational security following, well, recent unfortunate events. The Directorate's task is to ensure that history doesn't repeat itself. We're interviewing lots of people, you understand. Your presence here does not denote any suspicion on our part. Consider it like another round of vetting. Are we quite clear on that before we start?'

'Yes, of course.' Scarlet didn't believe a word of it. They were interviewing potential doubles, the names in line to join Kim in exile. She tried to recalculate. Was Archie the reason she was called back from Moscow? Or did he simply want an excuse to get rid of her? Was he embarrassed at the role they had all played in Hercules? Was this a directive from the fifth floor to extinguish a twenty-year-old secret?

Archie opened a manila file and handed a sheet of paper to Oldfield. It was Archie, now, who took charge of the interrogation. The details man, the inquisitor. Oldfield sat back, his arms clasped against his operatic belly, watching on with detachment.

Scarlet could hear the noise of feet and ringing phones outside. Despite the bland surroundings, she was fighting for her life.

'Well, Miss King,' said Archie. 'I want to start by asking about your time at Cambridge.'

1964
The Cambridge Spies

The question rocked her. She was about to point out their mistake. Scarlet King was an Oxonian, Lady Margaret Hall, proudly on the arts rather than science side. Archie, however, got there before her with a knowing smirk.

'You attended the Joint Services School for Linguistics before your first operational posting as part of the Intelligence Branch, is that correct?'

The JSSL. Of course. Scarlet had taken an intensive six-month course in Russian, an interlude before she was sent to Moscow. 'Yes, that's right.'

'You're aware, I presume, that our comrades in the Security Service have recently identified the JSSL as a potential recruiting ground for KGB agents in Britain?'

'No. I was not.'

'Rather a bizarre omission, don't you think?'

'I'm not sure I follow.'

'Let's see. You attended the JSSL in '63. By that point you'd spent seventeen years with us, including four separate foreign postings. Jolly nice too. Now you were joining the Intelligence Branch proper, the first woman to do so. Quite the achievement. Given that aptitude, I struggle to believe that you had no inkling, not even the tiniest suspicion, that Cambridge was a Russian hunting ground?'

'That's not what I said.'

'I see. My misinterpretation. So you *were* aware of Soviet recruitment while studying at Cambridge?'

'Not in the way you're implying.'

'And what way would that be?'

'I was there to learn Russian. I was more than happy to leave spying behind for six months and concentrate on my studies. It was something of a relief.'

'You were attached to Trinity College during that period, correct?'

'Yes.'

'Was that Mr Philby's recommendation?'

'No.'

'But, indeed, you were close friends with Mr Philby after your time together in Section IX, correct?'

'I wouldn't say close, exactly. We knew each other professionally and occasionally socialized. As did most of the other people in this building. You included.'

Archie brushed the comment aside. 'And, as a distinguished alumnus of Trinity College, Mr Philby had no thoughts to share when he heard the news?'

'Kim was out of things by that point. I was hardly updating him on every incident in my private life, nor in my professional duties. We hardly spoke at all.'

'No?' Archie turned to another page in his manila file. He handed it across to Scarlet. 'How curious. Perhaps, then, you could explain the origins of this chappie.'

Scarlet looked at the piece of paper. It was a copy of a letter written on thick cream notepaper. It was addressed to Scarlet. Archie had a second version and proceeded to read out the contents.

'Dear Scarlet, positively thrilled in the back of beyond to hear about Trinity etc. I shall try to enjoy myself without getting into any sort of trouble. Intelligence Branch at last! And a woman, to boot. Much love to all, Kim.' Archie put the piece of paper down. 'This was found during a search of Philby's premises in Beirut after he fled. He clearly didn't have time to get his affairs in order before he made a dash for it. Carefully written but, alas, seemingly never posted.'

Cornered, then. She'd underestimated Archie. 'Clearly.'

'It seems he knew of your acceptance at the Joint Services School and Trinity. The result of telepathy, perhaps, or divine intervention?'

'It's possible he heard about it, yes. We had mutual friends in common. After the kindness he showed me at Section IX, I felt obliged to show some kindness back. News may have travelled. That's hardly my doing. This place has always been like a sieve for personal gossip.'

'What else did you feel obliged to do for Philby? Or, I'm sorry, "Kim", as you call him in your young, intimate fashion.'

'He was my boss. He'd given me a break after Vienna. My work in Section IX got me the Intelligence Branch promotion. In many ways I owed him my career.'

'So you felt sorry at the way he was treated, is that it? Or were you more sympathetic to his cause? An ideological fellow traveller as well as a friend?'

'I liked him as a human being. I felt betrayed by him as a spy. It's quite possible to separate those two things. One doesn't invalidate the other.'

'No, no, I suppose you're right. Pity about all those agents he betrayed, though, wasn't it? The networks he burned. Those poor Albanians slaughtered. Do you think they felt invalidated?'

'None of us knew about that back then. Neither did you. Those rumours were recent. As soon as I heard about them, Kim became someone different for me.'

'So, to recap, the Oxford graduate and the first woman clever enough to be promoted to the Intelligence Branch didn't know her long-time friend Kim had any communist sympathies, despite the fact he was questioned on television in the fifties about his possible identity as the Third Man? Nor did she have any awareness that Trinity College, Cambridge, or the Joint Services School, was used as a recruiting ground by the Russians? Does that sum up the state of things?'

'Awareness and knowledge are quite different states of consciousness.'

'For those of us not blessed with an Oxford education?'

'I may be aware of many things I can't prove, Captain Grenville. But perhaps you've been out of the field too long.'

'Have I indeed?'

'My job as an intelligence officer is to gather intelligence that I can stand up. Embassy gossip helps no one. During my time at Cambridge, I never had any direct evidence that students were being recruited by the KGB. To report otherwise would have been professionally negligent.'

'Let's change the focus then,' said Archie, shuffling more paper and gazing curiously at the contents of the manila file. 'Forget the other students. Who tried to recruit *you*?'

Don't flinch. Calm, composed. 'No one.'

'What about romantic liaisons? I see you're still unmarried.'

'Does that make me a communist spy?'

'No, but it does make you untypical of your gender and your age. A puzzle, Miss King. We're not overly fond of such things in this building.'

'Shall I overlook the casual prejudice of that remark?'

'There was nothing casual about it, trust me. It was absolutely and thoroughly intended. My job is to spot anomalies. This seems to be a fairly obvious anomaly to me.'

'My marital status is a personal choice. It has nothing to do with my chosen career.'

'The Russians have enhanced their recruitment methods. The handlers no longer look like handlers. They're graduate students now, operating under deep cover. Charming PhD researchers who couldn't hurt a fly. Perhaps they even have British nationality and just the merest smidgeon of Russian ancestry.'

'I never met anyone like that.'

'During your entire six months in the city?'

'No.'

'You're sure?'

'Positive.'

177

'How strange. I have written testimony in this file from other students who confirm they witnessed aggressive recruitment tactics directed at JSSL, particularly those studying Russian.'

Scarlet thought back to her meeting with Control and the new source codenamed KAGO. This must be coming from him. Who else could it be? Anatoly Golitsyn. This was all his doing. Persuading his new masters to search for more moles in the Cambridge undergrowth.

'I can't speak for others,' she said. 'You'll have to ask them.'

'Don't worry, we have. Your account, like your good self, Miss King, stands aloof from the pack.'

Maurice Oldfield unclasped his hands now, flexing the knuckles like a boxer about to enter the ring. He had a different file to Archie, slimmer and frayed at the corners. He opened it now.

'Time, perhaps, to move to the rest of your career,' said Oldfield, his diplomat's tone contrasting sharply with Archie's. He looked at the file, careful about pronunciation. 'What can you tell us about Professor Maria Kazakova?'

1964
Jericho Memories

There was no room for weakness now. She stared at Oldfield. There was a slithery, darting intelligence behind those apple cheeks and Hank Marvin spectacles. He reminded her of the younger dons she'd known at Oxford, prematurely aged, waiting for the grey hairs and sense of elderly wisdom, as if youth was a mistake that must never be repeated.

Start strong. Put them on the defensive. 'It's quite simple,' she said. 'I owe everything to Aunt Maria.'

Oldfield nodded. 'Kazakova, of course, is not a biological aunt, is she?'

'No. My parents were both killed when I was young. I had no other immediate family who could take me in. Aunt Maria was a friend of my mother's, almost sisterly in fact. I moved back from Kenya and Aunt Maria became my de facto guardian. She and her husband, Professor Maurice Anderson, have a cottage in Jericho with a small garden. I'm very fond of them both.'

'Did your parents frequently consort with Russian nationals?'

'Aunt Maria was a White Russian who sought refuge in England after the revolution. She's taught at Oxford for most of her life. More patriotic than the British. My parents always were thwarted academics themselves. They enjoyed socializing with the real thing. Aunt Maria foremost among them.'

Oldfield paused for a moment, framing a question in his head. 'And, just to double back, Miss King, the first time you ever met Mr Philby was *when* exactly?'

' 'Forty-six. Yes, I think that's correct. I returned from Vienna, debriefed an asset at Spedan Towers in Hampstead and was then summoned to Broadway to receive a new posting with Section IX. Kim became my boss. That was the first time I set eyes on him.'

'Had you heard of him before that?'

'Rumours, possibly. Everyone thought he was on the path to becoming Chief one day. One of those rising stars. I imagine most people in this place had heard tales about him. I'd heard no more than most.'

'Strange, then.'

They were flicking between subjects now. 'How so?'

Oldfield produced another piece from his file. It was a contract with the logo of *The Times* newspaper at the top. Beneath it read: 'KAZAKOVA, MARIA – ADVISER'.

Scarlet feigned ignorance. 'I'm a linguist not an ancient historian,' she said. 'You'll have to explain this one, I'm afraid.'

Oldfield smiled in his self-satisfied way. Yes, just like an Oxford don. That same, rather treacly grin. 'The document in question shows that Maria Kazakova, your childhood guardian, worked as an adviser to *The Times* on international relations in the thirties. That happens to coincide with Mr Philby's stint as a foreign correspondent at the very same newspaper during that whole regrettable business in Spain.'

'Fascinating. I fail to see what that has to do with me.'

'There's no chance, I suppose, that your Aunt Maria had contact with Mr Philby then? A family friend or at least a nodding acquaintance. After all, they *were* in each other's territory.'

'You'll have to ask Kim. I was still in school.'

'But you can't deny that both of them worked for the same newspaper in the same department.'

'I'd hardly call Russia and Spain the same department.'

'International affairs is a rather broad term,' said Oldfield. He was bored now, hurrying onwards. He found another section of the file. 'You left Oxford for a role with the Baker Street Irregulars, I see. How very exciting.'

'What about it?'

'During the war, of course, Mr Philby served as a trainer at the Beaulieu Estate in Hampshire. Beaulieu was used as a group B training centre for SOE agents right up until '45. SOE records show you making numerous trips to Beaulieu during your period of service with the Special Operations Executive. Do you deny that?'

'No. Beaulieu was a big place.'

'And yet you claim never to have met Mr Philby until '46?'

'I didn't.'

Oldfield was silent, arching his luxurious

eyebrows instead. Silence was always a spy's most effective weapon. Assets scrambled to fill the void. Instinct trumped rational thought.

'Let me put an alternative theory to you,' said Oldfield, clasping his hands together, affecting a priestly smile. 'You were taken under the guardianship of Professor Kazakova, or "Aunt Maria", as you knew her following your parents' tragic accident. As with most Oxford academics, and despite her own personal history with the revolution, Maria's sympathies were leftish, if not downright socialist. Her husband's leanings certainly were. That is undisputed. Your upbringing was cosmopolitan, bohemian even. During the thirties, Maria Kazakova ran with quite a starry crowd. Back then, of course, Kim Philby was just another young buck. Your aunt knew him, you possibly knew of him. Later, on a visit to Beaulieu with SOE, the connection led to one of those funny wartime friendships. That, I venture, is why he put in a word with the Chief after the war and had you transferred to Section IX.'

'That's quite a theory.'

'We're simple souls, Miss King. Lies get awfully wearying. Be honest and we can help clear this whole confusion up.'

Scarlet looked at them both: Archie Grenville and Maurice Oldfield. Major and minor. Ascetic thinness and Falstaffian rotundity. Roundhead and cavalier. They were an unlikely pair, one making up for the other's deficiencies. He was right about lying. Yes, she'd heard of Kim before the meeting at Broadway in '46. Yes, she even suspected him of batting for Team Moscow. Of course Kim pulled the strings for Section IX.

What if she told them? Well, no return to Moscow for starters, or anywhere else for that matter. Pensioned off to the outposts of London Station, most likely, playing mother to lamplighters and pavement artists, just another middle-aged female housekeeper. Scarlet heard the phone call from the embassy, the two paroles on her tongue. To give up all of that now.

She gathered her thoughts and said, *'Post hoc ergo propter hoc.'*

Oldfield looked confused. 'I'm sorry?'

'After that, therefore because of that.'

'That doesn't sound like a confession.'

'You've become intellectually lazy, gentlemen. You've forgotten the basic principles of logic. You see conspiracies where none exist. Hunting for signs that are, in fact, mere human coincidence.'

'Miss King . . .'

The momentum shifted. Oldfield had the reputation of a spy-scholar, part of the reason he'd been appointed to lead the new Directorate. She was challenging him on his own turf.

She said, 'First, Aunt Maria advised many journalists with her widely acknowledged historical expertise on Europe. She did so by letter or telegram. There is no proof whatsoever that Philby and Aunt Maria ever met. Why? Because they never did. Kim was a low-level correspondent. Aunt Maria was a highly regarded Oxford professor and fellow. She was far above Kim's station and, frankly, you both know it.'

'That doesn't mean . . .'

'As regards my time at SOE: yes, hypothetically, it's possible I did meet Philby without knowing it.'

'Only hypothetically?'

'SOE never used real names. Agents, trainers, even the cooks never revealed their true identities. Philby didn't use his real name, and neither did I. To do so would have been a basic failure of operational security. During my time at Baker Street, I met hundreds of agents, trainers and military co-ordinators, all of whom hid behind an alias. You are putting two and two together and getting five.'

'That still doesn't explain the other facts.'

Scarlet smiled ruefully. 'I was sent to the Joint Services School in Cambridge by this Service. I was assigned to Section IX by the Chief, your former boss.' She looked at Archie now. 'And I believe, Mr Grenville, that your exact instructions when I arrived at the Vienna Station were to follow orders or prepare to run the tea trolley.'

Archie looked uncomfortable. 'I don't recall saying that.'

'I thought you might not.' She switched from sarcasm to seriousness now, lowering her voice to a whisper. 'Look, I know you two have an impossible job. But inventing connections that don't exist and tarring innocent people with half-baked theories is exactly what Moscow wants us to do. The Kremlin would like nothing more than to see us chase our tails for the next ten years. If you want to blame anyone for what happened, then blame our lords and masters. They trusted Philby. They put Kim in charge of Section IX. They sent Nick Elliott out to Beirut and let Philby escape to Moscow. They should be sitting here being judged for their sins. Not me.'

'The old Chief is dead,' said Archie. 'Long live the new Chief.'

'Yes,' she said. 'Well perhaps his mistakes should die with him too.'

Maurice Oldfield closed his manila file, shuffling the papers straight. He looked at his watch. 'Well, that will be all for now, Miss King.'

'Thank you.' Scarlet got up. She wondered if it was enough. 'And my return to Moscow?'

'Not yet,' said Oldfield. 'Stay in London for a few more days. Rest assured, Miss King, we'll be in touch if we require anything further of you. Good day.'

1964
New College

Oxford was different now. After the war, very little changed. The elderly dons trooping to high table; the Latin graces and dusty sherry; the same BBC accents echoing round the ancient quads. Perhaps it was the aftermath of the Kennedy assassination, or all those copycat Beatles haircuts. The city had been remade in Aunt Maria's image.

Scarlet left the station and walked towards New College. Then again, maybe politics had nothing to do with it: the Pill, guitar bands, legions of floppy-fringed and enjoyably earnest grammar school types. Age was the great divider. Oxford in the forties had been her city. This place was for another generation. She walked down the High and detoured through Magpie Lane and Merton Street, checking her tail constantly to try and draw out any watchers. She saw more students with their untucked shirts and Heathcliff hair. Scarlet King was middle-aged. Her student days were historical, as ancient as these buildings and bare brick walls.

Scarlet quickened her pace. Her stomach heaved dryly. She checked again and saw the same woman from the train turning on to Merton Street, a minute or so behind. One of the new watchers. Yes, women were their secret weapon now.

Scarlet calculated the best route from here. It was like this ever since the airport. Each morning a tiresome exercise in separating the civilians from the spooks. Her temporary accommodation was bugged. A team of three watched her every move. They rang the changes regularly, maintaining good watcher hygiene. Young, agile.

Scarlet headed left, back on to the High Street, and then up towards the side of All Souls. Quicker now, using everything to her advantage: the traffic, crowds, even the wintry sunlight. The watcher was stranded on the opposite side of the High. Scarlet veered left towards the arches of the Bodleian and found a place to hide – a small, shadowy nook behind the main library entrance, her face wreathed in shadow.

Minutes later, the watcher emerged, out of breath and visibly annoyed. Scarlet waited, maintaining her line of sight. Seconds later, a second man in a brown trilby joined the woman, both of them conferring. Scarlet didn't recognize the man from the train carriage, only from the station. Local, then, tailing her ever since.

Eventually, the two watchers turned and drifted away. Scarlet reached into her handbag and changed her shoes from flats to heels. She took off her cream jacket and put on a gown instead, adding a pair of thick spectacles for effect. She was a don, now, not a tourist, several inches taller and with an entirely different aspect, especially from a distance.

All watchers were instructed to wait thirty minutes after losing a target before regrouping. Scarlet waited, then finally slipped away. She reached New College without a tail, slipping in through the porter's lodge and reaching the right room moments later. She gave a silent signal to indicate the college room wasn't safe.

They would have to conduct the debriefing elsewhere.

The New College chapel was loud but intimate. Sound splashed off the sides. They sat on a pew near the front. The chapel organ played, masking the conversation between them. Aunt Maria had grown fatter and greyer over the years, her facial symmetry drowned by skin. Her titles had fattened too: Pro Vice-Chancellor for the Humanities, possibly on the path to a damehood, a fixture of the academic establishment. Maurice, likewise. And yet, when she spoke, Scarlet still heard that old idealism. Scarlet told her about the summons and the interview and the watcher on the train. Then the brief skit near the Bodleian.

'You're certain?'

'Yes,' said Scarlet. 'I assume they've bugged my accommodation too.'

'Yes, yes. I see.'

'Is there any news on the KAGO source? Is it Golitsyn?'

'The Centre is sulking,' said Aunt Maria. 'But Anatoly is deeply paranoid too. He's filling their heads with more theories about the Cambridge Spies and others. They're stupid enough to believe in fairy tales. He's entranced them with his mole theory.'

Scarlet prickled. Aunt Maria was too casual sometimes, a general absent from the frontline. Here, in the stony magnificence of the chapel, it

188

was hard to imagine danger. Impossible to feel the grimy streets of Moscow, the half-starved looks and the slimy tentacles of paranoia.

'What about other networks or sub-agents?'

'The Centre never changes. They tell me what I need to know. Nothing else. I'm as blind as you are.'

'And the exfil plan?'

'Your parole was specific on the phone. It's too late to begin the emergency protocol. It's long-term or nothing now.'

'Which is?'

'You would be smuggled out of the country via Dover. But it's a one-way ticket, Ana. Everything you've worked for would be over. A journey with only one destination.'

The old name felt so strange, like another human being. 'How soon would it take place?'

Aunt Maria looked up at the organ, basking in its noise. 'Why did you really come here, Ana? It wasn't just to tell me about some wide-eyed amateur pavement artist.'

'You know why.'

'No. If you were certain your cover was blown, you could have given me the codeword for the twelve-hour exfil over the phone. It would already be done. Something is stopping you, Ana . . .'

Scarlet looked sharply at Aunt Maria. 'Maybe I've already sacrificed too much.'

'Is that a question or a statement?'

'What if it's both?'

'I'll try not to mention that in my next report.'

Scarlet thought of that night in Moscow, the blip of normality with Caspar. She longed for that again. 'I'm sick of looking round corners. Sick of pretending.'

Then, as the organ built to a crescendo, Aunt Maria said, 'And Otto? What about him? You barely mention him these days.'

It was the one part of her life she kept hidden, even from herself. 'That's not his name any longer.'

'Well, it's my name for him. What does Otto say?'

'He doesn't know. About me, you, any of it.'

'Will you ever tell him?'

'No.'

'Is he the reason you're staying?'

'Let's leave Otto out of this.'

'You were once in love with the man, Ana. Someone's replaced him in your affections then?'

She couldn't do this. Not now. 'Please . . .'

'Is there someone else?'

Otto, Caspar. She clutched at failed attachments. The alternative was already gone. Her future was governed by lies and desperate snatched liaisons. 'What happened between us is history.'

'History, my child, is the most powerful motive of all.' Aunt Maria rested her hand gently on Scarlet's shoulder. 'Now, I'm afraid, we must leave.'

The chapel organ died away. The doors opened behind them. Suddenly, students filed in like an invasion. They wore choir robes and chattered loudly as they occupied the stalls.

The two of them left by the side entrance and walked through the fellows' garden, drinking in the beauty of it.

'You must tell him,' said Aunt Maria. 'Before it happens, you must find a way. Trust me.'

1964
Kensington

She waited until the family departed. The four-bedroom house in Kensington, hidden off a side street about five minutes' walk from the Victoria & Albert Museum, was tasteful in a ramshackle fashion. Mum and the two children departed in the run-down family Volvo. Scarlet checked there were no eyes on her, crossed the street and rang the doorbell for Number 9.

It took an age for the door to be answered. Eventually, Otto appeared in the doorway with his ink-stained shirt pocket, like an animal emerging from hibernation. His glasses perched on his forehead like goggles and tobacco stained his olive-green cardigan, or 'thinking garment', as he always called it in that thickly accented English. He had his usual mug of extra-strong coffee which, with idiosyncratic flair, he preferred cold.

'They've just left for orchestra practice,' he said, scratching at his scalp. 'My eldest has quite a flair for the violin, you know. Come in, come in. I hope this visit isn't official?'

Otto shut the door. Having done his time at Porton Down, he had moved into secular academic life and risen swiftly through the ranks at Imperial College London. He now held the Regius Chair in Biochemistry and wrote scholarly papers for obscure academic journals alongside the occasional op-ed for Sunday newspapers on all matters scientific. His legend was always suitably vague: the Austrian childhood, the early escape in the thirties, unspecified war work in England, then a glittering academic career. None of the colleagues or students knew of his past. His name, like his history, had been entirely erased.

The house was even scrappier inside than out. Books dominated the eyeline in every room, tottering at precarious heights and angles. They sat in the living room with its second-hand coffee table and scarred, weathered furniture. It was hard to imagine that first meeting in Café Landtmann now. Everything was so suburban, shabbily genteel, in this safe London street next to a prestigious university. That old life was a mirage.

'To what do I owe this pleasure?'

His English was fluent. Most of the other scientists recruited as part of Operation Hercules – those ranks of chemists, biologists and physicists kidnapped by the Allies – still fumbled with the basics. Otto's speech, however, was musical and sibilant, part of the professorial charm. Scarlet remembered teaching him his first English word at Spedan Towers, those nursery steps with grammar and writing. The closeness of those days – both young and galvanized by war – had never left them. It was like family, picking up where they left off.

'A case officer is allowed to speak with their asset,' said Scarlet. 'Welfare is part of my job now. Blame Service cutbacks.'

Otto smiled, as if understanding the game. 'I see. So this *is* official.'

'If you like.'

'Did you get my latest submission?'

Under the terms of Otto's resettlement, he was obliged to share any new research with SIS first. He was their eyes and ears within the scientific community, a leading light in academic conferences across the globe. Where possible, he even copied crucial documents and photographed papers, all to gain a minuscule advantage. No, that hadn't changed since Vienna. With his shiny new name and tenured position at Imperial, Dr Otto Spengler was still Broadway's secret weapon.

'Yes,' she said. 'I passed it on to the JIC.'

'And?'

'It sounded like something out of science fiction. You really think cellular profiles could be used to identify criminals?'

Otto was in his element now. He gesticulated wildly, coffee slopping over the carpet. 'After Crick and Watson, you see, that much is inevitable. No more Sherlock Holmes. And not just criminals too. It will transform spying, Scarlet. The days of assuming someone else's identity, of going under deep cover, will be eradicated. You will be able to pinpoint a person's identity just from their biological trace. Imagine it!'

'The mark of the beast?'

'Something better. The mark of biology. Trust me, DNA profiling will be the next big thing. Get ahead of it now and the others will never truly catch up.'

'I'll try to bear that in mind.'

Otto sipped his cold coffee. He looked at Scarlet

with that unblinking stare again, those unworldly eyes. 'Scientific chitchat is not, however, the reason for your visit, no?'

'Well deduced, Mr Holmes.'

'Why then?'

Scarlet wondered how to begin. She had dissembled in the chapel to Aunt Maria. Otto knew fragments, enough to make an educated guess. They had been so close at Spedan Towers and became closer when she was made his permanent case officer. She had been young, naïve even, and let her guard down. He knew more than either would ever like to admit.

'There's a chance I will be moving on,' she said. 'The Service may soon assign you a new handler.'

Otto looked perturbed. 'Do I have a choice in the matter?'

'I'm afraid not.'

'And what if I refuse to work with this other handler?'

'That wouldn't be a wise decision to make.'

'No?'

'Your legend, your position, this place, all of it is entirely at the discretion of the British government. Tit for tat, I'm afraid. If you no longer carry out your side of the bargain, we won't carry out ours.'

A chilly silence grew. Then, almost invisibly, it became mournful instead. There was so much to say, and no words in which to say it.

'Will you be away for long?'

'I'm not sure yet. It looks like a long-term posting. Possibly a permanent relocation.'

He nodded, translating the deeper meaning. 'Is there no way you can stay?'

Scarlet rose from the armchair and moved towards the mantelpiece and the row of framed family photographs. Otto's marriage had been sudden, the confirmed bachelor shocking everyone with an impulsive registry office wedding. Elsie was a secretary at the Imperial science department, then Otto's personal assistant. Scarlet picked up one of the photos. Otto, Elsie, and the two children.

Scarlet regretted coming here now. Why had she done so? Their handler–asset liaisons were usually conducted in parks or anonymous hotels. No, visiting the house had been reckless. And yet she couldn't think of escaping to Moscow, exiled forever, without a final reckoning with the past.

There was no more to say. They were at the door now. Scarlet wondered if this was the very last time she would ever see him. For a moment, the secret chronology of their relationship flashed through her mind: the photo, the café, the debriefing, the agent meetings, the brush passes, safe houses, intimacy blooming into passing fancy, the terror of exposure, then the cover up. She was so good at turning fact into fiction. The truth didn't hurt like it used to.

Otto watched her closely, frowning with concern. 'You don't look well, Scarlet,' he said. 'You should see a doctor.'

'I'm sure it's nothing.'

'Sickness, yes? Any other . . . irregularities?'

He was a scientist first, a human being second.

195

She was just another specimen in a lab. 'I'm fine, really.'

Otto retreated back into the house and returned with a business card. 'This man is a friend of mine. A very good doctor. What do you English say? Better to be safe than always sorry.'

She smiled and kissed him lightly on a stubbled cheek, then headed home and stared at the card. It was the next morning before she dialled. The receptionist at the surgery was austere but polite. Scarlet explained her symptoms, including the sickness.

An appointment was booked for the following day.

1964
Exfil

The long-term exfil protocol was simple. After leaving the doctor's surgery, Scarlet found a payphone in Chelsea. She dialled Aunt Maria's home number and mentioned the agreed codeword. From that moment onwards, she had one week to survive before the exfil from Dover. After that, she would be smuggled to Moscow and safety. Survival was all that mattered now. The decision was taken.

There was another letter when she got back. It requested her attendance for a further interview, just as Oldfield had promised. This time, however, the location had changed. Not Broadway, but BIN, SIS's London Station in Vauxhall Bridge Road. An escalation, then. The basement at Broadway was the gentle introduction. London Station was the Directorate's main base. The confession chamber for suspected doubles.

She lay awake and considered her options. Not showing would trigger the deployment of immediate search teams, a sure-fire signal of guilt. Even with the exfil already in motion, she would struggle to evade detection for so many days. She cursed herself for leaving it so late. But this was always how it happened. Spies weren't caught because of grand mistakes; it was the microscopic weakness. She had dithered, over-thought it, let her feelings for Otto blind her. She was to blame; no one else.

It was daylight already. Tiredness weighed heavily now. Her mind echoed. She thought of Otto and Aunt Maria and saw the doctor in that sterile room yesterday confirming what she long suspected, hearing the words like a physical blow. It was two months, almost eight weeks, since that night in Moscow.

She changed her clothes, washed, and then set out for Vauxhall Bridge Road. There were three watchers this morning. One locked in step as she left the house. A second as she approached the Tube station. Another as she reached Pimlico. Yes, they had rung the changes well. She didn't recognize any of their profiles. Two men, one woman. They buzzed like insects, dragging after her.

She reached Vauxhall Bridge Road. Broadway, at least, had some trace of imperial grandeur. BIN, or London Station, was functional. This was the business end of spying, fitted out to listen in on foreign embassies across London. It reminded Scarlet of a medieval scriptorium. Whole floors were filled with hunched copyists and their headphones, feverishly transcribing the latest exploits of cultural attachés and deputy ambassadors. It was noisy and stark. She nearly longed for head office.

The Directorate of Counterintelligence and Security resided on the third floor with a loyal army of secretaries and analysts. The basement rooms at Broadway were merely cover, lulling each interviewee into a false sense of security. London Station was operational, strictly detached from the rest. There were no high-ranking Chiefs or other grandees to sweep things under the carpet.

Both of them were waiting for her. Maurice Old-field looked even more donnish than before, adjusting his spectacles and smiling uncomfortably. Archie was stern, ascetic, that puritan grimness. Scarlet was ushered inside the room and told to sit down. Both the interrogators had different files this time. Escape was similarly impossible. There were guards at all the doors, probably armed. The jumble of floors was more difficult to navigate than Broadway. The streets outside in Pimlico were less open than St James's, which might help, but getting there would be more of a task. No, this was a concrete prison. Lies were her only weapons now. Her one chance to escape.

Innocent people protested, kicked up a storm. She must get on the front foot again. Strike first. So she did. 'Well, I didn't think it was possible. But your watchers were even more hopeless than usual this morning.'

Oldfield glanced up, a gleam of interest. 'You noticed them?'

'Fifty-something man in a grey raincoat. Thirty-something chap in shirtsleeves. And then the woman in that hideously dumpy cardigan by the station. Standards seem to be slipping, Maurice. Where are you recruiting these people?'

Oldfield sighed and opened the file. 'I see you also managed to escape their clutches in Oxford too?'

'Yes, well, I thought they should be taught a lesson. Learn the hard way, just like at Arisaig. Anyway, the woman on the train was far too blatant. And the other man helping her was scarcely any better. Say what you like about the KGB, but at least they know how to mount a decent tail. This was frankly embarrassing.'

'Did you notice anything else?'

She was on a roll. Press home the advantage. 'Well, my apartment was clearly bugged, though not particularly well. My phone, too. The post always arrived a day late, so no doubt you've had a good look at all my boring correspondence. Pity the sap who did that. And a new gardener popped up for the shrubbery outside the building. Another one of yours, I presume? Staged cigarette breaks as he goggled my window. I mean really.'

Oldfield looked at Archie. 'Is that all?'

'No, I almost forgot about the phone call I made from the embassy. I presume your listeners here enjoyed hearing chitchat with my Aunt Maria. That's not to mention the documents.'

'The documents?'

'Yes, those forgeries you showed me last time round. Tolerable for a garden-variety asset, I suppose, but hardly watertight. *The Times* don't draw up contracts for advisers, far too vulgar. It's a three-course lunch at the Savoy and a lifetime's free subscription. Not to mention that dreadful letter supposedly drafted by Kim in Beirut. Orthographically bearable, I suppose, but all wrong otherwise. He never called me Scarlet. His nickname for me, if you must know, was Prynne.'

Oldfield smiled. 'Of course. *The Scarlet Letter*.'

'Well done, Maurice. Alpha-minus all round.'

'Yes, he always was rather fond of nicknames. One of his only redeeming features.'

'Look, gentlemen, I'll say this once. I am a loyal servant of my country. I returned when called for. I dealt with watchers. I put up with your amateurish attempts at entrapment. But even I, frankly, have my limits. Either explain why I'm here and what's going on or let me resume my duties. If not, then you give me no choice but to resign.'

'Very well. Grenville . . .'

Archie took over now. The mood altered. He extracted a form from his file and handed it to Scarlet. He said, 'I apologize for the confusion, Miss King, but we have to take certain precautions when it comes to vetting. I assured Maurice and the Chief that you'd understand. One of the perils of the trade.'

Scarlet picked up the form and read the words across the top: 'SECTION V'. There was a signature box at the end.

'Vetting?'

'Yes.' Archie coughed. 'Section V have been looking for a new recruit for some time. They asked us to put various candidates through their paces. It was vitally important none of the candidates understood the reason for their recall.'

Scarlet thought back through everything that had happened: the watchers, the bugs, the basement interrogation. Suddenly it all made a new kind of sense. Section V was the most sensitive part of SIS, even more elite than her old counterintelligence role with Section IX. Counter-espionage. The mole hunters. Not hunting Russian spooks, but British doubles.

'Section V doesn't recruit lightly,' continued Archie.

'They need a female officer to carry out certain operational requirements which can't be fulfilled by men. As the first serving female officer in the Intelligence Branch, and after your work in Vienna, you were one of the only people to fit the profile. Naturally we had to be sure you were the right candidate from a security standpoint.'

'I see,' said Scarlet. She could forget Dover, Moscow, even Caspar. She was about to join the most secretive part of SIS. Tasked with finding traitors from within. Ensuring her own survival.

Oldfield now. 'Is there anything else you'd like to ask, Miss King, or indeed tell us?'

Scarlet smiled. There was a pen offered and she signed her name. She was escorted out and told to return Monday week at 9.30 a.m.

She walked down Vauxhall Bridge Road and, for the first time in weeks, didn't bother to check for a tail. Cars hooted nearby. Buses rattled. Smoke rose, pedestrians jostled. The world ignored her. Instead, she saw the doctor in Harley Street again, the Victorian disdain in his voice.

She touched her stomach briefly, then lost herself in the Tube. Moscow flickered, then died. Exile vanished. Secrets thickened. She saw the ceiling from that Moscow room again and the sound of Caspar smoking beside her. She closed her eyes, inhaled the smell of tobacco, and felt almost free.

PART THREE

16

Everything had changed. Nothing had changed.

He was guilty. He was innocent.

The blood was still on his hands. No matter how many times he washed them, the blood simply wouldn't disappear.

This was a nightmare, a tangled fever dream. And yet it wasn't. The world was different while still being the same. All except for one unavoidable fact.

Scarlet King was dead.

Max felt sweat trickle down the side of his neck. He gazed out at the rows of faces. His legs buckled. He looked at his lecture notes again and tried to find his place. Acting normally was everything now. He'd returned home, showered, dressed, turned up for work, presented a face to the world. This was a lecture he'd given at least five times before, one of his classics in fact: 'British Intelligence and the "Special Relationship" 1945–2001: New Perspectives'. He knew the text by heart.

He coughed, took a sip of water, and then forced himself to get through the final paragraphs. The words were blurring on the page, syllables slipping from his mouth.

'So, in conclusion: although the unique US–UK intelligence-sharing relationship was established in a time of war and continued largely unchanged until the events of September eleventh, the specific use of the term "Special Relationship" must be grounded in specific historical context or, indeed, "con*texts*".'

He could hear Emma wince at that last line. Academic ordure, in her words. Adding an 's' or an 'ism' to everything for cheap bonus points; or, worse still, speech marks. Or even all three. There was a reason academic books weren't bestsellers.

'Whether during Vietnam, the Falklands crisis or indeed the Gulf War, the precise paradigm of that "intelligence partnership" – whether through the Five Eyes arrangement or bespoke bilateral intelligence-sharing between SIS and the CIA or the FBI and MI5 – was conditional upon a matrix of factors, not least domestic political considerations and the relevant strengths of each country's diplomatic network or, indeed, "networks".'

Max looked up. He was relieved to see some students making notes. No half-time exits or cries of 'taxi for Dr Archer'. He was an associate professor, after all, not a B-list stand-up. He was about to push through the final paragraph, desperate for a hot cup of coffee and some ibuprofen, when he saw her.

'The task and the challenge of all intelligence history,' he said, clumsily turning the final page of his lecture notes and trying to process what he'd just seen, 'is that espionage never stands alone. Our subject area is a melting pot of political and military history, international relations, sociological and anthropological factors and, all too often, the basic facts of "geographies" and "biologies".

Whether through interviewing eyewitnesses or handling documents in the archives, finding the balance between such a range of disciplines is what makes intelligence history – or, should I say, "histories" – the most exciting new arena in historical studies for a generation. Many have said that historians are really detectives of the past. Our job, however, is even more complex: we must become the spies of the past as well. Thank you very much.'

There was the usual flurry of noise as over a hundred second-year history students began their exodus from the lecture theatre. Max dabbed his forehead and folded his lecture notes. He hadn't slept last night. He could still see the traces of blood washed off in his bathroom sink. He'd paced his small studio flat for hours debating whether to call the police, finding an excuse not to every single time. This was his first and only 9 a.m. lecture. He would do so now. The local station would be fully staffed. He would invent some excuse about the delay. It was his duty as a citizen.

Max zipped up his bag and put his jacket on. He looked up and saw the woman with the scar from the Holland Park flat walking down the stairs towards him. She was dressed like a postgrad or mature student, returning to university to take a different path in life. Her arms were covered with long sleeves but he could still trace the contours of the scar, the lethal proximity to the vein. Max wasn't sure whether to ignore her or seek help.

Had she killed Scarlet before he arrived? Had she just found the body?

What if she'd already contacted the police?

The terrible, career-ending possibilities were almost limitless. Max had always wondered what he would be like in a crisis. He'd spent his entire childhood listening to thinly disguised tales of Oliver's exploits as a journalist: evading bombs, ducking snipers, tunnelling his way into war zones, each one lightly embroidered, no doubt, but with the wounds to prove it. Did he have his father's courage? Could he hold his nerve? A lifetime of reading about spy exploits was no help in reality. If anything, it only made it worse.

'Dr Archer.'

Max was near the exit now, already reciting the cover story he would give to the police. He didn't turn. 'I'm sorry. My office hours are on the intranet. Better still, email me with any queries and I'll do my best to get back to you.'

She was beside him now, keeping pace. She had a bag in her left hand. He looked at the sleeve, almost waiting for it to ride up. 'What if my query is sensitive?'

'My office hours are only for current students.'

'And prospective ones?'

He looked at her. 'First I need their name.' Max pushed through the double doors and out into the hallway.

'Cleo,' she said. 'Pleasure to meet you.'

'Is that a real name or an alias?'

'Does it matter?'

Max was walking fast, elbowing his way through the crowd, seeking fresh air. He was on alert, ready to see blue lights and police cars surrounding this part of central London. He had visions of being detained by the police in full view of both students and faculty, securing a front-page splash in the weekly student newspaper. His entire career would go up in smoke.

'I'm sorry,' he said, 'but I have a seminar starting in fifteen minutes. I really can't help you.'

'Your next seminar isn't until this afternoon at three. After that your diary is free.'

Max stopped. 'How the hell do you know my diary?'

'Please, enough of the surprise. The same way I know that you were followed last night. The same way I knew your financial records and marital history.'

The anxiety was ice-cold. It was as if his skin had been scraped clean. Every tiny movement provoked a reaction. 'I have no idea what you're talking about.'

'You're probably still debating whether to call the police, am I right? Convincing yourself that if you make the call now everything can be put back in a box. Spot the naïve academic. It was over the minute you stumbled out of that flat. The minute you found the body.'

The bustle of students thinned. Max was about to continue walking, pushing through towards the double doors and out into the street. This couldn't be happening. Last night was a bad dream. His head throbbed. His body tingled. This was a hangover. That was all. Surely. There was still an innocent explanation.

'They have five watchers on you already,' she

said. 'Two of them trailed you from your flat to the campus. Three of them are waiting outside. An old man with a Tesco shopping bag. A middle-aged woman in running gear. And a young woman fixing her bike. Look outside. Tell me what you see.'

Max approached the double doors and looked through the glass. He spotted the old man first. He was loitering by the local newsagent, Tesco bag in hand, wondering how to fill the rest of the day. To the left was the young woman supposedly fixing her bike, helmet on. Ready to move. Then, finally, on his route up towards the History faculty was the middle-aged woman in running gear, currently sipping water and talking on the phone, jogging on the spot.

Max returned to the hallway, trying to find adequate words. His mouth was dry. 'Who are they?'

'Come on, Dr Archer. You can do better than that. You're the intelligence expert. You know exactly who they are.'

'Security Service. A Branch.'

'Yes.'

'If they followed me to the flat, why not just bring me in this morning?'

'Why do you think?'

The Socratic method. One of his favourite teaching techniques, providing questions not answers. His nerves were raw. 'I don't bloody know. A few days ago, I was just an ordinary academic. Now you're saying there are watchers from MI5 tracking me from my bloody flat. I have no idea what happened last night. I was drunk. Completely out of it.'

'C-minus, Dr Archer. Try again.'

He looked at Cleo now and truly hated her. He thought back to receiving the invitation card. He should have binned it. Walked away. None of this would ever have happened. All the things he used to hate – lecture schedules, essay marking, departmental meetings – were suddenly innocent and precious. No blood, no bodies.

'The memoir,' he said. 'There's something in the memoir.'

'And?'

'They think I have it.'

'Bravo.'

'How do I know you're not one of them?'

Cleo checked her watch. 'Is your phone off?'

Max had taken basic precautions before coming to the lecture. 'Yes.'

'Battery out?'

Max nodded. 'Who are you?'

Cleo eyeballed him. 'You have to make a choice now, Dr Archer. A choice only you can make.'

'No. This is ridiculous. I've done absolutely nothing wrong. I was invited to meet a former senior member of SIS and I did. There has to be a calm, sensible way out of this. I'll go to the police, explain what happened and let justice take its course. I have nothing to hide. This can all be smoothed over. Like grown-ups. Like civilized human beings.'

It was Cleo's turn to nod now. 'Okay. Then it sounds like you don't need my help. You're right. I'm sure there is a calm, sensible way to explain why you boasted about breaking the Official Secrets Act, turned off your phone and took out

211

the battery and broke into an old woman's flat last night while drunk and left your DNA all over the crime scene.'

'This can't be happening.'

'It *is* happening, Max.'

'It's ludicrous. Everyone can see that. What possible motive would I have for killing a woman in her nineties? For heaven's sake, she was the one who asked *me* to come to the flat.'

'Can you prove that?'

'Yes.' Max reached for his mobile, then remembered the self-deleting message. 'No, actually, it was –'

'Think about it. You're a mid-career academic with a serious cashflow problem and a desperate need for a big break. You get offered the chance to be part of a spy revelation that could be as big as Gordievsky or Mitrokhin, a once-in-a-generation scoop. But your source is playing hardball. She wants your expertise but doesn't want to share the royalties. This is probably the last chance for big money and getting out of debt.'

'That's hypothetical.'

'So, what do you do? You hatch a plan using all your intelligence expertise. After all, she's old, mid-nineties, she will die soon anyway. What's the harm in speeding things along a bit? You illegally insert a tracking device in her handbag. Then you summon some Dutch courage, track her back to her flat. You murder her, steal the memoir and then make it look like a robbery gone wrong, trashing the flat in the process.'

'No, no . . .'

'You publish the memoir. You make the millions. Her murder remains unsolved. Everyone's a winner. I've seen good QCs secure convictions on flimsier evidence than that.'

Suddenly it sounded horribly plausible. His hands started to shake. 'That's insane.'

'No, it's not. Get a decent Treasury counsel, a pliable jury and you're facing a life sentence for murder. That's not to mention the DNA and trace evidence at the flat.'

He was drunk. That was as much as he could remember. He'd touched the body. The door handle. Tramped through the entire place. 'I saw her lying there. It was instinctive. That was all. I was checking for a pulse, just to see if she was all right.'

'What about your flat? Will they find anything there?'

Max saw himself washing his hands last night, the coppery water staining the sink red. The clumsy attempt at bleaching the surface afterwards. 'Yes.'

'They were watching you last night. They will have it all on file. The only reason you're not sitting in a police cell right now is because they want to see what you do next. Do you have the memoir? Is it hidden somewhere else? Once they have the memoir, they'll go in hard for the arrest. After that, you're on your own. Once that happens, Max, I really can't help you.'

It was only hours ago, but it seemed like days since Max had been standing in the private room at the Goring Hotel trading insults with Oliver and Emma. How could things possibly have changed so much since then?

'You still haven't told me who you are,' he said. 'Why did Scarlet trust you?'

'We don't have time for that now. The A Branch team will be wondering why you haven't emerged. We have about thirty seconds before they walk through that door. A minute before the police are called and they decide to move in for the arrest. Two minutes tops before you never see a clear sky again.'

'You said it yourself. We're surrounded.'

'Which is why you need to follow my instructions exactly,' said Cleo. 'One moment of hesitation could get us both arrested. Deviate even slightly from what I tell you, and I'm gone. Agreed?'

Max glanced at the glass exit doors. Then summoned the last of his courage. There was no other way out of this. 'What do you want me to do?'

17

By the time Saul arrived at the crime scene, it was almost cleared. The forensic team had been working on it overnight. Police vans were parked outside, neighbours glancing anxiously at the commotion as they passed. A ring of uniformed officers protected the flat complex from photographers and reporters.

Saul never used his real name when interacting with police or civilian staff, at least not those below Assistant Commissioner level. He took out one of his many aliases – 'Nicholas Graves' from the Home Office – and showed it to the PC on logging duties. Then he ducked beneath the outer cordon and saw a figure in a full forensic suit waiting outside the property entrance.

'Mr Graves?' she said. 'DCI Laura Bishop. HSCC.'

Homicide and Serious Crime Command. The murder squad, as it was more commonly known. 'Nick, please. Home Office Liaison Team.'

She smiled thinly. It was several hours since the call came through from the office of the Assistant Commissioner in charge of Counter Terrorism Command. The scene had a sensitive national security aspect to it. She was to expect a visit from the Home Office, including a senior officer at Director level. Thirty minutes later, three Special Branch officers and two civvies rocked up, the warm-up act. This was the main billing.

'Suit up and follow me.'

'Thank you.'

Saul put on a full forensic suit, more out of good manners than any desire to protect the scene, and then followed DCI Bishop inside. The flat complex was a tall red-brick affair with views on to Chelsea Embankment. Inside was a bare stone hallway with a staircase reaching up to the flats on the upper levels. It was starker than Saul had imagined. Usually, these sorts of buildings had porters and acres of marble. From memory, Scarlet King had bought the flat in the seventies, snapping it up for a song. He wondered how much it would be worth now.

'Has the body been removed?'

'Not yet. Your team asked us to keep it in situ until you arrived.'

'Good.'

Following his call with the Home Secretary, Saul had stayed up most of the night. He received the A Branch alert about Max Archer's movements just after two-thirty. He'd dispatched Charlotte to supervise the scene while he made sure everything else was in place. As they moved into the flat itself, Saul saw Charlotte similarly suited up and examining exhibits. She looked bleary-eyed, carefully sifting various items of interest.

'One moment,' said Saul to DCI Bishop.

'Of course.'

He headed into the main sitting area. The three Special Branch officers were still checking the room. Under sofa cushions, floorboards, drains. Anywhere that could be used as a hiding place.

'Found the smoking gun yet?'

'We've searched everywhere, boss. Bathroom, cistern, showerhead, underneath the carpet. But I'm fairly sure there's nothing here.'

Saul wasn't surprised. Scarlet King was old school. She was a past master of Moscow Rules, when the phrase still meant something. She survived the Cold War, running operations against the Russians when the KGB was in its pomp. Even so, old age took its toll. The most scrupulous spies became careless.

He looked at the collection of items already bagged. 'These are the best you've got?'

'Yep.'

Saul crouched down and looked at the exhibits. There was a collection of old crosswords from *The Times*, a few books, a list of important phone numbers (plumber, electrician, builder) and then other workaday items: clothes, shoes, jackets, kitchen items.

'No laptops or any other digital items, then?'

'Nothing we've seen. She was ninety-odd, after all. The digital age seems to have passed her by completely. The flat doesn't even have wi-fi.'

Another piece of tradecraft, then. Charlotte was wrong in her diagnosis. Scarlet King wasn't analogue. No, she was savvy. The lack of wi-fi was to avoid any digital intrusion, from her own side or from older enemies. He sympathized.

Saul stood upright again. 'Check the phone

numbers just to make sure. Then give the rest back to the HSCC team. Keep me posted.'

'Of course, boss.'

Saul returned to DCI Bishop. 'This way?'

'Uh-huh.'

The single bedroom was the largest room in the small flat, still decorated in an early-noughties style. It was tasteful, slightly bland, but offset by the scene on the bed. Scarlet King looked even smaller in death. Her feet barely reached three-quarters of the way down the mattress. Her frame was slight enough, Saul thought, that even a serious breeze could snap her. He'd seen enough dead bodies that the sight of blood alone didn't shock him. But he marvelled all the same: this fragile old lady, all five foot nothing of her, had once been the chief antagonist of the Kremlin, the thorn in the side of the mighty First Chief Directorate. He felt a sudden stab of pride tempered by sadness.

'Do forensics have anything yet?'

'They found some dabs around her neck. And some other hairs. We're fast-tracking them as we speak.'

'Cause of death?'

'Tricky one. The blood's misleading. Looks like a heart attack to me. Nasty bash, which she dragged through here.'

Saul stepped closer to the bed and inspected the body. Scarlet's head was turned away. The blood came from a gash on the skin, probably as the body jerked during the heart attack. There was no obvious sign of violence in the rest of the room, however.

The bedroom still had a vestigial order to it, despite the best efforts of the forensic investigators.

Saul had seen enough. He left the flat and walked back to the front of the building, sucking in a lungful of open air. He unzipped the forensic suit and took off the mask, glad he didn't have to spend his days in those things. DCI Bishop kept her suit on, lowering the mask to speak.

'We're about to ship the body out for the post-mortem,' she said. 'I can keep your team looped in on progress.'

Saul nodded and took off the last of the feet coverings. This was always the bit he hated. Some spooks enjoyed striding into a crime scene and throwing their weight around. He felt mildly guilty. These people were professionals, trying to do a job. His dad had been a beat copper with thirty years of pounding pavements and railing against smarmy suits and politicians. Personal feelings, though, could never compromise an operation.

'We're going to need all your files,' he said, sterner now, no longer their friend. 'Deliver the body to Westminster Mortuary and then we'll take over from here. Log it in with Counter-Terrorism Command for the records, and then put your feet up. We'll let you know when we're done.'

DCI Bishop looked confused, wondering if he was joking. 'You can't be serious.'

'Who says?'

'This is a police investigation, sir. A suspicious death.'

'No. This is a national security matter and far, far

above your pay grade. Log it with CTC, then step away.'

'I'll take this to the Assistant Commissioner.'

'Be my guest. The AC has already given his permission for us to step in. Let the FIs in there finish up and then pack your bags and scarper. None of us want the Home Secretary to start phoning the Commissioner and bandying your name about now, do we?'

'Who was she?'

'I can't answer that.'

'You'll have to. Or perhaps you'd like to see this on the front page of the *Sun* tomorrow? Home Office hushes up murder case. Not a great look for your side.'

Saul almost admired the fight. Some of them caved immediately, desperate to fob off a case and save the legwork. Others battled. 'That would be illegal.'

'So would interfering in a homicide investigation.'

Saul could see other members of the murder squad leaving the building now. They would all have smartphones, able to video the whole encounter and post it on social media within minutes. He needed to close this down now. He moved away from the others, forcing DCI Bishop to follow, lowering his voice to ensure the sound didn't travel.

'What I'm about to tell you is classified at strap three. If you divulge it to anyone else, I will personally investigate you for breaching the OSA.'

'Who was she?'

'The woman in that flat used to be our chief Russia expert for the chaps across the river. She knew more secrets about the Kremlin than you or I have had hot dinners. The people who killed her were willing to poison an old lady. Just imagine what they'd do to the police officer, and no doubt her family, who tried to pursue them.'

DCI Bishop looked queasy. 'You think this has an international element? The Russians? Like Salisbury?'

She said it, not him. That was the trick of the trade: to lie without actually lying. 'It's the classic Kremlin MO. Heart attack that looks natural with nothing to find on the toxicology side. The quantity of blood was probably from a fall in the sitting area as the heart attack hit, a by-product of trying to reach the landline in the bedroom. By some estimates, they've killed upwards of twenty others on British soil this way.'

'You still didn't properly answer my question.'

'Would you like me to?'

DCI Bishop looked defeated. 'I'll get my team out and then transfer it to CTC within the hour. What about decontamination?'

'No, this was a private killing, not a statement to the world. Anyway, it's our problem now. Not yours.' Saul took out a card with his alias on and a burner phone number. 'Call me if you have any issues. Day or night.'

'Fine.'

Saul took a final look at the property, then ducked under the outer cordon again. He checked his phone and saw the string of urgent updates from the A Branch team.

He read them through and then cursed silently.

Max Archer was missing.

18

Max finished reading the second sheaf of papers and then closed his eyes. They narrowly avoided a delivery cyclist in a Just Eat fluorescent jacket. The car was old and jumpy, a ruby-red Renault sedan with a sensitive clutch. Cleo looked unfazed, clearly the beneficiary of some kind of advanced driving training, approaching the streets of West London as if they were as dangerous as Kabul or Tehran.

Max checked the wing mirrors again for a tail. For the moment, they appeared to be clean. His body was soaked through with sweat. His mouth was parched. The events of the previous thirty minutes were still an unfathomable blur. Cleo's instructions. The clothes hidden in the bag. Changing his profile in the lecture theatre toilets, emerging in a tracksuit with a student hoodie and baseball cap, and leaving via the fire escape exit. Cleo had already been waiting in a blacked-out Range Rover with the engine running. So this was what real fieldwork felt like.

The cyclist from the A Branch team had been sent to monitor the fire escape, but they managed to pull away just in time, screeching through the narrow streets just off Lincoln's Inn Fields until they lost her completely. The next change had been even more ingenious. Another vehicle was waiting near Holborn. They abandoned the showy Range Rover and switched to this old-timer. Different licence plate, different everything, changing the profile. No doubt false plates, too, jamming up ANPR.

Max saw the sweat from his hands seep into the paper. Moisture seemed to be dripping off every part of his skin. His breathing still hadn't returned to normal. It came in staccato bursts, trochaic rather than iambic.

Boom-boom-boom. *Boom*-boom-boom. *Boom*-boom-boom.

The hangover still throbbed, punching at the side of his skull. The pressure consumed him now. The shock lessened. His composure cracked. Fight or flight. 'Is Cleo even your real name?'

'It's my middle name.'

'What's your Christian name?'

'That I can't tell you.'

'Tell me something real within the next five seconds or I'll pull the handbrake.'

'And let us both die?'

'It's a chance I'm willing to take.'

Cleo shook her head. Max's right hand hovered over the handbrake. 'Okay, okay. What do you want to know?'

'Why don't we start with why you picked me? You had the change of car ready. You must have known something like this would happen. This has clearly been planned for a very long time. Of all the people in all the world, why the hell make *me* part of this?'

'Scarlet told you. She read your books. You know

more about Cold War espionage than anyone else. Your profile and background also matched.'

'Bollocks. I don't believe a word Scarlet told me.' Max held up the second sheaf of papers. 'I'm not sure I believe a word of this either.'

'No?'

'Third person rubbish. It could all be fabricated. It's a novel not a memoir. A decent thriller, but nothing more. How do I know she didn't make the whole thing up?'

'Scarlet explained that.'

'Look how that worked out. Defending herself against the Official Secrets Act appears to be the least of her problems now. Pretty hard to prosecute a dead person.'

'If the memoir was fiction, why would MI5 be after us?'

'You said it yourself. Perception is reality. They think I killed her.'

'That would be a police issue, not MI5.'

'Perhaps they're after me too.'

'Why would the Security Service care so much about a few pages written by an old woman if the contents were purely fictional?'

She had a point. Max unfolded the pages again. 'Where's the real notebook?'

'Locked in a safety deposit box behind enough layers of security that even Thames House can't easily access it.'

'Abroad?'

'Yes.'

'What about the rest of the memoir?' he said. 'Other sheafs?'

'Those were the only samples. It was all air-gapped and done without any digital connection at all.'

'How many other sections are there?'

'That's not important now.'

Max glanced at each page of the second sheaf again. Then he recalled the contents of the first part of the memoir. He spent his life combing through documents and hunting for historical clues. His entire career was detective work, an endless search through the past to better understand the present.

'Why were you working with Scarlet King?' he said. 'That flat in Holland Park was yours, I presume?'

'Presumptions are dangerous. You should know that. You're asking the wrong questions, doctor.'

'Are you always this obnoxious?'

'Are you always this impractical?'

Max bristled. She sounded like Emma or Oliver, chiding him over his latest failed attempt at DIY. They emerged on to the motorway now, picking up speed. Cleo brushed hair from her face. Up close, she looked slightly older than before. Late thirties, able to dress younger if the situation required it. She had shoulder-length black hair and a slight build. There was no ring or other ornamentation on her fingers. Other than that, there was nothing to go on. She seemed unfazed by this. Definitely not a civilian, or at least not an office-bound one. Her accent had few identifiers or regional giveaways, like some of the army brats Max had known. The sort of English that was taught abroad; a precise, unaccented fluency.

'Tell me something,' he said. 'Your background, at least. Who are you?'

Cleo checked the mirrors. She relented. 'Alexandra Cleopatra Watson. Alex until I was fifteen, then Cleo from then on. Dad was army, Mum worked for the UN, my entire childhood was spent in run-down military homes with bad wallpaper and even worse drainage.'

'After that?'

'Majored in Russian at Princeton, then a Masters in International Relations at Balliol, Oxford. Followed by a decade of government work in the Middle East and another five in private intelligence. Scarlet heard of my analysis work. That's how she ended up recruiting me. For the last two years, I've been her principal adviser.'

'Government work meaning SIS?'

'What do you think?'

'And the private intelligence outfit?'

'Grosvenor Strategy. Based in Mayfair.'

Max had heard of it. Grosvenor Strategy had an office near Green Park and were on the shadier side of things, renowned for working with legions of Russian oligarchs during the peak period of Londongrad in the noughties. They were staffed by former spooks and special forces types.

'Why would anyone give up a six-figure salary in private intelligence to work as a personal aide to a geriatric spy?'

'Because the geriatric spy doubled my salary and halved my hours.'

'That didn't make you suspicious?'

'I was working in private intelligence. Everything made me suspicious. At least this time I was doubling my money.'

'Who owns the flat in Holland Park?'

'We rented it through a shell company. Scarlet never liked to use her own premises. She thought it was poor tradecraft.'

'Where did the money come from?'

'Equity release on her Chelsea flat. She bought it cheap in the seventies and it earned more each year than she did. That's how she hired me.'

'Why though?' said Max. 'She'd kept silent all this time. She was entering the last few years of her life. Why do this now? Why risk everything?'

'You must have a theory. Academics, in my experience, usually do.'

Max felt that pang of irritation again. 'Money or morals. It's usually one or the other. That's if it's not medical, of course.'

'Scarlet knew she could only go public at the end of her life. She planned it for ten years, like one of her old secret operations. It made perfect sense for her. Her duty to her country was done. Now she could do duty to her conscience.'

Max almost laughed. 'From the evidence so far, it appears Scarlet King was a high-level double agent working for Moscow. I'd hardly call that duty to her country.'

'It depends which country.'

Max shook his head. 'No, sorry, I don't buy it. No Western leader murdered millions of his own people. Downing Street or the White House didn't condemn citizens to gulags or labour camps. If Scarlet King worked for Moscow, then she betrayed the very liberal values that protected her. She was as bad as Philby, Blake, Blunt, Cairncross and all the others. The champagne communists who thought their feeble intellects were more important than other people's lives.'

'Here endeth the lecture.'

'I'm serious.'

'No,' she said. 'You're not. You're just as hypocritical as they were. You're only here, Dr Archer, because you saw pound signs flashing before your eyes. You could have walked away at the very beginning. No one made you respond to our card. No one forced you to read the first section of the memoir or to meet Scarlet in the park. At least Scarlet followed her convictions. What have you done? You've built an entire career off the backs of the very traitors you condemn. You're not just lying to me. You're lying to *yourself.*'

The words lodged like bullets, right in the middle of his chest. She said it with such conviction that it was almost irrefutable. He heard himself over lunch with his agent pitching his first two books with undisguised glee: a history of British traitors and the biography of Kim Philby. He'd glamorized them, emphasized the sex and danger, even hoped they might be optioned in a splashy bidding war by Hollywood and hungrily consumed by the masses. He saw that letter in his pigeonhole at Cambridge again and those blank words of dismissal. Did that explain it? Was his entire career merely a petty act of revenge against the Service that had spurned him?

228

'Where are we going?' he said. He hardly had the energy to speak. His entire life, the last twenty years, flickered before him. Emma, the marriage, Oliver, Lily – one bitter act of personal revenge.

'I thought you wanted to get out of the car.'

Max thought about the next step. He could force the car to stop and hand himself in. He would be arrested, at the very least. His academic job would go. Even if he avoided a trial, the future would be bleak indeed. No university would rush to employ an intelligence historian who'd endured disgrace and got on the wrong side of the law. Emma gone, Oliver smugly triumphant, Max crushed on the wheel of misfortune. That was one branch of history. Perhaps there were others though. Counterfactuals.

'Tell me where we're going.'

Cleo checked the mirrors, changed lanes and then accelerated. 'To find the original notebook.'

'You said it was abroad?'

'It is.'

'We have the Security Service after us. Right now, our names will be pinged to all major national airports, private jet terminals and ports in Britain. There's no possible way we'll get out of the UK unidentified.'

Cleo smiled. 'Historians are always obsessed with the past. Spies live in the present.'

'What does that mean?'

'Just because it rarely happens,' she said, 'doesn't mean it can't.'

19

Lucas always felt fidgety without his phone. It was almost like a fifth limb. Ever since giving up his army career, he'd spent two thirds of every working day furiously hitting the keys of various devices – BlackBerries, the first iPhones, now boxy secure government mobiles. His life was charted through the contents of his inboxes.

The sign outside HOSR1 – Home Office Secure Room 1 – was unequivocal: 'ALL MOBILE PHONES, SMART WATCHES, FIT BITS AND OTHER DIGITAL DEVICES MUST NOT ENTER THIS ROOM'. Even ministers weren't granted an exception. Lucas read the wording and despaired at the lax syntax. He deposited his government mobile and personal phone in the grey tray outside.

He cleared his throat and buttoned his jacket, then entered with a signature flourish. It was like being head boy at school, sometimes. All the other participants rose from their chairs, before he magnanimously waved away the formality. He looked around the table: Saul Northcliffe, Deputy Director-General of the Security Service, was in prime position. Jo Harris, the Home Office's Director of National Security, was opposite. Straight ahead was Caroline Runcie from Vauxhall Cross, always equipped with the vaguest of titles: 'Director of

Whitehall Liaison', a free ticket to gatecrash any meeting she chose.

Lucas took his customary seat at the head of the small table and picked up a manila file with 'TOP SECRET – UK EYES ONLY' in red across the front. He scanned the one-page executive summary regarding the progress, or otherwise, of Operation Tempest then said, 'Where are we?'

Saul looked even gloomier than usual. He cleared the permanent frog in his throat and said, 'The A Branch team lost sight of Max Archer just after 10 a.m. this morning. From CCTV analysis, we believe he fled alongside an accomplice from the back exit disguised as a student. We have designated this a Cat-A incident and sent photos and ID to all MI5 regional officers and constabularies. Counter-Terrorism Command and D Branch are currently co-ordinating the manhunt.'

'What about airports and borders?'

'Border Force have also been informed, as have Transport Police. We should pick them up via ANPR, traffic cams, or as they try and make an exfil.'

'How the hell did this happen?'

'Last night we picked up further raw intelligence from a birthday party held by Dr Archer's father. We got on-the-record evidence that Dr Archer intended to help Miss King publish her memoir and violate the OSA.'

'So that's why you decided to let him escape?'

Saul didn't flinch, that usual spiky reserve. 'Late last night, the A Branch team monitoring Dr Archer followed him to an address in Beaufort Street, Chelsea, previously identified as the main London residence of Scarlet King. Dr Archer entered the property via the main flat complex and then exited it ten minutes later. If you'll refer to item EX4 in your files, enhanced versions of the surveillance photos appear to show blood on Dr Archer's hands as he exits. Forensic results are being fast-tracked as we speak.'

The room looked closely at EX4 from their files, studying the images in detail.

'Following Dr Archer's exit, the team leader for the A Branch unit entered the property and found Scarlet King deceased. An ambulance was subsequently called, but she was officially pronounced dead just after two a.m.'

'How did she die?'

'From an initial look at the scene, it appears to be a heart attack induced by poisoning. There's a significant quantity of blood and we're still trying to determine if that could have been caused by a fall or is directly related to the death. The post-mortem should give us more detail. I've also asked Porton Down to be copied in on this and give their assessment.'

'Please tell me this isn't Salisbury all over again?'

Saul shook his head. 'No. Scarlet King wasn't a public figure like Skripal or Litvinenko. In terms of MO, this will have been more akin to the London Fourteen murders. A sign to the secret community rather than an international outrage. Either it's been dressed up to look that way, or it's the real McCoy. At this stage it's impossible to tell.'

'You're positive?'

'We've sent various items for testing just to be on the safe side. But the manner of death and the lack of any immediate radiation suggest that's the most likely probability.'

'London 14' was the Whitehall abbreviation for the series of unexplained deaths on British soil that could be linked back to Russia. Most appeared to die from a heart attack, though no toxin was ever found in the post-mortems. The list of names haunted Thames House. Some had even become objects of press attention: Scot Young, the fixer; Boris Berezovsky, the billionaire; Alexander Perepilichnyy, the financier; Robbie Curtis, property dealer; Stephen Curtis, the lawyer. And then the case that still kept Saul awake at night: Dr Matthew Puncher.

Dr Puncher was a civilian nuclear scientist from Oxford who investigated the source of the polonium used to murder Alexander Litvinenko. In 2016, back in the UK from Russia and suffering from unexplained mental health difficulties, Puncher was found stabbed to death in his kitchen. The coroner had ruled suicide, but there was credible intelligence that it was Russian wet work. Two different knives had been used. Saul could still see the blood in the room, the anguish of the family, the heartless cruelty of it all.

'Did anyone else enter the property before Dr Archer?'

This was a slightly sore point. In order to catch Archer in the act at his father's birthday party, Saul had removed the detail watching Beaufort Street and pressed them into service at the Goring Hotel.

233

'We had limited resources last night,' he said. 'We had no visibility on the Beaufort Street premises prior to Dr Archer's arrival.'

'So, if your Russian theory is correct, it's possible that someone murdered Scarlet King before Dr Archer arrived?'

Saul sounded dyspeptic. 'Let's just say we're investigating all hypotheses.'

20

It was Caroline Runcie's turn now. She was one of the last of the old guard at Vauxhall Cross, recruited at a time when social pedigree and a tap on the shoulder still ruled. Her CV included a spell as foreign affairs adviser at Number 10 during the Cameron years; in typical SIS fashion, she was as much a politician as a spy.

Across the table, Saul experienced that familiar itch as she spoke. He had the permanent sense of being talked down to. Ridiculous, at his age, but also inescapable.

'Saul's too polite to say it,' said Caroline, 'but a little birdie tells me he doesn't think that's when Scarlet King actually was murdered.'

And there it was. In one sentence Saul could see himself as twenty-one again and arriving in Whitehall for the first time. He had shielded himself ever since. Put up a shell and played the bruiser.

'Too polite. Too thick. One or the other.' There was a scatter of smiles and laughter. The self-mocking humour had become an automatic reaction. Saul wished he hadn't said it.

'Is Caroline correct on that, Saul?' said Lucas.

'If you'll turn to page ten in your files,' said Saul, 'you'll find surveillance photos of Dr Archer's first meeting with Scarlet King at a safe house in Holland Park. From what we know from the other

London Fourteen cases, the poison is usually deposited in a drink or food several days prior to death occurring. If Max Archer wanted to kill Scarlet King, slipping something into her tea would have been the perfect opportunity.'

'And the visit to Beaufort Street?'

Caroline beat Saul to it. 'I hesitate to speak on behalf of Saul again, but I imagine he thinks that was a check-up, yes? Archer wanted to make sure she was dead. And, if the memoir theory is to be believed, try and find where she'd hidden it. That *is* why you think he killed her, Saul?'

Lucas again. 'Saul?'

Calm, now. Don't react. 'Well, it certainly provides motive, opportunity and means. We know that Max Archer is in serious financial trouble and has just gone through a very costly divorce. He is an expert on double agents and could well have heard rumours that Scarlet King had written a memoir. He speeds along that process, steals the memoir, claims Scarlet entrusted it to him and then reaps the full financial rewards. It's certainly a credible hypothesis.'

Caroline smiled and nodded ominously. 'I hate to be the party-pooper, Saul, but it does leave one rather relevant question. Max Archer is a career academic. Forgive me for being obtuse, but junior lecturers don't – I think I'm correct in saying this – *generally* have access to weapons-grade biological or chemical weapons. Or have I missed something?'

Saul was determined not to be outdone this time. 'Page sixteen in your files.'

The room turned to page sixteen. There were

surveillance photos of a woman entering an LSE lecture theatre date-stamped for earlier that morning. Another photo showed the same woman exiting the safe house in Holland Park.

'On his own? No, indeed, Caroline is correct on that. This woman, however, is a different matter entirely.'

'Who is she?'

'She calls herself Cleo Watson now. From what we gather, she spent time studying in the States and at Oxford. She went off-the-grid for a decade before popping up at a private intelligence boutique called Grosvenor Security in Mayfair. For the last two years, we believe she's been Scarlet King's principal aide and adviser. She has dual nationality and spent most of her childhood in army bases around the world.'

Lucas looked at his watch, then said: 'How does a private intelligence consultant get access to state-level poison?'

'If she's not really a private intelligence consultant.'

'What is she?'

'A dual British-Israeli national recruited into the intelligence world at Princeton. MI5 have been monitoring Grosvenor Security for the past five years. We believe it's a front organization for Israeli intelligence. Grosvenor Security allows Mossad to keep an eye on the flow of illicit capital into and out of the Middle East and the Gulf, all processed by private banks in the City.'

The room went quiet at the mention of Mossad. Despite the prestigious history of the Western intelligence agencies, none matched those who trained

237

at Midrasha on the Haifa Road. Whether it was false-flag operations, hit squads or kidnaps, Mossad went further and faster than any other spy agency. Every spy chief viewed them with a mixture of jealousy and quiet awe.

'How dangerous is she?'

'Most likely, she'll have gone through IDF training and then further instruction at Haifa Road before working under non-official cover in the Middle East. Grosvenor Security and the delights of London are usually a reward for serious hardship postings. She'll be trained in all forms of counter-surveillance, tradecraft and wet work.'

'What about Dr Archer?'

'We have to assume she's using him. Mossad don't like to leave a trail behind. Once he's served his purpose, he'll be disposed of. They have various methods now. Perhaps, like Scarlet King, it will be presented as death by natural causes. We'll probably find his body sometime after Cleo Watson has fled the country and changed her identity. Suicide is their usual framing for a civilian asset. Hanging, I suspect.'

'But this woman was the closest person to Scarlet King. What possible purpose could she have for using and killing Max Archer?'

'That's a question we still can't answer.'

'And this fits in with the Russian theory how exactly?'

'It doesn't,' said Saul. 'We're looking at two separate hypotheses. Either this was Russian wet work akin to the London Fourteen killings. Or it was made to *look* like Russian wet work. Cover, if you like. Based on Miss Watson's involvement, it could well be the latter.'

Caroline again, the arch-sceptic now. 'Try this. What would Israeli intelligence want with Scarlet King in the first place? Surely they have more pressing matters on hand. A nuclear Iran, for instance.'

Saul looked around the table. The next bit was the most sensitive. These were the parts he hadn't even put in the file. The details that were rarely, if ever, committed to paper in any form. Instead, they were passed down verbally from one generation to the next in Thames House, always kept strictly deniable.

The truth about Scarlet King. And the truth about Operation Hercules.

'There are two possible reasons,' he said. 'What I'm about to say must never be repeated beyond this room.'

21

It was several hours after leaving London that they arrived at the destination. Max ran through every possible escape route out of England. He'd spent twenty years researching how double agents did it. George Blake had escaped from Wormwood Scrubs prison by climbing over the outer wall. Donald Maclean and Guy Burgess boarded the SS *Falaise* from Southampton to St Malo. Kim Philby had fled from Beirut, either via Syria or on board a Soviet freighter called the *Dolmatova*, it was still impossible to be sure.

Others, of course, had stayed in situ. Melita Norwood, the so-called 'Granny Spy', was still flogging communist flyers in Bexleyheath when the media came for her. Aldrich Ames and Robert Hanssen had both been stung by the FBI on American soil. Max had spent so long researching this world that these characters seemed almost like friends or acquaintances. He would wake up, he was sure, surrounded by books. This was a research proposal that had got out of hand; academic fieldwork taken to extremes.

Cleo still wouldn't tell him where they were going. She kept to the speed limit, careful not to get pulled over by the police or caught on camera. Max checked the wing-mirrors, trying to make himself useful, but there was still no sign of an active tail. He tried to plot the route in his head and then saw the sign for the town of Gosport. The south coast. Cleo drove on until they reached a sign for 'Haslar Marina'.

'You look worried,' said Cleo, as she parked the car and turned off the ignition.

'Gosport? That's your great plan?'

'Do you have another one?'

'The home of Fort Monckton? The training centre for SIS?'

'Yes.'

'Right next to Poole and the SBS?'

'At least it's not Hereford.'

'This is madness.'

'Why?'

'The Fort has close links with local police. If cameras picked us up, you've just handed them our location.'

'All the more reason to ensure cameras didn't pick us up.'

Max stared out at the grey-blue water lapping against the shoreline. He saw the unobtrusive activities of the boat owners and marina employees. He could still stop now, somehow creep back towards normality. He glanced at Cleo and realized how little he still knew about her. His entire future in the hands of a stranger.

'I've spent fifteen years as a professional intelligence officer,' said Cleo. 'You've read about this stuff. I've lived it. At some point you're going to have to trust me.'

'No professional spook would pick Gosport as the exfil site.'

'Which is exactly why Scarlet picked it. Basic

241

tradecraft. It's the quickest exit route too. Gosport gets us straight out. Plus, I know enough about espionage office politics to know that spies hate sharing information. Thames House have full control of this. SIS won't get a look-in until it's too late. Fort Monckton is not a problem.'

'At least tell me where we're going?'

'Would it make a difference?'

'Tell me and we'll find out.'

'Where do you think?'

Max was finally tired of the games. 'Enough with the bloody questions. It feels like a bad episode of *Mastermind*.'

Cleo looked out at the marina. 'Spying is waiting. But it's also planning. Scarlet knew her memoirs might get her killed. She treated her own country like a denied area: hiding the product, planning an exfil route and having a fallback. Hence the vehicle change. Hence Gosport. Hence this.'

'Where is the original memoir?'

'Paris. It's locked in a safety deposit box.'

'A bank?'

'Not exactly.'

'Why there?'

'First, because Anglo-French rivalry ensures the DGSI will never do the Brits a favour and hand it back. Second, SIS won't let the Élysée discover the secrets in that notebook and, therefore, will never reveal its location or existence. Third, it's close enough for relatively easy access at short notice. Any other questions?'

Max thought back to entering Scarlet's flat and touching the body. He felt sick at the very thought.

'Why would the British government want to kill Scarlet King?'

'I thought that much was obvious. Or have I been talking to myself?'

'Why not just release the two scanned sections and be done with it?'

'You know why.'

'Perhaps. But I want to hear you say it.'

Cleo sounded exasperated. 'Because the only way the memoir has any impact is if the world accepts it's *authentic*. Scanned pages could be forged by anyone. Her notebook contains her original handwriting and other documentary evidence establishing its provenance. Why else do you think you're here?'

Max hadn't slept for over twenty-four hours. Tiredness gnawed at him. He was no longer capable of coherent thought. He looked at the Rolex, the surprise gift from his father at the party, still snug on his wrist, and yawned heavily. 'So that's the reason you decided to ruin my life?'

'You're a credible figure on intelligence issues. You've written books and consulted for documentaries. No one outside the secret world knows Scarlet's name. You're the only one who can make sure this is taken seriously. Verify the notebook, verify the claims in the notebook. It's really quite simple.'

Max felt both flattered and used. 'And once I've done that, what happens then? I'm no use to you any more. I'm dispensable.'

'Look, I'm a shadow,' said Cleo. She sounded softer, more sympathetic now. 'I can't even use my real name. You're the only one who can break the story, Max. You're the one who can claim all the glory. Without you, the memoirs are just pieces of paper or scrawls in an old notebook. No one knows as much about double agents during the Cold War as you do. You'll be the public face of the whole thing. You're anything *but* dispensable.'

It was the spy in her, Max knew, that silky method that all intelligence officers learned at the Fort. He should remain sceptical. And yet, despite himself, it almost worked. He was committing the ultimate sin of any asset and letting himself be flattered. One thing, however, still didn't make sense.

'What is it?'

'MI5 doesn't kill British citizens for being double agents,' he said. 'If that was all Scarlet was planning to reveal, she'd have been questioned by the police and then seen out her days in obscurity. Anthony Blunt kept working as Surveyor of the Queen's Pictures once he admitted being a Soviet mole. John Cairncross never faced prison time. The Home Secretary ensured Melita Norwood got a slap on the hand and a half-decent movie out of it.'

'So?'

'If it happened in the past, then it usually stays in the past. The embarrassment of a trial is enough to ensure the CPS turns a blind eye. Why would the Security Service have an A Branch team on Scarlet King? What are they so terrified of? Why would they break protocol and risk taking out one of their own?'

Cleo looked pensive. 'Scarlet never told me.'

'I don't believe you.'

'She was paranoid as hell. That's all I know. My job was to arrange the safe house, the shell company and the calling card. But she preserved strict need-to-know on the contents of the memoirs. That was her domain.'

'A wild goose chase, then. A secret without any clues.' Max felt like laughing, all hope drained from the world. 'Not one single bloody clue.'

'She told you the same thing she told me.'

Max remembered Scarlet sitting in St James's Park. Those cryptic final lines: *I gave you all the clues when we first met. You already have everything you need to solve the puzzle of my life. It's just a question of seeing what's in front of you.*

It was the riddle he returned to every time. 'What else was Scarlet hiding?' he said. 'What secrets did she have left?'

Cleo reached for the door handle. 'I guess there's only one way to find out.'

22

Max had spent a misbegotten year preparing a book project on links between the FSB and Russian oligarchs. As part of the research process, he'd become tediously familiar with yacht specifications and technicalities. It was now his party piece. This particular specimen was an S-line Prestige 420S with single-level flooring and a cruising speed of 23 knots. It was 13.06 metres in length, with a 1,170 litre fuel capacity, and contained a double bedroom and private bathroom. It wouldn't rank alongside the truly plutocratic types, but it was enough to cross the Channel.

'First the safe house in Holland Park,' said Max, 'now this. Either Scarlet had a hidden fortune, or the KGB paid much better than the historical record suggests.'

'The flat was rented through a shell company. This is leased through a different shell company. Scarlet owned the flat in Beaufort Street. No reptile funds, I'm afraid.'

'I'll pretend to believe you. Can't they track us through the on-board navigation?'

'One of my old contacts kitted this out,' said Cleo. 'We have a sat-phone which is encrypted end to end. The navigation is also protected. Cheltenham would need some serious man hours to break it. By that time, we'll be long gone.'

'You said you joined SIS fifteen years ago?'

'Yes.'

'Back in the Century House days, then.'

She was busy getting the boat prepared. 'What about it?'

'I'm just curious. The canteen was as bad as everyone says?'

'No. It was worse.'

Max tried to clear his head. He set up a temporary workstation in what was technically called the aft master stateroom. It seemed to function as kitchen, lounge area and mission control. The on-board navigation plotted the route to the French coast. From there it would be a perilous drive to Paris. That, of course, was if they weren't detained in between.

Cleo put on cruise control and left the driver's seat. There was an L-shaped sofa around a small, square table directly to the left of the control panel. Max sat on the left and spread the scanned notebook papers across the table as best he could.

Cleo sat nearest the controls and tried to discern some pattern in Max's design. 'Tell me you've cracked it.'

'Not quite.'

'What, then?'

You already have everything you need to solve the puzzle of my life.

'The sample chapters aren't much to go on. But, based on the limited available data, I do have three hypotheses.'

'Of course you do. You can take the academic out of university, but you can't . . .'

'Theory one,' said Max, 'is the double agent theory. Both parts of the memoir make clear that Scarlet was working for Moscow during her time as an intelligence officer. Date of recruitment unknown. Agreed?'

'Agreed.'

'The association with Kim Philby is confirmed in part one. And the fact she had an exfil route planned when under interrogation by the Directorate of Counterintelligence and Security. Those are two things we *do* know. It's also clear that her handler was Professor Maria Kazakova working out of Oxford.'

'Still not enough to get her killed, surely?'

'No, agreed. Let's bank theory one and return to it if we need to.'

'What's theory two?'

'Chronology,' said Max, slipping into what Emma always called his 'lecturer voice'. It was like a cross between David Attenborough and Jeremy Paxman. 'Abandon chronology and the volume of research material becomes overwhelming. The cardinal sin of all archival research.'

Cleo frowned. 'It's already chronological. What's your point?'

'Not quite. There's chronology in terms of time, yes. But there's also chronology in terms of cause and effect.'

'That sounds like academic logic-chopping.'

Max picked up the opening chapters from the first scanned sheaf. 'For example. The memoir starts when Scarlet has already been recruited into SIS and is working out of Vienna Station. She mentions

248

training at Arisaig House, which is consistent with the historical record. But, and this is the crucial point, there's another little detail that isn't.'

'We're back to the fact versus fiction debate?'

'No.' Max reached for the start of the second sheaf. 'At the start of part two of the memoirs, Scarlet writes about an off-the-books meeting with a figure she calls Control. He briefs her on the defection of a Soviet source codenamed KAGO and asks her to help track down Philby and find the name of the Fourth Man.' Max took out a pen and highlighted a section, puzzling over it.

'What is it?'

'This exchange here,' he said, handing the page to Cleo. 'It's nicely hidden, almost teasing us. But it hints at something else.'

She glanced at the words and read:

'And after that? You will go through with what we originally discussed?' He nodded. 'Of course, of course. After that, you can come in from the cold. You have my word on that.'

'It could mean anything.'

'Possibly.' Max was in his element now, briefly able to imagine this boat as a floating seminar room. He could tease out the mysteries of the past. 'But these words suggest a prior chronology, a hidden timeline beneath the documentary record. Something which isn't stated fully in the archive, as such, but which can be put together alongside other pieces of knowledge. It allows us to build a hypothesis and rejig the chronology.'

'Is this how you teach your students?' said Cleo.

'It's the foundational principles of working with documents. What was the author's intention here? Who are they addressing? What are they trying to conceal and reveal? What is the context in which this document is being read? Without that, it's just words on a page.'

'Do you have an answer or am I meant to guess?'

'Scarlet King lived her life in code. We can agree on that. In her day SIS wasn't even avowed. Nothing is ever stated bluntly. She plays games with people, leaves clues that only the initiated can pick up. What if this is one of those?'

'The identity of Control, you mean? We put a name to Control and we have the answer?'

'If only it were that simple.' Max had debated this point with himself. No, he was sure this was far more deviously complex, layers wrapped upon layers. 'The most obvious candidate, of course, is Sir Stewart Menzies, the Chief of SIS during the Second World War and the architect of the Ultra secret. Mark Strong played him in *The Imitation Game*. Military background, trusted by Churchill, all round good egg.'

'Why do I sense a qualification coming?'

'Menzies didn't die in 1964. Scarlet is quite explicit here that Control died as she went back to Moscow.'

'So?'

'The identity of Control can't be key to the secret,' said Max. 'We go back to first principles. Scarlet King's purpose in this memoir was to reveal a secret. She disguised that secret so the right people – namely us – could find the answer to the puzzle but made it difficult enough that the secret wouldn't fall into the wrong hands. Control was probably higher even than Menzies. The Chair of the Joint Intelligence Committee, maybe, or a senior figure within defence intelligence. If his name was important, Scarlet would have given us clearer identifiers to match to the historical record. No, the figure of Control isn't what she wants us to see here.'

'What does she want us to see?'

'The fact of the meeting itself.'

Cleo sounded sceptical. 'That helps us how exactly?'

'At this point in the memoirs, Scarlet King is the only serving female member of the Intelligence Branch. She's been assigned the plum posting of Moscow Station. Ordinarily, she wouldn't even speak of such things to anyone other than the Sovbloc Controller and the Chief.'

'But we know she spoke of operational details to the Aunt Maria character.'

'Her Russian handler, yes. But that's different.'

'It doesn't sound that different to me.'

'Aunt Maria was on the payroll of Moscow and using her position within the Oxford establishment to run double agents inside Whitehall and academia. She was the enemy, so to speak. But Control wasn't. He was on the side of British intelligence. Why would she confide in him so intimately and not others within SIS?'

Cleo checked the navigation panel and then

resumed her focus. 'Why does this feel like a wild academic goose chase?'

She sounded almost like his doctoral supervisor at Harvard. Full immersion was one of the perils of academic research. Back then, Max had dulled the pain of the MI6 rejection by hibernating in the historical archives, getting so stuck in the thickets of detail that he sometimes slept in the library. Finishing his PhD thesis required a detox programme. He had to ration himself to one book read to one page written.

Max turned one of the pages over and began making notes on the back. 'Okay, fine. That's theory two examined and dismissed. The Control hypothesis. Let's park that for a second.'

He heard Cleo getting impatient. He ignored her and scrawled 'THEORY 1: DOUBLE AGENT' at the top of the page and then 'THEORY 2: CONTROL???' beneath it. Then he wrote down a third line: 'THEORY 3: OPERATION HERCULES??'

Cleo perked up. 'Hercules was the codename of the operation run out of Vienna Station in 1946?'

Max nodded. 'Twenty years researching this period and I've never once heard of any British operation to rendition Nazi scientists back to Britain. The American programme, Operation Paperclip, is reasonably well known. Practically the entire brainpower behind space exploration was Nazi. But the British side has always been either non-existent or extremely classified.'

Cleo had other papers from the second sheaf now. She flicked through them before reaching the section she wanted. 'Here,' she said. 'The chapter where Scarlet meets Otto in Kensington. She talks about a new legend and his work as a British asset within the scientific community.'

'Which suggests that SIS, and other British intelligence agencies, went even further than the Americans. The Yanks didn't try and hide the fact they'd cherry-picked a bunch of German scientists and put them on the American payroll. This memoir suggests the British side didn't want the world to know.'

'Standard operational protocol? The Brits were more hostile to Germans than the Americans.'

'Possibly. But creating an entirely new identity for someone takes serious effort and investment. To fully erase Otto Spengler's past meant help with every step – accommodation, jobs, even rudimentary surgery of some kind to avoid facial recognition. SIS wouldn't sign off on that just to avoid negative public reaction.'

'Why then?'

Like all serious historians, Max had a terror of speculation. He worked purely on facts, the evidence in front of him. But, right now, there was no other choice. 'Dr Otto Spengler must have been worse than the others,' he said. 'The Americans had people like Arthur Rudolph, Wernher von Braun and Georg Rickhey. Rocket scientists who'd worked for the Nazis, but who weren't necessarily Nazis themselves. Their past could be whitewashed within limits. They could hide behind the only-following-orders defence.'

'Otto couldn't?'

'Who knows? Scarlet is clear that British

intelligence faked the death of Otto Spengler in Vienna and released the death notice to the media. The only credible reason to do that is if Otto Spengler's crimes simply weren't able to be explained away. A deal with the devil.'

'And yet,' said Cleo, flicking to a different page, 'Scarlet hints at a relationship between them. Here, look.'

Max took the page and read the section again:

'Let's leave Otto out of this.'

'You were once in love with the man, Ana. Someone's replaced him in your affections then?'

She couldn't do this. Not now. 'Please . . .'

'Is there someone else?'

Otto, Caspar. She clutched at failed attachments. The alternative was already gone. Her future was governed by lies and desperate snatched liaisons. 'What happened between us is history.'

'History, my child, is the most powerful motive of all.' Aunt Maria rested her hand gently on Scarlet's shoulder. 'Now, I'm afraid, we must leave.'

Max took a moment. 'I think it's a red herring,' he said. 'If it was important, then Scarlet would have given us more detail. It's a cul-de-sac. The Otto–Scarlet relationship can't be the secret.'

'What about the Caspar–Scarlet relationship?'

Max shook his head. 'No, MI5 cares about many things, but Scarlet King's love life isn't one of them.'

Cleo looked put out. 'So your working theory is that MI5 want to stop the truth about Operation Hercules getting out?'

It sounded credible, but not enough. They were still missing something. 'On its own, no. There *has* to be more. A bigger secret, somehow. Something the Home Office and British intelligence are still terrified of. Something which keeps them awake at night.'

'A wider programme?'

'If Otto was given a new name and identity, perhaps others were too. Scarlet makes clear that she was sent to Vienna for the specific task of recruiting Otto. He was particularly susceptible to female company. What if he was just the tip of the iceberg? What if SIS and MI5 kidnapped more Nazi scientists and gave them new identities? Let them live normal lives in the UK as academics and researchers. What if British intelligence convinced the world that those scientists had died and helped them escape justice at Nuremberg or elsewhere?'

'A national scandal, then. That's what they're covering up.'

'A scandal is a government minister caught with their trousers down. This would be a total historical re-evaluation. Britain's entire post-war identity is built on its role in the 1939–45 conflict. The darkest hour, standing alone against Hitler, the voice of moderation against US domination and Stalin's sociopathic purges. If it emerges that Britain helped senior Nazi war criminals evade justice and live out a peaceful life in the West, the textbooks will have to be rewritten. It will change the entire outlook of twentieth-century history.'

'More than enough to kill the messenger,' said Cleo. 'Scarlet blew the whistle, you authenticated it. That sounds like enough of a motive to take her out and frame you for her murder. Two for the price of one.'

It sounded worse out loud. Max saw himself stumbling out of Scarlet's building on to Beaufort Street. He imagined being tailed all the way there. Was it possible? A memory surfaced now. Walking through Thames House during one of MI5's annual lecture days. There to promote *The Cambridge Five* series on BBC2, supposedly a launchpad to other broadcasting work. Entering the rabbit warren, marvelling at the scale of the place. All that now set against him. There was no way to outrun that, no escape.

'Yes,' he said, collecting his thoughts. 'More than enough motive.'

And it was in that moment – the three hypotheses staring at him from the scrap of paper – that the thoughts suddenly collided: the memoir, Scarlet King, Control, Thames House, the Cambridge Five, Dr Otto Spengler. All of them jumbled up inside his brain until the single idea struck him with the force of a hammer blow. He saw Scarlet in St James's Park and the final words she ever told him; the same words repeated to Cleo right before the end.

It's just a question of seeing what's in front of you.
What if the real secret was none of the above?
Max thought he finally understood.

23

The phone rang, just like last time. History was repeating itself.

Everyone had told him it would be a bad idea, of course. That was the irony. Get a smaller flat of your own, they said. Hire a cleaner, hire a cook even, and live out the last few years in style. But they didn't know about the other debts. The secret excursions to the bookies, the desperate play on the horses, the football, rugby, cricket, the only way to recreate the excitement of the field. The sense of fate turning on a sixpence.

Yes, Oliver Archer had been convinced that no one other than his accountant knew the true state of affairs.

Or almost no one.

The envelope had arrived in its usual slot. Having a pigeonhole again was like being at university. Oliver planned his days now with a strict routine: waking at six, half an hour of gentle exercise in his room, then an hour or so with the morning newspapers. Veteran newshound that he was, he still read the full range, his 'news buffet' as Lily, his first wife, used to call it. He started with *The Times* as the paper of record, then moved on to the *Guardian* and the *Telegraph*. The gaudier thrills of the *Mail*, *Mirror* and *Sun* were kept for later, a sugar-rush of gossip before breakfast at eight-thirty. After poached eggs on toast, he would check his pigeon-hole and then retire for a morning of reading and writing, alongside any general admin. It was a tolerable existence, if not a thrilling one.

That's when he'd first spotted the envelope. It was brown, formal, the impression only altered by his name scrawled in black ink. The key to retirement was to expand activities, squeezing the full amount of pleasure from each one. Rush a daily routine and the days stretched interminably. Supper became almost impossibly distant. So he studied the writing closely, lingered over the details of this new arrival like a connoisseur. This is what counted as an eventful day now.

He heard that boyhood refrain from Kipling, a relic from an earlier Afghan war:

When you're wounded and left on Afghanistan's plains
And the women come out to cut up what remains
Jest roll to your rifle and blow out your brains
An' go to your Gawd like a soldier.

Yes, that sounded about right. Retirement was similarly bleak. A rifle could prove useful.

He looked at the items on the desk now. The envelope had contained a copy of his latest bank statement and then photos of him entering the local bookies. Oliver had looked in vain for anything else: a hidden message, identifying markers of some kind, anything which could give him a clue about the sender. He'd tipped the envelope upside down, shaken it, even resorted to some of those old field tricks to bring secret writing to the surface. But nothing emerged.

The phone call came later that same evening on the dusty landline in his room. It made a change from the scam calls he usually got. He'd string them along for the fun of it; and, though he loathed to admit it, for the sound of another human voice. He'd picked up the receiver and been prepared for another bout of verbal boxing, when the voice stopped him. It was anonymous, threatening.

'Mr Ryland?'

Oliver froze. An old name, a past legend. 'Speaking?'

'We have a spot of courier work we need a hand with. We can offer a day rate, slightly more than you're used to.'

Oliver was about to say they were mistaken. He would put the phone down. Wrong number. Sorry. 'What type of courier work?'

And then they explained. There was never any overt link with the envelope in the pigeonhole, but the coincidence could hardly be missed. 'Mr Ryland' was one of the legends he used when working as a NOC in the field. It was the nom de plume for every odd job since, whenever they needed someone from outside; a plummy-voiced oldster for a surveillance gig, say, or some basic pitching work at an embassy in Belgravia for a potential asset with too many mouths to feed and seriously cold feet.

The phone kept ringing now. He knew it was them. It had to be. No one else held on this long. That was one of the problems of working unofficially. Most of the time it was a faceless message or nameless voice. If he ever tried to refuse their requests, he would get similar brown envelopes. Blackmail, pure and simple.

Last time was different though. Before it had always been curiously arm's-length. The instructions were neutral: collect a package from Gentleman A and deliver it to a safe house; drive Woman B in the boot of your car to the airport; let Family C stay at your house for two nights while an exfil plan is arranged. It was never personal. That had always been one of the terms and conditions.

Now they'd crossed a line. The first request had left him shaken. The party at the Goring, Emma on the invite list, the gift to Max. No, he wasn't up to this any more. He'd done his time. Surely they could let him die in peace.

Oliver picked up the receiver. It was instinct, nothing more. He always picked up.

'Mr Ryland?'

There was no point pretending this time. 'I did what you asked me to do. I can't help you any further. I'm sorry.'

'This is our final request.'

'And I'm the Wizard of Oz.'

'Double pay and the chance to bow out with a clear conscience. We can't say fairer than that.'

'And what do I get in return?'

'Listen carefully. There's one final thing we need you to do. One last person you need to call.'

Oliver looked at the photo of Lily on his bedside table. Her eyes tracked him across the room. He'd made too many mistakes in life. Leaving Lily was by far the worst. He wondered who the voice on the other end of the line was. Did they have a family? Or any kind of normal life? He imagined them leaving Thames House or Vauxhall Cross and catching the late train back to Reading, microwaving a ready meal and checking in on the kids without waking them.

He sighed. 'What is it?'

24

Max was on his feet and pacing the deck of the stateroom. He had the two sheafs of scanned notebook paper in his hand, furiously trying to find the right page.

'Max, seriously, calm down,' said Cleo. 'You're not making any goddamn sense!'

'It was right in front of us. This entire time it was staring at us.'

'What was?'

'The secret. The magical mystery tour. The whole nine yards. That's what Scarlet meant when she said we already had all the clues. She'd provided them on every single bloody page.'

Cleo looked nonplussed. She returned to the navigation panel. 'You said it yourself. Operation Hercules is the secret. A bunch of geriatric Nazis posing as welfare tourists with the help of MI6.'

Max was still thumbing through the pages. 'Operation Hercules is one secret,' he said. 'And certainly a big one. On its own it could be enough for MI5 or SIS to ensure it never sees the light of day. But to kill a British citizen? No, even that isn't enough. Not nearly enough. The real secret has to be even more damaging. Something worth killing for. Far, far bigger.'

'What, then? Secret Nazi gold? The location of the holy grail? The elixir for eternal life? No, let me guess. Scarlet King had proof that Hitler escaped to Argentina and is really still alive?'

Max finally found the references he was looking for. He took the two pages and set them down on the table again. He read them carefully, desperate not to miss anything. It was the chapter where Aunt Maria urged caution over the exfil in the chapel of New College, Oxford:

'No. If you were certain your cover was blown, you could have given me the codeword for the twelve-hour exfil over the phone. It would already be done. Something is stopping you, Ana . . .'

Max cursed himself for not spotting it sooner. He'd put it down as some kind of family nickname, the sort of illogical shorthand that all children acquired. But what if it was something more than family banter? Three letters that could change the entire nature of the investigation. He highlighted the word.

Cleo hovered nearby. 'Another theory?'

'If I'm right, then it means everything.'

'Max, seriously. When was the last time you slept?'

Sleep was a distant luxury now. It was days ago, surely, possibly longer. There were several stages of tiredness: the bone-aching grind, the weakness of movement, now a liminal state where the body ate into vital reserves, the last illusion of energy before collapse.

'Sleep has nothing to do with it.'

'You're not being coherent. There's a bedroom

263

back there. Get half an hour at least before we arrive, then perhaps you'll start making sense again. For both our sakes.'

Max was smiling, almost laughing now. He looked at the pages. The logic of it was so elegant, beautiful almost. It was the best type of tradecraft, the mark of a lifetime spent in the secret world. Genius, in fact. He could hunt in the archives for another fifty years and still not find anything as pure.

'My academic research is on double agents,' he said, steadying his voice. 'Intelligence officers who officially work for one side but secretly work for another. The thing is, technically, some intelligence historians dispute the use of the term "double agents" for professional spies like Philby and the Cambridge Five.'

'And this is relevant because . . . ?'

'Well, according to their theory, these spies always worked for the Russians before even joining British intelligence. So, strictly speaking . . .'

Cleo couldn't take it any more. She held up her hands in a surrender gesture to stop him. 'Max, Max . . . slow down. Please, I beg you, let's skip the academic theory.'

'Right, of course. Sorry. Occupational hazard.'

'What are you talking about?'

Max breathed deeply. 'What are spy agencies most afraid of?'

'I dunno. A mole, I guess. The enemy within. Being betrayed by one of their own. The fallen angel theory.'

'Right. Conventional wisdom says that the worst

embarrassment for any spy chief is to find a double agent in their own ranks. It's a myth perpetuated by films, books, TV shows. It's why I've spent twenty years writing about them. The general public thinks double agents are the end of the line. It's *Tinker Tailor Soldier Spy*. It's *Casino Royale*. It's *Where Eagles Dare*. Every great spy thriller focuses on the traitor. But that's the difference between spy fiction and real life. They're wrong. All of them. A mole – one of your own secretly working for the enemy – is actually only the *second* worst thing that can happen.'

'For someone who never served in a spy agency, you seem awfully certain.'

'There is one thing worse than a double. Only one.'

Cleo paused, mulling the options. Finally, she said, 'Let me guess . . . illegals.'

'Exactly.'

'Illegals' referred to foreign spies who worked outside the diplomatic network. Instead of being a Second Secretary or cultural attaché, they worked as journalists, bankers, consultants or posed as students. But that wasn't all. An illegal, as opposed to a regular NOC, appeared to be a native of the very country they were trying to penetrate. The accent, the clothes, the background, indeed the entire 'legend' was unimpeachable.

Max gathered his thoughts and continued, 'The greatest embarrassment for any credible spy agency is being penetrated by a foreign national without realizing it. Think of the Ghost Stories op. The FBI found a group of Russian illegals living in the US with jobs, children and social lives as ordinary citizens. Anna Chapman grabs the headlines, sure, but the others were just as lethal.'

'I know what Ghost Stories is, Max.'

'Fine. Now consider this. The Ghost Stories illegals hovered round the fringes of national security. But they never got further than that. No meal-ticket to Langley or the Hoover Building. Just imagine, though, if they did.'

Cleo looked deeply unsettled. 'What you're saying is impossible. There's no way it could happen. It's out of the question.'

'Now? I agree. The internet has made it impossible. All of us live too much of our lives online. Someone, somewhere, would discover your real identity with a few clicks of a mouse. But we're not talking about the present day. We're talking about almost a century ago.'

'Even so. Max, come on.'

'Case in point. In the mid-fifties a Canadian businessman called Gordon Lonsdale arrived in London. He owned a jukebox company and glad-handed every famous name in the city. He acted like James Bond himself, a daredevil and a playboy. Cars, women, luxury. Lonsdale had been born in Ontario in 1924. Everyone believed him. Sometimes he even believed it himself.'

Cleo conceded the point. 'Except his real name was Konon Molody from Moscow.'

'A KGB illegal right at the heart of London. A Russian who passed as a Canadian. That happened in the fifties.'

'Yes. But Molody just made decent contacts. He didn't manage to get into MI6.'

'Twenty years earlier, with the right language skills and without the playboy theatrics, he might have done.'

'You're serious? Really?'

Max held up the piece of paper. 'In this chapter, Aunt Maria calls Scarlet "Ana". It's the only time in the memoirs she does so. We know how carefully this was written. That inclusion is not accidental.'

'So what? It was probably a family nickname. My relations almost never call me by my real name. It's what siblings and relations do.'

Max smiled. 'Just what I initially thought. Except for one thing. Aunt Maria wasn't a sibling or a relation. In fact, she wasn't technically related to Scarlet at all. That's what we've been missing. It was right there in front of us.'

Cleo picked up the first page of the scanned sheaf from the table. She scoured it. 'You said Scarlet left a clue on the first page. That she'd already given us all the clues. I see nothing here at all. You're tired, Max, and too close to this. Please, trust me, you need to get some rest.'

'That's because you're looking at the content.'

Cleo sounded dismissive. 'What else is there to look at?'

'The form.'

'We're doing an English literature class now?'

Max struggled to contain his enthusiasm, convinced he was right. 'Look, the very first sentence reveals the secret. It reveals everything. That's what she was guiding us towards. That's how she encoded the message. Not the substance but the style.'

They both read it again:

It was on her fifth day at the Vienna Station that Scarlet King saw the target for the first time.

Cleo still scowled disapprovingly. 'Something about the fifth day, then? Or Vienna? Or the target?'

'No. Think about it. What is the thing most striking about the memoirs?'

'The fact she wrote them at all.'

'And?'

Cleo looked at the words again. 'The fact she describes herself in the third person.'

'Yes. A memoir written in the third person. Not the first person.'

'Scarlet explained all that. She's a spy. She doesn't do confessions. It's harder to prosecute under the Official Secrets Act. We've been through this. Moot point.'

'The OSA defence is a technical point, but still irrelevant in this context. Third person is most commonly used in novels rather than memoirs. Novels can still be based on truth, but the main characters in novels are distinguished by one central thing.'

Cleo was losing patience, unable to see where this was going. 'I'll take a moderate guess ... they're fictional?'

'Exactly,' said Max. 'Don't you see?'

'See what?'

' "It was on her fifth day at the Vienna Station that Scarlet King . . . ". That doesn't sound like a memoir. That sounds like the introduction of a fictional character or the opening of a nineteenth-century novel. Not just "Scarlet", but the whole name.'

'And?'

'That's the clue. It was there right in front of us. *That's* the secret.'

Cleo stopped now. The various pieces coming together: 'Ana', the memoir, the third person, the puzzle. 'You mean –?'

'Yes,' said Max, marvelling at the simplicity of it. 'Scarlet King was always a work of fiction.'

25

Professor Vernon Kessler wiped his lips with a napkin and then drained the last of the Pinot Noir. He had just finished his usual historical party-piece on the evils of private education and class-based privilege – taking in Freud, Marx, E.P. Thompson and Eric Hobsbawm – when one of the club wait-ers tapped him on the shoulder.

'The phone for you, Sir Vernon. It's St Paul's School. Something about your son?'

Vernon smiled at his two guests and got up. 'One moment. I'm so sorry.'

He walked through the coffee room of the Athenaeum – a typically gnomic title for what was, in reality, the main dining room – and hurried towards the entrance desk in the main hall. The Athenaeum, like all the best clubs on Pall Mall, had a strict no-phone policy. Any guests wanting to take calls or talk business had to use one of the cof-fee shops in Haymarket. The only way members could be reached in an emergency was via the club landline.

Vernon picked up the receiver by the reception desk and looked at the unknown number. It was probably Theo begging a mobile off a friend and wanting a lift from school after his debate rehearsal. Mrs K was still otherwise engaged, and the au pair had gone on strike last month over poor pay and conditions. For now, Vernon was the family's de facto taxi driver.

'Theo?'

'Vernon, it's Max.'

'Max?'

'Sorry to disturb. I thought you might be at the club. I have a very quick favour to ask.'

Vernon rubbed at his eyes. Hadn't he been clear? There were yet more rumours about missed tutorials, office hours and even departmental meetings. There had been no messages, no emails, not even a line on the faculty WhatsApp group to explain the absence. Rumours of student grumblings were getting back to the Vice-Chancellor's office. It was a shame, really. Once a bright, almost glittering future. But middle age had done for him. Marriage, too.

'I see,' said Vernon. 'The Mysterious Max! We've been sending search parties out for you, Archer. We even have a public hotline open. Some students are putting together a petition for your safe return. The Vice-Chancellor's office think you might be dead. We've even had the police nosing around the department asking to see your office and computer.'

'I can explain everything, Vernon. I really can. All I need is time.'

'No, Max, I'm sorry. I warned you once. I can't do so again. Either return to work by the end of the day or please don't bother coming back at all. That's my final word on the matter.'

'A research lead came up which I couldn't ignore. Something which could secure major funding for the department. I'm talking Mitrokhin or Gordievsky money. A chance to show Cambridge

271

and Christopher Andrew that the LSE means business.'

'Big claims, Max. Very big claims.'

'And I can back them up. All I need is one small favour.'

'Which is?'

'I need you to find a computer which isn't registered in your name.'

'You've lost me.'

'It's why I'm calling on this line. The computer cannot be registered or connected to your personal devices. Can you do that?'

Vernon saw the bank of computers behind the club's entrance desk. One monitor and keyboard at the end was free.

'You're playing me, Max, and I don't like it. Why on earth would I do such a thing? Why are we even having this conversation?'

'One search, Vernon. That's all I'm asking. If I'm right, then we'll have grant money on tap. Trust me.'

'And this is something you can't do for yourself?'

'Ten seconds. I promise it will all make sense very soon.'

'And the subterfuge?'

'This research is sensitive,' said Max. 'The sort of research that could make your department, Vernon, the world's leading centre of intelligence research in Europe. Possibly even a contender for the next Vice-Chancellor.'

Vernon debated for a moment then signalled to the club porter. He squeezed behind the counter and shook the mouse to life.

'Is your mobile switched off?'

'It's docked whenever I enter the club.'

'Do you have anything else digital connected nearby?'

'Not presently, no.'

'Good.'

'What exactly am I searching for?'

Max read out the name of the website address and then the search term he wanted Vernon to enter. It was like the old days of being a doctoral student, thought Vernon. Nowadays it was all perky postgrads eager to spend their summer holidays mining the archives and sorting through the tedium before he took all the credit. No, this was sleeves up, nose to the grindstone, back on the frontline. It was almost enjoyable.

Vernon found the website Max requested. Some kind of digital history project from the University of Stirling digitizing all death certificates issued prior to standardization by the Home Office in the sixties. Then, reluctantly, he typed in the search term: 'KING, Scarlet Joanna'. He pressed enter. The old browser buffered laboriously for a minute, then a result emerged.

The phone crackled into life again. 'We're looking for any links to the twenties.'

Vernon clicked. A PDF document of a digitized death certificate filled the screen. It was tagged as part of the Colonial Office:

FULL NAME: KING, Scarlet Joanna
DATE OF BIRTH: October 5, 1926
DATE OF DEATH: January 9, 1929

CAUSE OF DEATH: *Bleeding on the brain*
NEXT OF KIN: *Mr and Mrs D. King / Mombasa, Kenya*

'I thought you researched spies,' said Vernon, balancing the receiver between his right ear and shoulder, 'not infant mortality. Or have you changed specialism now as well without informing me?'

'I promise you this all has a purpose,' said Max. 'Scarlet King is key to the whole thing.'

'Despite dying at the age of two and a half from a serious brain injury in Kenya in 1929?'

'I'll explain when I get back. Trust me, it will all make sense.'

'And the police? What do I tell them?'

'I need another twelve hours, Vernon. Keep them at bay until then and soon you'll know everything.'

'Where are you, Max? That sounds like –'

The line went dead. Vernon placed the receiver down and clicked off the browser. He apologized to the club staff for the inconvenience before returning to the coffee room. As Vernon sat down and considered his pudding options, he massaged his right ear, making sure he was still hearing normally.

It was absurd, surely. He must be imagining things. Yes, that had to be what it was.

For a minute there it almost sounded like Max Archer was calling from the sea.

26

Saul left Westminster Mortuary on Horseferry Road. He found the driver waiting outside. Usually only the Director-General got chauffeured around like this, all other ranks having to make do with public transport or shoe leather. But time was against them now. No expense spared.

The Jaguar XF navigated the busy streets of SW1 until they reached Marsham Street and the hulking modernism of the Home Office. Saul reviewed the contents of the pathologist's fast-track post-mortem report for a final time, and then entered the building by a side entrance, avoiding the long queues in security and the daily stream of visitors. The pathologist was reliable and experienced. He trusted her judgement. He thought of Scarlet King's body on that table and knew the image would never leave him. Saul was almost ashamed of his own sentimentality. But the frail, snowy-haired, bird-like woman reminded him of his parents.

One of the private secretaries accompanied him to the top floor and the Secretary of State's office. Saul gave firm instructions that no one was to be admitted – whether diary manager or personal protection detail – until he gave the nod. The instruction was duly relayed to the rest of the private office.

Inside his grand ministerial lair, Lucas Harper

adjusted his tie in the mirror then turned to face Saul. He was due to give a keynote speech at the Carlton Club in forty-five minutes. 'Better late than never,' he said, flattening his hair. 'As bad as we feared?'

Saul sat on one of the squashy cream sofas, grateful to avoid the stone-like hardness of the desk chairs. 'The body's been given the once-over,' he said, producing two copies of the post-mortem report. 'The pathologist can't give us a definite answer, probably few in the world can, but the basic signs match those of some of the other London Fourteen cases.'

Lucas finished primping himself. He joined Saul on the opposite sofa. 'Poison leading to the appearance of a heart attack?'

'Yes. Do you remember the case of Badri Patarkatsishvili?'

Lucas nodded. 'Georgian. Fifty-two. Died in his mansion. Nothing showed up in the post-mortem or toxicology report. But the Yanks were sure he'd been poisoned. That was a heart attack too, yes?'

'Yes.'

It was the Russian specialism, Saul knew. Moscow excelled in poisons that made death look natural. Yasenevo, the current headquarters of the SVR, viewed it almost as a matter of national pride. Only a few other intelligence services boasted similar capabilities: Mossad, the IRGC in Iran, elements within the military hierarchy of North Korea.

'Your theory stands, then,' said Lucas. 'The Israelis take out Scarlet King and make it look like a Russian hit.'

'That seems the most likely scenario.'

'Likely, perhaps. But why? Scarlet King would have died soon anyway. Why would Israel risk provoking a diplomatic storm?'

Saul had wrestled with the question ever since he'd seen the file on Cleo Watson. 'They want control of the memoir,' he said. 'With Scarlet King dead, no one stands in their way. Mossad use Max Archer as a cut-out, in effect, a neutral academic figure to validate the material and send it out into the world. But the Israelis make sure the story lands with maximum effect.'

'To embarrass us?'

'For a variety of reasons.' Saul saw the faces round the table earlier as he'd briefed them on the two secrets. An old dog with a few tricks still left. 'Operation Hercules is one of the last undiscovered secrets of the Second World War. The Americans have had to confront the ugly truth about Operation Paperclip. We've never been held to account in the same way.'

Lucas sounded sceptical. 'That's still not enough, though, surely. Even Mossad doesn't assassinate citizens in a Western nuclear-armed power just to set the history books straight.'

'Unless the timing's right. I take it you've been briefed on recent events in Neuruppin?'

'Seventy-odd million Britons cause enough trouble, Saul. Northeast Germany is slightly outside my portfolio.'

'The last of the Nazi prosecutions are about to begin. State prosecutors in Neuruppin recently announced the trial of a hundred-year-old man accused of complicity in the murder of 3,500 prisoners in the Sachsenhausen concentration camp.

277

Another secretary from Itzehoe has been charged with accessory to murder for 11,000 prisoners at Stutthof concentration camp. With a new regime in the White House, and anti-Israeli sentiment growing throughout the West, this represents a once-in-a-generation moment to remind the world of Western complicity in covering up anti-Semitism. Perfect timing, in effect, for the release of an historically authenticated memoir exposing Hercules.'

Lucas tapped down his hair, checked his tie again, anxiety building. 'Did you get a chance to look at the Hercules file?'

Saul nodded. He withdrew a manila file from his bag. 'I found the full background on Dr Otto Spengler,' he said. 'Apparently he was resettled in England under the name Thomas Hegel in 1946. He worked at Porton Down for a decade or so before working as a legal traveller for SIS helping them gain scientific intelligence. He ended up as Emeritus Professor of Biochemistry at Imperial until his death in 1992.'

'Is there anyone from Operation Hercules still alive?'

'Scarlet King was the last of them. She was only twenty-one when sent to Austria. Most of the scientists themselves died in the late nineties and early noughties. The support workers were mostly in their thirties at the time. The youngest, other than Scarlet, passed away two years ago.'

'And there's no chance we could deny the whole thing?'

Saul always felt uncomfortable with those sorts of questions. They were political, questions of strategy and tactics. His job was to collect the facts and deliver them to the elected leaders. Or, at least, that's what he told himself.

'Not if the memoir is already out there. And, even without that, we have to assume that Israeli intelligence has a list of the German scientists we renditioned and put to work. All they need is first-hand confirmation from a surviving witness. The memoir is the final piece of the puzzle.'

Lucas was up again now, pacing the office restlessly. 'What about the other issue you raised?' he said. 'Surely we can stop the other secret getting out at the very least. Someone at Thames House must be still doing their damn job and protecting this country.'

Saul understood the brusque tone, even if he didn't approve of it. Operation Hercules was bad enough. But the other matter could potentially cause even more embarrassment for Her Majesty's Government. Far more.

'Again, Minister, that rather depends on the contents of the memoir. If Scarlet King chooses to reveal –'

Lucas erupted now. 'For god's sake, Saul, please let's stop calling the bloody woman by that bloody name! At least use her real name. There *is* no Scarlet King. There never was. Or am I wrong about that too?'

It had taken a direct order from the Home Secretary to force Vauxhall Cross to pass over the unredacted file on the Scarlet King case. Caroline Runcie had tried every trick in the book to delay. Saul had the file with him now and opened it. He looked at the details of the asset and then the name at the top.

'No, you're right,' he said. 'Her real name was Anastasia Chekova, "Ana" for short. Born in Moscow in 1923 to a father who worked as a clerk for the KGB. Nothing more is known of her after 1936. We believe that's when she arrived in England.'

'Moscow really used kids to spy on us?'

'Yes. Children attracted less suspicion. We can presume that Scarlet's father or mother were also Directorate S employees. They would have been her first handlers. Later she must have used the tombstoning method of acquiring the birth certificate and passport in the name of Scarlet King. That was the identity she used at Oxford, by which time she could also speak English without any discernible accent.'

'So she lied about who she was. She lied about her own nationality. She lied about her own name. And yet we're all meant to take her so-called memoir as god's honest truth, are we?'

Lucas was back by the fireplace and the armchairs. He sounded different. No longer a minister trying to charm a crowd, but a political survivor, someone who had fought too hard and come too far to see it all slip away like this.

'What do you need to stop it?' he said, standing over Saul now, pleading for his political future. 'Tell me. What would it take to stop the entire damn thing?'

Saul considered. Alongside collecting intelligence, his job was also to anticipate ministerial wishes, laying the groundwork so swift action could be taken. Like last night, for instance, and the prior work with Oliver Archer, softening him up for that very moment. Yes, just like last night.

'The asset you authorized yesterday managed to carry out our request,' he said. 'I have them on standby to complete any further requests if we need them to.'

Lucas was seated again, calmer now. 'Good. What else?'

'With the asset's help, we can trace Max Archer and Cleo Watson's progress. But we'll need full ministerial authorization to activate our resources on the ground. If we move now, then we might be able to intercept them before the contents of the memoir are discovered and made public.'

'What are you asking me, Saul?'

Saul leaned closer. The details already worked out in his head. 'Three things. First, full use of the RAF Voyager from Brize Norton. Second, authority to direct the French Ambassador and Head of Paris Station. And, third, an agreement to deploy force if the circumstances require it.'

'Only the Foreign Secretary can authorize operations conducted outside British territory.'

'The Foreign Secretary's currently tied up in a NATO meeting. He's incommunicado. According to protocol, emergency authorization falls to you.'

'How soon do you need me to give the go-ahead?'

'How about five minutes ago?'

Saul could see Caroline Runcie's smug smile in the secure room during the last briefing. He heard all the accumulated slights from thirty years of toiling in the same patch: jumped up policemen, glorified stalkers, domestic drudgery versus foreign

281

adventure, the eternal battle between MI5 and SIS. Oh yes, what he would do to bring this home; watch their collective jaws drop as he masterminded the biggest face-saving operation in recent intelligence history.

'I'll have to run it by Number Ten. Just as a precaution.'

'Of course. It's also true that operations stay with whichever agency has overall control of them,' said Saul, on a roll now. 'Operation Tempest was our op from the very beginning. Our manpower, our intelligence, our resources. Five are the only ones with the knowledge to complete the mission. Hand this over to the FCDO and Vauxhall Cross and it will be too late to get them up to speed.'

'Let me run it by the JIC and the NCA,' said Lucas. 'Get everything ready and wait for my word.'

'Thank you, Home Secretary.'

The meeting ended. Lucas was spirited away to the Carlton Club while Saul left the Home Office and returned to Millbank. He instructed Charlotte to move Operation Tempest to stage three.

Several hours later, he was travelling down through the Oxfordshire countryside to Brize Norton where the RAF Voyager, usually reserved for senior government ministers, was waiting to fly to Charles de Gaulle.

Twenty minutes after that, Lucas Harper called Saul on an encrypted line to confirm that Number 10 had given the green light.

The final stage of Operation Tempest could now proceed.

27

Scarlet King died twice. That was the truth of it. She was dead and alive at the same time.

Before confirmation of the death certificate, it still felt unreal. Max hoped for some kind of get-out clause. Somehow, an innocent explanation would surface. Not now, though. They sat in silence for several minutes. Max excused himself and used the on-board bathroom. He stood at the basin and splashed his face with cold water.

It's just a question of seeing what's in front of you.

He dried his face and dreamed of sleep. As he emerged, one of the alarms went off at the back of the boat. A high-pitched shriek. Cleo got up. She left the stateroom to tend to it. Max did what he needed to do, then returned to his seat. Minutes later, the alarm died.

Cleo returned to the stateroom and sat down at the controls. 'How bad would it be?' she said. 'If what you think is true, how bad on a scale of one to ten?'

'If British intelligence had to admit that a Russian illegal managed to rise to the top floor of SIS and was even in the running to be Chief?'

'Yes.'

'It would make Kim Philby and the Third Man saga look small fry. Profumo and Christine Keeler, Blake and Wormwood Scrubs, David Kelly and Iraq – none of them would hold a candle to this.'

'And non-historically?'

'It would mean wholescale intelligence reform. A complete re-evaluation of Five Eyes and the Special Relationship. Every other major intelligence agency would have to assume that any projects with MI6 involvement landed in the lap of Moscow. Compromised from the very beginning.'

'Putin's greatest victory?'

'Yes.' Max hadn't even thought about that yet. It was like a pebble in still water. He wondered if the ripples would ever stop spreading. He looked at Cleo and saw her glance towards the navigation controls. Here he was, facing the biggest crisis of his career, and he still knew so little about her.

Max prepared himself, knowing the next move was final. It couldn't be undone. The alarm stunt. The car journey. All had led to this moment. 'Unless, of course, that's what we're supposed to think.'

Cleo seemed puzzled now. 'More academic theories?'

'Possibly.'

'When do the theories stop and the facts start?'

'You sound like my ex-wife.'

'Perhaps she had a point.'

Max nodded. 'True. Though there is one final theory. Hear me out.'

'Fine. What is the final theory?'

'What if this is a false flag op?' he said. 'It looks so Russian because it's designed to look that way. The lady doth protest too much. What if it's another intelligence service entirely?'

'Why would any other intelligence service want to get hold of an old woman's memoir?'

Max knew he should stop there. Hold his tongue, run through his options again. But the time for caution was over. French border patrol could stop them at any moment. Even if they managed to land undetected, getting to Paris and finding the original notebook presented too many obstacles. Then there was the minor matter of getting the media to bite before the lawyers descended.

No, caution was no use to them now.

'Spying is warfare by other means,' he said. 'It's not really about stealing secrets. Or not only that. Secrets are only of any value because they give one side power over another. That is the point of spying.'

'Is that a line from one of your lectures?'

Max ignored the jibe. 'This secret, of course, is the ultimate weapon. MI6, the oldest and grandest spy agency in the world, penetrated by an illegal at the very highest levels. Whoever held that evidence would have British intelligence at its mercy.'

'Blackmail, then?'

'Yes. Having that notebook would be like holding a gun to MI6's head. They would do anything to stop that secret getting out. It would ruin them.'

'Who, then?'

'Logically, there are only six major intelligence players. Historically as well as currently. Britain. America. France. Russia. Pakistan. And Israel. The others – Egypt, Germany, Saudi Arabia, North Korea – are either limited by strict privacy laws or by a total lack of global alliances. Realistically, the

Big Six are the only ones who would mount an operation like this.'

'Perhaps that's the difference between intelligence historians and actual spies. You guys talk about spying. We actually get on and do it. In my experience, the North Koreans or the Saudis can do anything they want.'

Max didn't rise to the bait. Instead, he said, 'But say it wasn't British intelligence that killed Scarlet. What if it was one of the others?'

'This is absurd, Max. We'll arrive in about twenty minutes. We don't have time for more theory.'

'We have another minute. That's all I'm asking for.'

Cleo didn't hide her frustration. 'Fine, fine. So, Professor, what's the new theory? If the Brits didn't do it, who did? The Avengers? Superman and Wonder Woman and the rest of the DC Cinematic Universe?'

'Moscow would be the obvious contender. Poison that looks like a heart attack and doesn't leave anything for a toxicologist to find. It's textbook Kremlin MO.'

'Great. So now we have British intelligence chasing you, and Russian intelligence chasing the notebook. Once they rope in the DGSI, we'll be battling half of the Big Six all by ourselves.'

He was getting to her. That much was clear. Cleo's tone was angrier. He decided to keep pushing, the thoughts building on each other.

'The Russian theory almost works, but it lacks something in the way of logic. What did the SVR or FSB or GRU have to gain by her death? Perhaps they forced her to tell them where the memoir was

286

hidden. But, even so, the Kremlin gained more from Scarlet being alive than dead. The PR coup was outing a living spy as an illegal, sparking total humiliation for Britain. A dead spy becomes history almost overnight. Why not just take her back to Moscow for the TV cameras? No, killing Scarlet like that only makes sense if the memoir is the ultimate aim. Ergo, it cannot logically be the Russians.'

'The ISI then?'

'Unlikely. Pakistan has enough problems of its own. Getting one over on the British has its appeal, but hardly gives them much immediate advantage. Which just leaves us with the last three.'

'France, America and Israel. Shall we toss a coin?'

'I prefer logic and deduction.'

'I thought you might.'

It was like a seminar, Max thought, the sort of exercises he used with his students. So much of history focused on research and archives and the endless grunt work of documents and admin. Too often it ignored basic rational analysis. History wasn't just about hoovering up material. It was about logically teasing out clues, using the brain as well as just the eyes.

'The French have a clear motive,' said Max. 'Britain and France have been duelling across the Channel for centuries. Now Brexit has given the Élysée even greater motive. The notebook in Paris would provide France with a lifetime of blackmail material. The perfect plan, then. Except why go to the bother of taking out Scarlet or Ana if the notebook is already on French soil? There's no need.'

287

'Maybe they don't realize it is. They're waiting for us to lead them to it.'

'Possibly. Then we come to the second major flaw. The method.'

'French intelligence doesn't use poisons?'

'They would if they could. But the DGSE, or the DGSI for that matter, don't have that kind of money. The investment to manufacture poisons which can go undetected by even the best forensic pathologists and toxicologists in London doesn't come cheap. They're only worth buying if your service goes in for hits in a major way.'

'The CIA all over, then. The Special Activities Division Ground Branch. The best assassins in the book.'

'A strong case, for sure. But what's the motive? The Special Relationship already means Langley has Vauxhall Cross in its pocket. The UK and US share more intelligence than any other spy agencies on earth. Why risk jeopardizing the work of the NSA and GCHQ for the sake of acquiring power you already have? No, I discounted America at the start. It was never them.'

There was silence. Only the rhythmic pulse of the waves beating against the boat. A light wind knocking on the sides, the rumble of the engine.

Then Cleo said, 'How long have you known?'

'That you're a professional intelligence officer or that you're not working for British intelligence?'

'Either. Both.'

'I knew you were a spy as soon as I saw you at the Holland Park flat. You checked your six without realizing it, basic counter-surveillance. An unconscious twitch. Not to mention that wound on your left arm. You deliberately antagonized me when we first met too. Dismissive one moment, slowing me down the next. You realized I had my suspicions and decided to try some mind games.'

'And the other part?'

'You said earlier that you joined SIS fifteen years ago.'

'So?'

'I mentioned Century House, the old SIS head-quarters on Westminster Bridge Road. You didn't correct me. SIS moved out of Century House in the nineties. Vauxhall Cross is the first building you would have known after IONEC. No real SIS offi-cer would make that mistake.'

Cleo smiled regretfully. One tiny verbal slip. 'Why didn't you say something?'

'Why didn't you tell me about killing Scarlet King?'

'You have no idea what you're talking about. Why would Mossad be interested in an old notebook?'

'How about a bargaining chip? First, the Israeli government leaks the information about Operation Hercules. Then threatens Downing Street with an even worse revelation about Scarlet King being a Soviet illegal. The US is still largely on your side, but the British have fallen away. This is the perfect means of rectifying that. You picked me as a cut-out. Once the Hercules story is out it can all be blamed on me. You wash your hands of the whole thing and I end up added to the Mossad body count. You kill me like you killed Scarlet. Just another piece of collateral damage.'

'And how exactly did I kill Scarlet?'

'Mossad are the best assassins in the business. Silent killing is second nature. A woman in her nineties is easy prey. You befriended her, gained her trust, then dispatched her when her usefulness expired. Poison, most likely, presenting as natural causes and impossible to detect.'

'That sounds like the perfect plan.'

'It was,' he said. 'Except for one mistake.'

'Which was?'

'Never let an absent-minded academic take a bathroom break. You never know what alarms they might set off and what other curiosities they might find.'

Cleo reached into the handbag by her feet, a split second, trained to absolute perfection. A handgun. Glock 17. Aimed squarely at his chest.

Max reached into his pocket and took out the bullets he'd removed earlier.

'Checkmate.'

The Scarlet Papers
1992

1992
The Archivist

They were the words she dreaded. Four words, a mere six syllables. But they changed everything.

'I think he's credible,' said the Head of Station.

She tried not to react. This was it. This very moment. 'You're sure?'

'As far as I can be. Everything he's said checks out so far. I've made some calls. He is who he says he is.'

Scarlet King listened intently on the secure line. The dip-tel had arrived twenty-four hours earlier. The sort of urgent, priority message that arrived once in a blue moon from Moscow Station. Not the standard plea of a former KGB grunt to defect, but the promise of serious treasure. This was the first chance to speak to H/MOSCOW without being overheard.

'And he's really just a walk-in? There was no pitch or hard sell from our side?'

'None whatsoever. Rumour is he tried the Americans first and got turned down. That's why he came to us.'

'Any chance this could be a dangle?'

'Honestly, I'm not sure there's any agency left to set a dangle in motion. It's every man for himself out here. But it's your call, ma'am.'

Scarlet paused. She looked out of her corner-view office at Century House. It still surprised her when they said things like that. Stupid, of course. But she had toiled for so long in the foothills that reaching the summit was a giddy, almost airless experience. She sometimes stopped as she saw the plaque on her office door: C/ECE.

Controller, Central and Eastern Europe. She was now in charge of all operations within Russia and beyond, the master of Sovbloc.

'Why Riga?'

'It's safer than Moscow. And it's also his current bolthole.'

'What about the source's claims?'

'The job description checks out, as far as I can tell. I have two sub-agents confirming that the source did work as a librarian and archivist for the First Chief Directorate. Takes time without blowing his cover.'

'He's still claiming he has all the files? Not just some of them?'

The Head of Moscow Station checked something, flicking through the pages of a notebook. Then he came back on the line. 'He claimed to me, and I'm paraphrasing here, that he had every file on every mole and penetration agent ever run in the West.'

'Birthday and Christmas at once. Sounds too good to be true. There's still nothing further on why the Americans passed on this?'

'Nothing concrete. They're slashing all Sovbloc budgets and personnel. The past doesn't interest them as much as the future. They were so scarred after Angleton and the mole-hunt before, I think they'd rather not know.'

Yes, Scarlet thought, that sounded right. The

pillars of her life smashed to pieces just like those chunks of the Berlin Wall; every shibboleth called into question. The Americans were drunk on their victory, Moscow disintegrating with defeat. And now, just when everything was over, old ghosts returned to haunt them all.

'I need to meet him,' said Scarlet. 'Say we need to see as much material as possible. We can't give a firm answer until we've verified some of the material.'

'Of course.'

The old spy in her felt uncomfortable with her next question, but her curiosity demanded it. 'And the source's name?'

'You really want to know?'

The line was secure. This office was bulletproof. 'Yes,' she said. 'I really do.'

The Head of Station cleared his throat, breaking an almost religious oath of silence. Finally, he said, 'Mitrokhin, ma'am. The source's name is Vasili Mitrokhin.'

1992
Mr Mitrokhin, I Presume

The old world was gone. All hail the new world.

The Cold War was over. Exit stage left for James Bond, George Smiley and all their tribe. Century House would be mothballed. Scarlet and the rest brutally cashiered. Even John le Carré was rumoured to be working on a book about organized crime and arms dealers. The press had read the last rites. The funeral wreaths were already planted. MI6, the residue of empire, the last gasp of the Second World War, even the twentieth century itself in its full blood-drenched glory – all for the knacker's yard.

She flew commercial and landed in Riga. She barely had time to take in the scenery. She was reminded of Vienna after the war, the same sense of aftermath. The world had changed yet was nearly recognizable. The human spirit indomitable and amnesiac. Her passport was in a different name. Her profile was altered by thick-rimmed glasses and a greying wig. Her cover was a trade mission, a lifer from the Foreign Office looking to establish business ties.

The car waited outside. Only hours after arriving, she was looking at the blank smudgy-grey walls of the Riga safe house. Lunch was a bad sandwich and weak tea. No, this was all the same. The tap in the bathroom was broken. The room smelled of sweat.

Riga maintained its Soviet staleness. Scarlet already missed the cardboard comfort of the plane.

In the flesh, Vasili Mitrokhin was older than she predicted. He was wiry and twitchy, with tufts of thinning grey hair and a nervous smile. He seemed at home in these surroundings, a career spook used to the drabness of safe house habitation. There was nothing of the wide-eyed civilian about him. He knew the dangers, the moral compromises. There was no court-jester brightness that usually signalled a dangle or a plant. He was one of them.

Today she was Susan Napier, a director from the British Foreign Office. Her passport said so, as did two other forms of identity. Mitrokhin sat on one side of the table, Scarlet and H/MOSCOW on the other. As the senior figure in the room, Scarlet led the interrogation. She was back in her handler mode again, now, dusting off the techniques of all agent-runners. Family, hobbies, the weather, sports. Then – and only then – would they get down to business. Spying was a human relationship, or it was nothing. Miktrokhin's English was poor, so they talked Russian, ensuring no nuance was missed. Finally, they got on to the files.

How? she asked first. How did he smuggle such treasure from under their noses? Why did he succeed when so many others failed? Why was he sitting here sipping Earl Grey tea rather than begging for his life in the Lubyanka?

Mitrokhin was smooth, prepared. It all happened with the transition when the First Chief Directorate moved from the Lubyanka to Yasenevo. The archive moved with them, and that was his job. He had to prepare every file for removal. The opportunity emerged.

All in one go?

No, no, too risky, over time. But the move provided an opportunity to secretly copy all the major files. Assets, double agents, illegals, that kind of thing. A rollcall of Russian foreign intelligence during the Cold War.

He was serious. Scarlet did everything to keep her composure. But there was no denying it. These weren't the words of a wind-up merchant looking for an easy payday. This quiet, unassuming figure was in earnest. This was happening.

'You copied – or are claiming to have copied – all the files of the First Chief Directorate?'

'Yes.'

'I am told you have a sample to show me?'

'Yes, yes. It is authentic, you will see. Completely authentic.'

He had two bags with him, and both were filled with papers. Later they counted over two thousand pages of notes. And this was just the sample. The full treasure trove would fill libraries many times over. To think the Yanks had passed. Langley's blind spot was Century House's windfall. One of history's fatal missteps.

'You will allow me to take this sample for authentication back in London?'

Miktrokhin sounded reluctant. 'These pages are my life,' he said. 'If word gets out, then I am a dead man. If you lose these, then I lose everything. You understand me?'

'Yes.'

298

'How do I know I can trust you?'

Scarlet smiled warmly. 'You saw the lengths we went to with the exfil of Oleg Gordievsky.'

He nodded. Of course.

Yes, the coup that had secured her promotion to Controller level. Made Britain an attractive home for the legions of former KGB types trying to defect. Operation Pimlico had been Scarlet's ticket to the top floor.

She continued, 'If we can protect Gordievsky in the heart of Moscow at the height of hostilities, then we can do the same for you in Riga. You have my word on that.'

'I hope so.'

'This development is being kept strictly deniable. The only ones briefed on these papers are sitting in this room now. This sample will not be shared with anyone else within our organization. I will personally verify the documents and then contact you regarding the rest of the archive. Do we have a deal, Mr Mitrokhin?'

There was silence and the background clank of bad plumbing. Then the figure opposite broke into a wary half-smile and said, 'Yes. I think we do.'

1992
The New Chief

They saw the asset off and then regrouped in the safe house gardens. Scarlet sipped from a cup of potent embassy coffee. The Head of Moscow Station smoked one of his heavy Soviet cigarettes, a prerequisite for any Russian posting. They said nothing, letting the meeting settle, hunting for the error or the anomaly and, so far, finding none.

It was H/MOSCOW who spoke first. He was mid-forties, a former Marine turned spook. Scarlet's brigade, as they were known in the Service.

'Rumour on the block,' he said, 'is that this is the Chief's last hurrah and you're next in line. After Rimington took over at Five, Number Ten want to repeat the trick at Century House. Perhaps I should be bowing to you right now.'

Scarlet waved the thought away. 'Rumours are dangerous beasts.'

'The Gordievsky exfil gets you bumped up to Controller. Mr Mitrokhin and his secret files propel you all the way to the Chief's chair. You're either a lucky devil or a genuine mastermind. Someday you'll have to pass on the trick.' He blew out a volley of smoke, acidic on the nostrils. 'The throne room really doesn't tempt you?'

Oh yes, she was tempted. Even that seemed too meek a word. The only woman serving in the Intelligence Branch. Now an intelligence baron in her own right, the leading Kremlinologist and Russia House expert; the most senior female officer in SIS history. But to sit in that chair, sleep in that serviced apartment, sign documents with the famous green pen. No longer a name, as such, but merely an initial: 'C'. To become a whisper in the halls of power. No longer mortal. Yes, she was more than tempted.

'Or the opposite,' she said. 'If it turns out our archivist friend is seeking an easy payday, then both of our careers could go south very quickly. We'll be cleaning Century House rather than running it.'

'The reverse is also true.'

'Is it?'

'Just think about it. All those rumours we can finally check. Wilson, the Cambridge Five, Fuchs and the nuclear side. Those files will give us the keys to the castle.'

It was a historian's idea of paradise. Was Harold Wilson really working for the KGB as Prime Minister? Were there any other senior members of the Labour Party or trade union movement recruited by Moscow as students and parachuted to the top of the British government? And then the other questions: was Anatoly Golitsyn right all those years ago? Was there really another senior SIS mole who still hadn't been caught? Was there a Sixth or Seventh Man still waiting for a knock on the door?

Her body was creaky, dog tired. She hadn't slept on the plane. She was too haunted by the dip-tel and the call. The past, for her, was already boxed up and gathering dust. Scarlet King could make the final step up to the Chief's office and then retire with battle honours: damehood, peerage, Order of the Garter, the memorial service at St Margaret's, Westminster. That was to be her reward. Now, in an instant, it could be cruelly snatched away. Those files would contain everything.

'Has anyone else got an inkling of this?' she said. 'Are there any junior station staff we need to worry about?'

'Mitrokhin knows the rules of the game and came straight to me. You're the only person I've told.'

'Good. I want you to keep it that way. I don't want the Ambassador, the Foreign Office or even the Chief getting wind of this until I'm absolutely certain that the product is genuine.'

'Of course.'

'I also don't want a dead archivist on my conscience. Neither do you.'

The Head of Station took another drag of his cigarette. 'And the Americans? How do we handle their remorse?'

'Let me find out,' said Scarlet. 'Act normally. Keep appointments. Forget Mr Mitrokhin and his library of files ever existed. Do nothing until I give the word.'

'Spoken like a true candidate for Chief.'

Scarlet finished her coffee. 'Everyone thinks the world changed overnight and the Russians have become our new best friends. But some things never change. Get this wrong and we'll both be strung up by our ankles.'

The Head of Station nodded. He looked newly anxious. He finished his cigarette and stubbed it out on the dirty concrete patio. 'Don't worry,' he said. 'My lips are sealed.'

1992
Blackheath

Back at Century House, the project went without a codename or strap grade. Officially, it didn't exist at all. Scarlet shut the blinds, locked her office door and cancelled all but the most important meetings. For the next week she waded through the two-thousand-page sample from the Riga meeting. The files from the KGB archive had all been laboriously copied in Mitrokhin's spidery black handwriting. She was overwhelmed by the sheer volume of names, operational details and progress reports. It was the closest a spy ever came to post-mortems, opening up a patient and removing the vital organs. She was careful, precise, methodically checking every dot and comma.

But, already, her worst fears were confirmed. Vasili Mitrokhin was a rarity in the spy business, someone who was what they claimed to be. The entire archive of the KGB's First Chief Director-ate was now for sale. No one would be spared; no one was safe. It was all finally here in smudgy black ink on cheap disposable paper. An inventory of an experiment's secret excess. A roll call of treachery.

After verifying the first two thousand pages, she waited for the right moment to approach the top floor and play in the Chief. She kept details scant, and offered no rash promises, but observed protocol. It was vital for what followed that her conduct couldn't be questioned. She had three key asks: first, a safe house paid for by the reptile fund, completely deniable and with no paper trail leading back to the Firm; second, additional resources to facilitate the exfil of Mr Mitrokhin from Riga and an all-expenses-paid place on the SIS resettlement scheme; and, finally, that the mere existence of these papers be kept secret even within the building. No Foreign Secretary, or Number 10 Foreign Affairs Adviser. Not yet. They needed time. No political PR games, either. Moscow Rules.

The Chief looked confused. 'If you want to get this chair, Scarlet, you have to play politics occasionally. Why not let news of your latest triumph reach the ears of the key decision-makers? Nothing operational, mind, just a headline.'

'Too risky.'

'The other contenders might not be so bashful.'

'Mitrokhin is trusting us with his life, sir. I gave him my word. This has to be above reproach.'

'The spy's code of honour.'

'Yes.'

'As you wish then. Just don't say I didn't warn you.'

The money from the reptile fund was transferred to a numbered account which only she could access. Scarlet rented a two-storey house in Blackheath, far away from the usual SIS stamping grounds of Pimlico and Victoria. The estate agent knew her as Mrs Hawkins, a teacher who'd recently stumbled into a fluke inheritance and wanted to sample London life before buying. She bought a mattress, a kettle, some soap and enough food to stock the fridge. Then she left her house in Fulham, telling the neighbours she was going abroad for work. They knew she was Foreign Office, something hush-hush, and rarely batted an eyelid at her frequent disappearances.

Four days later, Scarlet gave the go order on the exfil. New chatter had come in suggesting old KGB hands were getting suspicious of Mitrokhin and trying to hunt him down in Riga. Lose the asset, lose the treasure. Scarlet insisted the exfil happen first, then the document retrieval later. For maximum effect, the exfil was carried out on the anniversary of the Russian Revolution. Once she got news that Miktrokhin was safely out of Riga by boat, she authorized the Deputy Head of Moscow Station to visit the dacha where the documents were hidden. Four members of Moscow Station, heavily protected by members of the Increment, endured a night-time of gardening work and left with six trunks of documents flown back to London by diplomatic bag.

Only weeks after first hearing Mr Miktrokhin's name, the archive was securely delivered to the safe house in Blackheath. One of the Firm's usual heavies – a former Increment member from Northern Ireland known only as 'Paddy' – took up residence in the basement flat, monitoring the fringe of security cameras around the building entrance. Whenever Scarlet popped out, Paddy was in sole charge of ensuring the intelligence goldmine didn't vanish. He watched, drank and never said a word.

He reminded Scarlet of a samurai or one of those ancient and silent warrior classes.

At Century House the word soon spread that Scarlet King was on sabbatical. Illness, apparently. Something personal, at the very least. Profound thoughts and condolence. The Deputy C/ECE took over day-to-day duties. Scarlet, meanwhile, established a new routine: up at 5 a.m., half an hour run around Blackheath and Greenwich, then a solid morning reviewing files until a light lunch of fish and vegetables. She wouldn't pause again until 8 or 9 p.m. Often she woke in the night with a sudden thought and padded sleepily to her attic study to review more files. It was like being back at Oxford again. Or completing the DPhil she'd always dreamed of. The weight of material was almost incalculable. The archive laid bare the entire machinery of the First Chief Directorate. She was like a biblical scholar, fussing over syntax, grammar and foreign vocabulary, anything to peel back the mystery. She longed for divine revelation.

The Cambridge Five, senior politicians who spied for the KGB, Soviet operations in London, Madrid, Washington DC, Paris, West Berlin. The information contained here would ruin reputations; slay old ghosts and make new heroes. She could reframe history: editing bits out, ditching inconvenient truths, storing away facts that best remained hidden. She was Head of Russia House. The Firm's leading Kremlinologist. The next Chief of the Secret Intelligence Service. For this moment, she controlled the past, the present and the future too. History was hers.

It was a week and a half before she finally found the section covering Directorate S. The notes were organized by department: the Forgers (Department 2), in charge of creating false identities alongside documents, passports, driving licences and visas; the Recruiters (Department 3 and Department 10), winnowing down possible new recruits through surveillance and false-flag ops, targeting both Russian nationals and foreign nationals in Russia; the Americans (Department 4), overseeing all illegals operations in Latin America, the United States and Canada; or the Bloodhounds (Department 9), the counterintelligence chiefs sniffing for a hint of treachery. The most prestigious by far was the Veterans (Department 1), including the elite cadre of Special Reserve Officers also known as 'travelling illegals', those who had proved themselves battleworthy as sleeper agents, now dispatched for bespoke missions around the globe. The deadliest part of Directorate S was the Assassins (Department 8), the expert wet workers. The file also covered Line N officers stationed in embassies around the globe, the postmen and welfare officers who served and nurtured the illegals.

Then, near the end, the files turned to the most sensitive information of all: the identities of deep-cover illegals working around the world. Directorate S were present in every corner: Europe, the Middle East, Central and East Asia, North and South America. Scarlet turned to the Europe section, narrowing it down until she reached Northern Europe, then the United Kingdom of Great Britain and Northern Ireland.

She scrolled down the list of names until she found the entry she was looking for. She turned to the page number indicated, and read the name as if it were that of a stranger:

COL. ANASTASIA CHEKOVA
Directorate S
London, United Kingdom
Order of Lenin 1985

She turned the page and saw the type on the other side:

Date of recruitment: September, 1936
Current legend: Miss Scarlet King
Current employer: Secret Intelligence Service (UK)
Current handler: Professor Maria Kazakova
Current grading: PRIORITY 4/ULTRA
Current status: ACTIVE

Her other self. A separate person.
Ana.

1992
Professor Hegel

'How is he today?'

The nurse's face was neutral, as usual. She was chubby and austere, like an Edwardian governess. 'He was complaining about the food for most of yesterday.'

'Lasagne?' said Scarlet.

'Not his favourite. He's turned the rest of the ward against it too.'

'Blame his childhood. He's never got on with Italian food.'

'He was also asking again for a private room.'

'Is that a possibility?'

'Only if he's on the verge of going and we don't want to disturb the other patients. Until then, the ward's the best we can do. I told him to take it up with the consultant.'

St Thomas' Hospital was busier today. Every corridor echoed. Trolleys wheeled at high-speed, patients groaning, relatives sobbing, porters and orderlies laughing. Scarlet managed fortnightly visits. She was still his handler, after all, or at least that was her justification, forty-six years to the day since that fateful meeting in Café Landtmann.

'I take it he didn't respond well to such tough love?'

'The lasagne and the tray went flying. Sister had to remind him of the ward rules. The others

309

cheered. He's a folk hero to them now. It would be easier dealing with children. I'm putting in for a transfer to paediatrics.'

'Give me the Sister's name and I'll make sure I send flowers.'

'Save your money, love. We'll get the sequel next week.' The nurse stopped outside Ward 9. 'He really was a professor then? A proper one?'

'Still is, I'm afraid. The retired kind. Emeritus Professor.'

The nurse laughed. 'Poor thing kept telling me he'd signed the Official Secrets Act. Licence to kill and all. Our very own James Bond.'

Scarlet's insides curdled now. It was becoming a problem with many of the old Operation Hercules assets. All those fresh-faced scientists recruited after the war were in their dotage now, desperate for an audience and with threadbare inhibitions.

'Something about old age and delusions of grandeur,' she said. 'He spent his life as a chemist helping companies refine their stain-removal products. Nothing official, or secret, I can assure you.'

'There was me thinking he was some kind of spy.'

'The only way Thomas could kill someone is by boring them to death.'

The nurse laughed, then caught herself. 'I'll try reminding him of that next time I give him a bed bath.'

'Just don't tell him I said it.'

'Mum's the word.' The nurse wandered off. Scarlet prepared herself. She had seen dead bodies, massacred flesh, photos of assets tortured out of their skin. And yet the sight of snowy-haired people of a similar age lying in thin gowns on a hospital bed – displayed, she always thought, like second-hand toys in a junk shop – filled her with insurmountable horror. It was like staring at her future. One with no hope of escape.

Professor Thomas Hegel CBE, formerly of Imperial College London and now Visiting Professor for the Public Understanding of Science at Queen's College, Cambridge, was lying in his usual space at the end of Ward 9, slightly apart from the other beds. Typical Otto. He refused to join in even now. Scarlet had her usual haul of magazines and newspapers, along with a continuous supply of 4B pencils. She handed the loot over.

Otto eyed them sceptically. 'They're all there?'

'They are.'

'Even the *TLS* ?'

'Yes.'

Otto had a bizarre fascination with *The Times Literary Supplement*. He claimed the letters page was the best read in literary London. He relished the sight of prestigious colleagues tearing chunks out of each other. It was the closest academia came to a contact sport. Scarlet searched local newsagents every other week to find a copy.

'How are we today? Good, bad or exceedingly average?'

Otto was still immersed in the stash of newsprint. He sorted them into order. 'You know me.'

The lung cancer diagnosis had been sudden and brutal. And she knew how much he hated all of this. It was the one problem brainpower couldn't fix. Otto had spent his life condescending to others – students, colleagues, the public. Now he was ordered this way and that by nurses, talked down to by doctors half his age. His status was gone. His achievements moribund. There was a point, six months after the diagnosis, where he gave up completely. Now he would eke out the days in a semi-slumber. Soon he would move to a hospice.

'Is this visit work or play?' he said.

'Which would you like it to be?'

'Work is hardly logical. Unless you want the inside word on what's happening in this ward. I'm not much of an asset now. Though the man in the bed opposite has a slight accent. Russian, if you ask me. Probably armed too. Definitely NKVD.'

Scarlet pulled the curtain around the bed. At least it gave the illusion of privacy. She sat down opposite the bed and said, 'I've been talking with the bean-counters at Century House. Part of the package for all resettled assets is limited financial help with medical costs. They've finally agreed to stump up for the private hospice. Not Rolls-Royce treatment, but better than being henpecked in this place.'

Otto tried to laugh, then started coughing. The sound hacked out of him. 'Ah, they're getting nervous. The suits want me to go quietly.'

'You've been on the books for almost fifty years. You deserve some dignity at the end.'

'How very thoughtful. Next time they might even acknowledge my letters.'

Scarlet ignored the sarcasm. The facts were undeniable. Century House usually preferred private hospitals too, but Otto had refused. The last thing they needed were senile spooks unburdening their innermost secrets just before the end. The nurse laughed it off now. But how long before other details escaped him? Vienna, Hercules, the past.

She removed a brochure from her handbag and placed it on the bedside table. 'Promise me you'll look at it. You'll have your own room and a television. The food's nicer. There's a better staff-to-patient ratio too. I did a recce for you. Four stars, in my books. All the mod cons but no jacuzzi or shops.'

Otto didn't look up. He was currently staring at the contents page of the *TLS*. 'I promise nothing.'

'Just consider it. That's all we're asking.'

He lowered the newspaper and glared at her. 'And my house?'

Otto had arrived in Britain with nothing. The Thomas Hegel legend came with a house from the resettlement fund, alongside a basic stipend for the first five years, a recklessly profligate scheme from a previous generation. The accountants on the second floor of Century House were keen to recoup any such assets.

'You promised me.'

'I'm still working on it.'

'Those bastards have no right to disinherit me. To swindle my family. To boot out my own children. To separate a family from their own home.'

Scarlet saw Otto in Café Landtmann again, the emaciated figure in a tatty overcoat reading a second-hand copy of Shakespeare. Now he was fat and old, kept alive by a country he'd once tried to destroy, complaining that the taxpayer-funded house in Kensington would be reclaimed by the very state who'd paid for it. She thought of her own sacrifices and those details at the bottom of the Mitrokhin Files. Anastasia Chekova, born in 1923, run by Maria Kazakova, Order of Lenin. She had no mews house to show for it, no inheritance and no one to pass it on to. Her obituary wouldn't feature in *The Times*. She had no titles to boast of. Nothing.

'Leave it with me. I'm sure we can work something out.'

'Fine, fine. See that you do.'

Otto was engrossed in the *New Statesman* now, breezily waving her away. He was in one of those sulky, impossible moods. Scarlet left the ward and took the lift down to the ground floor. She bought a coffee at the hospital café and decided to take an extended break from reviewing documents. Normality, at last.

'Excuse me.'

Scarlet glanced upwards. A small, round young man hovered by the table. He was casually dressed with sky-blue eyes and a meringue of coppery hair. 'Yes?'

'Sorry to disturb and all that but, well . . . you're a friend of Thomas's, aren't you?'

She was alert now. 'I'm sorry?'

'I don't mean to pry, but I just saw you up there with Professor Hegel on Ward 9. The German gentleman right at the end. The one who's always reading.'

'What of it?'

'I just wondered if you were a friend?'

Scarlet had all manner of covers she could use. But she hesitated, tracking back through her movements. She had dry-cleaned herself routinely before arriving here, the counter-surveillance techniques just a force of habit now. Was it possible she'd missed something? Or someone?

'Who's asking?'

The young man blushed. 'Sorry, of course. My name's Christopher Sewell. I work for the *Sunday Times* Insight team. I'm keen to talk with friends and colleagues of Professor Hegel for a little piece I'm working on.'

Suspicion now. Fear, almost. 'The *Sunday Times*?'

'That's right.'

'The Insight section is investigative material, yes?'

'Usually.'

'Do you often gatecrash hospitals and stalk patients? Or is it just today?'

'Ha, well. Do you mind?' Christopher didn't wait for an answer. He sat down on the chair opposite. He was confident, insistent even. Perhaps late twenties or early thirties. Scarlet detected a West Midlands trace in the vowels. State school, at a guess, one of the smarter red-bricks, naturally bullish but allergic to charm. A fighter, then.

'I'm looking at Professor Hegel's early career,' he said. 'I'm working on a story about the role of foreign scientists in British industry. I'm particularly interested in a specific programme run out of Whitehall after the war. I believe it was called Hercules. Also its links with Russian double agents during the start of the Cold War. Spies and science, basically.'

Scarlet was midway through sipping her coffee when the word landed. She struggled to keep hold of the mug. She coughed loudly, finding a paper napkin and dabbing her lips as distraction. 'Gosh, that sounds like quite a story.'

'It is.'

'More of an airport thriller than a serious news article, though.'

'The difference is this one's actually true.'

'As far as I know, Professor Hegel left Germany in the thirties. What was the other part again?'

'Russian double agents,' he said, eagerly. 'Philby, Blunt, the Cambridge Five, all that jazz. I've got a theory that they all connect. Most of the evidence too, now, actually.'

'I thought the Cold War was all a bit passé these days, surely.'

Christopher smiled. 'Yes, that's the official version. And the record does say that Professor Hegel fled Berlin in the thirties. But, between us, I'm just not sure the official record can be entirely trusted.'

'I'm just an old friend. One retiree visiting another.'

Scarlet returned to her coffee. The *Sunday Times* Insight team had broken the original story about Kim Philby's defection. The paper maintained close links with the Security Service. Ever since Stella Rimington had been announced as the new Director-General of MI5, the strict secrecy surrounding senior figures within the Firm had grown laxer. Scarlet looked into Christopher's eyes. He knew Scarlet, though. Yes, he knew full well who she really was.

Here it comes. 'You don't look retired,' he said. 'If I may say so.'

'I wasn't aware one could look retired.'

Christopher took out a business card. He slid it across the table. 'My number's on there. It wouldn't have to be on the record, of course. I can do deep background if that's what you're comfortable with. As secret as you lot, probably.'

Yes, there was no doubt now. Scarlet picked up the card and read:

CHRISTOPHER SEWELL
Senior Reporter
Insight Team
Sunday Times

'When is the story running?'

'Within the next couple of weeks,' said Christopher. 'That's the hope at least. I want to ensure we cover all sides of the story.'

'I see.'

Christopher leaned closer, as if imparting a secret. 'This story really does have it all, you know. Nazis on the run, faked death certificates, MI6 double agents. Do call me if you change your mind.'

Christopher left before Scarlet could respond. She tucked the business card into her wallet and took a last sip of coffee.

Age was catching up with her. It took a while before her hands stopped shaking.

1992
The Military Man

The cottage was tucked away down a single-track country lane. It was bordered by a neat series of oak trees, standing at attention like soldiers on parade. Scarlet found the small wooden sign that said 'Malvern Cottage' and then parked on the roadside. She was still somewhere in the Cotswolds, presumably, in between the maze of small chocolate-box villages with their dusty pubs and cobwebby post offices.

She got out and admired the view. Greenery filled the space on all sides. Behind her were rolling fields that built towards a steep incline. In front of her were flat open fields and the distant tinkle of a small stream passing through. She heard bleating, too, and wasn't sure whether she'd imagined it. She wondered if much had changed here for fifty years or whether it was a time capsule, transporting visitors back to the middle of the century. She thought of that line from Orwell again about bicycles, holy communion and old maids. People revealed themselves by the places they chose. Yes, looking at this now, it was as if Archie Grenville had written himself into the landscape.

She had written first and then called. Sir Archie – the K had come upon retirement, naturally, alongside a position as Chair of the Travellers – was in his late eighties now. His wife had died eleven years earlier; his only son lived in Australia. According to Scarlet's researches, there was a carer who popped in several times a week. The only other company at the cottage was a cleaner and a small cat named Wellington. Archie himself, meanwhile, still dressed as if there was a war on: checked shirt, regimental tie, tweed jacket and cords. His moustache was precisely trimmed, his hair combed with rigorous symmetry. Age was the only change in him. The rest stayed frozen in time.

The cottage inside was cramped, almost mouldy. Everything was neatly stowed away. The place hadn't been refurbished for several decades at least. A bank of photos bleached with age lined the mantelpiece in the main sitting area. Archie rattled around in the kitchen trying to make tea before bringing in two old teacups and saucers alongside a plateful of questionable biscuits.

Scarlet played mother and poured for them both. Archie took up his pipe and lit it, wreathing the room in a greyish fug. The ancient grandfather clock in the hallway chimed the hour with sing-song formality. There was a radio in the sitting room but no television. A copy of the *Daily Telegraph* was open at the sports pages, alongside a well-thumbed copy of the *Racing Post*. Scarlet patrolled the bookshelves while Archie was in the kitchen and spied the latest offerings from Ken Follett and Jack Higgins. The old soldier was reliving the past vicariously.

Archie unfolded a copy of Scarlet's letter and put his spectacles on. He read it again with painful slowness. 'From what I hear, congratulations might soon be in order.'

Scarlet added a dash of milk to her tea. 'Oh yes?'

'The first female Chief. That would be quite a statement. The old place thundering into the modern world.'

'I'm too old.'

'Nonsense. Churchill was still Prime Minister in his eighties. Gladstone too. You're barely getting started. A veritable whippersnapper.'

'We'll see.'

'Does this unexpected visit herald positive news or the opposite? I was trying to remember the last time we clapped eyes on each other.'

'Sixty-four,' said Scarlet. 'When you vetted me for Section V.'

'Ah, yes. And you passed with flying colours, if I recall.'

'I don't know about that.'

'It hardly seems to matter now, does it? According to Mr Major and his kind, the Cold War is a relic of the past. Who needs spies any longer? Philby's dead, thank the Lord. Mother Russia will curl up into a ball and play nicely from now on. What, pray, was it all for, I wonder?'

There was no time for academic reappraisals of the past. Her needs were more urgent. The ghosts that haunted them both. 'I need to ask you something about the old days.'

'How old exactly?'

'Right back to the very beginning, I'm afraid. Our time in Vienna.'

Archie became more serious now. He clenched the pipe in his teeth and scowled. 'Practically ancient history, surely.'

320

'Until recently, that's exactly what I thought.'

'Well, I'll do my best, old girl, but I promise nothing. Age does that to a chap, you know. The little grey cells not quite what they were.'

Scarlet told him about being approached by the *Sunday Times* journalist at the hospital café. Archie digested the news. He didn't say anything for several minutes. Then he got up and walked over to the mantelpiece, puffing in rhythm with his steps.

'No, no, sorry, that's quite impossible,' he said, the argument in his head spilling out into the room. 'The file on Hercules is strap four. There's no way some reporter could have found out about it. Hardly anyone without the damn building knew of it even then. Quite, quite beyond reason.'

'He used the codename, Archie. He mentioned Nazis, science, the works. He *knew* about Hercules.'

'He was bluffing then. Giving you bait and watching you take it.'

'Or he has a source who's given him everything. He also seemed to know who I was. He said they'd run the piece in the next few weeks.'

'Who have you told?'

'No one yet. I wanted to check with you first.'

'The Chief doesn't know, I presume? Those wretched politicians haven't stuck their clumsy oars in yet?'

'Not that I'm aware.'

'Do you know who else this so-called journalist has been approaching in cafés? Who else he might have blabbed to?'

'No.'

Archie returned to the armchair and sat down

stiffly, tapping his left hand against the top of his knee in thought. 'What about a D-Notice?'

'They're only for use about contemporary operations which pose a danger to national security. We'd never get it through without causing a stink and letting too many people into the circle of knowledge. It would leak out somehow.'

Archie looked melancholic now, dragged back from his pastoral idyll to the murky depths of the secret world. He clenched his pipe again. 'I rather thought better of you than that, Scarlet, I must admit.'

'Better than what?'

'Conning a chap with a nice handwritten letter and a pleasant phone call. Popping down to the Cotswolds on short notice.'

'I'm not sure I understand?'

'Come now, please don't play the innocent. You said it yourself. You're far too old for those sorts of games.'

'Archie . . .'

'You think it's *me*, don't you? That's why you're really here. My name's in the frame. You want to plug the leak and you imagine I'm it.'

There was a cold, sober silence. The cottage creaked. Gusts of country wind tapped intermittently on the windowpanes. There was the faint sound of the cat clawing across wooden floorboards.

'I never said that.'

'You didn't need to. It's what you're thinking.'

'No. It's just logical thinking. After all, so few of us knew about Otto. The reporter knew which ward he was on. I presume he must know Otto's real name.'

'I see. So, in your theory, following the death of my beloved wife and the emigration of my only child, I decide to torch my posthumous reputation by leaking details of a deniable post-war operation.'

'Wait . . .'

'Thereby losing my knighthood, my positions and whatever legacy I have left within the intelligence community.'

'That wasn't what I meant.'

'You're accusing me of treachery, no less, of betraying the very country I spent forty beastly years serving.'

'Perhaps it isn't like that,' she said.

'Oh, I see, I committed treason accidentally, did I? In my forgetful old age. Clumsy, clumsy me.'

Scarlet framed it delicately. 'Your local pub. The club when you're in town. It starts as just a natural conversation, a few old soldiers sharing war stories. You're in your cups, they are too, and you think nothing more of it. We've all been there.'

'I taught you how to spy, Miss King. Thankfully I don't need a refresher.'

Scarlet was still undecided about her next move. Finally, she went for it, braced for the backlash. 'I know the recession hit you hard,' she said. 'Your investments crashed, you lost almost all your savings. This cottage is practically the last thing left standing.'

Fury boiled in that jowly, ascetic face. Archie's eyes were almost incandescent now. He didn't shout or get violent but sat silently. 'How dare you. How *dare* you snoop on me like that.'

'It's part of my job, Archie.'

'How did you even get that information? Dirty tricks, is it? Bribing bank managers. Spying fit for the sewers. I remember a time when dignity and respect still meant something. When there were *rules*.'

'The Firm keeps tabs on all former employees, Archie, you know that. The tricks weren't any dirtier than usual. We monitor all senior officers to see whether they could be targeted financially. You've been on that list for some time now.'

'It's intrusion. Gross, squalid intrusion.'

'It's spying, Archie. You spent your life doing it. You were the one who taught me how to play the game.'

That shut him up for a moment, as if he'd never quite thought of it in that way before. He went back to his pipe. 'My generation were gentlemen,' he said. 'We had our limits. Your generation are voyeurs. I like to think there's a difference.'

'I would understand,' said Scarlet. 'We all would. The system was ludicrous and unfair. Otto Spengler, German scientist, gets a mews house in Kensington and a chestful of awards and commendations. We toiled in the shadows and retired with a schoolteacher's pension. A quick tip, a brown envelope, and some threadbare luxury in retirement. None of us would judge you. I mean that.'

'Nor would you have reason to.' Archie glanced at his pipe. 'You haven't even mentioned the good stuff yet, either.'

'The good stuff?'

'Dr Spengler's war record.'

Scarlet shifted uncomfortably.

Archie spotted her hiccup of doubt. His eyes became triumphant. 'Ah, yes, Miss King, it turns out you *don't* know everything. Old timers like me still have some secrets up our sleeve.'

'What about his war record?'

'That was a file that really *was* burned into a thousand pieces. Let me tell you. Truly, truly terrible stuff. Dante had nothing on our Dr Spengler.'

'You told me Otto was just a minor biochemist. A functionary. Those were your exact words. You told me he was basically harmless.'

Archie guffawed. 'Please, honestly, don't be so naïve. What else was I going to tell you? Little Bo Peep had lost her sheep and found her way to Vienna Station. You were a walking liability. I was hardly going to indoctrinate you into the whole thing, now, was I? Hardly going to tell a child the full horrors of what our Dr Spengler did during the war.'

'So it wasn't true?'

'Broadway sent me a girl to do a man's job. I didn't think you could cope with the truth. You wouldn't have gone through with it if I'd told you everything. I was, what did you call it – ah, yes, that's right – *playing* the game.'

It was like stitches in a wound being prized open. The wound had always been there – patched up, of course, medicated and dressed – but in the background. Ever since their boat trip back, Scarlet had regarded Otto as a friend, occasionally even more than that, a lover. He was a bit older than her, caught in the wrong place at the wrong time. It was their shared tragedy. The misfortune of circumstance and bad timing.

'What was in the file?' she said. The tea tasted foul now. The biscuits were truly disgusting. She wanted to get out into open air. This fusty cottage with its Edwardian pretensions sickened her.

Archie smiled with those crooked teeth. Tobacco ash lodged at the corners of his moustache. 'It's all in the past.'

'Tell me. What was in the file? What did Otto and those other Hercules assets do during the war?'

Archie checked the time and got up. He'd regained the advantage now. That was all he really cared about. The morals of the trade were secondary. The only thing he couldn't stand was being beaten by a woman.

'The sun has gone over the yardarm,' he said. 'It's drinks time for me and leaving time for you. Come now, Miss King, bad manners aren't the done thing around these parts. London may be liberated, but the Cotswolds is still the last bastion of Western civilization. I hope I taught you better than that.'

Scarlet knew when she was beaten. They walked back down the hall and towards the front door like strangers, as if the years had rolled away. Scarlet was suddenly the junior again, cowed by the towering figure of Archie, while he was back as sergeant major, amused by frightening his troops.

The sun was dimming outside. Scarlet stepped

out and saw Archie fill the doorway. Like that, the spell was broken again. He was no longer the sergeant major, just an old, lonely man with only death to look forward to.

'Remember,' said Archie, straining for his old pomposity, 'only two people knew the exact minute-by-minute details of the recruitment of Otto Spengler. If I didn't leak it, that only leaves one candidate.' He smiled bitterly; his eyes drooped. '*You.*'

'Goodbye, Archie.'

A sniff of disapproval, then the door shut. 'Goodbye, Miss King.'

Scarlet drove off and headed back to London. She reached Blackheath and the safe house and spent a sleepless night pacing the attic. Every part of her own life felt new and strange. That one suspicion – always there without being there – grew until it was all she could see. She felt dirty. All those old feelings soiled. She hated herself.

There was only one person who could help her now.

1992
The Centre Cannot Hold

The bookshop was hidden in an alley off Cornmarket Street. It was one of those gems of old Oxford. Books were piled as far as the eye could see. They spilled from the shelves and were loosely congregated by theme. Biography on the first floor, fiction on the second, everything else spread messily across the ground floor. Visitors navigated narrow wooden staircases, until it was almost time-travel, spectral figures with their frock coats and lamps creaking their way through a haunted house.

It was what kept her busy, too. Scarlet entered Magpie Books and heard the tinkling bell that announced each new arrival. Aunt Maria was seated behind the counter, wrapped in a scarf and buried in a book of her own. Her legs were arthritic, and the stairs were beyond her. But she eked out an existence behind the main counter. Scarlet was always reminded of the eighteenth-century philosopher Jeremy Bentham, his waxy figure immortalized in the entrance hall at University College London. Getting book recommendations from Professor Maria Kazakova, the eminent cultural critic and humanist, was reason enough to visit this place. Magpie Books was a tourist attraction of sorts, a chance to see the famed Oxonian in the flesh.

They left and found a café on the High Street and

drank strong coffee, then took a stroll past Christ Church and through the fields bordering Merton and Corpus Christi. There was paranoia all round, now. Predators lurked behind the beauty. Every enclosed space promised danger. Strange faces were to be avoided. Before, when the struggle was still in progress, there had been something to gain. Now the news showed nothing but anarchy. The dream was dismantling; the only possibility was loss. Liberty, reputation, legacy – all of it snuffed out with a few simple words, one denunciation.

'They want to interview me,' said Scarlet. Although, truthfully, these meetings were the one moment when she allowed herself to break character. She was Ana again. The character she'd played for so long – the respectable Miss Scarlet King – receded, if only for a breath. She was Colonel Chekova now. Daughter of the party, child of the revolution, always a spy of the first and highest order.

'And you're sure, my dear Ana, that it's not a trap?'

'You can never be sure. But it's unlikely.'

Aunt Maria smiled. 'One of my girls and boys becoming Chief. Even the idea seems incredible. Back in the day they would have built statues of both of us. Our chests would have been garlanded with medals.'

'There's also another development. One that our friends may want to hear. The Office recently received a series of files copied during the move from the Lubyanka to Yasenevo. The entire operational history of the First Chief Directorate. I have a safe house in Blackheath to verify the material. So far, it all checks out.'

Aunt Maria didn't say anything for some time. 'Why are you telling me this?'

'What do you mean?'

'I am an old lady, Ana, who works in a bookshop. I am a former professor at the university. I am nothing now.'

'Don't say that.'

'It is true.'

'You've been my handler since the very beginning. My only channel back to the Centre. We agreed it was the cleanest way to do business, and so it's proved.'

Scarlet wondered whether to tell Aunt Maria about the *Sunday Times* and the Hercules operation. But she decided not to. That was her problem. Only she could fix it.

'I mean what I say, Ana. You should listen to me. Don't be stubborn, child.'

'The Centre has cut you off?'

'There is no Centre. There is no KGB. There is no First Chief Directorate. There is only every man and woman for themselves. Moscow is in chaos. They have flung us all out into the wild. Everything is being sold to the highest bidder. Your archive, our names, sooner or later it will all be sold for thirty pieces of silver by some Judas in uniform. It is just a matter of time. We are defenceless now, left to the wolves.'

'You're getting pessimistic in your old age.'

'No. I have stopped dreaming. Forget the state, the party, the Centre. They are just words. When they come for you, Moscow won't answer your call. There will be no exfil or diplomatic exchange. You will be locked away just like I will be. It will all have been for nothing.'

They walked back through Merton Street and along the cobbles. The street was still the same as it had always been, unchanging through the centuries, and yet so much was now in flux. Otto, Hercules, the Firm, Aunt Maria. It was as if every anchor in Scarlet King's life had come loose.

They reached the outside of Oriel and Aunt Maria checked they were clear. Then, without warning, she reached out and clung to Scarlet's shoulders. Her face looked deeply wrinkled. She had that sharp, old-lady scent.

'My journey is nearly over, Ana,' she whispered. 'Next week, next month, next year. But you still have life to live. And I want you to promise me something.'

Scarlet saw fear buried in those eyes. Aunt Maria was the only real family she'd ever had. The others, as she always thought of them, had grown faint over time, the contours of their faces blurring, until they were the memory of a memory, tarnished and second-hand.

'What?' she said.

'Protect yourself, Anastasia. Moscow is now over-run. It is being led by the looters. I can no longer help you, and nor will they. Forget me. Leave the party behind. Reinvent your life as you have reinvented it before now. Be free of all of this. Above all, do not make my mistakes, child. History doesn't have to be repeated. It can be escaped. I'm sure of that now.'

'How?'

'Find her, Ana. She is yours. Tell her who you really are and make peace with her. Don't go to your grave unreconciled. I have done all I can for you and for her. But she is your responsibility now.'

It lurked beneath the surface of every conversation. The secret that could never be wished away. Scarlet had become Aunt Scarlet, and Aunt Maria had become parent and guardian. The child never knew, of course, though she was no longer a child now. She had long since left for the glitter of the capital and a life removed from the bitter squabbles of academia. Scarlet thought of little else at night. The face of her only child. Half her, half Caspar. A living, breathing souvenir of that desperate night in Moscow.

'You've given your life to a cause,' said Aunt Maria. 'The cause has given nothing back. A life is to be lived. Forget the world. Think for yourself. I've lived with regrets, but I don't want to die with them too.'

For Scarlet, it was always the image she would carry with her, long after that day was over. They returned to the bookshop. Aunt Maria resumed her place behind the counter. She picked up her paperback. Scarlet saw it wasn't Chekhov or Dostoevsky or any of the usual suspects. Aunt Maria was reading *The Strange Case of Dr Jekyll and Mr Hyde* by Robert Louis Stevenson. The story of a respectable middle-class man who harboured a secret second self, a demon that would ultimately destroy him.

It was four weeks later that the news came

through. The doctor was matter-of-fact, as if the news was expected. The patient had been diagnosed with leukaemia twelve months ago, after all, and was rushed to hospital after picking up an infection. The doctor thought it was probably from another customer at the bookshop. One of those things, a tragic accident, part of life's grand and bewildering tapestry.

Aunt Maria was gone.

1992
The Cousins

It was impossible not to be overawed by the difference between London and Langley. The permission for the US trip came from the Foreign Secretary and the Chief five days after Aunt Maria's death. Scarlet boarded a diplomatic flight to Washington DC. She was greeted at the airport by a motorcade of blacked-out SUVS and burly ex-military figures with earpieces and crewcuts. The drive to Langley felt almost presidential. Back home, Scarlet King got the Tube to Westminster then made her way on foot until she reached 100 Westminster Bridge Road and the dreary view of Century House. Only the Chief got a chauffeur and a car. The rest trooped in like civil servants. This was another world.

Langley's mood was giddier than Century House. As Sovbloc Controller, Scarlet made biannual visits across the Atlantic. She enjoyed walking through the famous atrium, seeing the memorial wall to the fallen officers. Century House still had its tap-water furnishings and a sense of gloomy decline, the Firm forced to beg Downing Street for a stay of execution. Langley toasted the Soviet surrender and was now focused on the spoils of victory.

She was shown to the top floor. The building whirred with computers, fresh carpeting, the chug of fax machines and the smooth, electronic tinkle of secure phone lines. A handsome young aide

knocked on the door of the 'Deputy Director/
DO' – Head of the Directorate of Operations, overseeing the CIA's teams on the ground. She heard
the familiar voice before she saw him. Vienna and
the rubble of total war was a distant dream, or a
bad nightmare. She felt her age. This was no longer
her world.

'Scarlet!' He was weightier now, Churchillian
chin rolls and a waddling midriff. 'My, my, looking
as radiant as ever. You don't seem to have aged a
day since Moscow. What's your secret? You *must*
reveal all.'

She shook his hand, resisted the kiss on either
cheek. 'Hello, Caspar. Clean living and prayer usually does it. You should try it sometime. I'll send
you tips.'

His laugh was nuclear, condemning all in its
path. 'I'll make a note of that. Come in, come in.
How was the flight? Not too wearisome, I hope?'

His office was the size of several football pitches.
Up close, his waistline really had expanded, the
thighs plump and juicy. All those lunches with
Senators, no doubt, and a lifelong aversion to exercise. He looked like a corporate executive, Scarlet
thought, rather than a spy. The red braces, white-
and-blue striped shirt, an expensive gold Rolex,
pearly-white teeth and surgically smooth brow –
Caspar Madison was preparing for a future in the
private sector, according to gossip, soon to earn top
dollar as consultant, lobbyist and board member
for hire.

There would be two meetings, as usual. The first
was the official business conducted in Caspar's

palatial office. Scarlet was here with the approval of the British high command to brief Langley on the contents of the Mitrokhin Archive, as it was now known, and to share a timetable for release and publication. She had samples of the material relating to the US side – all of it far too sensitive to be transferred by electronic means – and watched as Caspar scrolled through each page. The official meeting meant others were present. Like the best Senators, Caspar had an army of staff covering all geographical regions and specialisms. They were waspy Harvard types, mainly, forming a horseshoe around their dear leader, eyes aflutter.

'This is dynamite,' said Caspar, finishing reading, placing the pages down.

Scarlet nodded. 'Alongside an insight into the Centre's methods, they also provide information about Russian agents-in-place operating in the West. The names we haven't caught. It will be delicate political work to apprehend them.'

Caspar nodded. 'Lock 'em up and throw away the key, say I. The sort that deserve nothing less. Their sins come home to bury them. And not before time, either. What's the distribution plan on this?'

'Several stages,' said Scarlet. 'First, we allow time for the political machinery to get their heads round the information. Second, we find a way to disseminate it to the general public in the new spirit of openness and transparency. My personal suggestion is in book form.'

'A book?'

'Um. Someone neutral, but independent. A reputable intelligence historian, say. We give them full access and produce a book revealing the extent of the find. We, of course, get a final glance at the manuscript to ensure no live operations are compromised. But the public, and our political masters, pat us on the back for embracing the modern age.'

'You have anyone in mind?'

'There's a professor at Cambridge who we think might be up for it. Currently a Fellow at Corpus Christi and senior member of the History faculty. His name is Christopher Andrew.'

Caspar glanced at one of his staffers in charge of comms, who gave the nod. 'Sure, sure, we can live with that. What about Mr Mitrokhin himself? Do you trust him?'

'We do.'

'Where is he now?'

'Where no former KGB wet worker can get to him. We promised him a ring of steel if he gave us his co-operation. That's what we've delivered.'

Caspar reclined in his executive desk-chair. He looked stern, angry even, like a pantomime crusader vowing to wreak vengeance. 'Just imagine,' he said, his voice actorly and loud, playing to the gallery around him. 'Time to bring some traitors in from the cold, wouldn't you say? Give them a taste of real justice. Separate the righteous from the guilty.'

Scarlet thought of Aunt Maria in the bookshop and the tattered paperback of Jekyll and Hyde. She marvelled at Caspar Madison's ability to compartmentalize himself. He said it with such conviction, almost like he believed it. He would have been an incredible politician. He made Clinton look like a puritan.

'To the victor goes the spoils,' she said.

'Yes,' said Caspar, his faultless teeth winking at her. 'Amen to that.'

1992
The Garden Meeting

The second meeting took place that evening. As Head of the Directorate of Operations, Caspar Madison travelled in considerable style: an armour-plated SUV, driver, secure comms inside the vehicle. There was a guard permanently stationed outside his four-storey brownstone. Inside was one of the world's most elaborate alarm systems. It was duly christened Fort Madison, and almost as secure as Fort Knox.

The set-up was simple. Scarlet arrived at eight o'clock, nodding politely to the guard outside. The food was good, the wine even better, though Scarlet limited herself to one glass and, even then, sipped slowly. By ten it was time for port and cigars. The caterers cleared up. Caspar's wife headed off for a bath and bed. Caspar and Scarlet, meanwhile, went out to the garden. Scarlet was on coffee; Caspar was on port. There was a furthermost section of the large garden safely out of sight. They were two friends chatting about old times. Vienna, Moscow, the glory days of Checkpoint Charlie and the red phone in the Oval Office.

'That was quite a performance today,' she said.

'Thank you.'

Caspar puffed at his Cuban cigar, looked up at the starless night sky. There was a tell-tale hiccup in his voice. Scarlet was now the only thing between Caspar Madison and total ruin. She sensed his fear.

'Is the personal grooming in aid of something?' said Scarlet. 'Please don't tell me she's blonde, six foot one and just graduated college.'

Caspar didn't smile. He was wound tight. 'Last month I thought I was being followed. There were three of them tailing me while I was out with the family. Pros, too, built like tanks.'

'Moscow?'

He shook his head. 'No, closer to home. That profile is usually the Feds. I had to deflect attention and put the heat on Ames instead. But the whole place has got mole mania again. They'd love to find a few more high up the nest. He's just the starter. Believe me, I'm the main course.'

Aldrich Ames was a mid-level agent-in-place currently working at Langley in counterintelligence. He was expendable, useful for local colour but nowhere near the upper echelons.

'Do you have a plan?'

'The start of one, at least. Let Ames soak up the attention and then get the hell out as soon as possible. I've been offered a berth with a private security outfit in DC. I'll stay for another six months then jump ship. That's if your damn archive doesn't stop me first.'

The eyes were the same. That was the thing she always noticed. The child had Caspar's eyes. 'The distribution list was kept tight.'

'How tight?'

'Just me, Head of Moscow Station and the Chief.'

'The three amigos.'

'The Chief had to let our political masters know something. But that's it. The archive was delivered to a safe house. I'm the only one with access. No one else knows the contents. With any luck, they never will.'

'Is that an offer of friendship or a threat?'

'Perhaps it's both.'

Caspar considered. He looked defeated now. 'I take it you have a price in mind,' he said. 'To remove my name from the documents?'

Scarlet let the question linger. The theatre of this was important. She saw herself surgically removing all references to 'Colonel Anastasia Chekova' and burning the relevant papers. From the six trunks of documents, including over three thousand leads abroad and two hundred in Britain alone, one or two deletions would never be noticed.

You have a child, she wanted to say. We have a child. She's beautiful and angry. We failed her. We were good spies and terrible human beings.

She thought again of Caspar in Vienna. She looked at the older version, surviving on a diet of lunchtime liquor and nicotine, terrified of every knock on the door and dreaming about prison cells.

'I don't want money,' she said, at last. 'I want something else.'

The envelope arrived a week later. Scarlet was back in London, still staying at the safe house in Blackheath. There was rarely any post, only flyers and local restaurant menus. The envelope contained two items: the first was an unmarked cassette tape; the other was an official report dated '1946'.

She read all three pages of the report closely and then returned to the attic and the section about the Russian embassy in Washington DC. She concentrated on the activities of the PR Line specializing in political intelligence from Congress, the Hoover building or Langley itself. There were multiple mentions of the codename 'JEFFERSON' and one mention of the asset's real name: 'MADISON, C.' Scarlet did what she had to.

By the end of the day, the next stage was set in motion.

1992
Survival

Christopher Sewell looked less threatening outside the hospital. He was squat and broad-shouldered, like a rugby prop, and younger than Scarlet remembered, a junior reporter trying to find his big break. Her background research indicated an unremarkable secondary education followed by Russian at UCL and then time spent grazing at various regional papers. No, this story hadn't yet gone past the lawyers. There were no invitations to regretful lunches in Pall Mall between Scarlet and the Editor. No threats exchanged over weak coffee or bunfights over the bill.

'I'm sorry for the brush-off at the hospital,' said Scarlet, easing in with an overt display of humility. They sat round her kitchen table, both drinking tea. First impressions were always vital, and the Fulham flat was homier now, all soft furnishings and bland colours. 'I was having one of those days. Thinking it over, I've changed my mind. Perhaps we can help one another.'

Christopher was nervier than before. He looked undone by the confined space, her friendliness, his mask in danger of slipping. 'I do have one question.'

'Of course.'

'Is there a reason your name isn't on the diplomatic list?'

'What's your theory?'

'You're not really Foreign Office or Ministry of Defence. You're one of the shadow people. A spook. You were friends with Philby as well, is that right?'

Questions were always the best form of defence. Baldly stating classified information was treasonable. Gently steering someone towards conclusions was murkier but not punishable by exile. Scarlet never committed before she had to.

'And why would a spook invite a journalist for a cup of tea?'

He relaxed slightly, happy to grandstand. 'To silence the freedom of the press. Bury embarrassing stories and ensure joe public never finds out what its spies really get up to. That sort of line might just have worked in the Cold War. But the big bad Russian bear's gone now. The public have a right to know.'

'I agree.'

'You do?'

'It's why we're a democracy. It's what it was all for. It's why Churchill got kicked out in '45. He saved liberal democracy so liberal democracy could boot him into the great beyond. I haven't spent my life fighting tyranny and a muzzled media to condone such practices at home, believe me. We're on the same side.'

Christopher looked unsettled again. He'd expected hostility and rebuttals. But he was being seduced, like all assets, slowly drawn into a web. He didn't know whether to play along or capitulate.

'But people are also tired of war,' said Scarlet.

She'd prepared this meticulously, careful to sound offhand and improvised. 'This is the nineties. A new dawn, a new Britain. Soon, of course, a new millennium.'

Christopher wasn't buying it. 'Forgive me, but Russian traitors sell. Nazis sell. World War Two sells. Just look at all that palaver over the Hitler diaries. People lap this stuff up. Nice try, 007, but I don't frighten that easily.'

Now for the hard push. The sort of ammunition that could only be used once.

Scarlet smiled, took another sip of tea. She toyed with a digestive. 'It was the *Sunday Times* that went big on the Hitler diaries, wasn't it?'

'So what?'

'Your paper hired Trevor-Roper. You splashed on it and broke the story and made colossal fools of yourselves all over the globe. Very embarrassing. Some thought Murdoch might pull the plug entirely.'

'I wasn't at the paper then. I had nothing to do with that.'

'Imagine those who were, though. That's their obituary, right there. They thought they had the scoop of the century. From now on, they'll be lucky to write for the school magazine. Poor sods. One mistake and it's all over.'

Christopher's perky confidence dimmed. 'What are you trying to say?'

'I know who your source is,' said Scarlet. 'I know categorically that your source is even less reliable than the fantasists who conned the world with the Hitler diaries. Your paper survived one forgery

345

scandal. It won't survive a second. You've just got a seat at the grown-ups' table. Take my advice and don't give it up so rashly.'

Christopher grew rigid. 'Is that your usual tactic to scare off journalists?'

Scarlet shrugged. 'There was no Nazi conspiracy plot dreamed up by the British government. It's too good to be true simply because it isn't true. The names you've been given are impossible to verify. Why? Because the source made them up. Bogus source, bogus story. This is single-sourced, yes?'

'You made sure of that, I suppose.'

'Take your chances. Write the article. See your career implode before it's even started. Just don't come crawling back to me and say I didn't warn you.'

Christopher stared at his half-empty mug. He breathed heavily. He said, 'So the secret world protects its own at the expense of the poor British taxpayer. Yet again.'

'You're wasted in journalism. You should try politics instead.'

'I'm also not naïve. MI6 Controllers don't invite journalists to tea unless they have something they want to exchange. What are you offering?'

'You clearly have done your homework.'

'I'm green. But not *that* green.'

Scarlet knew the Controller jibe had been a lucky guess. Age conferred wisdom or respectability. Flattering or accurate, one of the two. 'How about a former KGB archivist escaping from Riga with six trunks of documents copied from the archives of the First Chief Directorate at Yasenevo. The

346

archive sheds new light on the disintegration of the Soviet Union. Between us, it could change our view on everything.'

'You're serious?'

'No, I'm joking. Why?'

Christopher tried to look sceptical, playacting at detachment. 'Heavy geopolitical analysis doesn't always go down well with our readers. We're in the entertainment business. I'll need more than that to forget about fugitive Nazis and science experiments.'

'Your paper broke the story about Kim Philby and his escape to Moscow,' she said. 'You have a proud tradition on this stuff. Now you're about to have another one.'

'I'm a junior reporter. If you're serious and this is even halfway verifiable, why come to me? No editor would even give me the by-line. This is a top-floor job.'

Scarlet picked up the teapot and decided to make another batch. 'Perfect cover, then. More tea?'

1992
The End

Stepping away was the hardest thing. The Permanent Under-Secretary at the Foreign Office looked stunned, checking his calendar to see if it was an early April Fool's. The Chief begged her to reconsider. No one turned down the top job. She would give Stella a run for her money. Show the world that MI6 wasn't the fossilized dinosaur of caricature. Reconsider, Scarlet. Take a holiday, sabbatical, shake off the cobwebs. Even the Foreign Secretary invited her for sherry and dehydrated nibbles at King Charles Street. But the answer remained the same.

She was too old, she said. Ten years ago, maybe. But she had done her stint, won her war. She would retire to the countryside and nurse her vegetable patch. Fortune favoured others, all conspicuously male. Colin McColl, the current Chief, agreed to stay on for another two years. David Spedding, SIS's Controller of the Middle East, was groomed as regent. Scarlet would be pensioned off with a memorial plate and a decent dinner. Her secret war was almost over.

She waited for the blowback from Moscow, but none ever came. Aunt Maria was right. She wondered if they even knew. There was an empty feeling afterwards. She paced her flat and replayed each operation. And yet there was still one more obstacle lying in wait. A final loose end to make good.

Otto and Caspar. The plan. She had to stick to the plan.

Professor Thomas Hegel was officially transferred from St Thomas' Hospital to a hospice in Kensington a week later. His wife visited, as did his two grown-up children. But the Professor was different now, his old enthusiasm withered, his intellect dulled. He seemed frustrated. They chatted and read to him, but their father was already gone. The figure in the bed was a different man.

It was four days after the move that Scarlet found the back entrance. The hospice was lightly staffed at night. She avoided the security cameras and headed soundlessly to the room on the third floor. She wore the same navy-blue shade of uniform as the other staff. The doctored ID pass was authentic to all but a specialist. This was her final mission. The last of thousands. No more aliases, plans, pocket litter or sheer invention. One last curtain call.

There were two more care workers to avoid on the third floor, then finally the corridor was clear. The doors were left open for emergency access. Scarlet counted along until she found Otto's room number. She withdrew a thick set of gloves and slid them on. She opened the door and locked it behind her, muffling the metallic click.

The room was dark and she could just make out the thick shape on the bed. He had been so gangly once upon a time. His body had thickened with age and his posture shortened, until the loose-limbed young man became the stooped and squat grandfather, never seen without a walking stick, his nose angled permanently at the ground.

Scarlet advanced towards the bed. The corridor was patrolled by night-shift care workers every fifteen minutes. She'd watched the on-duty staff members take their break, fiddling for a cigarette and lighter. The timing had to be exact.

The figure on the bed didn't stir fully. Only his eyes flickered open. Scarlet checked the curtains were drawn tight and then reached for the lamp switch on the bedside table. The room filled with light. Otto lay on his side, eyes open, blinking quizzically at the figure of Scarlet standing over the bed.

Scarlet put a finger to her lips to shush him. He looked worried now. She reached into her jacket pocket and removed the three pages; the treasure Madison promised in the garden. The joint OSS and CIG archive was still at Langley and required sign-off from Director-level or above. The pages were from a single file dated '1946' and marked: 'TOP SECRET / US EYES ONLY'. Beneath the security grading was a name: 'SPENGLER, OTTO (Dr)' and a black-and-white photo.

The report contained a brief résumé of Dr Otto Spengler's likely whereabouts, a section regarding his educational achievements and then a report from an OSS case officer regarding Dr Spengler's activities during the war. Scarlet had read the file so many times over the last seventy-two hours that it was branded into her. She could repeat the paragraphs word for word, name for name.

She held the first page up by the lamp. Otto's eyes flickered. She saw him absorb the first page, slowly understanding. She held up the second page and his eyes flickered again. When it was done, Scarlet folded the two pages back into her jacket pocket. She took out the next exhibit and held up Christopher Sewell's business card against the lamp. Otto's eyes constricted. He looked glassy, panicked. Scarlet removed the final item Caspar had sent. It was a SIGINT intercept from Fort Meade which had been passed to Langley. The voicemail message had been left seven weeks earlier for a number linked to the *Sunday Times* newspaper. Scarlet had a Walkman and turned up the volume to maximum. The voice was male, elderly, with that residual Germanic inflection.

'Mr Sewell, I have a tip-off for you regarding an operation carried out by the British government just after the war which was codenamed Hercules. I am dying and believe my story should be known to the world. It is time to redress the historical record, defend the achievements of the German people. I am calling from a public phone in St Thomas' Hospital. Do not try and call me back. I can be visited between the hours of 11 a.m. to 1 p.m. on weekdays at Ward 9. When you arrive, ask for Professor Thomas Hegel. Do not mention this call to your colleagues. I will explain more when you visit. It is vital that you treat this information with the utmost seriousness.'

Scarlet stopped the recording. She replaced the Walkman. He looked so insubstantial now. It was impossible to think this frail little old man had committed the acts detailed in that file. That the awkward figure in the Café Landtmann, the shy romantic in her Vienna flat, was responsible for so much blood, so much suffering.

She withdrew the last few items from her bag. First, she put on the mask, checking the straps were tight. Second, she took out the medical case. It was a gift from Aunt Maria seven years earlier, fresh from the Centre: the pipette, the toxin, all brewed by those wizards in the southwest, the Kremlin's own Shikhany Sorcerers. The project was code-named Foliant. During one of their asset–handler meetings, Aunt Maria had broken protocol and revealed its true name: Novichok.

Scarlet followed procedure exactly. Otto's mouth was dry. He tried to utter a cry for help, but the sound buffered on his tongue, the phlegm of his throat like static. The pipette was safer than spray. When she was finished, Scarlet removed the thick gloves and, finally, the mask. Otto's eyes were wide, full of childish terror. He knew what happened next. The choking, the suffering, the absence of relief. He was both torturer and victim. He knew his own fate.

The fifteen minutes were nearly up. Scarlet left the room, careful not to contaminate anything as she went. She disappeared through the back exit. She was home twenty minutes later. She followed the rest of the safety protocols: multiple showers, sterilizing clothes, eliminating all trace of the material, deep-cleaning the house. She lay awake in bed and heard the traffic outside. She counted her sins.

She saw Otto's eyes and the sense of infant terror.

Scarlet King was a murderer. Anastasia Chekova was an innocent.

Tonight, she was Ana again.

1992
Fallen Angel

The first sign of trouble came just before 9 p.m.
The Editor of the *Sunday Times* was spotted leaving the door of 70 Whitehall, the redoubt of the Cabinet Office and the Joint Intelligence Committee. He was closely followed – this time via a back exit not in public view – by the Chief of the Secret Intelligence Service, the Director-General of the Security Service and the CIA's London Chief of Station, all of whom disappeared into chauffeured cars and made their way back to Westminster Bridge Road, Gower Street and Grosvenor Square respectively.

By Sunday morning the front-page story graced every newsstand in Britain. The splash was written under the by-line of the newspaper's top security hand Oliver Archer, veteran of Hungary, Cuba, DC, Afghanistan and Moscow. Owing to the time difference, and furious backroom diplomacy between the White House, Langley and the Hoover Building, the news wasn't reported stateside until just after 8 a.m. in New York when CNN broke the story. By then, it was 1 p.m. in London and Century House – usually a ghost-town on a Sunday – was packed with counterintelligence personnel and liaison officers summoned personally by the Chief for an all-hands meeting.

By evening in London, and lunchtime across the

Atlantic, the first photographic evidence emerged of Caspar Madison, the former Deputy Director of the CIA, being led away by federal agents in handcuffs. All the major networks hurriedly recruited new legal consultants and intelligence specialists. Confirmation of the arrest came from a Department of Justice spokesman at 3 p.m. US time, verifying media reports that Caspar Madison had indeed been arrested on suspicion of conspiracy to commit espionage and spying for the Soviet Union.

In London, SIS media liaison and the D-Notice committee were locked in furious rows about how Oliver Archer could possibly have gained access to such classified information. In Washington DC, an internecine turf war ensued between the CIA and FBI, defused only by the personal intervention of the President from Camp David.

At Century House, the Chief issued a stern instruction to no-comment and called Scarlet into his sixth-floor office. 'Quite a day.'

She shut the door. 'Now you can see why I don't want this job. Too much stress, not enough pay.'

McColl's eyes were grey and puffy. He clearly hadn't slept for several nights, ever since the first suggestion that the story could break. 'I can't argue with that.'

'Any formal response yet from Langley?'

'Nothing further. Let's just say we won't be on their Christmas card list for some time to come. The one thing they can't stand is being embarrassed. We just humiliated our closest ally with very little warning. The PM's climbing the walls.'

'We're a democracy. We don't control our news-papers.'

'Try telling that to the National Security Adviser.' The Chief yawned then reached for a cup of cold tea, draining the last of it. 'The media firefighting is just the start, Scarlet. We both know that.'

'What do you need?'

'A holiday?'

'Apart from that?'

'I need someone who I trust to comb through every operation Madison worked on with us and could have betrayed. I mean everything.'

Scarlet nodded. 'Of course.'

'Frankly, it's lucky we caught this now. A few weeks further down the line and this could have been several magnitudes worse. If you catch my meaning.'

'Quite.' The Firm was preparing to move loca-tion to a new complex at 60 Vauxhall Bridge Road. As part of the transfer, the entire SIS archive was going to be digitized and scanned indelibly into history. The process was scheduled to start in five weeks' time. That gave them a window to make some final amendments.

Scarlet phrased it delicately. 'And what are my instructions if I find anything that Madison did touch? It will be hard to avoid given his position and length of service.'

The Chief sounded conflicted. He glanced towards the door, as if frightened a journalist could barge in unannounced. 'I never said what I'm about to say and this little chat never happened. You understand that?'

'Yes.'

'Burn the lot of them,' he said. 'The files are still in paper form with no digital trace. What future historians don't know really can't hurt them. We're in enough of a wrestling match as it is with White-hall. Only yesterday I heard one analyst on the JIC proposing to combine us with Five and Chelten-ham. The very last thing we need is to be haunted by old files compromised by an American double. The Cold War's history. Perhaps it's time our arch-ive reflected that.'

'I understand.'

'I wouldn't ask anyone else to do this, Scarlet. Get a burn bag, dispense with anything you find, and then make sure there's no trail. Neither of us got this far to lose our pensions over another man's crimes.'

Scarlet nodded again. The Chief opened his drawer and took out a Mars bar. She was about to leave him to it when the question came.

'By the way,' he said, 'any theories about how this hack reporter got wind of Mitrokhin?'

She had prepared for this. Nonchalantly, sum-moning half a century of experience, she pretended to think for a moment and said, 'My guess? Brief-ing Langley was a mistake. There were more people in that room than sit around the Cabinet table. Plus, the counterintelligence types who flew across have never liked Madison. They've wanted him out for yonks. This gave them a chance.'

The Chief took another bite. 'I'll try floating that theory with the White House. See if it calms them down.'

'The lesson of history. The Cold War kept them disciplined. Now the decline can begin.'

'Let me know when it's done.'

For the next three days Scarlet lived in the basement of Century House. A guard stood outside. All entry was restricted. She began in 1946 with the first mention of one 'MADISON, C' in a file relating to OSS and CIG operatives working under diplomatic cover. She moved through the decades, catching her own shadow, like a trip down memory lane. Moscow Station, Philby's defection, the wilderness of mirrors in the seventies, the downfall of James Jesus Angleton, the Soviet invasion of Afghanistan, the fall of the Berlin Wall. Every time Caspar Madison was mentioned, and a few times besides, she committed the file to the burn bag. It all went: 'King, Scarlet', 'Madison, Caspar', 'Hercules'. The ghosts extinguished, all on the direct orders of the Chief.

It was six months later that she stepped out of the building for a final time and on to Westminster Bridge Road. She had been Scarlet King for so long. She shed tears for her colleagues and for this old place, knowing she would never darken its doors again. She listened to the Chief's speech, heard the clink of champagne glasses, gave a rousing and witty farewell to her team. She was Scarlet to the very end.

It had been quite a performance. Now, finally, the curtain closed for the last time. Scarlet King – Head of Russia House, veteran of the post-war years, a vanished breed raised in the age of empire – melted into the busy crowds around Pimlico Tube

Station, one elderly face among many, hoarding her anonymity.

The files were burned. Otto dead from a heart attack. Caspar behind bars, any wild accusations discounted as the ravings of a pathological liar. The Cold War was over. The Soviet Union dismantled. Aunt Maria was dead. Moscow Centre was no more.

Her mission was complete. There was only one thing left.

The child.

PART FOUR

28

It was just after midnight in Paris when the call
came through. It had been one of those days when
the job seemed finally worth it. After all those years
in Kabul Station or enduring the misery of the
Green Zone in Baghdad, tonight was what spying
should always be about. The Ambassador's leaving party had drawn out the good and the great, all
dolled up in penguin suits and bespoke finery.
Senior ministers, business tycoons, editors and
other functionaries, all of them getting along famously. Stephanie Porter, the newly appointed Head
of Paris Station, tiptoed back to bed with a woozy
head and the prospect of six good hours. Not quite
James Bond, but almost. Just almost.

That was until the call.

'Paris Station?'

It wasn't a voice she recognized, certainly not
Vauxhall Cross. The formal greeting was only used
by those on the outside. Strangers, in the jargon.

'Speaking?'

'Are you secure?'

Stephanie rubbed sleep from her eyes and stifled
a yawn. She leaned across to the phone line and
changed channel, adding an extra layer of encryp-
tion. Even her own team wouldn't be able to snoop
on this one.

'Go ahead, caller.'

'This is Thames 2.'

Stephanie saw her husband stir and quietly slipped out of bed, taking the hands-free receiver into the bathroom. THAMES 2 was the official callsign of the Deputy Director-General of the Security Service, someone who usually only called their equivalent at Legoland, never a mere Head of Station.

'How can I help, sir?'

'Stephanie, right?'

'That's correct, sir.'

'Saul Northcliffe here. Let's dispense with all the Jason Bourne bollocks, shall we? Speak like normal human beings. Think you can manage that?'

'I'll certainly give it a try.'

The British spying community was small and, against type, intensely gossipy. Saul Northcliffe's reputation preceded him. He was the scourge of the British class system, the terror of all things entitled, known to go blow-for-blow with even the most senior politicians. His lack of diplomacy reportedly cost him the top job, though many said he never wanted it. He was a born deputy and enforcer, the bruiser who could tell the emperor he should put on some damn clothes.

'Good,' said Saul. 'I arrive at Charles de Gaulle in twenty minutes. I've flown diplomatic and need the full works on arrival then some time alone with you in the secure room. Apologies for the unholy hour but it can't be helped.'

'Of course, sir. May I ask what this is about?'

'Ask all you like. I can't answer. Not until I brief you in person.'

364

Stephanie hesitated. The turf war between SIS and MI5 was bitter, and she had no desire to get stuck in the middle of it. 'I'll have to clear this with my side first.'

There was an ominous silence. 'This is a Security Service operation and I have the full backing of the high command. Last time I checked we were both on the same side.'

'Yes, sir. It's just . . .'

'Just nothing. One whiff of my arrival to the DGSE or DGSI and you'll be posted to outer Mongolia with drone attacks as mood music. Do we understand each other?'

'Yes, sir.'

'This is strict need-to-know. The Ambassador, defence intelligence and the other members of the station aren't on the distribution list. Only you. If anyone asks what you're doing, refer them to me.'

Stephanie evaluated all threats to national security on a daily basis. Migrant boats crossing to Dover, terror cells working across the Channel, ongoing trade disputes, rumours that one of the President's senior aides was passing classified information to the Kremlin. Even so. The second in command of the Security Service didn't fly out to Paris in the middle of the night on a diplomatic plane for an emergency briefing unless it was something out of the ordinary.

Her head was still fuzzy from champagne. She longed for bed again. 'I'll collect you from the airport myself,' she said. 'Are you expecting any other eyes?'

'Take all usual precautions,' he said. 'In the next

twelve hours we'll both be given peerages or be looking for other careers. See you shortly.'

The line went dead. Stephanie wondered if he was joking. She headed down to the kitchen and brewed a mug of extra-strong black coffee. It was only seconds ago, surely, that she had trudged upstairs.

Stephanie picked up the keys to the secure embassy vehicle and then made a note of the time. She parked at Charles de Gaulle and saw Saul Northcliffe emerge – true to form – with a single rucksack on his back and wearing a soiled cream mackintosh. His hair was thinning and unkempt from the wind outside. He looked hangdog tired and his forehead was creased like paper. Accompanying him were three others: one older gentleman who looked like an operator and remained nameless; a younger woman who offered only a first name, Charlotte; then another figure, also nameless for now, a civvy out of their natural habitat.

The travelling party was silent on the journey back. Saul revealed nothing operational until they were inside the secure part of the embassy, requesting only a cup of English Breakfast tea and a ham sandwich with crusts. The other three travellers settled into their embassy bedrooms and caught some shut-eye.

Once suitably nourished and hydrated, Saul took out a single manila file from his rucksack. Then he briefed her on the case and why he was in Paris. He waited for questions until she'd finished reading the file.

'Why do I feel like I'm still not hearing everything?' she said, closing the file.

'I don't know. You tell me.'

'I really should run this by Vauxhall Cross.'

Saul smiled. 'We're not flatfoot beat coppers, you know. You lot do the embassy cocktail circuit. My lot take out the terrorists. I'm not having the officer class trample all over my operation, no siree. If you can't follow my orders, then feel free to take a few days of paid holiday and catch up on some beauty sleep. My job is to catch a murderer. If that's beyond your pay grade, then my guys can take it from here.'

Stephanie noted the casual sexism. She could use that later if needs be. 'France is a notional ally, sir. We can't run an op like this on French territory without informing the DGSI as a basic courtesy. It breaks all protocol.'

'Spoken like a true Foreign Office lifer.'

'This is my patch. With all due respect, I have relationships to maintain.'

'And I have national security to look after. Your cover may say First Secretary, Ms Porter, but you're still a spy. Caroline Runcie, your notional lord and master, is already fully indoctrinated into Tempest. But the distribution list is tight. Spread the word wider and most of Whitehall will be chatting about it by teatime. Help me out or get off my back. Which is it?'

Stephanie saw her future go up in flames. But that was the inevitable fate of the foot-soldier. Spying was always politics by other means.

She looked at the time and made her decision. 'What do you need?'

29

After the storm, the calm arrived.

Max still felt the bullets in his pocket. Cleo's gun was nestled in her bag. Until they reached dry land, that was the best he could hope for. She needed him. He had few other options while still on the water. Staying alive was his only priority now. Antagonizing Cleo further was a ticket to the bottom of the ocean.

It was dark as they neared the French coast. Max could just make out the contours of a beach or jut of land. A smuggling route, most likely. He tried to place it geographically, but smuggling routes weren't his specialism. Plus, there were other things to think about. A small dinghy motored out to them. Two ex-military types emerged from the dinghy and clambered on to the Prestige 420S. Cleo and Max did the reverse. Cleo exchanged a few muttered words with the two men in Hebrew. Then both parties went their opposite ways.

'Here, knock yourself out.' Cleo flung a life jacket to him.

'And you?'

'We only have one. I'm replaceable. You're not.'

'I think others would beg to differ.'

The water was bumpy and pitch-black. Max pinched himself to stay awake. He'd sat across from countless spooks and agent-runners, soaking up details of life on the frontline. And yet this was the nearest he'd ever come to a real-life op. Those two men – both late thirties or early forties – were Mossad, no doubt, some of the NOCs stationed throughout Western Europe for moments such as this. They wouldn't be top drawer, of course, but oddbins types. The people who stocked safe houses, returned leased vehicles, conducted brush-passes and serviced dead letterboxes. The admin section, rarely getting any glory but helping the world go round. The invisible men and women of the secret world.

As they neared the shoreline, Max again tried to calculate roughly where they might be. He could pick out hotspots across the Middle East, happily navigate the cavernous geography of Russia, even identify areas of interest across China. But France wasn't part of his research. Before long he gave up the effort and trusted to Cleo's direction.

They reached the shore then trekked for what seemed like hours until they reached a small village where a silver Mercedes GLA 250 was parked on a gravel path. Inside were water bottles and food. Max drank greedily and stocked up on protein bars, sandwiches and fruit. If anyone asked, the detritus was the result of a recent picnic. Cleo avoided using GPS and, instead, relied on a hard-copy map.

Max drank coffee from a Thermos and was determined to keep awake, but his eyelids became heavy and, before long, he was gone. When he woke again it was already nearly daylight. Cleo was driving and he saw the first sign for Paris. He drank more coffee. The roads were filling up now. There was still that kick of surprise at being here at all. He'd dreamed of being back in his office at the LSE and the usual panic about teaching the wrong exam subject, a frequent nightmare which no amount of therapy or experience cured. There was music on the car speakers. He recognized 'Galway Girl' by Ed Sheeran.

'You've been out for hours,' said Cleo. She turned down the music.

'I'm an eight-hours man. Less than that and my brain starts to shut down.'

'You haven't missed much.'

'Who were those two guys back there?'

'Who do you think?'

So they had been real. 'Mossad irregulars. NOCs, probably. The sort that can't be traced back to any formal diplomatic mission or embarrass the Israeli government.'

'Well deduced, Mr Bond. Perhaps we'll never know.'

Max marvelled at her calmness. 'How does someone with a British passport and an RP accent end up doing off-the-grid jobs for Israeli intelligence?'

'Hypothetically?'

'Of course.'

'Do you think Mossad only uses people called Jacob who are fresh from the kibbutz?'

'I'm serious.'

Cleo turned the music down further. 'Do you want the highlights or the full ninety minutes?'

'I have a very busy diary right now, so . . .'

'My father was British-Egyptian; my mother was

Israeli. I have dual nationality. The pitch at Princeton promised decent pay and exciting work. No one with an Egyptian name like Alexandra Cleopatra is suspected of helping out Israel. I got to work as a consultant all round the world while doing odd jobs when called upon. I had no family money, so the retainer was an added bonus.'

'An enterprising way to get on to the housing ladder?'

'If you like. We all do what we have to do. This was my solution. I'd do the same again. What about you? How does someone with a double first from Cambridge and a famous father end up with no money, no wife and a junior lecturing job?'

Max hated it when they did that. It was a form of brain burgling. It was like being X-rayed without permission. 'Double starred first, actually,' he said. 'And I didn't want to sell out, if you must know.'

'I don't believe that.'

'You and my ex-wife must be related.'

'She's certainly done well for herself. What, then, you just didn't like sharing the limelight with a powerful woman?'

Max was getting tired of this conversation. 'Where was that landing spot?'

Cleo changed lanes, zigzagging between two other vehicles. 'The less you know, the easier it will be for you. Trust me on that.'

'If you won't tell me anything, why bring me along at all?'

'I told you. The notebook is worthless without

371

someone independent who can verify the contents. By itself it's just handwriting about old events. You're the missing piece of the puzzle. Without your endorsement, the operation fails.'

Max wasn't convinced. But he backed off. For now, at least. 'What's the plan when we get there?'

'Simple,' she said. 'We secure the notebook and anything else Scarlet left behind in the safety deposit box. Then we find a place to hide while you read through the contents.'

'And then?'

'Once you've verified it, we begin the process of getting the material out into the media. After that, the story should take care of itself.'

'You still haven't told me where we're going.'

'Does it really matter?'

'I'm risking everything for this.'

Cleo sounded frustrated. 'There's a safety deposit box company on Boulevard Pereire. Scarlet stored the notebook and some other papers there. I know the manager and he'll give us access as soon as we arrive. The whole thing will be over within twenty minutes.'

'Where do we go after that?'

'I've booked two rooms at the Hilton Hotel on Rue Saint-Lazare. The first is a decoy. The second is for a married couple. That's our cover. You'll have twenty-four hours to go through the material and then we strike.'

'It's really that simple?'

Cleo changed lanes again and then accelerated, always mindful of the speed limit. The last thing they needed was to be pulled over.

'This is real-world spying, Dr Archer. What were you expecting? DB9s and exploding watches?'

He was annoyed at being spoken to like a child.

But yes, he wanted to say. That's exactly what he'd been expecting.

30

The MI6 Station at 35 Rue du Faubourg Saint-Honoré now went into overdrive. Saul reviewed the latest piece of string and underlined the two key details:

> **ARCHER:** You still haven't told me where we're going.
> **WATSON:** Does it matter?
> **ARCHER:** I'm risking everything for this.
> **WATSON:** There's a <u>safety deposit box company on Boulevard Pereire</u>. Scarlet stored the notebook and some other papers there. I know the manager and he'll give us access as soon as we arrive. The whole thing will be over within twenty minutes.
> **ARCHER:** Where do we go after that?
> **WATSON:** I've booked two rooms at the <u>Hilton Hotel on Rue Saint-Lazare</u>. The first is a decoy. The second is for a married couple. That's our cover. You'll have twenty-four hours to go through the material and then we strike.

The three intelligence officers under Stephanie's command – supposedly a Second Secretary, in reality the Deputy Head of Station, and two cultural attachés – were told to follow Saul's orders. The two junior officers were dispatched to the Hilton Hotel on Rue Saint-Lazare, while Charlotte and the

Deputy Head of Station tracked down the safety deposit box company on Boulevard Pereire, eventually finding a small boutique storage facility. The website advertised its '24/7 world-class enhanced security' to high-net-worth clients from across the globe. The other two passengers from the diplomatic flight – the former special forces muscle and the civvy – were instructed to stay behind at the embassy.

Just after nine a.m., Saul and Stephanie Porter set up an OP in an unmarked embassy Range Rover with fake plates outside the safety deposit box company on Boulevard Pereire, connected to Alpha Team 1 and Alpha Team 2. Forensics alone wasn't enough to swing a jury. They needed photographic evidence of Max Archer carrying the notebook. That's if Max Archer made it this far at all.

Stephanie looked again at Max's profile on the London School of Economics website. She said, 'I still don't understand. Why would a history academic want to murder a retired spy?'

Saul kept a constant watch, barely even blinking. 'Money is the oldest motive. He saw the opportunity of a lifetime and he took it.'

'One small notebook is really that valuable?'

'The Hitler diaries almost went for two point five million dollars for American rights, just under a million for UK rights and did sell for nine million marks, or over two million sterling, for the German language rights. And that was in 1983. The media hasn't had a proper spy scandal since Litvinenko or Salisbury. They'll lap this up.'

'Even so. A retired MI6 officer isn't exactly Hitler.'

'Nor, as it turned out, was the Hitler diaries.'

'So several million is this guy's pension fund?'

'Many people have killed for a lot less.'

'You still won't tell me the name of the intelligence officer who died?'

'If this goes wrong, you'll know it soon enough.'

'And if it doesn't?'

Saul looked at the GPS dot on his screen. He didn't answer. The GPS tracker had stopped five minutes' walk away. Parking directly by the safety deposit box building was too obvious. Ditch the vehicle, make the final part of the journey on foot, collect the product and then dry-clean in a series of cabs, even public transport, until reaching the hotel. Basic tradecraft.

The radio crackled into life. 'Control, this is Alpha 1. Update on the target ETA?'

Saul picked up the radio and went secure. 'Received Alpha 1. Target ETA four minutes thirty.'

'Copy that.'

Saul professed a general allergy for all things digital. It was another part of his shtick, happy to play the office Luddite when it mattered, the last vocal defender of HUMINT and all things analogue. He still had the newspapers delivered as hard copy. He preferred paperbacks to Kindle. Online banking had been unavoidable and printing out emails long since frowned upon. But he still phoned up the local curry house rather than using an app and preferred laminated menus to QR codes. His daughters might roll their eyes, but he could hardly change now.

Ironically, part of his remit as Deputy Director-General was supervising the tech-ops division of Thames House. He paid them weekly visits and sampled their latest product: microphones hidden inside envelopes; cameras tucked into water bottles; GPS trackers smuggled into watches. Each item was scuffed and distressed until it looked like any other shop-bought version. The 'Saul test' had even become an informal benchmark for how easy a tech-ops briefing was to understand. They had moved quickly this time. So far, the plan had worked.

Saul went secure on the radio mic again. 'Alpha 1, this is Control. ETA three minutes.'

'Copy that, Control.'

He kept watching the small red dot crawling across the street map on his phone. Charlotte was stationed inside the building. The Deputy Head of Station was fully equipped with a long-lens camera in the tower block opposite. Shots of Max Archer entering the building, retrieving the notebook, then exiting would be enough. The arrest could occur later, once they'd surprised Archer at the hotel.

Saul did the calculation in his head.

With any luck, he'd be home in time for tea.

31

It was as they reached the centre of Paris that Max realized something was very wrong. Cleo pulled into a car park and then turned on the car radio. She dialled up the volume until the car vibrated with sound. Max looked across bemused. He saw Cleo signal for silence.

Max was about to speak, then stopped himself. Cleo searched in the car for some paper or writing material and eventually found the car manual stuffed inside the glovebox. She took a biro from her pocket and then scribbled something in large capital letters. Max couldn't make out the word, distracted by the din of French alternative rock blasting from the car speakers.

Finally, Cleo finished writing and held up the car manual. On a blank page near the back were six words. Max struggled to believe them even as he understood each one:

DON'T SPEAK. GIVE ME YOUR WATCH!!!

Max frowned. He shrugged in confusion, trying to mime a question. Then, with a horrible certainty, the various events realigned. He saw himself numerous glasses in at his father's birthday party. He remembered their brief conversation in the lobby of the Goring Hotel and the family heirloom and the black velvety pouch and those heart-tugging references to Lily and his grandfather's exploits during the war.

He shook his head. It couldn't be true. Oliver was a 'character', there was no doubt of that. He had abandoned the family with no obvious signs of guilt and treated Lily recklessly. Max had no illusions about his father's absence of paternal feelings or familial responsibility. But betraying him in plain sight? Invoking his dead mother's memory? Shopping his own son to the intelligence services?

No, that was something else.

The music on the radio changed. Noughties pop pelted out, filling the vehicle with manufactured drumbeats and synthesized strings. Cleo gestured again to the words and refused to back down. Reluctantly, Max gently unclasped the watch and handed it over to Cleo. This was absurd. The Rolex was scarred and battered after almost eighty years of continuous use. All the photos he'd ever seen of devices from Hanslope Park were new. This was a family treasure, handed down from grandfather to mother to son.

Max watched with frustration as Cleo scribbled down another phrase. She held it up:

STAY IN THE CAR!!!

He watched as Cleo exited the vehicle and disappeared. From his front seat, he saw her pick a target and approach a homeless man slumped on the street corner with a dirty guitar case for coins. She bent down, flashed a beguiling smile and then took out the watch. The homeless man gratefully took the watch and repeated some words back. Then Cleo crossed the street and returned to the vehicle. She turned off the radio, and ushered Max out, locking the car behind them both.

'What the hell was that?'

Cleo turned to him. 'I'll explain on the way.'

32

Max tried to keep up with her as they slalomed through the busy streets. The heat was tropical. His shirt stuck damply to his chest. This wasn't how his first foray into operational fieldwork was meant to go. He wanted the old days of three-martini lunches and afternoon siestas in clubland. Homeless men, paternal betrayal and messages on car manuals wasn't his idea of spying.

'You have to learn how to think like a professional,' said Cleo. 'Until then, keep quiet and follow my lead.'

Max absorbed the insult. Usually, he was the one telling others how to think. 'Ah, I see. So that little stunt back there was professional, was it? Amateur handwritten signs and then flogging a family heirloom to a guy on the street. Super-smooth. All that top-secret training, I suppose.'

Cleo wasn't fazed. 'You know this world in theory, Max. But theory is different from reality. Real spying is messy. It's dull and lethal at the same time. You have to change plans and improvise. That's what we're doing.'

'No. That's what you're doing.'

'Think. You once applied to join MI6. Time to show them what they missed.'

'That's classified.'

'According to you, I'm a highly trained Mossad

officer with nearly two decades working under natural cover. You think I let you meet Scarlet without full vetting?'

Max thought back to that very first meeting and wondering how Scarlet knew so much about him: the marriage, the finances, Emma's pregnancy. MI6 files were impossible to hack; everything after that was child's play.

'Why the watch?' he said.

'Why do you think?'

'Are you ever capable of giving a straight answer?'

'I'm a spy. Of course not.'

There was a large crowd ahead queuing outside a cinema. Cleo was lithe enough to squeeze her way through. Max took a detour off the pavement and hurried to catch her again. The sweat puddled under his elbows, upon his brow, squishing between his toes.

'You think the watch is some kind of tracking device,' he said. 'From the song and dance with the car radio, I'm guessing a device with audio and GPS tracking capabilities.'

'Why would I think that?'

'That's what I'm asking.'

'The thought never occurred to you?'

Max got level with her again. He was almost breathless, woefully unfit. Once upon a time he'd played tennis every weekend. That was before the divorce. Now he could barely afford the club membership. 'A few days ago, the only thought that occurred to me was whether or not I would get tenure. Suspecting my own father of shopping me to MI5 wasn't a top priority.'

'Perhaps that's why you failed to get a place on IONEC. Spying requires permanent paranoia. Some have it, some don't. You want to believe the best of people. I'm happy to believe the worst.'

Trusting was hardly the word he'd use. He was a sceptic, an academic, always ready with a searching question. His job was to look under the bonnet of life until he understood the wiring.

'Rubbish. Why would my own father collude with British intelligence?'

'Your father spent his career under non-official cover, yes? He was a journalist. But really he worked for MI6.'

Max shook his head. 'NOC, fellow traveller, agent of influence . . . Look, there are many names for what my father did, or rather claims to have done. Most of it's just old war stories. The greatest work of fiction since Tony Blair's autobiography. He likes to embellish the truth.'

'You underestimate him.'

'No. I've just met my father.'

'Oliver Archer worked in Hungary in the fifties, South America in the sixties, DC in the seventies and reported from Afghanistan in the eighties before a final posting as Moscow stringer in the nineties. You honestly never joined the dots?'

Max was about to ask how she knew so much about Oliver's career. But it was pointless. The same way she'd managed to psychoanalyse him. It was true that Oliver's archive showed by-lines from Budapest, Mexico City, Capitol Hill, Kabul and Peshawar and, at the end, Moscow. But, like all sons, Max knew Oliver's career only in outline. Nothing was less interesting than your parents' CVs.

'So what?'

Cleo shook her head. 'I'm just the spy. You're the historian.'

'Are you going to make me beg?'

'The Hungarian Uprising. The Cuban Missile crisis. Watergate. Western support for the Mujahadeen. Putin's rise and Russia's decline into a criminal state. The dates and geography match. Your father wasn't just reporting on those events, Max. He was helping shape them.'

Max was catching up now. 'Gold-medal bollocks. My father was a stringer who liked too many women and always had a bottle in his hand. More *Our Man in Havana* than *A Perfect Spy*.'

'That was his cover, yes. But Oliver Archer was never some minor agent of influence, no matter what he told you. Those were the terms of his deal. He got access in return for providing a helping hand. He was one of the most effective NOCs that SIS ever deployed. Their ultimate go-to man for their deniable jobs.'

'How could you possibly know?'

'Simple,' she said. 'He was one of the case studies in Tel Aviv.'

Max reeled. He pictured Oliver in the Goring Hotel regaling guests with those war stories. He heard those endless conversations about writing a memoir without ever committing words to paper.

He'd never understood Oliver's reluctance. His father had been a convenient punchbag for so long: over Lily's death, the family breakdown, even the rejection by the SIS recruiters.

'Even if that were true . . .'

'Which it is.'

'You're a spy. You lie for a living. I don't trust a thing you say.'

'Suit yourself.'

'Why would my father deliberately trick me with the watch? He's been out of the game for decades. He owes them nothing.'

'For a clever man, Max, you can be remarkably stupid.'

Max was getting even hotter now. He was tired of being insulted. 'Stop. Just stop. Where the hell are we even going?'

'It's better you don't know.'

'Not good enough. Tell me now or I'm bailing.'

They reached a set of traffic lights. Cleo scanned the immediate horizon, trying to glimpse any possible tail amid the scrum of people.

'A deep dive of your father's financial records shows he's in difficulty,' she said.

'The finances of a retired journalist? Mossad really has nothing better to do?'

Cleo ignored the comment. 'Oliver's last Service psych evaluation showed his work took a heavy toll. That's why he was let go after Moscow. He started gambling. He hasn't stopped. Unless the Firm helps him out, your father will lose everything. They've had him on a string ever since.'

The lights changed. People started crossing.

Max was too stunned to move his legs. His first shameful instinct was a selfish one. That old three-bedroom house in North London had been Max's back-up plan, appreciating in value until it earned more than Oliver ever did.

'Blackmail,' he said, as they reached the other side of the road. 'That's what you're telling me. British intelligence blackmailed my father into carrying out one last courier job and bugging his own son.'

'Yes.'

'Why keep silent all this time?'

'Because I knew you'd react badly. Academics love arguments. Spies like solutions. I couldn't afford a fight in the car.'

'For a minute there I thought you might be being patronizing.'

Cleo checked the time and increased her pace. She was barely breaking sweat. 'I had my suspicions when you first mentioned the watch. The car journey confirmed it.'

'How?'

'Too quiet, too easy. The notebook contains secrets that the British government has spent the last seventy years trying to bury. The fact we didn't have a physical tail meant they must be tracking us digitally.'

'So everything you told me in the car was disinformation?'

'Bravo, doctor.'

Max stopped now. He was drenched in sweat. There was only the bitter aftertaste of coffee from the car. He longed for water, anything cool. There were too many thoughts. Oliver and the house. Those old by-lines kept in plastic boxes in the attic. The performance at the Goring. Fact became fiction. Myth alchemized into reality. Lies converted to truth. Nothing seemed real any more.

'We're two people against two states,' he said. 'British and French intelligence have the best funded spy agencies in Europe. This isn't dodging a bullet in Palestine. By the time SIS and the DGSI get on the case, we'll have nowhere to run. One homeless man with a GPS tracker won't fool them for long. Tell me the plan or I'm handing myself in.'

'To be arrested for the murder of Scarlet King?'

'I'm innocent. I can prove that.'

'Even with your DNA on her body? Motive, opportunity, means. I'd convict you.'

'Then it's a good thing enemy spies don't sit on British juries.' Max was resolute, unafraid, the revelations about Oliver and the house and the watch bulldozing the last of his nerves. 'How do we get out of this?'

Cleo moved closer. 'You really want to know?'

Max swallowed and felt his heart rate tick upwards. 'Yes.'

And so she told him.

33

Even before he saw the figure in the dirty-grey hoodie and unwashed trousers, Saul knew he'd been duped. Cleo Watson, or whatever her real name was, had been trained by the most lethal intelligence agency in the world. Mossad counter-surveillance classes made those at the Fort look like hide-and-seek. Israeli intelligence was founded on myths about penetrating enemy camps and losing watchers. No spook would approach a target building in such a linear fashion or at such a slow pace.

They'd been played.

Saul cursed himself silently, invoking every oath he could think of. He should have gone with his gut. This, right here, was why he was sceptical of tech-ops. He'd been reluctant to deploy a full watcher unit because of the territorial challenge of operating on French soil and the inevitable political trouble with SIS and the DGSI. But the real business of spying could never be hacked. Shortcuts were for amateurs. He'd doubted his own instinct. Now he was paying the price.

He grabbed the handheld radio and went secure. 'Alpha 1, this is Control. Any sign of the target?'

'Negative, Control.'

Stephanie Porter glanced across from the passenger seat. 'Problem?'

'They've made us. The GPS tracker's been re-positioned for a decoy asset. Shit.'

'What about the wiretaps from the car?'

'False trail, it has to be. This place is a decoy, so's the hotel. They're trying to throw us off the scent.'

'You realize I can't help unless you indoctrinate me fully into the operation.'

Saul felt his body rattle with tiredness. The flight over, the lack of sleep, even the adrenaline of the operation itself – once he could take it all in his stride. Now his own body was his worst enemy. 'The retired spy who was killed wasn't just any retired spy. Hence the last twelve hours.'

'I'm guessing this is related to the notebook.'

'Yes.'

Saul could see it all very clearly now. Operation Tempest drawing to an ignominious close. The Home Secretary washing his hands of it. Saul would return to Whitehall as the scapegoat, forced to endure the mocking of all those bumptious wannabes from Vauxhall Cross. The message would travel around SW1 until Saul's entire career – thirty-plus years on the job – would be reduced to a mildly comic tale about how the old spook got outwitted by a middle-aged academic. A brutal end.

'Only two other people know the full truth about Tempest,' he said. 'You're about to become the third.'

'Should I consider it an honour?'

'Think of it more like a curse. After this, there's no turning back. It's snakes in the Garden of Eden time.'

Stephanie didn't hesitate. 'What's in the note-book, Saul?'

'Two state secrets which British intelligence has tried to keep hidden ever since the end of the war. Tube Alloy big. D-Day levels.'

'Let me guess. Harold Wilson was a KGB agent and we killed JFK?'

'Worse.'

'You're serious?'

Saul breathed deeply. 'First, that in 1946 the British government actively helped Nazi war criminals relocate to Britain. The Americans got the brightest and the cleanest with Paperclip. We were left with the dregs. The sadists and the torturers. We kitted these scientists out with brand-new identities, faked their death certificates and put them to work at Porton Down. Most of them rose to full profes-sorships and had comfortable lives. All of them were protected and fully funded by MI6.'

Stephanie flinched, absorbing the information. 'And the second?'

'SIS's most senior Russia hand during the height of the Cold War was actually a Soviet illegal named Anastasia Chekova. We believe she was the one who tipped off Philby before his escape in '64. She worked with Caspar Madison through the seven-ties and eighties. She was the mythic traitor Anatoly Golitsyn warned us about. Not a Fourth Man, but a Fourth Woman. She had oversight of everything: the Mitrokhin Archive, the Gordi-evsky op, even the location of defectors granted sanctuary once the wall came down. She makes the Cambridge Five look like schoolboys.'

Stephanie didn't say anything at first. She sat back against the seat, kneading her fingers together. Eventually she said, 'And the notebook?'

'A handwritten account by Ms Chekova, or "Scarlet King" as her legend was, of her activities during the Cold War. She was run by a handler in Oxford called Maria Kazakova. All this time we fixated on Cambridge. All that time they were being outdone by their closest rivals.'

'Why would the notebook be hidden in Paris?'

'At a guess, London was too risky. Plus, Anglo-French relations haven't exactly been smooth of late. Scarlet King, or Anastasia Chekova, knew we would never divulge this to the DGSI and that we had no legal authority to carry out a raid on French soil. It was easy enough to access but far enough away to stop British law enforcement.'

'So that's why the notebook is worth so much.'

Saul nodded wearily. 'The revelation about Philby crippled British intelligence for decades. Just imagine what this would do. Five Eyes, trans-atlantic intelligence sharing, even the agencies themselves – it could bring down all of it. Our armed forces are depleted, our diplomatic network has been gutted. Spies are all we have left. The politicians will do anything to ensure that notebook never sees the light of day.'

'Next time I'll forget to answer the emergency phone.'

'Wise advice.' Saul knew he'd been bellyaching. He was usually allergic to self-pity; yet another sign of age. A car horn blasted nearby and shook him back to the present. He looked at the safety deposit box company opposite and saw the GPS dot align perfectly with the target destination. The homeless man was settling down on a corner outside the building. He laid out his sleeping bag and guitar case. Saul picked up a pair of binoculars and looked closer. The watch from tech-ops was sitting on the man's left wrist.

He put the binoculars down. 'Can you get into the station system remotely?'

'Via secure laptop. It's not bulletproof but we can risk it.'

Saul nodded. 'Try. I need a list of any sites of interest within a five-mile radius that could be used as a storage facility or DLB.'

Stephanie took out her service laptop. On the surface it looked like any over-the-counter version, a MacBook-style device but without the semi-chewed Apple logo on the casing. When not wining and dining diplomats, the station monitored foreign nationals using Paris as a transit point into Western Europe: money laundering, drug smuggling, arms dealing, people trafficking, front companies. Paris Station regularly updated all key points of interest and fed them back to the Joint Intelligence Committee based in the Cabinet Office at 70 Whitehall.

'The list was updated two weeks ago,' said Stephanie, swivelling the screen round for Saul to see it. 'We have ten SOIs within a five-mile radius.'

SOIs were the office jargon for Sites of Interest, the dialect Saul still hated. He took charge of the laptop and scrolled down the classified list. The ten sites ranged from boutique asset managers to

392

dry cleaners used as fronts for trans-national drug dealing. All of them were graded Cat 1 and associated with a POI – person of interest – or a previous crime.

'Too obvious,' he said.

'I can expand the search criteria to a wider radius.'

Saul looked at the screen again. He was making the same mistake, relying on technology rather than instinct. Scarlet King, or Anastasia Chekova, was a veteran of the secret world. She didn't choose DLBs by algorithm or spreadsheet. It was the Amazon problem, recommendations similar to previous purchases. But Scarlet King wasn't a drug smuggler or money launderer or people trafficker. She was schooled in a world where tradecraft was a point of pride, an eternal duel with the other side; a time when enemies had grudging respect for their opponents. Proper tradecraft, as Saul always thought of it, had a dash of personality. It was a spy's signature, a wink and a nod to those in pursuit.

'It has to have some connection with the notebook,' he said. 'The best type of tradecraft is also a kind of statement. That's the way Scarlet King was trained. Safety deposit boxes and boutique banks are too blatant.'

'What do you want me to do?'

'Search for all major institutes or offices within a three-mile radius.'

'This is the centre of a major global city. There'll be hundreds.'

'Just try.'

Stephanie duly carried out the search. As predicted, the screen coughed up hundreds of entries. Saul worked his way down. He'd always thought of Paris as so much smaller than London, a monument to autocratic planning rather than the jumble of England. But that didn't stop the city's geography teeming with possibilities. Banks, corporations, think tanks, publishers, government offices, educational establishments. Saul scrolled endlessly, the minutes drifting by, ignoring the radio as the Alpha teams requested an update. The list was alphabetized. He was still on 'R'.

Then, at last, he saw it. One rung down, near the start of the 'S' section.

Saul memorized the address and then closed the laptop lid. He checked the mirrors and forced his way into the nightmarish traffic. He radioed the new address to the two Alpha teams. Then he speed-dialled the group waiting at the embassy station on hands-free.

'Control, this is Beta 1.'

'Beta 1, we have a new location.' Saul repeated the location address. He added one final coda, a last-ditch attempt to stop Max Archer in his tracks. It had worked once before; it could work again. 'It's time to prepare the asset.'

34

Simon Wiesenthal was arguably the most famous Nazi hunter of them all. According to some official biographies, he helped capture almost 1,100 Nazi war criminals. The most notable was Adolf Eichmann. A victim of the camps himself, Wiesenthal almost died at Mauthausen before being liberated by the 11th Armored Division of the Third US Army on May 5th, 1945.

Max had once written an academic paper on Wiesenthal and knew the rest by heart. After the war, Wiesenthal worked for the OSS, the forerunner of the CIA, and continued the hunt for the 90,000 or so Nazi war criminals still at large across Europe and South America. He was knighted by the Queen and awarded the US Congressional Gold Medal. He was featured in Frederick Forsyth's novel *The Odessa File*, which had barely left Max's bedside table as an undergraduate. The Simon Wiesenthal Centre was launched in 1977 and now headquartered in Los Angeles with regional offices in New York, Toronto, Miami, Chicago, Buenos Aires, Jerusalem and . . . Paris.

They approached 66 Rue Laugier. The front entrance of the Simon Wiesenthal Centre, the project's European headquarters, was smaller than Max imagined, just a simple building with a small sign outside. Wiesenthal's life and the hunt for former Nazis was irresistible material for any intelligence historian. Even now, nothing seemed to enthuse a commissioning editor more than Spitfires, Normandy, WAAFs and Churchill. Max knew the darker side too – that the list of Nazis Wiesenthal claimed to have brought to justice was wildly overblown. That he played little part in the Eichmann saga, and that whole chunks of his life story were factually inaccurate. Sometimes, though, he was happy to believe the myth, at least for now.

The building was like an oasis after the heat outside. Max tried to imagine Scarlet King here. She'd been politically conscious during the Holocaust, young amid the rubble of post-war Vienna, living on into an old age of iPhones and social media, the bathos of the twenty-first century, watching the past become mythologized. Scarlet's contemporaries were like veterans of the First World War, or survivors of the Great Depression. A whole generation, an entire chapter of history, soon to be extinct.

'Why here specifically?' he said, looking round at the photos and statements on the walls. There was a calm, meditative hush. It reminded him of a small hotel.

Cleo's shoes rapped loudly over the glossy floor. 'Why do you think?'

'Please stop using questions for answers.'

'How else will you ever learn?'

'I'm a teacher. I learned most of what I need to know quite some time ago.'

'Most, but not all. Consider this an education, Professor.'

'Associate Professor, actually.'

'You've read the first half of the memoir. You're the expert. Join the dots.'

Reluctantly, Max decided to play along. 'Fine. Scarlet was ashamed of her role in Operation Hercules helping Nazi war criminals like Otto Spengler escape justice. She saw the memoir as a way to atone for her sins.'

'Getting warmer. And?'

'Hiding the notebook at the Simon Wiesenthal Centre has a thematic link. Wiesenthal also worked out of Vienna for most of his life. If Scarlet ever returned to the city, there's a chance she could have met him, known him even.'

'Logical, if predictable. Still not the whole picture, though. Try again.'

They were at the reception desk now. Cleo asked for a staff member called Reuben and the receptionist nodded and picked up the phone. The lobby was eerily silent, as if any form of elevator music was inappropriate here. The stillness fused with the chug of traffic outside. It felt spectral and haunting.

Then, as he looked around, Max finally got it. He saw himself sitting in St James's Park next to Scarlet. He heard those lines again and the question mark that had followed him from the very beginning. Why would she want to publish the memoir? Why risk everything now? If it wasn't money, then what other possible reason could there be?

He remembered visiting the Jewish Museum and Tolerance Centre in Moscow, the largest Jewish museum in the world. Russia had been a home for Jewish people for over 1,500 years. Even today it was the fourth largest Jewish settlement in the world.

It was a guess, a supposition. But it was all he had. 'Anastasia was a Russian Jew,' he said. 'Operation Hercules wasn't academic to her. It was personal.'

Cleo nodded. 'Well done, doctor. You're finally thinking like a spy.'

35

It would be fruitless to deny it. When in the right mood with at least six hours' sleep behind him, Lucas Harper enjoyed the secret aspects of his job. The rest was mundane. Border patrols, immigration, drugs, policing – subjects that corroded the soul and sucked any joy from life. But MI5, the National Crime Agency, SCO19. That quickened the pulse of any red-blooded man or woman condemned to a desk. Those were the days he remembered.

He was forty-two minutes into an interminably dull briefing on possible fraud at the Passport Office when it happened. One of the private secretaries entered and passed a note to him. Lucas smiled neutrally at the assembled guests and indicated that the current speaker should continue. Meanwhile, he opened the note and glanced at it and felt unexpected relief. Finally, he could get out of this meeting.

'Excuse me,' he said, getting up and indicating towards one of the junior ministers. 'National security, I'm afraid. Felicity will see things out.'

And, like that, he was gone. The key with such swift departures was to maximize the theatrical effect. None of the assembled guests knew what the problem was, but they needed to believe it was grave. He always told the private secretaries to look suitably stern. The last thing he wanted was rumours to circulate that he used national security as an excuse to skip dull departmental meetings.

'Where do you need me?' he asked.

The Private Secretary handed him a briefing folder. 'We have everything set up in the secure room.'

'And he's sure this time?'

'Apparently.'

Lucas nodded politely to passing staff in the corridor, still relishing the automatic deference, and then walked into the secure room. This time he ignored the sign to leave his phone outside. The damn thing was encrypted. He was in charge of the building, not some naughty schoolboy.

The secure comms system was set up in the middle of the conference table. Lucas took a seat. Jo Harris, the Director of National Security, was standing behind the seat opposite, nervously clutching the rim of the chair. She leaned forward and pressed the speaker button. Lucas took a breath and prepared himself.

'Tempest 1, you're connected to the Principal,' said Jo Harris. 'Also present are DNS1 and SPS3. The line is secure.'

Lucas could never get used to Whitehall's obsession with acronyms. The Home Office was almost as bad as the MoD. They had entire novel-length briefing guides for new entrants.

'Home Secretary, this is Tempest 1.'

It was the routine designation for the senior officer on any Thames House op. The codename was followed by the level of seniority. Real names were considered classified. Bandying them about over a phone line, even if it was secure, was poor tradecraft. Lucas had enough enemies without the spooks on his case. He played along.

'Tempest 1, what do you need?' he said.

'Minister, the location of the targets should be on-screen with you now.'

The bank of screens ahead filled with a Google Earth map of central Paris. Jo Harris zeroed in on a red dot in the centre. The location caption read: 66 Rue Laugier.

'The briefing this morning indicated some kind of safety deposit place.'

'Yes, Minister.' Saul sounded tired; his voice was croaky. 'The intel was incorrect. Current thinking is that the Beta target made the surveillance during the course of the journey and tried to lay a false trail.'

'So what am I looking at? The next best guess?'

There was a pause, then, 'We're confident this is the correct location.'

'Do you have eyeball?'

'Not yet, sir.'

'Any camera evidence at all?'

'We're working on that.'

Lucas needed strong coffee, preferably some aspirin tablets. Anything to calm the agony in his head. 'What do you need?'

'Home Secretary, I believe we have the last window of opportunity to apprehend the Alpha and Beta targets and secure the product. But I need ministerial sign-off for both the use of force and operational deployment of a civilian asset.'

Lucas looked up at Jo. He pressed mute on the speaker, then said, 'This wasn't in this morning's intelligence briefing.'

'We weren't informed. It sounds like Tempest 1 is freelancing on the ground.'

'Who's providing firearms support?'

'They have CTSFO liaison from Hereford.'

'Armed with what?'

'They'll be in mufti, so just a Glock 17 with two mags.'

'Nothing automatic?'

'No.'

'And who's the asset he's talking about?'

'That's a new one for me.'

Lucas unmuted the line again. 'Tempest 1, please confirm the identity of the asset in question and the reasons for operational deployment.'

There was another pause. Saul Northcliffe's voice crackled over the line. 'I'm sorry, but I can't do that, Home Secretary. It could endanger the asset.'

'The line is secure.'

'I can't take the risk. We believe the asset could be the only way to neutralize the Alpha target, as we achieved before with the SIGINT drop.'

Lucas heard Saul on the line that night – hours or days ago, whichever it was – when he'd authorized the use of the first covert asset. Oliver Archer was firmly back on civvy street with no security clearance and it required ministerial permission to waive the usual vetting checks. Saul must have taken Oliver Archer to Paris as insurance. Damn him.

'I need your assurance, Tempest 1, that the asset

402

in question won't be in physical danger and will not – repeat *not* – knowingly contravene any domestic laws set out by the French government.'

'Copy that. The asset will not be in danger or break French law.'

Running a covert operation on French territory without informing the Élysée was bad enough. It could set back Anglo-French relationships for another decade. The Americans had only got away with it for the bin Laden operation because Pakistan was caught red-handed. One European ally working covertly on the turf of another could escalate into a full-on diplomatic incident.

Lucas made up his mind. 'Tempest 1, you have my permission to deploy a civilian asset under those strict parameters.'

'Thank you, Home Secretary. And firearms deployment?'

Lucas had been in the job long enough to know the worst-case scenario was always the most likely. Lifers in the police or intelligence world always overestimated their own abilities. He'd been burned by that over-confidence before.

'How many CTSFOs do you have with you?'

'Just one, Minister. Plainclothes, embedded as part of the team.'

Lucas had visions of a French civilian being shot by a plainclothes member of the Increment. It didn't bear thinking about. 'Alpha target is an academic,' he said. 'I fail to see on what grounds a CTSFO presence is required.'

'The Beta target is a trained IO, most likely with extensive firearms experience. We believe she may

403

well be armed. We need some firearms option to go ahead with the operation if things get noisy.'

The screens changed now. Jo Harris drew up the Security Service profile of 'Cleo Watson' and the activities of Grosvenor Security, the front company in Mayfair.

'The Beta target is a British citizen, is that correct?'

'Dual British and Israeli citizenship, yes.'

That made things more difficult. The Home Department's job was to protect British citizens, not shoot them. CTSFOs, meanwhile, were only permitted to use lethal force if there was an immediate threat to life.

'Are there no other options?' said Lucas. 'Taser, physical restraint?'

'No. The Beta target is too good. If she collects the product, and we go in unarmed, there's every likelihood she might use force to distract our attention. Or, in the most extreme scenario, shoot her way out.'

'I need to think on it.'

'I'm sorry, Minister. But we don't have that luxury. If we're going to do this, we need to move now.'

'And there's no way to allow French police or security services to make the arrest themselves?'

'Not without telling them why. Once they know about the notebook, we'd be handing them a diplomatic weapon that could be used against us for decades. Bearing in mind the ongoing negotiations around the security and foreign policy agreement . . .'

Lucas glanced at Jo again. 'What about Number 10?'

'The PM's tied up in Geneva.'

'The Foreign Secretary?'

'En route to Riyadh. He can't be reached at this short notice.'

So this was what it came down to. Twenty years of trying to become a Member of Parliament. Two failed campaigns, selection in a safe seat, two successful General Elections, the eighty per cent pay cut, the failed relationships, the drudgery of junior office, the sycophantic media interviews, the death threats on social media, now finally in a job which justified the sacrifice and two decades of sweat. All to be undone by a single wrong decision regarding an operation he didn't control in another country entirely.

Lucas thought of the notebook being made public. Of the humiliation of British intelligence letting a Russian illegal rise to the very top of SIS. It would reset diplomatic and security relationships. It could imperil the UK's permanent seat on the UN Security Council, undermine the case for a British Head of NATO, even end Five Eyes altogether. Lucas imagined standing outside the Prime Minister's den in Downing Street with the knowledge that it happened on his watch.

'Permission granted,' he said reluctantly. 'Tempest 1, the operation is a go.'

36

Reuben didn't have a last name. Or at least not one he was prepared to share. He was old and tufty with a boxer's shoulders. Max was reminded of those male French intellectuals on the Left Bank talking about existentialism and the meaning of life while sipping *cafés crèmes* and cheating on their wives.

Reuben wasn't old enough to have been a contemporary of Scarlet, surely, but not far off. Perhaps a child during the war, Max thought, one of the few who managed to survive in hiding; or a boy who had been shipped off to the camps but stayed alive until the liberation. He kept trying to catch a look at Reuben's arms to see if there was a number tattooed into the flesh. Then he felt horribly voyeuristic, the historian in him nudging out basic humanity. He regained self-control and followed Reuben and Cleo into the basement area where the Centre's archives were kept.

If Max knew anything, it was archives. He'd spent twenty years searching the world for bits of paper hidden in places like this. One of the drier games in the LSE staff room was to rank the best archives in the world. Amateurs imagined this would be down to aspects of history like how well each document was preserved, the smell of the pages, the feel of them through the white gloves.

Instead, the professionals squabbled over vending machines, lavatorial facilities, the pulchritude or otherwise of the archive employees – both male and female; academics were equal opportunity lechers if nothing else – and the reliability of the air conditioning. The American archives were the most luxurious. The Russian the most primitive. Max always had a soft spot for the Churchill Archives at Cambridge, marvelling at how a Victorian aristocrat born to the neo-classical glories of Blenheim had given his name to a temple of brutalist concrete.

Air conditioning certainly wasn't a problem here. The first thing Max felt was the cool gusts brushing his cheeks. Some archives tried to preserve the spirit of the wood-panelled university library. Others looked more like the USS *Enterprise*. This archive was somewhere between those two. There was a series of desks with angled lighting and a scholarly air of chalk dust. The perimeter, meanwhile, was metallic with an endless series of greyish storage units lining the room.

Reuben walked slowly, befitting his age, in a regimented shuffle. He reached the metal cabinet marked 'CTPE21'. He took a large keychain from his jacket pocket and searched for the right drawer.

Cleo was beside Max now. 'More secure than a safety deposit box,' she said. 'No one can get past Reuben.'

'What's his story?'

'Have you ever heard of the Nokmim?'

It was one of those liminal moments in history, a legend whispered about by intelligence historians.

The Nokmim meant 'Avengers' in Hebrew. Their mission was known as 'Nakam' or revenge. The Nokmim were a group of Jewish survivors determined to avenge the Holocaust and kill one German for every Jew who died in the camps. They planned to poison the water supplies in five key German cities. The group was led by Abba Kovner, later one of Israel's most decorated writers. The Avengers carried out reprisals across the world, tracking down Nazis and inflicting summary justice. The poisoning scheme never came to fruition. The young men involved soon peeled away and became respectable. The secret was only revealed in the mid-eighties. Some said there were other even more explosive tales that had still never been revealed.

Max imagined the old man in front of him as a teenager in that different world. The righteous thirst for justice. 'I'll try and keep on the right side of him then.'

Cleo smiled. 'Scarlet trusted him with her life.'

'How did they meet?'

'In Vienna, just after the war, I think. Lots of Nazis were in Austria. Scarlet was on her mission; Reuben was on his. They kept in touch ever since.'

Up ahead, Reuben pulled out a safety deposit box that was tucked inside the main steel container. Yes, Max thought, it would take some heavy machinery to get through those layers without the right key. Reuben heaved the box across to one of the desks and laid it down with a heavy breath. He took out a speckled handkerchief and dabbed his forehead. Even then, he didn't speak. Apart from the '*Bonjour*' earlier, and the occasional '*Merci*', he maintained a monkish silence.

Reuben unlocked the box with another key from the chain. Then he said, '*Voilà, madame.*'

'*Merci beaucoup.*'

Reuben took a step back with that antique courtesy. Max approached the safety deposit box in pilgrim-like fashion, remembering all those stories of penitents climbing stone stairs on their hands and knees, and even feeling a small adolescent thrill. It was ridiculous. He was middle-aged, an associate professor. Life should be viewed with clinical detachment. But, here, he was a schoolboy again, confronted with living, breathing artefacts from the past. Or at least he hoped so.

There was yet another layer to be unravelled. Inside the box lay a large, velvety bag with a pinched, frilly noose at the top tied with string. There was a pair of gloves – the sort of flimsy things usually found in archives – and Max squeezed both hands into them. He reached for the string, untied the knot and then eased the bag open at the top, slowly tipping its contents into the body of the box.

Several items emerged. The first, and the greatest relief, was the notebook itself. Max did little to hide his stationery fetish. The dinosaurs at the LSE could mock all they liked, but it was basic logic. Academics and writers spent fourteen hours a day with their laptop or fountain pen or notebook. Good stationery was essential, like a decent piece of willow for an opening batsman or expensive boots for a centre-forward. Scarlet, clearly, followed the same approach.

Max picked the notebook up and inhaled the musky scent. It was a Portobello notebook, based on the original Panama diary of 1908. The design was by Frank Smythson of Smythson's, Bond Street. The cover was black crossgrain lambskin; the pages were made of featherweight paper, pale blue inside and with a charming gilt-edge on the outside. The dimensions, Max guessed, were roughly about 20 x 25 cm. He opened the notebook and looked at the darker ink set against the bluish page. Scarlet had a sloping hand with lots of words crammed into every line. She wrote fluent copy with barely a smudge or crossing out, as if the tale had been brewed over many years and this artefact was the result, each part already drafted and refined. The scans becoming real.

He saw the two further sections – '1992' and '2010' – and forced himself not to begin reading but to concentrate, instead, on other things. The primary task of any historian was verification. Was the document what it claimed to be, or what others claimed it to be? Were there any tell-tale signs of a forgery? Paper type, ink type, giveaways on the physical artefact itself like incongruous dates or the wrong printer – Max checked all of these. He saw no obvious anomalies. It looked genuine: a Portobello notebook bought from London's most famous upmarket stationer and filled with selected memories from a life spent in the shadows.

'So?' said Cleo.

'Nothing obviously wrong so far. I'll have to get it under better light to be sure. Then there's the final two sections which need properly verifying.'

Max turned to the other four items. The first piece was old and fragile. Max was gentle with it, gradually smoothing the folds until the entire thing was visible. It looked like some sort of birth certificate. The text was Russian and the name 'CHEKOVA, A' stood at the top alongside the birth date: 'May 2, 1923'. The next item was a medal. Max recognized the red and yellow strap. There was a grey impression of Lenin's face in the middle, a gold fringe with a hammer and sickle and a red star. An Order of Lenin medal. Different eras had slightly different designs. This was the latest design, made for medals given out between 1943 and 1991. The next item was another notebook, but larger than the Portobello version. It had a similar leather cover but inside were photos preserved in pouches at the front and back, allowing the browser to skim through a whole selection, like a movie-reel.

Max felt almost overwhelmed. The text came to life here: Anastasia Chekova preparing to depart for England with her KGB father in the thirties; at Oxford in sub-fusc with a young-looking Aunt Maria; sitting in her Pimlico flat after the war with souvenirs from Vienna; holding up a wine glass in salute at some Service drinks party – probably the raucous Christmas variety – with Kim Philby of Section IX at her side; reading a copy of *Lady Chatterley's Lover* in the Moscow embassy in the sixties. He stopped at a photograph midway through of Scarlet with a small child, stunned by the possibility, reeling from seeing it confirmed in shape and colour.

The entire scope of Scarlet/Anastasia's life was

hinted at here. There were more photos from the decades of her standing outside the gates of the White House in Washington DC in the seventies; posing in a military aircraft on the way into Afghanistan in the eighties; then a group shot of Scarlet with other senior figures – one future Chief and one Chair of the Joint Intelligence Committee, if Max remembered rightly – at her leaving do in the early nineties. Finally, there were two more photos that looked more modern. Scarlet King back in Vienna and a slip of paper saying '2010'.

Max was trained to be sceptical. No historian ever declared anything to be 'true', only probable or likely, always terrified of certainty. But he felt that crabbed, tentative academic habit lift now. He was a child again handling some ancient object and looking at a world that was like the present but somehow wholly different. He was engaging with the physical reality of a vanished universe. Time at its most enchanting.

The evidence was right before him, lovingly curated over all those years. The mere existence of these photographs, of course, violated the Official Secrets Act in the same way as the notebook. But spies were people first and professionals second. They needed an imprint. This was hers. There were no photographs with assets or details which could endanger lives in the field. There was just the glimpse of history, a primary source second to none.

'She did this all herself,' said Cleo, joining Max now. 'She kept asking me to take packages to different dead drops. I think she had it all worked out in her head, ensuring that none of this got into the hands of the authorities. She'd planned it all for years.'

Max understood now. He'd always questioned the idea that the Security Service or SIS could actively try to suppress the past. But now, holding these items, he saw it all so clearly. The contents of this safety deposit box would be the biggest spy scoop of them all. The photos alone were unprecedented. The notebook, the Order of Lenin, the birth certificate – it would rewrite the history of the Cold War. The book would be bigger than Mitrokhin, Philby's memoir, Rimington's autobiography; more controversial than Richard Tomlinson or David Shayler.

Max imagined the phone call with his long-suffering literary agent. No more academic monographs to Oxford University Press for less than the price of a half-decent cappuccino. No desperate hopes of persuading publishers that a cradle-to-grave biography of the Soviet defector Anatoly Golitsyn had a realistic chance of breaking into the Richard and Judy Book Club and bossing every branch of WH Smiths.

No, this album alone guaranteed newspaper front pages and a decent serialization in the *Sun* or the *Mail*. Every TV producer this side of Soho would be able to envisage the eight-part co-production that would bring these images to life on-screen. No more hand-to-mouth consultancy gigs, either. This safety deposit box promised a new flat, the attention of the Vice-Chancellor, a sure-fire promotion. He would dine out on the story for years, 'the man who broke the Scarlet King story', joining Schama and Ferguson and Beard as media dons par excellence, part of the establishment furniture.

There was one last item. Max wondered what further treasures were left. This was another letter. It looked as frail as the birth certificate. The paper was yellowed with age and wrinkled on both sides. Max teased the fold open and saw the crest at the top of the page – 10 Downing Street. The rest of the letter was written in blue ink.

Max was about to read it, when one of the junior staff members hurried down the basement steps and consulted Reuben. She whispered something in his ear. Reuben looked over at Max and Cleo. He shuffled towards them with alarm.

'What is it?' said Cleo.

'L'ambassade du Royaume-Uni,' said Reuben. His voice sounded agitated. 'Ils disent que vous ne devriez pas être ici.'

Cleo turned to Max. 'They've found us. You know what to do?'

Max swallowed loudly. The plan. Just stick to the plan.

He nodded.

37

There was one consular official and another dressed in mufti. Max saw the Glock 17 visible at the man's waist. Hereford, then, the Increment. The consular official was young enough to be one of his students. She was intelligence, no doubt. The role play was duly enacted. ID produced in the name of 'Cass Temple (Consular Assistant)', Max and Cleo pretending to inspect it, both sides knowing the other side already knew. But the truth remaining unsayable, even so.

'Dr Max Archer?'

'Yes.'

'Miss Cleo Watson?'

'Who's asking?'

The consular assistant glanced at the armed officer and nodded. He began liaising with the staff and marching down towards the basement level.

'Are you arresting us?' said Max.

'Would you like me to?'

'That didn't answer my question.'

'A combined UK-French border patrol team spotted you transferring from an S-line Prestige 420S boat to an inflatable dinghy before landing on a beachhead on the coast. They alerted the DGSI, who had you tailed here and alerted the embassy. They asked the British embassy to intervene and help defuse the situation.'

'I see.'

'They've given us thirty minutes to bring you in.'

'Or what?'

The consular assistant smiled. 'Strip-search, detention, a bit of the rough stuff, then a deportation flight back to the UK mainland if you're lucky. Perhaps even a nice landing party when you arrive. Lots of photographers. First item on the evening news.'

'And if we're not lucky?'

'A long spell inside a French prison on charges of espionage. We won't try and get you back. Not with the Israelis involved. The Home Secretary's quite sure about that.'

Cleo spoke now. 'You have no authority on French soil.'

The consular assistant took out her phone. She held her thumb over a number. 'But I do have a DGSI team around the corner and the Minister of the Interior and the *préfet de police* on speed-dial.'

'You're bluffing.'

'You have ten seconds to accept the offer. I hear the Place Beauvau likes to keep suspected foreign agents in group cells while they have a long weekend. Rather you than me on that one. So?'

The embassy log later showed that a car with diplomatic plates left 66 Rue Laugier several minutes later and returned to the British embassy at 35 Rue du Faubourg Saint-Honoré. The two civilian passengers were formally identified as Dr M. Archer and Ms C. Watson. Both suspects were searched. Their hand-luggage was confiscated and analysed for any potential weapons. Dr Archer and Ms Watson were separated and led into different rooms for further interrogation.

Saul arrived ten minutes later, fresh from observing the entire scene at 66 Rue Laugier and then tailing the diplomatic car back to the embassy grounds. 'All set?'

Charlotte nodded. 'The team are going through the Centre's archives now. Their bags are also being searched as we speak. I'll let you know as soon as I have something.'

'Any chance they found another exit route?'

'We blocked off the entrance and exit. They had nowhere to run.'

'The optimism of youth.' Saul managed a deflated smile. 'I'll take Alpha. You're on Beta.'

'Any particular angles you want me to work?'

'Cleo Watson's spent over a decade working for a foreign intelligence service. That alone puts her British citizenship in doubt. Rattle her if she starts to clam up. I'll get Archer to sing for his supper.'

Charlotte looked at the three camera feeds on the monitors in front of her. Archer, Watson, then the mysterious asset from the plane. 'Will you use them?' she said.

Saul stared at the feed and looked despondent. Things had escalated. He was shutting out SIS, ignoring his own Director-General, stretching the rules to break a British national. Protocol had been abandoned. Morals already blurred. And yet he had no choice. This was personal now, even more so than before. The secret had to be carefully erased.

'Good luck,' he said, ignoring the question. 'Let me know if you get anything.'

38

This was how it always began.

The faceless embassy room stocked with faceless officials. The soulless quiet. Cameras hidden in the cornicing. Nation states liked to bury their traitors quietly. Ever since George Blake's escape from Wormwood Scrubs in 1966, British traitors had been squirrelled away in the damper corners of England, condemned to distant marshes and northerly gloom. The interrogation area here was at the back of the complex and as gloomy as this part of Paris ever got, which wasn't very much.

The embassy was one of the jewels in the crown of the diplomatic service, renowned in Whitehall for its parties and wine cellar. Apart from the interrogation room, the rest was similarly ornate. It was like the set of a French costume drama, Max thought, with its swirly patterning and dandified Regency plastering. There were no proper cells either. After finishing with him here, the worst they could do was imprison him in one of the lesser bedrooms. The sort of attic where they stashed junior functionaries or noisome ex-Prime Ministers.

The door opened. Not the woman, this time, but an older man with a hangdog expression and a tired suit. The less said about the tie the better. Like all spies, he was neither tall nor short, thin nor fat, posh nor commoner. Thames House picked people who were proudly average. They needed those who hugged the median like a prize. SIS dressed better. Genuine diplomats had charm. Only Security Service staff wore that trademark rainy expression, a skin-deep facial squall.

The man took out some ID. 'Paul Bilton,' he said. 'I'm a Counsellor here at the British embassy. Dr Archer, I believe?'

The name might be near enough, but the Counsellor rank was fake. Max had seen the production line of fake passports, government passes and other pocket litter pumped out at Hanslope Park. The question was whether to play along. Was Max an innocent bystander or co-conspirator? Did he talk his way out of this or wait for a lawyer?

'I still don't understand why I'm here,' he said, making the decision. 'Am I under some kind of caution? Should I not have a solicitor present? Is this criminal or off-the-record?'

'I'm a Counsellor, Dr Archer, not a police officer. And this isn't a criminal interrogation. Well, not yet at least. Our police liaison can walk you through the stages if that becomes necessary. For now, I just want to have a little chat.'

Max cleared his throat. 'There's clearly been some kind of misunderstanding.'

The man opened a manila file and glanced at the summary page. 'Gosport Marina to the French coast. Quite an adventure. Was that little jaunt your idea or someone else's?'

Max waited before saying the next part. It was all he could think of. 'I was under duress.'

Bilton glanced up sharply, his interest piqued. 'Duress?'

'Yes.'

'How so?'

'You know how.'

'Enlighten me.'

'I was approached yesterday by a woman who claimed to be working on behalf of the Security Service. She said I was being watched by Russian intelligence following a recent meeting with a contact called Scarlet King. She warned me that failure to comply with her orders would result in my immediate detention under the Official Secrets Act.'

There was silence in the room. The place was secure, Max realized, suddenly noticing the total absence of background noise. There was no shoe leather or chatter from the front desk. They were sealed off from the world.

'And you believed her?'

'Yes.'

Max needed stillness to think. He hated lying. There was only one cardinal sin in professional history, as in serious journalism, and that was to make things up. Max knew at least three senior lecturers who'd been fired from history departments for sexing up quotes or inventing witnesses, all in the quest for headlines. No, lying was an art form. One he hadn't mastered yet.

'Did you ask for any form of identification?' asked Bilton.

'Yes. She showed me a card from the MoD,' said Max. 'But I'm old enough and ugly enough to know

420

that no real spy produces chapter and verse to a civilian. I trusted her.'

Bilton was doing a fine job of looking bewildered. 'And that other name you mentioned. Susan –'

'Scarlet King.'

'Yes. She was some kind of secret agent too, was she? In on the great conspiracy?'

He was mocking him. The entire charade at the Simon Wiesenthal Centre was a farce. And yet they hadn't been able to resist. The operator with his semi-hidden Glock had seen to that.

'Let's cut the act,' said Max. 'You're no more a Counsellor than I'm the Prince of Wales.'

'No?'

'You know full well who Scarlet King is.'

'Dr Archer –'

'You know she was a Soviet illegal. You know her notebook confirms that fact. You know about the Hercules operation. You also know that both scandals will damage UK national security beyond repair. Let's ditch the dressing-up box.'

'What if I do?'

'You're the errand boy who mops the whole thing up. That explains the stunt back there. It explains the fake name and the Father Christmas act.' Max paused and longed for a drink of water. 'Stop me if you can't keep up.'

39

The man had talent. Saul had seen hundreds of interrogations. Suspects reacted in all manner of ways. The loud expressions of innocence. The sly and surly types. And then the charmers, those who would create a sense of intimacy between suspect and interrogator, playing mind games to wheedle their way out of trouble.

'If you insist,' Saul said. 'We can do it your way.'

'What's your real name?'

'You know I can't tell you that.'

'Security Service rather than SIS, yes?'

'Does it really matter?'

'I've interviewed enough SIS types in my time. None of them would choose that tie. These days none of them would even wear a tie.'

Saul felt aggrieved at the implication. Perhaps his wife and daughters were right after all. They'd been urging him to ditch this particular specimen for years.

'You're a clever man, Dr Archer,' he said, turning the focus back on Max. 'You know full well that an operation involving British citizens on UK embassy territory is run by the Security Service. I think it's time you cut the act as well. Both of us are professionals here.'

'Who said anything about an act?'

Saul reached into his bag. He took out another

file and tossed it across to Max. 'Have a gander. Knock yourself out.'

'Sarcasm and something to read. All I need now is a decent cup of coffee.'

'Not my specialty, sadly. More of a tea man. Or a decent pint. Take a look.'

Max opened the folder. He removed the series of photographs taken by the A4 surveillance team. Saul watched his reaction closely. This was the first time he'd have seen the extent of it.

'This is illegal.'

'On the contrary. It's perfectly legal. We have photographic evidence of you consorting with a former SIS employee to leak classified intelligence for financial gain. That is a clear breach of the Official Secrets Act and usually accompanied by a lengthy custodial sentence.'

Max was still flicking through the surveillance photos. 'How long were you tracking me?'

'As long as we needed to. 5B is my personal favourite.' Saul waited until Max reached the large print-out with the '5B' tag. 'You leaving the flat of Scarlet King in Beaufort Street, Chelsea, near the time of the incident which led to her death. Try the next one. Trust me, it gets even better.'

Max looked drained now. He turned reluctantly to the next photo.

'The forensic team did a decent job on this one. They found your DNA all over the scene. That, added to the prior photographic evidence and lack of any alibi, makes a very convincing package. The CPS already have the champagne on ice. Spy cases don't usually come this clean-cut.'

Archer was still fighting. 'No, sorry, impossible again. I've never been charged with a crime or convicted of anything. How could you possibly have a record of my DNA?'

'We're spies, Dr Archer, not charity workers. How hard do you think it is to lift prints from a coffee cup?'

'That is definitely illegal.'

'Are you a lawyer?'

'No.'

'Then why don't you leave matters of legality to those who are. I'm sure the Attorney General will happily provide you with a primer if, or should I say when, this gets to court.'

Max put the photos down. He was unsettled, Saul could see, and unsure where to put his hands. He folded them, then rested them on his knees. His eyes darted. His breathing quickened.

'It's absurd,' said Max. 'Scarlet King was clearly taken out by some high-level poison. Most likely untraceable in any kind of toxicology report. Just like all those Russians who died on British soil. The only people with access to that kind of material are current employees of state-level intelligence services. FSB, SVR, GRU, MSS, IRGC, Mossad possibly. You can't seriously be accusing a mid-career academic of having ready access to state-level chemical or biological weapons? It's nonsense. Any judge will laugh the very concept out of court.'

'You missed one.'

Max scrolled back through the list again. 'There's another intelligence service I don't know about who likes to poison their victims with nerve agent?

Twenty years researching you lot, but this I have to hear.'

'No. But you said *current* employees. The last group who has access to that kind of material are former operatives of all the services you just mentioned.'

'You've lost me.'

Saul saw the flicker of distress around Max's eyes again. No, he wasn't lost. He was afraid. Saul reached into his goody bag again and withdrew two books and an old-fashioned DVD case.

'Ah, so you're the person who bought them. I've always wondered.'

Saul held each item up, like an auctioneer. 'Let's see. *Double Agents: A History* and *The Honourable Traitor: An Unauthorized Biography of Kim Philby.* These are yours, yes?'

'You know they are.'

Saul admired the DVD case with the BBC logo. 'And this forgotten gem. A BBC2 documentary on the Cambridge Five. I searched for it on iPlayer but couldn't spot it. The team had to dig this out of the Amazon lost-and-found bin. Cost a fortune to ship.'

'Her Majesty's Security Service can't afford a Prime subscription?'

'This was shipped all the way from Canada. Or perhaps Australia. I can't quite remember. I hear the ratings were measured in single digits.'

'It was competing with international football. The televisual equivalent of Lord Lucan.'

'Vanished into thin air and never seen again.'

'No, dead before the search even began.' Max nodded to the two books. 'Those might be the only copies left in Britain. By the time my extended family bought the first fifty there were no more to go round. I'm told they make very useful doorstops.'

He was trying to buy time. Deflect the question and hope it went away. Saul thumbed his way through to the acknowledgements section. 'Yes, here we are. You don't mention their last names, quite sensibly, but we do get some of their first names. You must have tracked down every resettled KGB double this country has ever taken in. An impressive feat of detection work, if nothing else. Alexander, Yuri, Sergei . . .'

Max was impatient now, his voice alive with fear. 'It was an academic study of double agents. They were an invaluable primary source for the research. Of course I interviewed them. That's hardly prima facie proof of treason.'

Saul sniffed. 'Oh, I think you did more than interview them, Dr Archer. I think you became friends with some of them. You'd failed to get on to IONEC yourself. No Fort, no diplomatic postings, writing about this world rather than being in it. I think you liked sitting at the big boys' table. These former KGB types were bored out of their skulls, stuck in some provincial English backwater collecting their pensions. Plenty of vodka and tales about the old days was their perfect afternoon. You became their gofer.'

'I'm an associate professor. Not some intelligence groupie.'

'A mixed bunch, as well, if those first names are any guide. KGB, GRU, a few of them with a stint at the Shikhany military research base. That's how it all fell into your lap, I'm guessing. After all, you're a British citizen, an academic. You keep a far lower profile than the GRU heavies that Moscow usually sends over. So that's why you did it.'

'Did what exactly?'

'Scarlet King had a notebook. You had the chance for a big break. Now you had a contact book of connections with former Russian spooks. You get the poison through them, take out Scarlet King, hunt down the notebook and job done. Medals all round.'

'That's absurd.'

Saul removed another file. He held it up. 'Your bank statements for the last eighteenth months. Your good lady wife has taken you to the cleaners, I see. Those debts alone make convincing evidence for a jury. Eye-popping sums.'

Max opened the file and glanced at the documents. Then, just as quickly, he shut it again. 'This will never get to court.'

'No?'

'If it did, then I'd demand to have my fifteen minutes of fame on the stand. And I'd tell the world all about who Scarlet King really was and why British intelligence actively collaborated with Nazi war criminals in a desperate attempt to boost the biological and chemical warfare programme at Porton Down. By the time the trial was over, you'd be playing security guards in Bhutan with half your pension gone for gross misconduct.'

Saul placed the files and the books and the DVD case back into his bag. Then, with a last flourish, he adjusted his tie. 'That's not how I see it.'

'Really?'

'Scarlet King was a senior member of British intelligence.'

'That much I'd gathered.'

'The trial would be held in camera. No press reporting allowed.'

'I know what in camera means.'

'A healthy woman in her mid-nineties. No chronic conditions apart from mild arthritis. Ladies and gentlemen of the jury, Dr Max Archer was a friend of dangerous Russian defectors with access to chemical and biological weapons.'

'So far, so circumstantial. You'll have to do better than that.'

'We know the defendant entered the victim's flat on the night of the murder. We know he failed to report the body. We know he then took a boat across the Channel in the company of an enemy intelligence officer. We know he was apprehended at the Simon Wiesenthal Centre in Paris attempting to steal a safety deposit box belonging to the victim.'

'Interesting. But not beyond reasonable doubt.'

Saul nodded. 'We also know the forensic evidence is clear. This man was in the victim's flat. This man's DNA was found on the victim's body. No one else. None of us need a PhD to decide these are not the actions of an innocent man.'

Max was silent. He breathed heavily. 'If the evidence is so compelling, then why not arrest me now? Why are the Security Service questioning me and not the Metropolitan Police?'

'Do you have a theory, doctor?'

'Yes,' he said. 'As a matter of fact, I do.'

40

It was one thing knowing the evidence in abstract; quite another seeing it typed up in those official files. Max wondered where Cleo was. He imagined her in some equally faceless room being quizzed by the woman posing as a consular official. Could he trust her? Or was he just the fall guy for them all?

The man listened patiently. Once Max was finished, he said, 'That's quite a claim. Do you have any evidence?'

Max indicated to the bag. 'That's the evidence. The files, the bank statements, the photographs. You saw me visiting Scarlet King and spotted the perfect opportunity.'

'MI5 doesn't frame British citizens for murder.'

'History tells us that MI5 does almost anything it wants. British citizens or not.'

'You should clearly check your sources more carefully.'

Max knew he had to play for time. 'The British government wanted rid of Scarlet King. Porton Down has supplies for just this kind of emergency. You kill her and then set me up to lead you to the notebook. Then you threaten me with a secret trial and a lifetime behind bars if I ever speak out. I'm muzzled, the secrets are buried, the world is none the wiser. All very tidy.'

'MI5 certainly doesn't murder its own citizens.'

'But that's the beauty of it. Scarlet King wasn't a British citizen. She was a fraud. The real Scarlet King died in Kenya on January the ninth, 1929. The woman you murdered was a Russian national called Anastasia Chekova. She was an enemy agent operating on British soil.'

'Thames House isn't Langley, Dr Archer. We don't have the Special Activities Division to call on when we want to greenlight a deniable black op. Try dealing with the real world. You've clearly read too many spy novels.'

'No, I think *you* have. I know how closely Five works with Hereford on the Executive Action work you're too chicken to do for yourselves. Slipping into an old lady's flat would be the work of minutes. They get a suitcase of cash; you get a result. A grey op at its finest.'

'You clearly have a vivid imagination. You're wasted in the world of academia.'

Max decided to press the point home. 'Then, I ask again, why haven't you arrested me?'

The man – Bilton, or whoever he really was – looked weary now, as if the charade had gone on long enough. 'Because the minute we hand you over to Dixon of Dock Green, you'll start no-commenting and we'll all be in the dark.'

'Your guards searched me and my bags. Did you find anything?'

'The search isn't complete.'

'What about at the Simon Wiesenthal Centre itself? I presume the staff have afforded you every courtesy. Have you found it there either?'

'A ground team is still looking.'

'If history is any guide, I'd say this entire misadventure was cooked up between you and a minister. The junior ones wouldn't have the right authority. This would have to be Cabinet level. The Home Secretary won't be very pleased when he finds out he looked the other way on extra-judicial killing on British soil and your lot still haven't even recovered the bounty. Worst of all worlds.'

The man was tetchy now. 'Tell us where the notebook is and we can talk.'

'So my thesis was right then? You did kill her.'

'I didn't say that.'

'Let me guess. I tell you where the notebook is and Scarlet King suddenly becomes an old lady who died of natural causes.'

'I'm offering you a ladder and a way to climb out of your current hole. You'd be well advised to take it.'

Max maintained eye contact. For the first time in years, he felt fully alive. There was something magnetic about trying to outwit an opponent, using every ounce of intelligence to create a real-world effect. Despite the danger – the files, the threat of prosecution, the unholy tangle of his life – Max didn't regret what had happened. He would still take that taxi to Holland Park and answer the card from Scarlet King. This is what he should have been doing all his life. Not an academic; but a spy.

'Fine,' he said. 'I'll tell you where the notebook is hidden on one condition.'

The man waited. 'Which is?'

41

Stephanie Porter had never seen anything like it. She was used to interrogations in the wilds of Bagram or Baghdad. The suspects were almost always young men. There was the sweltering heat and the constant delay of translation. The answers were often little more than abusive grunts. Then Stephanie would produce her final option, invoking the Americans, tea towels, water bottles and simulated drowning. That always got them talking.

She watched both interrogations repeatedly on the monitor. Alpha was the more voluble, Beta more taciturn. The woman stonewalled each question and demanded to speak to the Israeli embassy. Mossad, Scarlet King, Operation Hercules, the Increment, grey ops – this was the grubby, under-the-counter knowledge that ended careers. Stephanie imagined being exiled to Uzbekistan or told to set up a new SIS Sub-station in Antarctica. She pretended to hear none of it and wondered again whether to contact Vauxhall Cross.

The searches continued throughout the rest of the day. Saul went through every item in the bags, searched each pocket. Both suspects were given spare sets of clothes. Saul searched through their jackets, jeans and shoes with similar results.

When both suspects were changed and locked in their rooms, Saul ordered Stephanie to accompany him to the Simon Wiesenthal Centre. Charlotte, one of the MI5 fast-trackers, was finalizing the scene search. They checked camera footage inside the building and were given a guided tour of the basement archives and the safety deposit boxes. Reuben, the usual guide, was off sick. Saul mustered schoolboy French but made little headway. They were shown to the safety deposit box belonging to Scarlet King and found it empty with no recent trace of ever having been used.

The basement archive itself wasn't covered by CCTV, only the main entrance and hallways. Saul and Stephanie studied the available footage. Here comes Max Archer and Cleo Watson with rucksacks. Ten minutes later, they emerge from the archive to be greeted by Charlotte posing as a consular assistant. Both still have rucksacks. There is no obvious bulge or protrusion from either rucksack or other items of clothing. If they have taken the notebook before leaving the archive, where have they hidden it? How can the contents of a safety deposit box simply vanish into thin air? Or was this another decoy location too?

Saul ordered a full search of the embassy vehicle used to transfer both suspects. Stephanie looked everywhere, but there were no signs of tampering. No, she was sure the notebook couldn't have gone missing during the drive back.

At the embassy, meanwhile, the Beta target continued her strident demands to contact the Israeli embassy, claiming it was her right as an Israeli national. Stephanie posed a hypothetical to a JIC legal adviser in London, all the facts suitably disguised, before Saul bowed to the inevitable and told her to inform the defence attaché – in reality the Head of Station for Mossad – at 3 Rue Rabelais, the Israeli embassy, that a citizen with joint British-Israeli nationality was currently being questioned and demanding the right to further consular assistance.

Two hours later, Stephanie was in conference with a Second Secretary from the Israeli embassy who supposedly ran the political desk. After the Second Secretary left, Stephanie found Saul in the embassy gardens. She handed him a cigarette and a cup of builder's tea and watched a yawn extend across the full length of his face.

'What happens now?' she said.

'That depends.'

'On what?'

'If you've beamed all this back to the desk jockeys in Vauxhall.'

'Silent as a nun. I promise.'

'I'm still missing something,' he said, blowing showily on his tea. 'Cleo Watson trained with Mossad. She's worked under natural cover. She knows how to do a bit of abracadabra. But she doesn't get the cavalry charging in behind her when things go wrong. She's on her own. That's the deal. That's what she signed up for.'

'Unless the notebook was never really there.'

'Why else come here? Why not just stay in England?'

'Alpha and Beta are both under 24/7 surveillance. Even Mossad can't defy the laws of physics.'

'You sure of that?' Saul risked a first sip of his

tea, wincing at the heat. 'They finally get hold of the product, we surprise them and, somehow, the product goes missing in between their return to the embassy and our searches.'

'What does the Home Secretary say?'

'He wants to avoid getting punishment beatings from Number 10. Ideally he wants the entire thing to go away.'

'Which means you have to let Cleo Watson go.'

'Only if she chooses to renounce her British passport.'

'Israeli spy breaks EU immigration rules with the assistance of top MI5 officer. Not exactly the Home Secretary's dream headline.'

Saul looked pained. His brow furrowed. His hair was flecked with grey and spilled into his face now. The coppery skin turned puce. 'You're the field operative,' he said. 'I'm just the jumped-up police-man. What am I not seeing here? What sort of tradecraft could pull this off?'

'I'm just the glorified hostess, remember. Or words to that effect.'

Saul smiled. 'I looked at your file.'

'Uh-huh?'

'Six months interrogating suspects at Bagram. Not much champagne there.'

'Perhaps the Beta target knew your focus would be on her. She distracts your attention while the Alpha target spirits the notebook to safety. After all, he's their secret weapon. Without him to verify it, the notebook has no propaganda value at all.'

'That's another thing,' said Saul.

'Another what?'

'Why him? Of all the academics Scarlet King could have chosen, why go for a relatively junior associate professor with no field experience?' Saul took another large gulp of tea. 'What?'

'You don't want my advice.'

'Then why am I asking for it?'

'Call off the hunt. Admit defeat. Shush the whole thing up, pray that the notebook – wherever the damn thing is – never sees the light of day and keep your hands clean on this one. You must be near retirement?'

'It's that obvious?'

'Steer clear, repatriate Archer and Watson on the next flight to London and spin the Home Secretary a tale about how you expertly defused a serious political scandal. Force the DG to put in a call to Tel Aviv and read them the riot act if the notebook is made public. You still get that semi-decent pension and a few nice budget holidays.'

'Are you trying to save my career or yours?'

'Both.'

Saul admired the gardens. He appeared deep in contemplation: about his life, his future, that elusive promise of freedom and the siren call of retirement. Then Stephanie saw a flicker of something in his eyes.

'What is it?'

Saul looked towards the compound again. 'A Hail Mary.'

42

Max wondered if he should be making notes. The rollcall of firsts was building: exfil (check); trade-craft (check); interrogation (check). The next round might be less glamorous. First time in court; first time accused; first night in jail. He had spent nearly two decades trying to get into the head of a spy. This, no doubt, was as close as he would ever get.

He got up from the bed and took another walk around the room. The embassy room was old and scrappier than the downstairs. The paintwork was chipped, the mattress sprung. Mould riddled the washbasin and the rest of the en-suite bathroom was twenty years out of date.

Relics from the embassy art collection covered the main bedroom. Anglo-French collisions like Waterloo and Trafalgar had been tactfully over-looked. Instead, there were so-so watercolours of Windsor and Buckingham Palace, even a piece of modern art nodding to the Bayeux tapestry. Max stood in front of it. He was always better with the written word, forever ashamed of his philistine preference for spy fare. Give him a re-run of *The Eagle Has Landed* or the glories of *Where Eagles Dare*. The painting defeated him. He returned to the bed. He tried to steady his heart rate.

He ran through everything again. He could picture

them in the basement archive. Reuben mentioned the visitors upstairs. The safety deposit box lay there with the notebook, the Order of Lenin medal, the birth certificate, the photograph album and that final piece of paper with the Downing Street crest. Cleo had an instinct for these things. They'd had mere seconds to decide.

Max could only hope that the plan worked.

His mobile was gone as was his work laptop. He imagined the screeds from Kessler about his unauthorized absence. The lack of office hours, the inbox of unanswered emails. Max wondered if he'd already been sacked and would only hear about it later. A conviction in a French court for illegal entry was hardly going to help matters, nor an anonymous phone call summoning the Vice-Chancellor to a meeting at King Charles Street.

Max had been so wrapped up in the drama of the last twenty-four hours that day-to-day concerns had melted away. But they consumed him now. The job was the only way of paying rent. He had no savings, only debts. The flat in Fulham was rented at mates' rates from one of his old Cambridge friends who'd made a fortune in private equity. The job, the flat – all of it could unwind very quickly. Moving out of London narrowed things further. The regional red-bricks wanted economic historians, social historians, gender historians – anything other than intelligence specialists fixated on posh white men in private members' clubs. The LSE was one of the few places where he was still employable. Lose that and a career teaching GCSE history and the six wives of Henry the Eighth beckoned.

He was about to search again for any reading material – book, magazine, cereal packet, anything would do – when there was a loud knock on the bedroom door. It would be Bilton again, the diplomat-spy, probably armed with a six-pack and trying to charm Max into submission. That was another time-honoured spy technique. The interrogator was hostile one moment and best friend the next. Prefect, then priest. Judge turned BFF.

Max stood up. He prepared himself. He couldn't cave in. He would sort the job when back in London. For now, he had to follow the strategy they'd agreed on. Cleo knew what she was doing, or at least he hoped she did.

Max tucked in his shirt. He coughed, walked to the door and opened it, ready for Bilton with a disarming smile and a look of unruffled calm. Except it wasn't Bilton.

'Hello, Max.'

It was the last person on earth he expected.

43

Max had that rabbits-in-a-headlight look, as he always did when startled. He was a poor actor, too, trying to bury it before she noticed. That was the thing with falling in love in your early twenties and falling out of it so many years later. You knew the history of those personal foibles, the fossil record of each one. Nothing was truly secret. Well, almost nothing.

It took a moment for him to speak. Then it was a whisper, stuttering out the words, 'I don't understand.'

She walked inside and closed the door. Max looked even more bewildered now. She watched him closely. His eyes reappraised her – the first date, the engagement, the wedding itself, assorted anniversaries.

Max Archer, poor thing, was having his entire personal history rewritten.

'No,' he said, eventually. He was sitting on the bed again now, kneading his head with his hands. 'No, this can't be happening. This can't be bloody happening.'

Emma had always imagined this moment. She would wake up, turn on the bedroom light and tell him. The words spilling out: legal adviser, three years, Security Service, Thames House, Treasury cover, paperwork mostly, rather dull. But, as the years went on, it became progressively harder. The secret about those early years snowballed until its very existence threatened everything. Fate, of course, had already seen to that.

Max was up again now, still kneading his head, the look of surprise turning into one of hate. 'This isn't possible. You're one of them. All this time and you're one of . . .'

'I think you should sit down, Max. Honestly, just try and relax.'

'Relax?'

'It's been a long journey. They called me very late last night. I barely had time to pack a bag.'

'It was you.'

'What was me?'

'At the party. You gave the watch to Oliver to give to me.'

There was no point denying it. 'You were always obsessed with that damn thing. The Great Escape, living up to the family name. One piece of metal was more important than the rest of life. Anyway, Oliver's been out of the game for years and Thames House don't air their dirty laundry to a former SIS NOC. You're an intelligence historian, Max. You of all people should know that.'

'How could you?'

'I asked Oliver to pass it on. It was easier all round.'

'It's not even the original, is it?'

Emma looked mildly guilty now. 'Hanslope do a good line in fakes. It is a Rolex 3525 Oyster chronograph. Just not *the* 3525 Oyster chronograph.'

Max felt even stupider now. He conceded defeat

and sat on the bed again. He rocked slightly, his mind still whirring. 'All this time?'

'Not exactly.'

'What does that mean?'

'I always meant to tell you.'

'You're an eloquent woman, Ems, I think you could have found the words.'

'I was thinking of you.'

Max let out a strangled snort of disbelief. 'How kind of you. You lied to me throughout our entire marriage. But, no, I completely get it. It was all for my benefit.'

'What else was I supposed to do?'

'I can't believe you're even asking that question.'

'If it's any consolation, the decision wasn't entirely mine. Oliver was insistent. He thought the knowledge would break you and break us. For what it's worth, I think he was right.'

Max looked up. 'Oliver?'

'Who else? We were broke, Max. You couldn't get a job. We had nowhere to live. I needed something to keep food on the table.'

'I see. Why does it feel like you're blaming me?'

'I'm not blaming anyone. Oliver knew some of his colleagues were looking for a lawyer. The pay was pretty good, the hours were fine, and it enabled you to keep on applying for the dream academic job. I did a few years with the government and then moved to the City.'

'I bet you and Oliver must have had a decent laugh about it.'

'It wasn't like that.'

'No, what was it like?'

Emma took a deep breath. 'This was always your problem, Max. You created some insane worldview where life could never be complete because you failed to become a spy. Everything else was second best.'

'That's not true.'

'Me, our marriage, your career, the books you wrote, the students you taught. It was all a let-down because it wasn't the life you dreamed of.'

'Rubbish.'

'You defined yourself by one event. You never moved past it. Oliver saw that. I saw it. You're the only idiot who couldn't.'

Max was silent. The shock was fading. But he wasn't stupid. He was naïve at times, idealistic even. But he felt the blow land.

'MI5 then,' he said.

'A few years on a government scheme after graduating. Just to pay the bills when we got married and moved back.'

'Why use the Treasury as cover rather than MoD?'

'MoD is a spy's cover. For lawyers, a secular Whitehall department allowed us back into normal work if the secret world lost its appeal. Which it soon did. Believe me.'

'Which section?'

'Let's not do this.'

'No. You've lied to me for twenty years. I think I'm owed this much. Which section?'

'I was a government legal adviser, Max. I went wherever I was sent. Counterintelligence, counter-terrorism, counter-espionage – it's not like I got to pick and choose.'

'What grade?'

'You know I can't tell you that.'

'Is that how you know Bilton?'

Emma looked confused, then remembered. 'Yes.'

'What's his real name?'

'I also can't tell you that.'

'He's senior, though, yes? Assistant Director. Possibly even Deputy DG?'

'See my previous answer.'

'Were you always spying on me?'

'I worked for the government for three years. Why would I possibly be spying on my own husband?'

'What was it? Occasional peek at my inbox, password for my encrypted email, quick back door into my laptop? Make sure I wasn't causing trouble?'

Emma knew she had to lie. 'British intelligence doesn't spy on ordinary citizens. That requires specific authorization by the Home Secretary or Foreign Secretary.'

'You didn't have to spy though. You just had to keep your eyes open. You had access to everything of mine already. Help MI5 keep tabs on a nosy intelligence historian.'

'Yeah, you're right. Forget the terrorists, the drug kingpins, the arms dealers. The people MI5 are *really* after are bitter academics who can't get a promotion.'

'Wow.'

'I'm sorry. That sounded harsher than I meant.'

'What about moving into the private sector?'

'That was genuine.'

'Genuine as in true, or genuine as natural cover?'

'I can't talk about operational details.'

444

Max thumped his forehead, a comical version of stupidity. 'Silly Max. Of course.'

'Don't be like that.'

Max laughed humourlessly. 'If it was really only three years, why are you here now? Why fly all the way to Paris?'

'Part of the exit deal,' she said. 'Extramural work as and when the Service needs a favour. Rare, but useful.'

'So that's what I am to you, Ems?'

'Max –'

'Just a piece of extramural work? A favour for your old bosses? Just another asset who needs to be brought in line?'

'Of course not.'

'Then why are you here?'

Emma sighed. 'Because, Max, you're about to make the biggest mistake of your life.'

Saul adjusted the headphones. He turned the volume up a fraction. The listening station was hidden in the bowels of the embassy. The bugs had been planted earlier, concealed in everything from bookcases and paintings to lamps. Saul had requested both an audio and visual feed, providing back-up should one of them conk out.

'Is that true?' Stephanie said, seated beside him.

'Most of it.'

'She was one of yours back in the day?'

'Entry level graduate work mostly. A lawyer not a spook.'

'How much does she know about the notebook?'

'Enough to be convincing.'

445

'And if this doesn't work?'

Saul ignored the question. He fiddled with the headphones again and concentrated more intensely on the monitor. It was like watching Spurs. The fancy footwork, the extravagant play, and yet still one nil down at half-time. He had a call with the Home Secretary in twenty minutes. They must have something by then.

'Zoom in on camera four.'

44

Max felt disorientated. He was the intelligence guru. Emma was the one who hated that world. She yawned every time he droned on about it, refused to entertain spy movies or thrillers in any form, bingeing on competitive cooking formats instead. That had been their identity as a couple. The nerdish flair meeting lawyerly coolness.

And yet, now, it was gone. Every yawn meant something different. His expertise was second-hand. She had spent their marriage humouring him, pretending, living her cover, laughing off her own achievements with jokes about the excitement of tax law and IR35s. All that time, all those car rides home, she'd denied a part of herself to make the marriage work. Someday, he knew, that simple truth would haunt him. Now he was too blindsided to care.

He said, 'What have they told you?'

'That my ex-husband is having a mid-life crisis of truly epic proportions.'

'How so?'

'Something about going to jail because of an old woman and a seventy-year-old notebook.'

'You're worried that might hurt your image?'

She laughed despairingly. 'I'm worried they'll have a quiet word to the American embassy and stop my visa going through, yes. After they put you in Belmarsh for the next forty years.'

'Well, there are some things even Cristiano can't buy.'

'Is it true?'

Max felt a stab of nausea around his stomach. It wasn't meant to be like this. Emma was meant to see the news in the *New York Times* or in *Vanity Fair* or MailOnline. This wasn't victory; this was ritual humiliation.

After all, that was the point of this. It was why people went into politics, took to the stage, became TV presenters, wrote newspaper columns, published vanity novels – they wanted that moment of revelation. When Mary Jane Watson discovers Peter Parker is Spiderman or Lois Lane recognizes Clark Kent as Superman. It was childish and pathetic. But true.

'Yes,' he said.

'Max . . .'

And so he told her. About Scarlet King, the memoir, his collaboration, her death, his escape with Cleo. It sounded even more outlandish now.

Emma absorbed it like a therapist dealing with a difficult patient. She said, 'What happened to the material from the safety deposit box? Tell them that and they'll let you go.'

'Oh no they won't.'

'They can't keep you here without charging you with something.'

'I've read the first two sections of the memoir already. Scarlet had them scanned and printed. I know too much.'

'I'm telling you this as a lawyer, Max.'

Another classic line. One he wouldn't miss. 'They can't risk the French charging me with flouting immigration laws, in case I start blabbing to the DGSI in exchange for some kind of immunity deal.'

'You don't know that.'

'They'll fly me back to Britain, hammer me with the OSA charges and, if they feel like it, murder or manslaughter. I rot in jail for the next thirty years. The memoir is forgotten. They win. I'm just a low-grade Wikipedia entry.'

'They told me you'd asked for a deal?'

Ah, yes. His final demand. It was petty, stupid even. But he couldn't help it. 'I'm sorry. But I can't discuss operational details.'

'I can't help you if you refuse to help yourself.'

'You want a visa to America to start a new life. I'm the only thing standing in your way. Help isn't the word for it.'

'Then what is?'

'You're the lawyer and the former spook. You should know.'

'The ball's in your court, Max. They won't give you a deal. There's no precedent for it. British law doesn't do immunity deals or plea-bargains. This isn't an end of season double-episode of *The West Wing*.'

Max stood up. He glanced round the room, trying to aim for the nearest bug. It was the moment he'd been waiting for. The last card he had. 'You're wrong.'

'I've spent two decades as a lawyer. Fairly sure I'm not.'

449

'It's why everyone should study history.'

Emma rolled her eyes. 'You're unbelievable.'

Max continued regardless. 'On the twenty-third of April, 1964, Sir Anthony Blunt, Surveyor of the Queen's Pictures, confessed to MI5 that he'd been a double agent for the Soviet Union. He admitted being the Fourth Man.'

'This is the real world, Max. This isn't a seminar.'

'The Home Secretary granted him full immunity from prosecution and kept the secret for the next fifteen years.'

'So what?'

'The point of studying the past is to understand the present.'

Emma looked confused. 'You're not making any sense.'

'Those are my terms.'

'What are?'

'Call the Home Secretary, Ems. Tell him I want what Blunt got,' he said. 'Give me full immunity and then I'll talk.'

45

The catalogue of errors started early. If the middle child hadn't been ill; if Mrs H hadn't been absent on a long-planned work trip in Rome; if their usual nanny – a charming Parisian twenty-something called Claudette – hadn't been on honeymoon and the agency's phone lines hadn't been down; and if every living grandparent hadn't been either incapacitated or conveniently refusing to answer their mobiles – then the Rt Hon Lucas Harper MP, Secretary of State for the Home Department, wouldn't have been standing in his kitchen juggling calls about drug smuggling and potential terrorist attacks while brewing a Lemsip and trying to remember the family password for Disney+. The call would have been landline rather than mobile, answered by an adviser and not the principal. It would have been bogged down in the labyrinth of his private office. The request would have been delayed. History would have branched off on to another course entirely.

The call from the Paris embassy came just after 2 p.m. Saul was brief. At that very moment the middle child was complaining about the beans on toast that Lucas had served up for lunch and his private office were trying to contact him regarding an urgent call from the Deputy Prime Minister.

Lucas eventually lost patience. 'Saul, please say you're kidding me.'

'With respect, Minister, this operation is being kept on a deniable footing. Unless we widen the distribution list, I'm not sure what other options we have.'

Lucas considered. Thames House was leakier than many Whitehall departments. Number 10 would get jumpy and Lucas would take the political hit. He was cornered.

'How would it work?'

'Precedence, mainly. The AG's office don't want this to go to trial and, frankly, the courts are full enough as it is. Dust down the Blunt deal in exchange for his co-operation.'

'Or?'

'The Israelis get hold of the material, if they don't already have it, and a full-blown propaganda war emerges.'

Lucas heard the sound of a tray being dropped and a plate tumbling on to the cream carpet in the living room. He imagined his wife's face. 'The Blunt deal. As in –'

'Sir Anthony Blunt. Surveyor of the Queen's Pictures. The Cambridge Five Blunt.'

'How did you not anticipate this?'

'I've never been up against an intelligence historian before.'

'And the Blunt deal was authorized personally by the Home Secretary?'

'Yes. There's also one other thing regarding the woman. A little suggestion.'

'Yes?'

'One thought to make the problem go away.'

Lucas listened to Saul's proposal. He tried to retain some equanimity. He hated this job. The spies and civil servants made the real decisions; he just got the blame for their mistakes. The call ended. Lucas spent the next twenty minutes with a bottle of Dettol and a cloth wiping the living room carpet. Finally, he conceded to the middle child's demands for a Deliveroo. He ordered burger and chips for two.

By four-thirty he was speaking to the Director of Public Prosecutions via a secure line installed at 102 Petty France, Westminster, and setting out the need to resurrect the Blunt deal for covert use in an MI5 operation currently underway at the British embassy in Paris. Next, he spoke with the Permanent Secretary at the Home Office regarding Saul Northcliffe's second proposal.

The Permanent Secretary sounded sceptical. There was her usual teeth-sucking gasp of disapproval. 'And this woman is a dual citizen of Britain and Israel?'

'Yes.'

'Well, I suppose it's theoretically possible.'

'I need more than theory, Isabel. This needs to be done within the next few hours.'

'We open ourselves up to legal action. We'd have to demonstrate reasonable cause.'

'I think committing espionage for a foreign power while on British territory more than qualifies, don't you?'

'Leave it with me, Minister. I'll make some calls.'

By five-thirty Lucas was heading towards Highgate to pick up the eldest child and youngest child from orchestra practice. For all personal errands he still had to navigate the traffic himself, even if he did have an armed member of the Met sitting beside him. At least it helped keep the kids quiet.

By eight-thirty, any further evidence of lunchtime chips had been bleached from the living room carpet and the Charlie Bigham ready-meals gorged on. Homework was completed and the extra thirty minutes of evening telly – a customary bribe for good behaviour – duly enjoyed. Teeth were brushed. A bedtime story was recited to child number three. Then lights out.

The only subsequent disturbance was the sound of Lucas's ministerial red box being couriered to the house and the bell ringing loudly. Eldest child used the interruption as an excuse to hover around the TV in the living room on the unlikely pretext of needing water.

Forty minutes, and several pocket money-related threats later, Lucas sat at his kitchen table with a gallon of black coffee while going through the contents of the red box. The first item was from the Crown Prosecution Service. It outlined the terms of the Blunt immunity deal and sought sign-off from the Home Secretary and Attorney General. The second item was from the Permanent Secretary at Marsham Street regarding the decision to strip 'Miss Cleo Watson' of her British citizenship for committing espionage activities for a foreign power.

By midnight, Lucas took a final call from Saul Northcliffe confirming his requests had been granted. He had just reached his bedroom and slid beneath the bedclothes, careful not to wake the kids, when he touched his forehead and felt it burning. The middle child was ill and now so was he.

Lucas blamed Saul.

46

The news came through just after 1 a.m. By five-thirty Cleo Watson was informed that her British citizenship had been stripped following her admission of spying for a foreign power and she was being transferred into the care of a consular official from the Israeli embassy. By six forty-five, Max Archer was presented with the immunity deal drafted by the Crown Prosecution Service and approved by the Director of Public Prosecutions, the Attorney General and the Home Secretary.

'You understand,' said Saul, 'that signing the immunity deal is a direct admission of guilt regarding offences committed under the Official Secrets Act and that failure to comply with the exact wording of the agreement renders it null and void.'

Max Archer nodded. 'Yes.'

'We've kept our side of the bargain,' said Saul, 'and now it's time for you to do the same.'

Embassies were like old country houses, Saul often thought. There was the rattle of housekeepers, kitchen maids rising at ungodly hours, lawnmowers strafing the gardens outside. Breakfast was being prepared downstairs. He should have joined the Foreign Office. A knighthood, deluxe ambassadorial quarters, working lunches, cocktail parties, five-course dinners – yes, that was his big career mistake.

Max hesitated. The pen hovered over the page. 'You won't be able to bury the truth forever, you know.'

'We can certainly give it a try.'

'You're not even slightly curious?'

'About what?'

'Scarlet King. Operation Hercules. Anastasia Chekova. You're really content to see the truth suppressed?'

'This isn't a tutorial, Dr Archer. And I'm not one of your students.'

'No, but you are an MI5 officer who enjoys getting one over on your rivals across the river. That notebook is a loaded gun. Surely it's tempting to pull the trigger.'

Saul had underestimated Max Archer. The psychological profile suggested a mid-career academic passed over for a chair of his own and struggling to revive the promise of his early years. His wife had divorced him; his father outshone him. But there was a tungsten quality to him nonetheless. He was accused of involvement in Scarlet King's death. He had gone on the run. And he'd been apprehended by British intelligence and subjected to mind games and questioning, including being doorstepped by his ex-wife.

Yet, somehow, he still looked composed.

Saul had seen similar pressure break other assets. Seasoned fieldmen often cracked when the physical challenge became mental. But Max Archer kept his self-control. He was treating this like an enemy interrogation, Saul realized, refusing to show weakness. He thought back to Max's application for IONEC and his failure to get through the final stage. It still bugged him. Dr Max Archer looked less like an academic and more like a spy with every passing moment. Fate was a curious thing.

'Where is Emma?'

'She flew back to London on a diplomatic flight. Her role here was over.'

'Was all that true?'

Saul thought about playing ignorant. 'She was seconded from the Government Legal Department to work as a Legal Adviser for the Security Service in the early 2000s.'

'She was never a spy?'

'She was a legal eagle, far more useful than most spies. No, she wasn't operational, if that's what you mean. A desk job, nothing more.'

'And you can't touch her after this. The immunity deal takes her out of the equation too. No more after-the-fact agreements or exit terms. She's rid of you all now. We're agreed on that?'

'A last attempt at chivalry?'

'Just answer my question.'

'That really depends on you. Tell us where the notebook is and the other items from that safety deposit box and we can consider the matter closed. Lie to us again and the immunity deal is tomorrow's fish and chip paper.'

'What about Scarlet King's death?'

'It's still being investigated. If you fulfil your obligations as described in this document, it's possible the coroner will find it occurred via natural causes and merits no further investigation.'

457

'Is that what usually happens when MI5 clean up after themselves?'

'You're the intelligence historian, Dr Archer. You know better than me.'

Max looked down at the document again. He'd read through every clause three times, pausing over each line with professorial slowness. 'I need my own lawyer to look over this.'

'She already did. Your ex-wife approved every word. The DPP put a deadline on it. Unless it's returned to them within the next twenty minutes then it will expire.'

'How do I know you're not bluffing?'

'You don't.'

'And once I've signed?'

'We'll act on your information. Providing it's correct, we'll smooth things over with the French regarding the border violation and then taxi you back to London courtesy of Her Majesty's diplomatic service. After that, you'll be free to continue your life and career.'

Max examined one particular clause. His eyes paused over the last paragraph. 'As long as I never again refer to the existence or activities of Scarlet King or the notebook?'

'Yes.' Saul looked at his watch. 'The DPP is waiting for it and the embassy wi-fi can be temperamental. Waste any more time and I can't guarantee we'll meet the deadline.'

Max looked around the interview room. He took a final moment to consider his options. 'Who will this go to?'

'We scan a copy back to Marsham Street, the CPS

and the Attorney General's Office. They acknowledge receipt and this piece of paper gets locked away in a drawer with exemption from the thirty-year rule and strict instructions never to be released into the National Archives.'

Max nodded. 'I see.'

Saul felt unusually nervous. This was all his doing: he persuaded the Home Secretary to push for the immunity agreement; he advocated stripping Cleo Watson of her British citizenship; he'd led a private operation on French soil without the direct authorization of the Director-General. Yes, this was his Waterloo. His endgame. If Dr Max Archer, Associate Professor of Intelligence History at the London School of Economics, played more mind games now then Saul would lose everything.

He prepared himself and stared at Max. It all depended on the next few seconds. 'Where is the notebook?'

Max looked pensive. He took a deep breath. He signed his name at the bottom of the page and handed it back.

Then, at last, he began to speak.

The Scarlet Papers
2010

2010
The Return

She saw him after the interval. He had just arrived, which was always a cause for concern. People sometimes walked out of theatres and concerts. Very few walked in halfway through. He didn't look sweaty or rushed, which was the second give-away. The man was tall and cadaverous with a brush of ash-blond hair and a studious, almost angular bone structure. He had no girlfriend, wife or partner and sat on the end of the row behind her. He didn't make much noise, only clapping politely at the end.

She had invited this upon herself, she supposed. Her fortnightly trips to the Royal Court Theatre in Sloane Square, within walking distance of her flat on Beaufort Street, were her only concession to habit. She had no landline and existed solely on burner pay-as-you-go mobiles. She changed her locks every six months and, even now, always positioned a hair in the doorframe, just as she did in Vienna after the war. She paid in cash, rarely by card, and avoided using the same ATM machine too often. Her council tax was paid by cheque, as were other utility bills. She had no online presence, social media profiles or digital subscriptions of any kind. She walked to the newsagent most mornings to buy the papers, counting out the coins and ana-lysing the paper receipt. She was untraceable. The only secrets left were locked in the safe under her bed and accessible by retinal scan. Otherwise, she was off-the-grid entirely.

The play ended and the literati shuffled from the theatre. Scarlet always felt out of place here. Everyone else looked like polished investment bankers. They had entourages with them, usually friends and family, sometimes clients or guests. She was alone. Some of the theatre staff knew her by sight now and nodded. She nodded back. They stood at a respectful distance and never treated her like an old lady. She admired that.

Scarlet walked through the front entrance and blinked at the lights of Sloane Square and the glassy bulk of Peter Jones opposite. The walk down had exhausted her. She should call a cab. But weakness was alien to her. No, she had to walk it now. It might kill her but, then again, something had to. Taking a tumble would beat staring gormlessly at a care home wall. She shivered again at the mere idea. To breathe one's last while staring at the lights and glitter of Chelsea and the King's Road. There were far worse ways to go.

She was about to start, when there was the tap of brogues on the pavement and a male voice behind her: 'Miss King.'

She had been right, then. Seven decades of practice, and she could still spot a spook at fifty paces. Her antennae mercifully intact. She turned now and looked at the man behind her. He suited the darkness better, as if that was his natural habitat. He had both hands lodged squarely in the pockets of a dark formal coat. He must be late thirties,

Scarlet guessed, but with a face that could pass for a decade older. He was handsome in a crooked way, the face of a scholar, angular like a mathematician or a poet.

'That depends who's asking,' she said.

The man approached, careful not to broadcast the next part too loudly. 'Robert,' he said, reaching out a hand. 'The Office asked me to pay you a visit.'

Yes, it was always the Office now. She preferred the Friends or the Firm, but time moved on. The former was probably deemed too clubby, the latter too antiquated. The world had professionalized, yoked under the tyranny of HR, the old-timers of Personnel now ruling the world. The Office it was. No more drinks trollies, expense accounts, two-bottle lunches or routine board appointments in the City. Life was duller somehow.

'Did they indeed? And what office would that be exactly?'

'The night's still young. Can I buy you a drink? I've booked a table for two at Colbert if the mood takes you.'

'How very forward of you.'

'The Chief asked me to roll out the red carpet.'

'Name-dropping too. Am I on the naughty step this time?'

Robert smiled. 'Just a welfare catch-up call,' he said. 'Nothing more.'

There was no last name, of course. Despite being retired, she still kept an ear open for decent Service gossip, especially concerning her old fiefdoms. He was probably one of her successors in Section V, the master of all things counterintelligence and counter-espionage. Not that it was still called Section V. It had some meandering title, like a bottled goods firm. Even the new SIS building at Vauxhall Cross looked like a children's theme park. Legoland, apparently. God preserve us.

'Shall we?'

It was over two decades since she'd left Century House. She'd waited for this moment ever since, wondering if death would take her first. She'd often thought about the knock on the door, police officers outside the flat building; or, like this, sneaking up on her, caught unawares.

A welfare call.

Did they have surveillance on her already? Was this the final part of a long operation she hadn't noticed? Was this really the moment?

It was nearly seventy years since her first SIS operation and yet safety still eluded her.

'Of course,' she said, smiling wearily. 'Lead the way, young man.'

2010
Robert

The restaurant was shedding its dinner crowd. They sat at a corner table, well out of earshot of other diners. Robert ordered a strong coffee, Scarlet a mint tea. To avoid seeming cheap, Robert added a mousse au chocolat and proceeded to pick at it, almost willing himself to take a proper bite. No wonder he stayed so thin.

'I presume welfare didn't send you to check on my dietary habits,' said Scarlet, taking a first sip of mint tea. 'Or to sample my small talk.'

Robert gave up on the chocolate mousse and pushed the bowl away. He wiped his lips with a napkin. 'No.'

'Knowing your tricks, the Office will already have a full overview of my financial situation and investments.'

'Everything seems in order.'

'Does the Chief want to check I'm not talking out of turn or joining the local history group? I've written a bit of bad poetry, admittedly, but that hardly calls for a personal visit from the Office ratcatcher now, does it?'

Robert concentrated on the coffee instead. 'There's a situation,' he said. 'Quite a delicate one as it happens.'

Relief was sharp. It nipped at her body. No, it was always a silly idea. They wouldn't send someone this young to arrest her. It would be one of the old guard. The Firm would do it gently: dispatch a former comrade, ply her with wine, tease out a confession and then swear her to eternal silence. They didn't offer mint tea and chocolate mousse. Well, not in her day.

'What sort of situation? Anything I might find in the newspapers?'

'I'm afraid not. This is too delicate even for the JIC at this point. You're still the most experienced Kremlinologist the Office has ever had and, well, truthfully HMG needs a helping hand. There's really no one else to turn to.'

'You carefully sidestepped my question.'

'I hoped you might not notice.'

'I'm elderly, dear, not stupid.'

'It involves your old stamping ground. And some of your former acquaintances. The Chief wants to brief you in full tomorrow. He's sending a car at nine a.m.'

'Do I get any choice in the matter?'

'Would you like to decline?'

'What exactly would I be declining?'

Robert took a gulp of black coffee. 'It's nothing trivial, if that's what you're worried about. It's big. One of a kind. The Chief has asked for you personally.'

'He knows how old I am?'

'He has the file.'

'And what do you know about me?'

'I've also read the file.'

'Then you'll know I was the one who prepared and published the Mitrokhin Archive in the nineties.

I helped reveal the names of every surviving KGB spy in Britain and beyond. Let's just say I'm not exactly guest of honour at the Kremlin these days.'

'This wouldn't involve the Kremlin. At least not directly.'

'Then who would it involve?'

Robert took out his wallet. He signalled for the bill. 'The Chief can give you the running order when you speak to him tomorrow. I'm just the messenger.'

Scarlet saw the half-eaten plate of chocolate mousse. She picked up a spoon and took a mouthful. She allowed herself treats now and again. Death was funny like that. It lingered like an hourglass, grains of sand slipping through with unstoppable momentum. Pleasures must be seized, opportunities taken. The bill arrived. Robert paid. They emerged again into the greyish evening just as the waiters began shutting up. Robert called for a taxi.

'I'm quite capable of walking,' she said.

'The Office still has its uses.'

'Bribing me already?'

'Naturally. Tomorrow at nine, Miss King. Grey Mercedes with an S reg. The parole is Ottawa.'

'Duly noted. And the designation?'

'Off-the-books,' said Robert. 'Moscow Rules all the way.'

'I see. Just like the old times then.'

'Yes.' Scarlet hesitated and Robert caught the expression. 'Is there something else?'

She wasn't sure whether to say it. The name lurked behind everything now. This could be her only chance. 'May I ask for a small favour, in return? Nothing major, just a name I'm searching for.'

Robert looked intrigued. 'Of course.'

'I want to trace someone. The child of an old acquaintance. Technically, I'm a godmother. But we've fallen out of touch.'

'Give me the name and I'll see what I can find.'

Scarlet repeated the name as casually as she could, hoping the slight uptick in her voice wasn't noticeable. Then a taxi stopped near the pavement. Robert slipped money through the window and asked for Beaufort Street. He opened the passenger door and helped Scarlet inside. There was a studious, old-fashioned courtesy to him, and Scarlet warmed to it. Robert shut the passenger door and then tapped on the top of the vehicle. The cab pulled away.

'One of yours, is he?' chirped the cabbie, indicating Robert on the pavement, the thin figure receding into the distance. 'Giving his old mum a night on the town?'

It took a moment for Scarlet to comprehend. Then she shook her head. 'No, just a friend,' she said.

She watched the world blitz past the window and felt a sudden cramp of intense, overpowering loneliness. Back at the flat, she poured a large whisky and then went to bed. Regret was for amateurs. There was work to do.

Tomorrow could still change everything.

2010
Carlton Gardens

The unmarked car arrived at Beaufort Street the next morning. Scarlet gave the correct parole and noticed the number plate. The car was from the SIS pool, the driver suitably anonymous in a dark supermarket suit. There were no earpieces or Glocks either. SIS preferred subtlety. The car would be decked out with enough weaponry to invade a small country, but there was no merit in display. Even now, some things were best kept in the shadows.

Scarlet had spent the night wondering where the meeting would take place. The Chief had a large Georgian manor in the country somewhere, blessed with plentiful acres and rambling, tussocky fields. But the driver wound his way through the familiar streets of central London. They stopped just off the Mall in Carlton Gardens. Scarlet noticed there was no welcoming party. This felt operational, rather than personal.

The memories hit her straight away. The card arriving at Baker Street signed by the 'FCO Co-ordinating Staff'; the panel of four Edwardian squires here with their toothbrush moustaches and country tweeds; the questions about her likelihood of marriage, her German language skills, a brief overview of her work with the Special Operations Executive. Then Arisaig House, learning the rudiments of tradecraft at the hands of a peppery sergeant major: secret writing, brush passes, dead letterboxes, book codes and agent-running. After that, she'd been sent to Vienna and Otto and Archie. She'd never returned to 3 Carlton Gardens since. It was like travelling back in time.

Robert waited for her inside. He took her coat and led her through to a large drawing room at the end of the corridor. The décor was different, of course, spruced up in modern shades of diluted blues and greenish greys. Seventy years ago, the house boasted royal reds and wood-panelling, somewhere between a minor royal palace and an officers' mess. Now it looked more like a school classroom.

Scarlet entered the long drawing room. The Chief stood by a pair of cream chairs facing each other. The long table at the end had gone, replaced by comfy-looking furnishings and upmarket coffee tables. Robert closed the door behind them. The Chief did his usual politician act, a peck on both cheeks and a waft of pricey aftershave. He was the new type of Service chief – Victorian breeding with barrow boy manners. Scarlet still preferred the old-school versions, speccy types with beady stares and library-like minds, the products of Bletchley and the seminar room.

Yes, in another life the current Chief would be Home Secretary or a gadfly backbencher, a rent-a-quote popping up on every major news channel before charming constituents at church tea parties and village fetes. Instead, he had rebuilt the Service after the disaster of Iraq, WMD and extraordinary rendition. He spoke the same language as the Cabinet, visited the same Pall Mall clubs, displayed the same chameleon-like ability to sniff the public mood and change accordingly. Scarlet had selected him for IONEC. In the end, she had only herself to blame.

The first twenty minutes were all smiles and bonhomie. Tea was poured, biscuits offered, bland questions asked about the drive, the play last night, what Scarlet was getting up to these days. She parried each one, wondering if she'd been too complacent. They were being curiously nice. What if they were coaxing her into an indiscretion? The Chief pausing, solemnly announcing that he'd spoken to the CPS, her last hope of freedom snuffed out. He was capable of that. He was a politician, after all. They knew how to charm and kill in the same breath.

Scarlet accepted the offer of more tea, then snared another chocolate biscuit. The Chief put down his cup and glanced at Robert. Something was astir. The tired formalities over. Scarlet busied herself with the biscuit and wiped crumbs from her front. She was playing the old woman now, the dotty crossbreed of Miss Marple and the Queen. It was always her best disguise.

'I imagine you're wondering why the sudden call to arms,' said the Chief. 'I must apologize for the subterfuge of it all. The usual Service theatrics.'

'Not at all.'

'What I'm about to say is, granted, a rather unusual request. But do hear me out. I sent Robert here to roll the pitch just in case there were any issues we should know about. Plus, this isn't

473

something we want to broadcast widely. Hence why we're meeting here rather than at the mother ship. I'm sure you understand.'

A request, then, not an arrest. That was the first interesting part. 'I'm an old woman. Yesterday was the most exciting day for some time. Consider me duly flattered.'

The Chief smiled, nodding appreciatively. 'Do you still hear much on the grapevine, as it were? The sort of stories that don't make it on to the front pages?'

'Most of my old contacts are long dead. I hear the occasional muttering but not much more. Why?'

'Have you, I wonder, heard anything from across the pond regarding an operation codenamed Ghost Stories?'

Yes, she has. She knows chapter and verse, actually. The Centre is in crisis. Yasenevo has been badly burned. Purged, gutted, humiliated. But that is not Scarlet, no, that is Anastasia. Scarlet is an entirely different character, who looks innocent now, struggling with the mental burdens of age. She says, 'I must have missed that one. Though I see the codenames have certainly improved.'

'That along with much else. All of us have an eye to the media these days. The Yanks more than most, I fear.'

'You said across the pond. Langley or the Hoover Building?'

'Ah, well, the Hoover Building this time. Ghost Stories was on US soil. Langley, no matter how much they tried, didn't have the legal authority to

474

stick their oars in. Though they're helping with mopping-up duties.'

'I see.'

She must demonstrate some residual flair while not betraying how much she knows. It is a high-wire act. The Chief will miss the slip. Robert with his puritan intellect will not. 'Russians, I presume? Or the Israelis?'

'Russians, indeed. Ghost Stories is something of a coup. The Cousins have just snared a ring of SVR illegals working in the US. The biggest operation of its kind since the nineties. Rather an incredible haul.'

This, of course, is where it gets dangerous. Illegals, Directorate S. She is treading on icy ground now. 'I'm waiting for a but to arrive.'

'The truth is, Ghost Stories is both a riotous success and a colossal failure. These people have been living their lives in full view. Hauling them to court and risking the media circus of a trial – particularly an American trial – will do more harm than good. Both Langley, the White House and the FBI want a quieter solution.'

'A swap?'

'Yes. In exchange for the illegals, Moscow have agreed to trade some Russian nationals rotting away for helping us back in the day. Most of them for the Americans, of course, but we managed to get our request in too. There's one name in particular that's just been confirmed. A former airborne man in Afghanistan and one-time GRU operative who went under the codename Forthwith. He was recruited in '96, not long after you left. Worked under First Secretary cover at the Russian embassy in Gibraltar. His real name is Sergei Skripal.'

Scarlet knew the name. She remembered the footage too, a barrel-like figure with a leathery face and dirty-white hair being led out of his house by FSB men and bundled into the back of an unmarked van. December 2004, if she remembered rightly. Skripal had been questioned at Lefortovo prison, that notorious Moscow hellhole, and then sentenced to thirteen years in a Russian labour camp. From all accounts, his boxing skills – honed in the army – were all that protected him. Guards and other inmates didn't treat traitors kindly.

'Where is the spy swap taking place?' she asked.

'Vienna. Your old stamping ground. It's one of the reasons we thought of you.'

One of them. But surely not the sole reason. Vauxhall Cross had well-stocked departments with directors tired of manning desks and bursting to experience some action before they retired. No, the Chief didn't call on veterans just to deal with the likes of Skripal. Even if they had served in Vienna a lifetime ago.

'Who have the Russians requested? Anyone decent?'

The Chief accepted defeat. 'Indeed they have. That, as you've no doubt guessed, is the second reason we've asked for this little chat.'

'Who?' said Scarlet, though she was sure she knew. The idea nibbling away ever since arriving here.

'There's one prisoner the Russians have requested who isn't part of the illegals network. Someone that we, and Langley, want you to interrogate before the Vienna swap occurs. We're all agreed, from the CIA Director downwards, that only you can do this.'

Scarlet waited. Then she said, 'Do what exactly?'

'Your last mission, Scarlet. A final foray into the field. Consider it a swansong and, if you like, a retirement gift. We need you to fly to Vienna and interrogate one of your former colleagues and rivals.'

'I see.' Yes, Scarlet was sure now. The person she met in Vienna almost seventy years ago. The figure at the bar, both of them still playing at life, giddy, carefree, even young. 'And does this mysterious individual have a name?'

'He does,' said the Chief. He paused, glanced again at Robert. At last, he said, 'The Russians are demanding the release of Caspar Madison.'

2010
Vienna

The flight was private from London City under the name 'Helena Wright'. The plane was owned by a shell company based in the Caymans with no links back to Vauxhall Cross or the British government. A car waited at the airport and she settled into her hotel within the hour. The room was a top-floor suite also booked under the 'Helena Wright' alias – complete with passport, debit and credit cards – and was backstopped by tech-ops working out of a safe house in Marylebone. The CCTV footage of her entry to the hotel would be wiped after she left; the room deep-cleaned. The spy swap was shrouded in the highest possible secrecy. If anything leaked, then Langley or the Centre would call the whole thing off.

The heavies arrived three hours later. Scarlet was helped into the back of the blacked-out SUV and driven to a secure location within the American embassy. She was met by Langley's Chief of Station and SIS's H/VIENNA. The assembled team looked amused and slightly awed. The Americans seemed even more respectful than the Brits. Scarlet was seated at the top of a large table, offered all types of drinks, even checked over by a medical officer to assess the impact of the flight. Then, at last, the hangers-on were shooed out. Only the Chief of Station and H/VIENNA remained. Work could begin.

'Caspar Madison has been kept in solitary at the Federal Correctional Institute in Indiana for the last eighteen years,' said the American Chief of Station. A woman, fortyish, still rare among the CoS class at Langley, but very much the senior partner here. 'According to the prison officers, he's shown no signs of repentance and spends up to twenty-three hours a day in his cell.'

Scarlet looked through the file in front of her. She banished all emotion. This wasn't a former friend and lover. This was a target. 'I presume you've tried to get him to co-operate?'

'Yes, ma'am.'

'And?'

'He seems to enjoy the game too much. He gives us hints, then laughs as we chase them. Some of it may be true, much of it isn't. He had his favourites among our interrogators. Those favourites have tried to complete our picture of his activities up to, and including, his arrest.'

'Why not send one of the favourites to Vienna? Why me?'

'Page four in the file.' The CoS waited as they turned the pages. 'As you can see, our analysts believe Madison still knows the identities of other doubles working in the US. Some who may still be alive and, thanks to ongoing security clearance, passing information to the Russians. Before we make the trade with Moscow, the Director wants you to persuade him to talk.'

'What makes you think I'll succeed where your interrogators have failed?'

'With all due respect, ma'am, none of our

interrogators have any kind of history with him. You've known him for almost seventy years. From our recent psychological analysis, we believe an old colleague may be the only person he will open up to. Someone he considers an equal. Someone worthy of the knowledge.'

'You make him sound like a sociopath.'

'The man betrayed nearly a hundred assets working for the West. According to our most recent analysis, we believe over eighty of those assets were executed in cold blood. Caspar Madison may not have pulled the trigger himself, but he's responsible for more deaths than most serial killers.'

'Yes,' said Scarlet. She looked at page eight in the file now and saw the list of names. She could picture their faces, the ghoulish terror as they knelt in the stone-cold cell, the certainty of death. 'Yes, I see.'

'We've liaised with the Department of Justice and we can give you an hour with him tomorrow before the swap takes place.'

'Where?'

'Here in the embassy.'

'I see. Does he know I'm here?'

'We've told him an old friend is visiting. We haven't said who. We want to preserve the element of surprise.'

Scarlet flicked back through the file. It was bloodless. And yet the horrors within it were all too real: over eighty executions, twenty-three hours a day in solitary, eighteen years inside, now a final passage back to Moscow to be proclaimed a hero.

She shut the file. She'd seen enough. 'I have one condition.'

'Ma'am?'

'Caspar rose to the very top of your Agency. He might be old now, but he's certainly not stupid. He won't talk if he's inside. It's why he's said nothing of use until now. He knows you'll have ears all over.'

'Do you have a better suggestion?'

'The embassy gardens. And free of all audio surveillance. No long-range cameras, mics, or any other tricks. He knows what to look for. Without that, I can't get you anything. Those are my conditions.'

'I'll take it to the Director.'

'No.' She was fiercer, like before. 'You'll agree to it now. If it's my interrogation, then it's on my terms.'

The CoS nodded reluctantly. She glanced at H/Vienna, a flicker of something in her eye. 'Understood.'

'Good.' Scarlet stared at the Chief of Station, analysing the tension in her face. Life was short; age was eternal. The world was unrecognizable now. But here they still were, burdened with the past and trapped in the present. 'Why do I feel like you're still not telling me everything?'

'I'm sorry?'

'My dear, I sat in your seat before you were a gleam in the milkman's eyes,' said Scarlet. Yes, that flicker had meaning. She was sure of it. 'Let's drop the games, shall we. What am I *really* doing here?'

2010
Caspar

Scarlet slept badly that night. She woke early, washed and dressed, then sipped on lukewarm hotel coffee. Interrogations worked best on an empty stomach. Food was heavy, dulling the mind. She needed hunger. Scarlet checked the news, read the papers and then ran through her approach. How long was it since her last interrogation? Years, possibly, decades even. She'd been called back in occasionally to debrief former assets. But that was always informal. She would attend funerals, talk with relatives and spouses, general clean-up duties. This was on an entirely different scale.

The SUV arrived just after ten o'clock. She was whisked away to the American embassy again. The bonhomie of yesterday was gone. Tension rippled through the station. Scarlet was prepped and escorted to the embassy gardens to wait. The Chief of Station fielded endless calls from Langley. H/ Vienna was updating Vauxhall Cross. Then a strange calm arrived. Before long, a tall figure in handcuffs was led out into the sunshine, blinking at the sky like a stranger.

The first emotion was shock. Scarlet had seen everything, except this. Now, in the flesh, Caspar Madison wasn't a specimen to be observed with clinical detachment or a photo contained in a classified file, absorbed and then forgotten. He looked thin. His hair, once lustrous and buoyant, was shaved close. There was a pebbly spray of stubble around his chin. He had changed out of prison clothes now. The mufti provided was several sizes too large. The shirt sagged around his chest; the trousers trailed along the grass; the scuffed brown shoes were left unlaced, as if he'd forgotten how. For now, he was still a prisoner in US custody, part of the largest and most fearsome penal regime in the world. Soon, though, he would be a free man again. If defectors were ever truly free.

Caspar was walked to the garden bench. Two embassy Marines removed the flexi-cuffs. They nodded to Scarlet, then returned to the station entrance, as per the agreement. The temperature was high. Scarlet sipped from a bottle of water. She could smell Caspar next to her: sour and cheap, the smell of cut-price soap, institutional decay, the days before daily showers and compulsory deodorant. It was the taste of her youth.

Neither of them spoke and Caspar wheezed heavily. He was accustomed to the stale prison ventilation and the air here was too pure. His soul was gone. That was Scarlet's first thought. The ligaments, joints and bone structure were still recognizable. But the essence was absent. The twinkly charmer from the bar in Vienna was dead. His choices had destroyed him.

'Was it you?' he said, finally breaking the silence.

It was the question she expected. The question she'd debated for the last two decades. 'It's good to see you too, Caspar. I hear you've been living off the state. And here was I thinking the Madisons were all God-fearing Republicans. How very social-ist of you.'

'Even now, you can never answer a simple question.'

'Why else do you think I'm on the outside and you're not?'

He glanced over. 'Are they listening?'

'Would I have said that if they were?'

'I don't know these days. My spying skills are rusty.'

'Not to mention your hygiene. They don't have working showers in prison?'

Caspar shook his head. 'Once a week, if I'm lucky. They carted me out of the cell and pushed me on a plane. I've barely had the chance to breathe, never mind wash. You get used to it.'

'That bad?'

He sighed. 'It's a beautiful day. It's the first nat-ural light I've seen in eighteen years. Let's not talk about prison.'

'What would you like to talk about?'

'I wasn't aware I called this meeting.'

Scarlet had a bag beside her. 'No, my hosting skills are rusty too. Please, sit down. I managed to smuggle in some goodies. One of the few joys of old age.'

'Treats for good behaviour?'

'More like a final taste of the West before you live off gherkins and vodka.'

'I happen to like vodka.'

She took out the stash of sandwiches, crisps, chocolate, her own little picnic. She saw Caspar trying not to look impressed. 'I even managed to smuggle a favourite of yours.' She had a small hip flask and held it up. 'Johnnie Walker Blue. That *is* still your tipple of choice?'

'I haven't had a sip of the stuff for nearly twenty years.'

'Consider it a leaving present then.'

He took the hip flask. Despite prolonged abstinence, his eyes still had an alcoholic glow to them. He opened the flask as if he was undressing it, taking each action slowly: unscrewing the top, raising it to his eyeline, then the slow, delicate sip.

'Still got it?'

He closed his eyes, like a religious experience. 'You have no idea how good that feels.'

'Prison guards no longer take payments for special favours? I'm surprised. You were always good at letting other people have your way.'

'I've been in solitary. I don't get any favours. They do a good line in verbal abuse, though. Some of our shouting matches should have been televised.'

'I'll try and remember that.'

They started eating. Caspar munched on the chocolate and crisps with childish delight. When they'd finished, she brushed the debris from the bench and then zipped the picnic bag shut. 'How does a little exercise sound?'

'After sitting on my rear end for eighteen years?'

'That's what I thought. Slowly as you like, mind. We're in no hurry.'

The embassy gardens reminded Scarlet of an Oxbridge college. They were walled off from the world, like a private idyll. The grass was well kept and the flowerbeds alive with colour. For a moment she was nineteen again. Oxford was abuzz with war and men in uniform. Every second shivered with potential, the urgency of now. She felt that again here. Within hours, Caspar Madison would be gone forever. This was the last time they would ever speak. She thought of that night in Moscow and the child.

'You still didn't answer my question,' said Caspar. He walked awkwardly now, clasping his hands behind his stooped back. 'I've spent every day trying to figure out who gave me up. Why, after surviving intact for the entire Cold War, did I get ratted on at the very end? Was it you?'

'I'm going to pretend you didn't ask me that.'

'That doesn't sound like a no.'

She was angry, adding some spice. 'Too much Scotch and not enough spying. You got old, Caspar. You got fat. You got lazy. Don't make me your scapegoat. You fell because you thought yourself invincible. Icarus all over again. You flew too close to the goddamn sun.'

'I'm still waiting for an answer.'

'Why would I give you up?'

'Who then?'

'There were hundreds of them selling their souls to the highest bidder in '92. Take your pick. That's if anyone leaked at all. Most long-term doubles trip themselves up. You know that as well as I do.'

Caspar looked around, seeing just acres of green space. The entrance to the station receded into the distance. 'If that were so, how come your name never came up? I go to prison, you enjoy retirement. Why did every British double get outed apart from you?'

'It's hard to get caught if you don't exist.'

Caspar was closer now, the words rehearsed. His voice hummed with anger. 'Say I walk in there and announce that Scarlet King, the grand dame of British intelligence, Miss Bond herself, is actually a Soviet illegal? The crowning glory of Directorate S. The pride of Yasenevo. What if I do that?'

'The word of a traitor and a convicted criminal.'

'Don't tell me it doesn't keep you up at night. The tap-tap-tap on the front door. The public embarrassment. Blunt was a pariah in his final years. Even if you do avoid jail time, you'll lose everything. That's why you're here, isn't it? To see if I've talked?'

'Arrested on what proof?'

'You edited your name out of Mitrokhin. You spent forty years passing product through your handler at Oxford. You tomb-stoned the identity of a dead child. That should be proof enough.'

'You're ugly sober. I like you much better drunk.'

Caspar growled with frustration. He took several swigs from the hip flask. He gurgled the Scotch in his mouth, rolled it round, celebrating the taste. 'How do you do it? How do those ghosts not haunt you?'

'I'm a professional.'

They reached a tree and a long gravel path ahead of them. It was surrounded by ornamental gardens. Caspar stared at the beauty of it and took another sip of Scotch. 'You were beautiful back then. We both were. When did we stop being beautiful?'

'Our mistakes hadn't caught up with us. We were still too busy making them.'

'Is that what you think it was? A mistake?'

'Navel-gazing doesn't suit me, Caspar. I try not to think about the past.'

'So why meet me here? Why not let me disappear?'

She looked at the gardens again. She sniffed the freshly mown grass.

Yes, it was time.

2010
The Walk

They walked for another five minutes in silence. Then Scarlet said, 'Are you prepared for Moscow?'

Caspar smiled tentatively. He took another swig of Scotch. He shook the hip flask. It was almost empty. 'I'm prepared to drink myself to death, if that's what you're asking.'

'Blake is still alive. You could have dinner parties together.'

'I might just do that.'

'Is that what you fought for though,' she said. 'No freedom, summary executions of anyone who disagrees. Is that what it was all for?'

'I don't remember you making those objections at the time.'

'They'll ask me for something, you know. Names, dates, codewords. Throw me a bone and they can log it. Quid pro quo. Give them something to show Langley and everyone's a winner.'

Caspar had exhausted the hip flask now. He screwed the top back on and placed it in his baggy trouser pocket. 'You said it yourself. You saw all the stuff in Mitrokhin. You know more than I do.'

'Something, at least? For an old friend? What don't they know?'

Freedom was so enchanting. There was real terror in his eyes: of being taken back, caged like an animal again. 'Ames,' he said. 'Tell them I protected Ames.'

Aldrich Ames. The CIA counterintelligence officer caught spying for the Russians in the nineties, the next to fall after Caspar. 'How?'

'Everyone asked why it took so long to capture him. He wasn't smart, and his luck was rotten.'

'You buried the investigation?'

'I got an instruction from my handler to make sure Ames wasn't caught. Let's just say I kept an eye on things.'

'So how was he caught?'

'I was arrested. I couldn't protect him any longer. By that time, though, his game was done. Moscow was ready to turn him loose.'

Scarlet nodded. She looked at Caspar now, still trying to understand him. Most doubles were misfits and eccentrics; showmen denied their proper due. But Caspar was too smart to be an ideologue. His morality, like so much else, was dependent on the time of day.

'It's boredom, isn't it?' she said. 'That's why you did it. Normal life, the nine to five, a timid little wife and a three-bedroom house in the suburbs – all that was too boring. Just like monogamy, or being heterosexual, or sticking to a single faith. You don't believe in Moscow any more than I do. You didn't betray your country for a cause. You betrayed it as a way of staying alive.'

'Is that your psych assessment of me? Or is that Langley talking?'

A sociopath, she thought. The father of her child.

'I'm sick of just knowing who. Frequently, now, I want to know *why*.'

'Does there always have to be a why?'

'The Caspar Madison I met in that bar wasn't some misty-eyed ideologue intent on furthering the cause of socialism and building a better world. I know that much.'

Caspar was tiring now. He slowed down and then stopped, leaning against a tree trunk for support. 'Perhaps some of us have hidden depths.'

'No.' Scarlet saw those eighty names in the file. 'No, I don't think so.'

Caspar waved the implication away. 'I gave my life to a cause I believed in. I've paid a suitably heavy price. On that we can agree.'

The child. No, this was for the child. Everything now was for the child. Their time was nearly over. 'I want to know what I didn't see that day,' she said. 'In Vienna, or again in Moscow. All those trips to see you in the States. I want to know how normal people can commit abnormal acts. Eighty people, Caspar. Eighty souls.'

Caspar wiped his brow. 'No spy ever has their hands clean. We exist in the gutter. Only a fool thinks otherwise. And the girl I met in that bar all those years ago certainly wasn't a fool. Or was I wrong about that too?'

Scarlet didn't reply. She was surprised at herself. Seeing Caspar again triggered a cold, quiet fury. For a moment she wondered what would happen if she told him, lifting the lid on the last forty-six years. But it was hopeless. Caspar Madison only ever had time for himself.

491

Scarlet looked at her watch. She had loved him once, though not in a romantic way. Oxford and Baker Street were full of priggish public school-boys who couldn't talk to women. The American at the bar in Vienna was so insolently handsome, rudely charming. She always thought of Gatsby when she saw him, and still did. Maybe this is what James Gatz would have become. Someone who justified the worst human actions with the noblest moral intentions.

The ugly feelings faded. She turned off her emotions, like a rusty tap. 'What's past is past.'

'*Carpe diem. In vino veritas.* To love, life and unhappiness.'

'Youth is beautiful; age is ugly. That's what happened, Caspar. We lived too long.'

A pause, then, 'You would tell me, though?'

'Tell you what?'

'If you were the one who betrayed me?'

'They're waiting for us.' Scarlet moved closer to him. She rose to the tip of her toes and kissed his cheek, scrubbing away the mark instinctively. 'Goodbye, Caspar.'

2010
Spy Games

July 9, 2010. In the end was the beginning. Everyone here was young or middle-aged. Muscles
bulged; earpieces buzzed. There were Glock 17s
for the Brits and Beretta M9s for the Americans.
The spooks were wand-like, the operators squat
and bellied. The airstrip at Vienna Airport crawled
with CIA, SIS, Increment, Special Activities Division, FCO and State Department Liaison. If a
bomb dropped on them now, Scarlet thought, the
best of Western intelligence would be gone.

And what do they see? An old woman who
stands barely more than five feet now in her flats.
Someone who has done her homework. Who
knows about Skripal, his likes and dislikes, mulling how to handle her last asset, even if their
relationship will only last for a few hours. She has
done the other business, too, of course, as she
always does. The drafts folder in the anonymous
Gmail account with the usual crumbs about the
mood among the CIA and SIS, the talk with Caspar, the plans for tomorrow, initial timings. Before
it took effort. Now betrayal is only a mouse-click
away.

The event, when it happens, is brutally short. The
Russian plane arrives first. Minutes later the American plane lands with the Russian illegals – the
ghosts of the Ghost Stories operation; actor-spies

of the highest quality. Both sets of prisoners exit their respective planes. They cross over and board the opposite plane, like cars speeding past each other in broad daylight.

From a distance, Scarlet sees Caspar Madison dragging his feet along the tarmac. He joins the Russian nationals from the American plane. The swap takes minutes. The Russian illegals and Caspar are swallowed into the Russian plane; the Russian doubles disappear into the American plane. Headcounts are taken. Names checked. Cursory medicals undertaken. Then, when both sides are content, the signal is given. The CIA, SIS and SVR delegates acknowledge that the cargo has been transferred. Both planes are given permission for take-off. No movie showdowns; no Hollywood theatrics.

Scarlet is ushered towards the American plane and helped up the stairs. She's shown to her seat by a field officer from Vienna Station. Others soon fill the plane. Scarlet is seated next to two Russian gentlemen. They smell of forced labour and prehistoric hygiene facilities. She knows them like members of her own family now: Mr Sergei Skripal on the left; Mr Igor Sutyagin on the right.

The Russian plane departs first. Scarlet watches it arc into the distance. The American plane is heading to Dulles International Airport. The three of them, however, will stop at RAF Brize Norton. These two old men fresh from the Russian wilderness, gulags in all but name. First, though, business is tended to.

Are you both here of your own free will?

Yes, babushka, we are.

Do you know that you are being taken for a full debriefing to England where you will be rehoused as part of the SIS resettlement scheme?

Thank you, babushka, yes.

You will first be taken to Fort Monckton in Gosport where the Secret Intelligence Service, which you may know as MI6, has a training base. You will be met by the Chief and welcomed like heroes.

Yes, yes, thank you, yes.

Do you have any specific requests which SIS can accommodate?

The man on the right now. Mr Igor Sutyagin.

Dumplings, he says. *Pelmeni.* Proper, authentic Russian dumplings. He remembers how to smile.

The man on the left now. Mr Skripal.

Fresh fruit, babushka. The taste of fresh fruit.

And that is all?

That and clean clothes, babushka. Bright colours. Freedom colours.

Rest now, gentlemen. Soon we will be in Britain. Thank you for your service.

At Brize Norton a helicopter spirits them across the Oxfordshire countryside and down towards the south coast. They land on the small helipad at Fort Monckton where a fuller welcoming party – the Chief; the current Director for Central and Eastern Europe; and Robert, the youngest of the trio, presumably as Head of Counterintelligence – greets the two assets, shows them to their rooms.

The two assets shower, sleep and recuperate before the debrief. Scarlet receives an invitation for the 'Chief's Mess'. The Fort boasts a functional

495

military décor and the Chief's Mess has been redecorated on the public purse. There's tasteful art on the walls, signed photos of famous assets and officers, even spy memorabilia, ranging from the creation of the secret service right up to the modern day. The long twentieth century is all here: two world wars, the Cold War, the war on terror. Scarlet can't decide if it's a monument to failure or success.

The starters are cleared away. Scarlet wipes her lips and takes another sip of wine. She is bone tired, but game enough to smile and talk. And it is just before the main course that one of the case officers enters and passes a note to the Chief. He unfolds it, reads and then shows Robert. Both turn to Scarlet now.

The mission is finally complete.

2010
The Fort

The Chief passed the note across to her. 'Congratulations are in order, it seems,' he said.

Scarlet read the note then fed it into a nearby water glass, watching as the ink melted away. 'Toasting death seems rather macabre, don't you think?'

'Well, according to the FSB, he's still very much alive. I'm sure the Kremlin will claim baying crowds cheered his name at the airport. His hologram will be paraded through the streets. Autobiographies, speeches, just you wait.'

Scarlet risked a smile, then raised her glass half-heartedly, as did Robert and the Chief. They both took celebratory sips and watched as the main course was served. Once the plates were unveiled, and the door shut, the mood relaxed. There was always a drunken, boosterish mood among off-duty spies. According to legend, the Christmas parties at SIS were the most riotous in Whitehall. For a moment, in conditions of scrupulous privacy, tight-lipped professionals were allowed to unwind.

'And he really suspected nothing?'

'No.' The lie came fluently. Scarlet had debated the point. She saw herself passing the hip flask to him, watching as he sunk the lot, letting him keep the flask, then informing the CIA Vienna Station Chief that their request had been completed. The

Office of Technical Service, or OTS, was the CIA's resident magician service. Scarlet hadn't asked what type of poison was used. She didn't want to know. Within hours of ingesting it, Caspar Madison had suffered a fatal heart attack on board the Russian flight to Moscow. His remaining secrets would never be divulged. She thought about the way he drank from the flask: desperate, greedy, fatal.

I'm prepared to drink myself to death, if that's what you're asking.

Robert speared a piece of fish and said, 'Did you get much out of him during the talk?'

Scarlet focused again on the present. 'Some idle gossip. He told me quite a bit about protecting Aldrich Ames. It was always a mystery how Ames survived so long. Having Langley's second-in-command in your corner probably helped.'

'And nothing more?'

Scarlet met Robert's eye. Yes, he was the real deal. Some spies existed only to be liked. They fed off others' approval, desperate for it. Others were flintier, colder people. Scarlet remembered a line from Graham Greene, an old acquaintance back in the early days – every great writer needed a splinter of ice in the heart. Robert didn't blink.

'No,' she said. 'Caspar wasn't exactly in great shape. Eighteen years in a federal prison isn't conducive to mental sharpness or enhanced social skills.'

'Do you think there are any more?'

'Any more what?'

'The old guard. Russian doubles or illegals or

498

fellow travellers. The student communists who became high-ranking politicians and Permanent Under-Secretaries at the Foreign Office. Any more moles still out there?'

'If there are, they must be ancient by now.'

Robert's eyes didn't flicker. He still held her gaze. 'Age doesn't confer innocence, of course. Old people can still be guilty. They can still pay for their crimes. The past is never really over, is it?'

She knew then that he didn't buy the old lady routine. Robert saw her mind, admiring it like a sculpture. How much did he know? How much could he prove? The lingering suspicion stayed with her.

The dinner ended. Scarlet returned to her room. She didn't sleep again. The secrets – so many secrets – felt heavier than ever. Anastasia Chekova and Scarlet King were becoming one again. The swap in Vienna and the death of Caspar and the helicopter ride back to this place signalled the end. After this, she would become a hermit in her Chelsea flat and emerge only for bare necessities.

She got up early. She took breakfast in the mess. There was a dip-tel from the Director of the CIA, no less, thanking her for the heroics in Vienna and her service to the intelligence community. She was strong-armed into several training seminars and watched as young IONEC recruits – children, really, all of them – sat open-mouthed as she regaled them with sanitized tales of Vienna after the war and her time in Section IX with Kim and Section V with Archie and Maurice Oldfield. They raised their hands like a school class and quizzed her about the Mitrokhin Archive and the fall of the Berlin Wall.

She was a museum piece to them now, a relic from a previous millennium. Scarlet remembered her first days at the Firm and those Edwardians with their showy manners and bumptious eccentricity, eager to tell tales of the Boer War and their struggles on the frontline of empire. That was how distant she was now. Europe in ruins, Stalin's hidden crimes, Churchill licking his wounds, Attlee building a New Jerusalem. It was like the pharaohs and the pyramids, a vanished age.

When the seminars were over, Scarlet was given a full send-off. The Chief was master of ceremonies. As the car pulled out, Scarlet glanced out of the window for a final time. In the middle of them all, stony-faced, stood Robert with those eyes still watching her. The one heretic among them. She unfurled the note he'd given her just before she left. It was the name she'd mentioned in Sloane Square.

ANDERSON, E.

Scarlet saw the maiden name, the married name and then the dates: 1964–2009. She looked blankly out of the car window again. There was a line underneath the name of the deceased. She read the name and clutched it to her.

'Pleasant stay, ma'am?' said the driver.

'Yes,' she lied. 'Very pleasant indeed.'

2010–present
The Watchers

The eyes were everywhere after that. She didn't go out most days, pottering round the flat instead, watching bad breakfast television and reading books she'd never finished. But that didn't stop the paranoia. Her neighbours were spying on her. The shuffle of feet on the stone staircase outside provoked a day of anxiety. She searched the flat for listening devices every morning, as if ghosts could have planted them during the night. She dusted in corners, unscrewed light bulbs, checked the corners of every device and appliance. But the terror remained. They were watching.

Colonel Anastasia Chekova of Directorate S of the KGB.

Miss Scarlet King of Baker Street and the Secret Intelligence Service.

Frau Isabel Charlemont at Café Landtmann in Vienna.

Miss Sarah Webber, humble secretary to the Deputy Ambassador.

Dr Susan Napier, a senior functionary from Her Majesty's Foreign and Commonwealth Office.

She was friend, lover, colleague, traitor, spy.

And so she started. She took the bus to Peckham, bought a notebook and a set of pens and enough blue refill cartridges to last. She returned to the flat and set up her workstation. The flat didn't have wi-fi. Nothing was connected. And, as the paranoia built, she started writing. There was no 'I' this time, only 'she'. This would be her therapy. Not a talking cure, but a writing cure.

She stored each day's work beneath the bed. Slowly, the pages built. The daily paragraphs became pages. The pages turned into chapters. Eighteen months after starting, she had the first section complete. She granted herself a two-day holiday, then started on the next part, returning to the world of the sixties and Kim and the point at which the modern world – in all its messiness – truly began.

The routine kept her going. She slept longer now and rose later. Cooking was too much of a chore, and she existed on hand-cooked ready-meals from one of the food shops on the King's Road. The owner was handsome and young, and treated Scarlet with filial delicacy. She talked to herself, now. Sometimes she took the child's part and talked about the news, the weather, crafting her own biological imprint until the child with Caspar's eyes and her smile was almost sitting before her.

The routine slowed as the years advanced. She wrote one paragraph before supper, then another afterwards if she still had the energy. Once she'd been so fluent. Now every clause was scratched out several times. She reordered sentences until they sounded musical. Whole paragraphs were gunned down in a blaze of fidgety blue ink. The words that survived were the lucky few. But speed didn't matter now. She had nothing else. There was no family. Her friends were dead. Only her secrets remained.

She dry-cleaned herself on her walks down the King's Road. She stopped and looked in shop windows; she bent down to inspect her shopping bag; she took sudden diversions round the many small roads branching off from Sloane Square. Everyone – shopkeeper, bus driver, cabbie, police officer – was a potential threat. Dodging the glare of one intelligence service was hard. Blindsiding three – the Brits, the Americans and her old Russian handlers – was surely pushing things. She couldn't outrun them forever.

They would kill her, of course. She'd always known that. The FSB wouldn't hesitate, nor would Langley. The Brits would wring their hands and consult lawyers, but in the end find a way. She had lived a risky life. Agents died, case officers too, children demolished in drone strikes, innocent academics and tourists bundled into stinking prison cells. The secret world reeked of collateral damage. She had no illusions. Few would ever know she'd died. Even fewer would crowd round the graveside.

The world moved on. Robert, the mole hunter with those haunting eyes, was thrown out of Vauxhall Cross and condemned to exile. The Chief was implicated in an illegal UK–US black op and sent to tend his cabbage patch somewhere in the backwaters of France. There were terrorist attacks in Manchester and Westminster. Sergei Skripal, the man Scarlet had shepherded back from Vienna, was poisoned and recovered. Putin changed the constitution. The 45th President of the United States was accused of being a Russian mole. And the new Chief of the Secret Intelligence Service, 'C' himself, started tweeting.

Scarlet observed it all and ignored it all. She kept writing. The single paragraph a day became her quiet time. She grew older. Her body failed. Pain was permanent, fatigue constant. And yet she never stopped. Sometimes she could only manage a handful of sentences. At other points two paragraphs filled an entire page. She was beyond the sixties now, into the nineties and memories of Mr Mitrokhin, Professor Andrew and Otto. One chapter in particular upset her, and she took a sabbatical. A week later, she finished the third section.

Peace descended with the final part. She knew what she had to do. She began contacting old assets, NOCs and bureaucrats from Tel Aviv to Toronto. For her plan to work, she needed an assistant and a cut-out. The assistant was the easy part. She had a contact at the Israeli embassy who might know of someone.

The cut-out, meanwhile, was already chosen. Her thrice weekly trips down the King's Road expanded to include a visit to John Sandoe Books on Blacklands Terrace. She worked through the spy history section: Ben Macintyre, Nigel West, Gordon Corera, Luke Harding, David Omand, Henry Hemming, Mark Urban and her old acquaintance, Professor Andrew of Cambridge University. It was on her seventh visit that she saw the two volumes. She spoke casually. This next move must appear coincidental. After all, they would follow the trail later. Of that she was certain.

'Are they new?' she asked.

The bookseller smiled. 'Hardly. We have a bet on. How long will it take to shift a single copy? Manager went for two and a half years. Wildly optimistic, as it turns out. These have been in storage.' He held them up. 'Half a decade of dust. I went for seven years. It's getting damn close.'

Scarlet bought both volumes. The first was called *Double Agents: A History*. The second was titled *The Honourable Traitor: An Unauthorized Biography of Kim Philby*. Scarlet turned to the first page and saw the brief biographical paragraph for the author: 'Dr Max Archer is Associate Professor of Intelligence History at the London School of Economics . . .'

The bookseller was still hovering. 'The author actually came here once for a signing, I think. Did a BBC documentary a while back on the Cambridge Spies.'

She had a sudden urge to tell him about her times with Kim, the drinks with Anthony Blunt, what it was like to be in Moscow during the mole-hunt years, that the Cambridge Five were amateurs compared to her. Saying it out loud would make it real.

But, instead, she merely nodded and left. She spent the next three days immersed in both books. She re-read the Philby biography twice over, combing the pages for errors. But each episode was recorded with unerring accuracy. Next, she turned to the history of double agents, skimming through the index to find the names she'd known personally. By the time she'd finished her fourth read, she'd decided.

She had failed before. But she wouldn't fail again. Her last secret mission was almost complete.

PART FIVE
One Year Later

47

The lecture theatre was empty. That was the first odd thing. Then there were the cameras, which was the second. This was a pre-record, due to be broadcast later. A live audience would give the game away.

Max looked down at his lecture notes. He took a sip of water. He was in the final furlong now. At the back, the Harvard media team whispered together. They were paying attention. His nerves rose again. He was so close. This was championship point.

He breathed deeply and changed the slide on the screen. It showed a tubby, bespectacled and genial old man, with Einstein hair and Harry Potter glasses, dressed in a crumpled shirt with the sleeves rolled up. He looked grandfatherly. He was surrounded by books. The caption read: 'Professor Thomas Hegel, Emeritus Professor of Biochemistry, Imperial College London'.

Max continued. 'Professor Thomas Hegel was the foremost biochemist of his generation. He was a devoted family man with two children and a loving wife. The official record shows that Thomas Hegel escaped from Germany in the thirties and devoted his life to scientific discovery. After a brief period working for the British government after the war, mainly at the Porton Down research facility, Professor Hegel settled in Kensington,

London, where he stayed until his death in 1992. He was a Fellow of the Royal Society. His obituary was featured in *The Times*. A memorial service was held at St Mary Abbots Church. There is currently a laboratory at Imperial named in his honour. He was a pillar of the academic establishment, a refugee who rose to the very top of British science.'

Max changed the slide again. The genial face was replaced by a familiar wartime scene: children with hollow cheeks dressed in striped uniforms and standing next to barbed wire. He could sense the media team becoming more intrigued.

'This is a scene from Auschwitz III. Auschwitz I was the main death camp. Auschwitz II housed the Birkenau gas chambers and crematoria. Auschwitz III, meanwhile, was run not as a state facility, but as a corporate facility and labour-concentration camp by the chemical firm IG Farben. It was, in the words of one intelligence historian, "the first corporate concentration camp in the Third Reich".

'Even today, IG Farben is still relatively unknown. But it was the biggest company in Europe during the forties, and the fourth biggest in the world. The scientists who worked for IG Farben were designing chemical weapons. And they had two secret advantages: a workforce of slave labourers and the use of concentration camp inmates as human guinea pigs for testing.'

Max changed the slide again. With an audience there would have been an audible gasp of horror, even though the image was horribly familiar, paraded in countless documentaries and history books. It showed the gas chambers. But there was an even creepier silence now.

'Make no mistake,' said Max, still looking at the main camera, 'Auschwitz and the other Nazi death camps weren't just a monument to human evil. They were also a monument to human science. The Holocaust depended on scientists devising new methods of mass murder. The chemists of IG Farben were more than equal to that task. None more so than a young scientist with a first-class degree in Chemistry from the Friedrich Wilhelm University in Berlin. His name was Dr Otto Spengler. He was an employee of IG Farben and he worked at the camp known as Auschwitz III. He was the Deputy Plant Manager of Buna-Werk IV. His task was twofold. First, to oversee the slave labour used to create the weapons; second, to test those weapons on human inmates. According to official war records, Dr Spengler died in 1946 while on the run in Vienna. Just another Nazi who never faced justice for his crimes. Case closed.'

Max paused. This was the moment that would go viral on YouTube. He had rehearsed it endlessly in front of the mirror in his Harvard room, making sure the timing was exactly right. Now, finally, he changed the slide again. Two photos emerged: the earlier shot of the twinkly professor and another grainy black-and-white headshot of a young barrel-chested man dated 'April 2, 1942'.

'Except Dr Otto Spengler didn't really die,' he said. 'His death certificate was issued. But his body was never found. In fact, Dr Spengler was abducted by T-Force and renditioned to Britain. He was sent for interrogation at Spedan Towers in Hampstead, run by the British Intelligence Objectives Sub-Committee, often used as cover for MI6. While staying as a "Visitor" at Spedan Towers, Dr Spengler was debriefed and given a new identity, or "legend" as spies call it. Dr Otto Spengler was dead. Long live Dr Thomas Hegel. Dr Spengler was one of the first assets of an SIS operation code-named Hercules.

'The man formerly known as Dr Spengler was issued with a new passport, official papers and the guarantee of permanent residency in the UK. Then he was put to work at the Chemical Defence Experimental Establishment, or what we know as Porton Down. His residency terms mandated fifteen years of service there. Afterwards, Dr Hegel was found a role at Imperial College London. He spent the next thirty-one years as an agent of influence for MI6. His job? To spy for the British. He attended scientific conferences across the world and reported back to his handlers at the Secret Intelligence Service. China, the Soviet Union, the Middle East – Dr Hegel was MI6's best-kept secret.

'Like all such legends, this one was backstopped thoroughly. The papers were official. The records intact. The creation of Dr Thomas Hegel, and the death of Dr Otto Spengler, were among the finest espionage achievements of the post-war era. They were also among the most morally and ethically reprehensible.'

Careful pause now. Max shuffled his notes, took another sip of water. Two more paragraphs. Academic immortality beckoned.

He continued, 'Porton Down is today considered one of the best chemical and biological weapons facilities in the world. Rightly so. It played a vital role in Salisbury in 2018. It is on the frontline of the global fight against biological or chemical weapons, protecting billions of lives against biochemical terrorist attacks. And yet our national, and indeed international, security rests partly on the work of a brilliant scientist who committed mass murder eighty years ago.

'Operation Hercules in many ways symbolizes the dilemma of all intelligence history. Is it ever right to lie in search of the truth? Can evil people be used for decent ends? Can deception be pressed into the service of accountability? As Edmund Burke famously didn't say: all that is necessary for the triumph of evil is that good men do nothing. But what if the opposite is also true in spy history? All that is necessary for the triumph of good is that evil men do something. That is our puzzle, ladies and gentlemen, and that is our challenge. Thank you very much indeed.'

There was silence. Then, without warning, a figure on the back row stood up and gently started clapping. Suddenly, like a contagion, the rest of the camera crew followed. Soon the photographers were joining in as well. Until, within a matter of seconds, the standing ovation spread throughout all those stationed in the lecture theatre.

Max took a moment to realize it was aimed at him. The Harvard media team kept the camera rolling. The photographer on the left turned on the flash and began snapping photos of Max soaking up the applause behind the lectern.

The slide behind Max changed:

PROFESSOR MAX ARCHER
Visiting Professor of International Relations
(Harvard Kennedy School)
Professor of Intelligence History
(London School of Economics)

He would blink awake now and find a pile of essays to mark and an inbox full of emails from Vernon Kessler about the faculty rota. But the applause continued. Max took another hasty glug of water, half-wishing it was something stronger, and then tucked his lecture notes away.

He checked his watch and saw the time. By tonight, of course, it could all change again. He just prayed his literary agent's prediction was right this time.

The circus was only just beginning.

48

As the Jaguar XF pulled in to the MI5 headquarters, Saul couldn't help thinking that the Thames House basement entrance looked more like a shopping centre car park or a council multi-storey. There was that same sound of water dripping and the eternal smell of urinals and concrete. The car drew to a halt and one of the guards opened the right-side passenger door. For any enemy surveillance, the number plates of this particular vehicle led back to the government carpool. The vehicle itself was registered to an obscure junior minister in the Department of International Trade.

In reality, the saloon car was fitted with bullet-proof glass. Hidden in the touchscreen was a control panel allowing secure video-conferencing with the Cabinet Office, while the DAB radio was, in fact, a secure line to the Joint Terrorism Analysis Centre. The cabin lighting, meanwhile, contained cutting-edge sensors developed at Hanslope Park in Buckinghamshire that blocked any external digital interference. The Director-General of MI5, along with the Chief of the Secret Intelligence Service, was one of the few Crown servants granted a permanent chauffeur and a dedicated vehicle. Even most Ministers of State, these days, had to slum it by car-sharing with their ministerial colleagues. Sometimes it still paid to be in the shadows.

Saul Northcliffe – or 'Sir Saul', to be strictly accurate – got out of the car and felt that ripple of excitement again. The family jokes would never stop, of course. He was now the Knight Commander at home, fulfilling his new chivalric duties with endless tea refills or learning how to bake vegan brownies. The official letters after his name were GCMG, technically known as the Most Distinguished Order of Saint Michael and Saint George. Or, as *Yes Minister* once quipped, 'God Calls Me God'.

Still the feeling of fraud stayed with him. He was only Acting Director-General. He fully expected to be shafted for the top job in favour of someone younger, better looking and with a far more enviable social media presence. According to the papers, he had unwittingly committed the cardinal sin of being pale, male and stale. None of the above seemed likely to change in the immediate future.

For some time, at least, he occupied the top corner office. The days of crowded Tubes, rain-drenched macs and cereal bars as a midday snack were gone. Now he was ferried to endless three-course lunches, wined and dined by everyone from the Prime Minister at Chequers to the Chief of the Defence Staff. He was spared the evening commute thanks to a small flat just off Westminster Abbey reserved for the Director-General when duty called. Which, somehow, it always seemed to.

He rarely walked the corridors alone, either. Every step was shadowed by assistants, department heads and diary managers. His usual strolls through Thames House now elicited almost regimental formality from staff. The lure of retirement, replete with lazy mornings on the crossword, pints of English breakfast tea and copious supplies of toast, became weaker. He breakfasted out, almost exclusively, and his waistline had duly expanded. His wife banned him from eating all forms of fried food, and he was reduced to going continental just in case a newspaper photographer snapped him in the act. The domestic strife simply wasn't worth it.

He entered the main building, shaking off a scatter of rain from his coat. The security detail shepherded him into the lift. They motored to the top floor. Charlotte, now his staff officer, was waiting with the latest briefing folders. Today had already been of gale-force intensity. First a breakfast meeting with the Commissioner of the Met, then a morning of meetings with visiting intelligence heads from Saudi Arabia, Egypt and Iraq, followed by lunch with the Editor of the *Daily Telegraph*, an hour with the National Security Adviser and then an appearance before the Intelligence and Security Committee in Parliament on everything from MI5's budget to plans for celebrating International Women's Day.

'We've just received the latest from the Élysée regarding the French President's state visit next month,' said Charlotte, walking with him to the office door, 'and there's a note from the National Crime Agency about some new links on Operation Gambit. The Director of Special Forces would also like to schedule a call about Executive Action capabilities on the planned raid in Birmingham tomorrow.'

Saul heard the thud as Charlotte placed the folders on his desk. He removed his coat and admired the view from his office window, far more scenic than that old cubbyhole.

'Fine, fine. But I'm clear for the rest of the evening?'

'The Security Minister said he might try your mobile. But, other than that, yes. Should I ask the team for anything?'

'I'd kill for a decent cuppa if there's one going.'

'Milky?'

'Biscuit too. Something chocolatey. Strict state secret, of course.'

Charlotte nodded. 'I'll get someone to bring them through.' She was about to leave when she turned and said: 'Oh, one last thing. There's been a development on Tempest. I put it at the top of the pile.'

'Thank you.'

The secure office door closed with a heavy clunk. Saul sat down, loosened his tie and then considered the night's-worth of reading material. The French President's state visit could wait, more fluff about Monsieur le Président's dietary requirements, accommodation preferences and request that all rooms graced with the presidential bottom would be heated to below room temperature. The Special Forces Director was probably a yes, always hunting for things to occupy his troopers, even if it did involve smashing down doors in Birmingham rather than abseiling into the Brazilian jungle. The National Crime Agency, meanwhile, was trying to poach some of his best analysts. That would be a very firm no.

Saul cleared the other files from the desk and laid them on one side. Instead, he picked out the top file marked 'OPERATION TEMPEST: TOP SECRET / UK EYES ONLY'. 'Tempest' along with 'Scarlet King' and 'Operation Hercules' were still the only words guaranteed to give him a sleepless night. He opened the cover and glanced warily at the latest intelligence report. Charlotte was the only person he trusted to evaluate and vet the raw intelligence. No one else in the building knew the case still existed.

Operation Tempest currently consisted of four separate lines of attack: first, intercepts of all email and cellular traffic from the offices of R.B. Wickham Literary Agency based in Holborn; second, a similar SIGINT monitoring remit for Rockefeller Talent Agency housed near Dean Street, Soho; third, ongoing surveillance of Professor Max Archer, Menzies Chair in Intelligence History at the London School of Economics and incoming Head of Department; and, finally, the premises of Trinity Care Home near Lambeth, following the death of resident number forty-eight, Mr Oliver Archer, from a suspected heart attack just under a week ago.

Saul focused now. There were yet more email chains about a manuscript entitled 'OPERATION HERCULES' alongside a submission letter introducing the book. Saul picked out various phrases: 'event publication', 'explosive new revelations', 'volcanic archival work', 'headline-grabbing global literary event', 'shattering personal story', 'reappraisal of Britain's role in the Second World War', 'seismic discoveries', 'Primo Levi meets Max

Hastings', 'bigger than the Hitler diaries', 'once-in-a-generation secret that reshapes the world's understanding of the 1939–1945 conflict'.

The manuscript consisted of 450 pages and around 130,000 double-spaced words. The first reply had come within twenty-four hours of submission, clearly written via iPhone and in the witching hour, with a US six-figure offer. By that stage, a UK auction was well into high six figures sterling. Saul stopped as he reached the thirty-first foreign rights deal, not even bothering to try and calculate the combined figure. Nazis, the Second World War, MI6, an establishment cover-up – yes, he could see the film now.

So, apparently, could Hollywood. Saul skimmed through further emails from film producers with unlikely names spraying around zeroes, calling the book the 'novel of the century, possibly of all time' and promising to attach a revolving door of A-list talent: Leo, Brad, George, the two Ryans, Ewan, Gerard, Colin, Hugh. All were looking for awards-worthy fare. Laurence Olivier had set the benchmark for playing Nazis in *The Marathon Man* and earned an Academy Award nomination for his troubles. This was the kind of IP streamers were looking for: Amazon, Netflix, HBO Max, Peacock, Hulu, Disney+. Precedent suggested there was no precedent. The consensus was this could go, in the technical jargon of the entertainment industry, 'totally gangbusters'.

The last email was dated four hours ago. It was a summary from Antonia Wickham to Max Archer, itemizing the events of the last seventy-two hours.

The email ended with a cumulative figure that ensured Professor Max Archer, penurious academic and occasional media don, now had a semi-decent retirement fund. Archer had replied at 5:01 a.m. with the details of an account in the Cayman Islands, set up under a shell company called 'ASHENDEN LTD'.

The last email was from the accounts department at R.B. Wickham Literary Agency confirming that the first tranche of signature fees had been deposited in the Cayman account. The next page showed the shell company account was quickly cleared and the money bounced around a variety of different tax havens before being parcelled up into fragments and lodged everywhere from the British Virgin Islands to a boutique asset manager in Monaco.

Saul heard his stomach rumble and then picked up his red pen – a counterpart to the Chief of SIS's famous green pen – and squiggled a note on the bottom for Charlotte to pick up tomorrow morning. Soon after, a tray arrived with piping hot tea and three chocolate Hobnobs. Saul ate all three and then glanced out of his office window.

Twelve months, one week and two days.

It was finally time to close the file on Operation Tempest.

49

The flight from Logan International Airport to London City was truly something else. Max always hated flying. He was a spy historian. He was meant to be a globetrotter, a roguish adventurer happy in anything from old Soviet gunships to battered Toyota SUVs. But the tedium of the departure lounge still brought him out in hives.

Thankfully the British Airways flight was punctual and, for the first time ever, Max turned left for first class. Ample leg room, ordering off the à la carte menu, free on-board wi-fi – he'd spent twenty years watching old university classmates ascend the corporate ladder, their wallets fattening along with their egos. No, he'd toiled in the weeds for long enough. He deserved a glimpse of luxury.

Max checked his emails. The first set of transfers had gone according to plan. He sank back into the seat, sceptically considered the packet of complimentary loungewear. Harvard was a daily grind of lectures, seminars, endless drinks receptions, and then compulsory faculty dinners that stretched into the early hours. He'd barely slept for a full night since arriving stateside. He seemed to be permanently yawning.

Max glanced at the rest of his inbox now. Following the four-day bidding war, there was yet another email from the Loch Ness Monster, his former editor at Chatham & Grey, simply *dying* to speak to him. Dinner at the Groucho this week? Coffee at the Corinthia? Max blocked the email address and deleted the other emails. He imagined *Operation Hercules* catapulting to the top of the *Sunday Times* bestseller list. Yes, revenge was a dish best served with a seven-figure advance.

The flight was over before Max realized. He dozed off in his private suite and woke up forty minutes away from London City. The complimentary loungewear and body care collection still lay unused. From habit, if nothing else, Max furtively squashed both into his on-board luggage. No academic ever threw away a freebie.

The demob spirit lasted until he stepped off the plane. He inhaled the stale London air and felt those old worries return. He waited in baggage collection and then made for the exit. He half-expected to see uniformed members of British Transport Police surround him, accompanied by plainclothes from Special Branch. His grand finale at Harvard was the first time he'd trailed the full thesis about Operation Hercules. The lecture wouldn't be released until the book deal announcement was public. But, no doubt, British intelligence would get an advance copy from their friends in the FBI.

He was so close, yet still so far. Like all secret operations, the infiltration was relatively simple. The exfil was where all operatives got caught. Max had spent every night reciting the details of the plan until he knew them backwards. He wheeled out his bags and tried to remember where his car was parked. The airport was thronged with passengers. Max used them for cover, hoping the cameras would struggle to isolate another middle-aged face in the crowd.

He reached the exit and stared round at signs for taxis. Then, as he was about to risk turning on his phone, a voice sounded behind him. Outside rather than inside.

'Max!'

He turned, squinting at a figure pushing through the doors, struggling with tiredness and confusion. Then, as the figure moved nearer, he saw who it was.

50

The briefings started several months ago. First it was a quote in *The Times*. Then it became gossip fodder in the *Mail*. Finally, the *Telegraph* ran an editorial calling for the Prime Minister to shake up his top team and sort out British domestic policy. The final blow was a snide one-liner in the *Daily Star* which eliminated all doubt. The next reshuffle was due any moment now and Lucas Harper was about to be publicly fired.

To lessen the trauma, Lucas started moving things from his large ministerial office back to his shabbier digs in the Houses of Parliament. He cancelled non-urgent diary appointments. He shelved plans for new legislation. Instead, he decided to use his final weeks to smooth over any legacy issues. Like all Home Secretaries before him, Lucas had been buried by the graveyard of ministerial departments, still bearing the scars of every controversy from immigration to terrorist attacks. #RIPLucasHarper was already trending on Twitter.

In his quieter moments, the exploratory calls began. He tapped up some old City contacts to see if anyone was looking for a board member. Failing that, how about a shiny tech start-up. He was fluent in the world of cyber security and data protection, with a sideline in fraud prevention and digitizing public services. There must be an app developer who needed an A-list name for their letterhead. He would gladly trade his Jermyn Street suit for dad jeans and a hoodie. After all, he still had three school-age kids and a mortgage. All offers were welcome.

The calls, so far, had yielded nothing. The only recruiter he'd met was a pinched, haughty type who'd once failed selection for the candidates' list and skulked off to the recruitment industry instead. Lucas had been midway through a second G&T when she lowered her spectacles and asked if he'd considered volunteering. He left early and let her pay for the drinks.

That was the riddle of politics – it was so crushingly temporary. Now he had an armoured car, a protection detail outside the door and the safest house on the street. He enjoyed total autonomy over who came into the country, who was forced to leave, who was arrested and who remained at large. He was in charge of MI5, the National Crime Agency, Border Force and could have half the SAS inside his office with one phone call to the right number.

The minute after the reshuffle, he would be an anonymous backbencher with two staff, a cupboard of an office and powerless to stop a planning application or fill a pothole in his constituency. No more free newspapers, either. He'd even heard stories of former Chancellors reduced to stealing a copy of the *FT* from the Members' Centre. He could hear the gods mocking him. Mocking them all.

There was a knock on the door. His Senior Private Secretary stuck their head in. Lucas wondered how many more times that would happen. Soon he'd be doing his own diary, scrolling through the Trainline app to book travel, condemned to the tea round, showing he was still a man of the people and watching the lobby journalists snicker at how far the mighty had fallen.

'Your next appointment, Minister. The Acting DG is here.'

'Thank you. Show him in.'

Lucas greeted Saul and ushered him towards the easy chairs around the glass-topped coffee table. The weekly MI5 briefings were one thing he would miss. They were the most varied part of his day. One minute there would be eye-popping evidence about the editor of a broadsheet newspaper and his on-off relationship with a Russian prostitute. The next minute some spine-chilling detail of an assassination attempt cooked up by rogue members of the ISI and due to be carried out within hours. Lucas even wondered about turning it into some kind of airport thriller if money ran tight. He could use a pseudonym. No one need ever know.

Drinks were delivered and the secure door was shut. Saul cycled through the headlines including the forthcoming state visit of the French President; security concerns regarding climate protestors and plans to storm into the Commons chamber; more details on a key Moscow money-launderer striking up an intimate friendship with a former Chief of the General Staff; then rumblings from the Chinese embassy about the UK's digital infrastructure and the rollout of 6G.

Finally, Saul closed the official briefing folder

and finished his tea – always a plain builder's brew, never anything as fancy as Earl Grey or, God help us, Darjeeling. Saul, despite the recent knighthood, hadn't changed. Few would ever know the truth about the prim superintendent father and Maths teacher mother. But all spies needed cover, and Lucas was content to play along. The act was almost done.

Saul checked his watch. They had five minutes before Lucas would be summoned for his next meeting. 'There is one rather more delicate issue I'd like to discuss, Home Secretary. Strictly off-the-books, this time, as opposed to the other items on the agenda.'

Lucas was intrigued. 'Oh yes?'

'Weapons-grade, I'm afraid.'

'I see.'

'It's concerning an operation from last year. You may remember it. Codenamed Tempest.'

Lucas tried not to show his panic. He kept his voice level. He still had nightmares about that one. 'I thought that was ancient history, Saul. Dead and buried. I'm sure I remember hearing those exact words.'

He remembered Saul returning from Paris last year with the contents of the safety deposit box including a notebook, a photo album, a birth certificate and a letter. There was some convoluted story about the Simon Wiesenthal Centre being a decoy location and the notebook hidden by one of Scarlet King's old acquaintances in a fourth-floor flat on Île de la Cité near Notre-Dame. Reuben something or other, a former child inmate at Auschwitz. A live letterbox, in the jargon.

'It was, Minister,' continued Saul. 'Recently, however, I came across raw intelligence suggesting that Dr Max Archer, the academic involved, has sold a manuscript revealing the full story behind Operation Hercules and the British state's complicity in hiding the truth about Nazi war crimes.'

'Just Operation Hercules. Nothing about Scarlet King?'

'It appears so.'

'Does the Attorney General have a view on this?'

'The lawyers glanced over the immunity deal. The specific wording only prohibited mention of Scarlet King and her work as an illegal, copied almost directly from the Blunt immunity agreement we used as precedent. The AG's view is we can't touch him legally.'

Lucas felt his blood pressure rising. 'I don't understand, Saul. You assured me personally that this was dealt with. That was the basis on which the DPP agreed to the immunity deal. You got the notebook. Case closed. End of story.'

Saul squirmed on the sofa, shifting his bulk uneasily. 'Minister, what do you know about a deception method known as the "Haversack Ruse"?'

'About as much as I know about the rest of Operation Tempest, apparently. Sod all.'

'In October 1917 an enterprising British intelligence officer named Richard Meinertzhagen allegedly helped win the Battle of Beersheba and Gaza by allowing a haversack full of supposedly genuine British battle plans to fall into the possession of the Ottomans. It was a minor victory, then, and no more might have come of it. Except that one admirer of the Haversack Ruse was Churchill.'

'Spare me the history lesson, Saul, and try getting to the point.'

'Churchill decided to set up London Controlling Section in September '41. Their sole job was to run all forms of Allied military deception. This is when the Haversack Ruse was dusted down. It became the basis of some of the most famous wartime secret operations: Operation Mincemeat in '43, using false documents as a smoke-and-mirror disguise for the Allied invasion of Sicily; and most infamously, of course, Operation Fortitude in '44, using phantom armies to convince the German high command that the real D-Day invasion was coming from the Pas de Calais rather than Normandy.'

Lucas nodded. *Eye of the Needle*. I read it when I was a teenager.'

'Precisely. The Germans were gifted sights of the dummy Sherman tanks and landing craft and thus failed to provide reinforcements. The materials might have been different, but the method was the same. Fortitude was the Haversack Ruse writ large.'

'Is there a point to all this?'

'Yes. I think Scarlet King used our best trick back at us. In fact, I think the whole operation was a Haversack Ruse of her own. The notebook was a decoy. A Pas de Calais rather than a Normandy. She wanted all our attention to be on that to ensure we missed the real landing ground. She played us right from the very start.'

Lucas barely took in the words. His head throbbed. Spies always seemed to make things so damn complicated. 'You've seen the papers, Saul. According to every lobby journalist in SW1, I'm about to be kicked out of here. I may not survive till the end of the week. I'm a dead man walking.'

'Max Archer is back on British soil. He's been untouchable under US free speech protections for the last twelve months. We may have one final chance to close this down. But I need ministerial authorization to do so. One last move. One final play.'

'How?'

'It's better you don't know the details.'

'And when it's done?'

'When what's done?'

'If this gets out, you're the one standing in the dock, do you understand? We never discussed this. This conversation never happened. You closed your folder and went on your way.'

Saul nodded. 'Thank you, Home Secretary.'

51

Max tried not to stare but there was no helping
it. Her hair was shorter now, the skin tanned
from the Californian sun. She was dressed differ-
ently too. The formal lawyerly outfits were gone.
Instead, there was the artful streetwear of a
Silicon Valley executive, complete with smart-
watch and the transatlantic twang in her voice.
The baby sat, pudgy and surprisingly mute, on
her lap.

'We decided on Jennifer,' said Emma, once the
coffees arrived, 'after my mum. Jenny for short.
Cris gets first dibs on the name for the next one.'

Max covered his surprise with a cough. 'The next
one?'

'Strictly speaking, we're not actually telling
people yet.'

'Don't worry. I'll try not to broadcast the news.'

Emma smiled. 'So how are things?'

Max looked at Emma now and realized it wasn't
the hair or the clothes or the tan. Or not really. It
was something intangible, abstract almost. She was
happy. That was the difference. It suffused her, from
the way she smiled to how she stroked the baby's
head to how she drank from the takeaway coffee
cup. She was at ease with herself, like a light switching on. The version he knew was a prototype, a

flawed early version; this was the model everyone would remember, the permanent version cleared for public release.

'Since almost getting jailed for life in the Paris embassy you mean.'

'Everyone has a mid-life crisis. Yours was typically extreme.'

'I think buying a Ferrari might be marginally less embarrassing.'

'But a lot more expensive.'

The life they'd had was already being airbrushed from history, like one of those old Soviet photographs. When all was said and done, he would be a vague reference point, merely a random name from the past. They had been everything to each other; now they were nearly strangers again.

She said, 'I heard you got promoted. Professor Max Archer. That has a certain ring to it.'

He smiled. It sounded hollow when she said it, like being made head prefect when you've already left school. It was nothing compared to the small bundle sitting on her lap. Age was such a mercurial thing. The dreams of a twenty-year-old were the shackles of middle age. Sometimes Max felt like a hostage to his younger self.

'I meant to send a note or something,' he said. 'I have a lot to be grateful for and we didn't exactly part on the best terms.'

In his mind, this was the point where he mentioned the book. He would dazzle her with his outrageous success and watch the torment build in her eyes. But it was immaterial now. She would say nice things and mean them, too, and he wasn't sure he could face that sort of kindness.

Emma nodded. 'Well, for what it's worth, I'm sorry I couldn't tell you. I should have done. Perhaps that would have made things easier.'

'Do you really believe that?'

'Why?'

'I spent so long sulking over something I never had, Ems, that I missed what was right in front of me. I was a fool.'

'You were young. We're all fools then.'

'Some of us seemed to grow wiser.'

The baby started fidgeting. Emma saw the time. There had already been one bizarre muck-up with their tickets, the airline computer system mysteriously forgetting their earlier booking, and they couldn't afford to miss the next flight.

They stood awkwardly, not quite sure of the protocol.

'Take care, Max,' she said. 'I mean it.'

They settled on a hug. Max watched Emma and her daughter head towards the departure gate and knew he would probably never see them again. That old life, in all its chaotic glory, was over now, a former existence to be boxed and stored, never to be reopened.

He left the airport and found a taxi.

'Where to, mate?'

Max sat in the back of the cab and wondered. Emma was gone. Oliver was gone. Scarlet King was gone too. What else was there left? He wondered if the taxi could be bugged and then felt tired of hiding, sick of the shadows. He would rather go down fighting than live on the run from ciphers and ghosts.

'Cadogan Hotel,' he said. 'Sloane Street.'

Following the weekly briefing at the Home Office, the Acting Director-General of Her Majesty's Security Service returned from Marsham Street to Thames House. He endured two further meetings before cancelling his diary for the rest of the day with muttered complaints of a stomach bug.

The official log showed the service car dropping the Acting DG off at his house in the village of Kingham, West Oxfordshire, just over an hour later.

The same afternoon a former member of the Special Air Service D Squadron received a call from a burner mobile while sitting in the corner office of a private security firm based in Knightsbridge. The voice didn't identify itself, but merely repeated a target name, an address and a time. The usual routine.

By that evening, as Saul Northcliffe tucked into a vegan shepherd's pie with mineral water, a team of former A Branch operatives and veterans of the Special Reconnaissance Regiment trailed the target to the Cadogan Hotel in Chelsea.

Third floor, single room, booked in for two nights.

The target didn't leave until 9 a.m. the following morning.

52

Max breakfasted lightly on fruit and strong coffee. He wanted to think clearly today. He left most of his belongings in the hotel bedroom and set out on foot, stopping first at a local florist and then continuing to Sloane Square Tube Station. There were at least three watchers he spotted last night, but they must have rung the changes this morning. He spotted one elderly figure with a newspaper, a second younger man in a tracksuit and then a thirty-something woman parked in a car nearby supposedly engrossed in her phone.

He put in place some basic dry-cleaning measures – getting on and off Tube carriages, heading back up the stairs, changing platform – before he darted out of the exit and headed towards Pimlico Tube Station instead, seeing how many still tailed him. One had dropped off, but the younger man was still active, keeping several paces behind in his dull grey zip-up top. Max reached Pimlico Tube and then darted away at the last moment and headed for Victoria Station, losing himself in the chaos of the main concourse, before taking the District line westbound and emerging from the Warwick Road exit of Earl's Court.

By the time he reached Brompton Cemetery, Max was pretty sure he'd lost them. That was always the risk with coming back to Britain. Ideally, he should have stayed at Harvard and tried to convert the visiting post into a permanent one. But Oliver had died only weeks before he started, and the lure of home proved too strong. Max reached the grave and saw the headstone was dirty already. He bent down and wiped it with his palms, then positioned the flowers carefully until he was happy. Lily, his mother, had been cremated. Oliver always had a terror of his flesh being incinerated. They were apart in death as in life. It had a curious symmetry.

Max took a step back. Even at the end, Oliver was always a reporter, preferring life from a distance. He was a freelancer, a stringer, sampling the most exciting parts of other people's lives and then leaving in his socks before the boredom kicked in. Or was that merely cover? It was impossible to know, separating the performance from the real thing. The man had been a living slice of history, a witness to the twentieth century, a secret source to beat all sources, sitting opposite him all this time. And yet Max had missed it.

He felt that familiar sadness now. He barely registered the crunch of leaves behind him or the snap of dried twigs underfoot. He caught the rustle of the old mackintosh, then the exaggerated throat-clearing. When he turned round, Max saw Saul Northcliffe standing three feet behind him, polishing his glasses and then looking at Oliver's headstone.

Saul finished with his glasses and put them back on. He looked tired, almost mournful. They nodded to one another.

It was time.

53

The café was almost deserted. Brompton Cemetery was near any number of five-star hotels, but that wasn't Saul Northcliffe's style. Max looked around the greasy spoon. The laminated menus were slippery with ketchup and someone else's fingerprints. Heart FM blared from the speakers. Any background noise was lost in the permanent oily sizzle behind the counter.

Saul was a regular, clearly, received with an in-the-know nod by the proprietor and taking his usual booth, the furthest away from the toilets. They ordered – Saul went for the full English, Max for a coffee – and the food arrived with surprising haste. Saul squeezed more ketchup on to his plate and then mixed it all in with the beans, mushrooms and black pudding. He slurped at his builder's brew.

'My old man was a copper,' he said, girding himself for another rasher of bacon. 'Always had a ritual before each big operation. A greasy spoon breakfast to start, a greasy spoon brekkie to finish.' Saul picked up a paper napkin and wiped eggs from his mouth. 'He also died of a heart attack in his early sixties. The two may be connected.'

Max looked at the other customers. Two middle-aged blokes with high-viz vests stuffed on the spare chair. An older man flicking through a copy of the *Sun*. Then a younger woman munching on toast as she scrolled through her phone.

'You brought me here to talk about your family?' he asked.

Saul smiled. 'I didn't bring you here at all. You came of your own free will.'

'Does the Acting Director-General of the Security Service usually take intelligence historians to greasy spoons?'

Saul was on to the fried bread now. He began using the bread to mop up beans and some leftover egg yolk. It was a nineties revival hour on the radio and 'Roll with It' by Oasis began, the Gallagher brothers at their throaty best. Max thought of school and sneaking fags behind the sports centre and felt like he was fifteen again.

'Blame the penny-pinchers in Whitehall. Soon running a secret service won't be cost efficient. We'll have to outsource it to the Chinese, if we haven't already.'

'Why am I really here?'

'I hear congratulations are in order.'

Max thought of the watchers trailing him from the Cadogan Hotel and the items still in his room. 'I have no idea what you mean.'

'I think you do. Six-figure American deal, six-figures for UK rights, now Hollywood calling. That overdraft should be cleared in no time. Not to mention your father's old gambling debts. Put a bit aside for a roof of your own.'

'You're still spying on me.'

'I'm a spy, Professor Archer. It's what I do.'

'Not without due cause.'

'Plenty of cause, I assure you. Or did you think we only watch other kinds of people? Not white middle-aged academics like you?'

'That's not what I said.'

'It's what you meant.'

'I rather think I'm the judge of what I do or do not mean.'

'That's the problem with you ivory-tower types. You think you can break the law and get away with it. One rule for the rest of us, another one for you.'

'We had a deal.'

'Check the statute book, Professor. The Coroners and Justice Act 2009.'

'Refresh my memory.'

'Clearly prohibits any monetary gain by the description of a crime. Little thing called an "exploitative proceeds order". Mainly ex-cons looking to cash in. But it comes in handy for us spooks now and then.'

'The immunity deal stopped me mentioning the notebook, Scarlet King or her work as an illegal for Directorate S of the KGB. It said nothing about Operation Hercules or Otto Spengler. I've had some of the best legal brains at Harvard scrutinize every single comma. I've kept my side of the bargain. It's time you kept yours.'

Saul took another sip of tea. Max glanced again at the other diners. More than ever, now, there seemed to be something off about this set-up. No customers had come in or out of the café in the last twenty minutes. None of the others had left. They were all still in position: reading the newspaper, chatting about last night's footie, scrolling through phones. It was too staged, too perfect.

Saul saw Max's gaze and the light of realization. He pushed his plate away. 'My people, Professor. All of them. Try not to make a scene.'

'Why?'

Saul smiled. 'Because it's finally over, Professor. After all this time . . . I *know*.'

54

Max tried to keep calm. But his hands were damp. He felt dizzy. He looked at the mug of coffee and suddenly wondered what had been slipped inside.

'What is this place?'

'Think of it like a safe house, Max. An outpost of the office canteen.'

Max loosened his collar, longed for outside air. The figures in the café remained unmoved. They were like wax exhibits, real but make-believe. He'd been prepared for arrest, interview rooms, even a custody suite. But this had been planned to the last detail. Emma at the airport, her ticket mix-up with the airline computer system, the watchers by the hotel, the music here – all of it was designed to unsettle him. Break him, even.

'What do you want from me?'

'Why don't we start with the truth.'

'You had the truth in Paris. I gave you everything you asked for.'

'No. You did a very good job of playing the innocent academic abroad. I fell for it then, but my eyes have since been opened.'

'I have no idea what you're talking about.'

Saul reached into his jacket pocket and removed a piece of paper. It was a copy of a letter from the oncology department at St Thomas' Hospital addressed to 'Miss S. King'. Saul placed it on the table for Max to read. 'Terminal cancer. The consultant only gave her months, a year at best. Did you know that?'

Max stared at the letter. It could be a forgery, of course, decked out with a fake consultant's name and a convincing impression of the hospital crest. But, somehow, he doubted it. He remembered his surprise at seeing Scarlet's face made up so heavily in St James's Park. She was hiding something then. Now he knew what.

Saul wiped his hands and continued. 'Scarlet King had two mortal sins in her life, Max. Two sins which she needed to expiate before she went into the great beyond. That's why she did what she did. That's why she picked you.'

'You've still lost me.'

'Mortal sin number one. Helping Otto Spengler escape justice in 1946. Scarlet King wasn't Jewish, but Anastasia Chekova was. Scarlet helped a killer of Jews escape punishment for his crimes. That was the first thing she couldn't live with. The first cancer of the soul.'

'And the second?'

'In 1964, Scarlet was stationed in Moscow at the same time as Caspar Madison. Records show Scarlet took a six-month leave of absence from the Service later that year. Back then it was written off as a break after a hardship posting. Now it appears she was pregnant with Caspar Madison's child.'

Max remembered the passage from the papers. 'Vetting must have been a nightmare.'

'But, back then, still doable. Especially if the pregnancy was never declared and the child was quickly hidden in plain sight. Maria Kazakova was

Scarlet's handler as well as being an academic at Oxford University. Maria took in the child as her own. The daughter she always longed for but could never have. No one else apart from Scarlet and Maria's husband ever knew.'

'Do you have any proof or is this just theory?'

Saul fetched a folder from his bag, withdrawing the first item. 'Try this for starters.'

Max looked at the document. It was far more modern than he was expecting. The document was a personnel file dated from June 2001. Max saw his own name at the top: ARCHER, M. There was a codename (Candidate 79B) and then a report from an IONEC training instructor. He read the words once, then again, struggling to comprehend it:

Candidate 79B has shown the necessary aptitude for secret work. He was fluent at interview and achieved top marks across all the examinations. Further improvement is needed on situational awareness, but that is a minor point that can be addressed at Fort Monckton. He achieved the top marks in this year's vetting, and, without hesitation, we recommend he proceed to IONEC in September.

Max looked up. He felt sick. 'I don't understand.'

'According to the SIS archives, this recommendation was sent to the chair of the IONEC recruitment panel in the summer of 2001. The recruitment panel was always headed up by a former Service grandee. It wasn't the recruiters who vetoed you, Max. It was the chair herself. Very unusual. No specific reason was ever given, and none was ever asked. But the chair of the panel that year was none other than . . .'

'Scarlet King.'

'The very one.'

Max needed a moment to register that. There was no point asking why. Max knew. Saul knew. That was why they were here. That was why everything had happened. Max had thought he'd uncovered every facet of this case over the last twelve months, the forensic academic barely missing a beat. But there was always one surprise. This was it.

The music on the speakers changed again now to 'Bitter Sweet Symphony'. The late nineties, Blair and Cool Britannia, that brief interval between the end of the Cold War and 9/11. Max's life flashed hazily in front of him.

Saul continued. 'I don't mind admitting that this had me puzzled. Why would Scarlet King veto you, Max? This woman who supposedly had no connection with you until a year ago. Why would she cast the candidate with the highest IONEC entry marks and the best recommendation into the wilderness? Why would she condemn you to a life of regret and academia instead?'

'You'll have to ask her.'

Saul took out a second document. It was a photograph. Max knew there was nowhere to turn now. This was it. 'Surnames let you down every time. That was the dinosaur in me, I suppose, the one fatal error I made. Kazakova wasn't Maria's married name, of course, it was her maiden name. Her husband was Professor Maurice Anderson, the communist mathematician and philosopher. The child adopted by Maria Kazakova was known by the surname Anderson. That was the final piece of the jigsaw. That was how everything connects. ANDERSON, E. Born November 1964.'

The old family anecdote. Their first meeting: the embassy ball, the music, Oliver in his Sunday best.

'First name Elizabeth, known to everyone as Lily. She became Elizabeth Archer upon marrying. Died in 2009 leaving behind one child. A son.'

Max didn't know what to say. He had known it in an academic sense. But hearing the facts take audible form made them feel real for the first time.

'You.'

55

The dynamic changed after that. Max still remembered the moment of realization at the Simon Wiesenthal Centre as he saw the photograph of his mother in the album, the small fair-haired child standing next to Scarlet. The moment he finally knew this wasn't a tale about a Russian illegal called Scarlet King, but about a Russian Jew named Anastasia Chekova.

'You were Scarlet's last secret operation, Max. Her final joe. Not just an asset. But family. Scarlet had neglected her own family in life. She was determined to rectify that mistake in death.'

Max saw Lily just before the end. She was tortured by something. But the cancer got there first. She died with the secret still in her.

'Scarlet thought she was protecting you by vetoing your application for IONEC,' Saul continued. 'In fact, she came close to ruining your life. She wanted to make amends. But she knew you'd never turn your life around unless forced to. That's why she set the plan in motion. The calling card, the email, the notebook, her own suicide, the safety deposit box, Reuben. Being framed by British intelligence for a murder you didn't commit was the only thing terrifying enough to jolt you into action. You were the only thing that could make her plan fail.'

'Sounds almost simple.'

'Scarlet even trusted you to think of the immunity deal. She'd seen your evaluation marks for IONEC. She knew what you were capable of. She'd also read your books. She knew you'd studied the Anthony Blunt case. You were the one who spotted the opportunity. We were the ones who fell for it. Once the Home Secretary granted the immunity deal, Scarlet's plan worked perfectly. Exposing the truth about Operation Hercules and helping her only grandson turn his life around. Now all the ducks were in a row: the secret, immunity, enough for you to publish the truth about Hercules and make some mega-bucks. There was just one final part.'

'The notebook was genuine,' Max insisted. 'You did your research. It all checks out.'

'Yes. Everything she wrote there was true, granted. But it was the wrong truth. The notebook was always a decoy, never the main event. Scarlet needed us to believe that her ultimate goal was to reveal the truth about her life as a Russian illegal. But it never was. This was always far more personal for her. Scarlet only had one thing to give – secrets. So that's what she did. This was her inheritance to you from beyond the grave.'

Max looked at the other diners now. They still hadn't broken cover. He couldn't see any side-arms or visible weaponry. But he bet there were Glock 17s tucked away, ready to take him out if required. He was tired of being on the back foot. Tired of all of this: Emma, the baby, the music on the speakers, Saul Northcliffe and his hardscrabble pretensions.

Now it was time to turn the tables. Prove he still had some fight.

'It's not just personal for me, though, is it?' he said. 'Mr Bilton, right? Or is it really Sir Saul Northcliffe? Or, no, perhaps . . . Christopher Sewell?'

Saul didn't react. 'I'm sorry?'

Max pressed on. 'I can do my research too. It's what I'm best at. My special skill. Saul Northcliffe, born January 1962. Joined Thames House in 1984 and part of K Branch in the nineties. It was your job to investigate suspected double agents working in Britain. Cold War traitors that needed to be cleaned up and prosecuted. Scarlet King was on that list, wasn't she? A person of interest. Your responsibility. You were the officer who let her slip right through your fingers. A career-ending mistake. Pension, titles, everything.'

'A charming story, Professor.'

'This isn't about covering up other people's mistakes.' Max saw the resignation in Saul Northcliffe's face. 'No, this is about covering up your own.'

56

Saul was silent. He knew what was coming. He'd always feared Max Archer was smart enough to make the connection. He saw Max reading through the rest of the notebook in that fourth-floor flat on Île de la Cité a year ago, verifying the find was genuine. That the details of the immunity agreement had been fulfilled. Reuben, Scarlet's live letterbox, had smuggled the contents out of the Simon Wiesenthal Centre for safekeeping, a basic deception ploy. Saul had always known this moment would arrive.

'Of course,' continued Max, 'no K Branch officer worth their salt would approach the Sovbloc Controller of SIS without some form of cover. So you pretended to be a reporter from the *Sunday Times* Insight team as a pretext for interviewing her about possible espionage activities for the KGB during the Cold War and her alliances in Vienna. You cosied up to Otto Spengler and got him to talk about Hercules. You used an alias to hide your real motive . . . Christopher Sewell.'

Saul could still remember his nerves before that first bump at the hospital. The friendship with Philby, the link with Professor Maria Kazakova and her communist mathematician husband Professor Maurice Anderson, the rise through Russia House – he'd looked at it all, one of thousands of names being re-vetted by K Branch. He remembered the call from Scarlet and visiting her flat and seeing that playful look in her eyes, stripping the armour from him, as if she could tell a lie just by the way he pronounced the words.

'What if I did?'

Max looked triumphant. 'That's why you couldn't arrest me. That's why the police were never involved. That's why you were so determined to get the notebook and bury this case. Not to help the nation, but to help yourself. Your job was to hunt down Russian assets working on British soil. You missed the biggest traitor of the Cold War. Your pension would go at the very least, reputation too. If that came out, you'd spend the next twenty years in front of official inquiries accusing you of gross incompetence.'

Saul felt that familiar weight in his gut. He remembered Charlotte mentioning Scarlet King's name for the first time and the flashbacks to almost three decades earlier. Yes, this had always been personal. Scarlet had outplayed him then. He'd been determined not to let history repeat itself.

Max looked at the other operatives now. 'Given that fact, I'm assuming your friends aren't official?'

Saul conceded the fact with a nod. 'Knightsbridge private security firm. Run by a former Regiment contact. They help us out with deniable jobs.'

'Does anyone else know?'

'That I had suspicions about Scarlet King in the nineties and let her bamboozle me with the prize of Caspar Madison and the Mitrokhin Archive?'

'Yes.'

'No. K Branch was amalgamated into D Branch in '94, just after SIS was avowed. We moved out of those rabbit warrens at Curzon Street and Gower Street to the promised land of Thames House. Some of the more sensitive K branch files never survived the move.'

'How convenient.'

'Accidents happen. Usually in our favour.'

There was silence, just the slow hiss of background cooking. Finally, Max said, 'So what happens now?'

Saul considered. There was one last play here. A very final move. Saul wondered whether Scarlet King had anticipated it, after all, a mind always five steps ahead. The self-deleting email, the notebook, the safety deposit box, Cleo and Reuben, the immunity deal, the live letterbox, the bidding war for Max's book – Scarlet had crafted all of it, he was sure, planned each strand in detail, an agent-runner to the last. He'd never faced another opponent like her. Scarlet King haunted him even in death.

Saul gathered himself. 'When Scarlet King vetoed you for IONEC, she was trying to save you from repeating her own mistakes. She didn't want you to endure the solitude and sacrifices of life as a spy. As irony would have it, by trying to save your life she accidentally ruined it.'

'The butterfly effect,' said Max. 'Change one small bit of history and you change everything. What if Hitler had been killed during the Battle of the Somme in October 1916? What if the Germans had never allowed Lenin back to Petrograd in 1917? Counterfactuals.'

'Yes.' Saul paused, then committed to the next part. 'But what if a counterfactual could become factual? Rewriting the sins of history?'

'Hypothetically?'

'No.'

'You're mocking me.'

'My time as Acting Director-General will soon come to an end. They're pensioning me off with a stint as Chair of the Joint Intelligence Committee at the Cabinet Office. Whitehall's idea of a golden goodbye. I have a small reptile fund that allows me to run my own off-the-books assets. Nothing too grand, mind, but a hand-picked network providing useful gossip and intel for HMG.'

'Diplomatic cover?'

'Natural cover. NOCs, fellow travellers, agents of influence. People in finance, the media, science and academia. The French would call them honourable correspondents. The sort of thing your father used to do for us. A chance to continue the family tradition.'

'And do what exactly?'

Saul kept his expression neutral. The bump at the graveyard, the gang-plank pitch here – yes, there was a chance this could work. 'Be our eyes and ears. Your access as an intelligence historian is the perfect cover. Old spies will talk to you, current spies will monitor you. You can talk to people we can't. The reptile fund is strictly deniable and held in a private bank in the City. As such, the terms are more generous than usual.'

'And the book?'

'It will enhance your cover. Max Archer the best-selling spy historian is more use to us than a mid-level academic. It will give you better access to key sources.'

Max's eyes narrowed. 'No strings attached?'

'We only ask for one thing in exchange.'

Max smiled. 'Of course.'

'The immunity deal stands. The Attorney General and the DPP won't try and prosecute you under the Coroners and Justice Act or any other piece of arcane legislation. You get almost everything you wanted.'

'Almost?'

'You can have everything . . . as long as the JIC gets full copy approval on *Operation Hercules* and all subsequent books and articles.'

Max laughed. He sat back, reeling from the blow. 'That's absurd. Totally out of the question.'

'The deal stands for the next twelve hours. There won't be another.'

'No academic could agree to that. It would be betraying everything I believe in. The entire principle of academic independence. Not to mention my own self-respect.'

'Then stop being so self-respecting, Max. Stop being a wide-eyed student wannabe. Work with us rather than against us.'

'It's not that simple.'

'Yes, it is. Your father served his country without betraying himself. Your grandmother too. Life isn't black and white. Surely Scarlet taught you that, if nothing else. Show us what we missed all those years ago. Stop standing on the sidelines and get your hands dirty. Take a tough decision for once in your life.'

Max was speechless. He stared around the café again, looking darkly at the speakers. The music now changed to 'Wannabe' by the Spice Girls.

Saul looked at his watch and signalled for the bill. 'Which reminds me.' He took a final piece of paper out of his jacket pocket.

Max looked down at the piece of paper. It was a hotel booking for the Ritz-Carlton in Vienna. 'What's this?'

'If you accept our offer, then this is your first assignment.'

'Do I really have a choice?'

Saul nodded to the others in the café to stand down. The four pavement artists got up now, breaking the act, pocketing their props and heading for the exit.

Saul rose from the table and buttoned his suit jacket. 'We always have a choice, Dr Archer. That's what Scarlet fought for. In the end, that's what we're all fighting for.'

57

Getting into the country had been easier than expected. The customs officer had looked at the passport for Dr Charlotte Weizmann, Assistant Professor of Biology at the Hebrew University of Jerusalem and asked a few cursory questions in broken English before letting her through. A taxi ride to the Ritz-Carlton passed without incident. Only a few hours after landing, Dr Weizmann was installed in a pleasant single room with her laptop connected to a secure server. Tel Aviv received the agreed parole signalling that she'd arrived safely.

She showered, changed and then reviewed the official programme for the '48th Annual Interdisciplinary Security Conference'. This year, apparently, the AISC conference was sponsored by an American social media firm hoping to boost their cyber-security credentials. Dr Weizmann checked the times again and then pocketed the programme and went for a short walk around the city. She took touristy photos with her phone, stopped in bookshops to browse, and even sampled some old-style European café culture with a copy of the *The Economist.*

She spotted no watchers so far. That didn't necessarily mean she was clean. The conference attracted experts from Beijing, Moscow, London, Berlin and

Paris, the Davos of the global intelligence community. Officers from all those countries could be searching through her hotel room at this very moment. Dr Weizmann had left enough red herrings to preoccupy them. After all, she wanted them chasing their tails.

Once the dry-cleaning was done, Dr Weizmann headed back to the hotel and lunched in the restaurant, silently noting the various eminent guests who'd already arrived with their minders and entourage in tow. She returned briefly to her room and noticed the dust patterns by the drawers. The hair in the doorway was gone too and the room safe had been searched. She would have to play this carefully, then. Either her legend was under suspicion or, more likely, various scalp-hunters wanted to know more about the research of the mysterious Dr C. Weizmann and the top-secret goings-on at Hebrew University.

The opening lecture began at six o'clock. She took a seat near the back and watched as various big names were ushered to the front row. Eminent professors from Beijing, academics from Harvard and Yale tipped for sensitive jobs at the White House, even a grey-haired sage from the University of Tehran flanked by two men posing as research students but displaying all the jowly arrogance of Quds Force, the special operations unit of the Islamic Revolutionary Guard Corps.

There was a brief introduction by this year's Conference Chair and the usual thanks to all the corporate sponsors. The first night was always lighter fare before the technical stuff tomorrow.

This year's opening keynote was given by a Professor of Intelligence History from the London School of Economics, a puff piece for his new book apparently. The lecture was entitled: 'Operation Hercules: Science, Security and History's Lessons for the Future of Global Intelligence'. A break from yet more interminable PowerPoint decks, at least.

Professor Archer had clearly rehearsed the presentation well. Dr Weizmann had googled the name beforehand and seen the online articles in the *Bookseller*, *Publishers Weekly*, *Deadline* and the *Hollywood Reporter*. Apparently, several big A-list stars were already rumoured to be in discussions about playing the Nazi war criminal.

The room tonight, however, was largely hostile. No academic ever welcomed another's success. There was silence at the jokes, energetic coughing at each anecdote, then loud, face-altering yawns. But Professor Archer ignored them. He could afford to. His appearance here, surely, was just to retain his academic status. Pretty soon he'd drop down to part-time teaching, buy a nice house in the country and continue producing bestselling works of espionage history that made his accountant very happy. The others here would be lucky to retire on half as much.

Dr Weizmann enjoyed people-watching. The German scientists bristled at the early part of the lecture on Nazi scientists and the spectre of Auschwitz. The British contingent looked equally displeased as focus turned to Operation Hercules and MI6's role in covering up war crimes. The French weren't much happier as Professor Archer set out the scientific advantage the UK gained from such perfidy, confirming Paris's own worst fears. Finally, the Chinese stared at their watches when the lecture turned to modern-day human rights abuses and the plight of the Uighurs. The lecture ended with three recommendations about the future of global security and a decidedly muted round of applause.

Afterwards, the delegates scuttled off for the opening night gala dinner, complete with the promise of a free bar. Dr Weizmann watched them go. This was her best time to strike. Each delegate was out of their room. The minders would be too preoccupied with events in the main hall to permanently man the corridors. They would drink too much, think too little. Perfect hunting time.

She slipped into the ladies and emerged several minutes later having made the changes. Then she took the stairs to the seventh floor. Tel Aviv was clear about the list of priority targets. Beijing was useful, anything from the Harvard types if she could get it. But the University of Tehran delegation was the jewel in the crown. It was also the riskiest. The MSS would put a bullet in her and leave the rest to the local police. The IRCG, however, didn't do drive-by assassinations. They liked rendition, torture, prisons so filthy they were more like human sewers. But she had a back-up for that. There was a pill hidden inside the lining of her dress, short-term activation. Anything – yes, truly anything – was better than waking up in Tehran.

Dr Weizmann reached the seventh floor. She was heading down the corridor now, the nerves already building. There was the sound of lift doors open-ing behind her. She slowed down, glanced behind her, then checked again.

The figure emerged from the lift and smiled in recognition.

'Hello, Cleo,' said Max.

58

Max looked round the inside of Café Landtmann. It was hard to believe the place was still standing, just as it used to be. A survivor of wars and recessions, romance and tragedy alike. He imagined Otto Spengler walking in the door nearly eighty years ago, Scarlet King sitting opposite, the city still fresh from war. Architecture was always the best type of history. The past was stitched into every detail here.

They were easing him in gently, or at least that's what they claimed. The Vienna Security Conference was an annual gathering of intelligence experts, international affairs academics, the odd political scientist and legions of actual scientists. He was here as a token, the media don parachuted in to entertain the troops without ever quite being one of them. Not that Max minded. The pay was decent, the room was deluxe and the company, barring a few notable exceptions, was rarely dull. Plus, there was an academic from Moscow State University that the JIC had an eye on, an early recruit for the Foliant scheme in the seventies. The information on his hard drive would help Porton Down assess the latest developments in Putin's nerve agent programme. He had his mission brief.

But that was all in the future. Max was focused on tonight. Cleo looked different from the last time they met in Paris. The 'Dr Weizmann' legend called for longer hair, presumably a wig of some kind. There were subtle alterations to her face: the nose longer, eyes pea-green rather than sea-blue, and the peak of the forehead lower than before. Max admired the attention to detail. Even her accent was different. The cosmetics, he knew, stopped advanced facial recognition technology ruining a mission before it began. The estuary English had been replaced by a convincing Israeli-American blend, like a postgrad at Princeton shaking off a past life.

The drinks arrived and Cleo looked around at the scattering of other diners. She said, 'You brought me here for a history lesson?'

Max admired her ventriloquism. Her accent was slowly shifting back. Once more the dual citizen from North London.

'Who says this isn't just a pleasant surprise.'

'Rumour is that Saul Northcliffe is recruiting his own private army at the JIC. You're one of them now?'

'If I was, do you think I'd tell you?'

'I'll take that as a yes.'

'What happened in Paris?'

'Apart from losing my British citizenship?'

'Yes.'

'The plan happened, Max. Just as I told you. My side did their bit of horse-trading and then I was released back into the wild.'

'Your cover was blown. I imagined you in Tel Aviv with a desk job and a nice two-bedroom semi in the suburbs.'

'Cleo Watson the British-Israeli political consultant is finished. Dr Charlotte Weizmann the Israeli scientist is not.'

'Does it ever end?' said Max. 'When do you stop being other people and start being yourself?'

'Is that a question or a statement?'

'Both.'

Cleo smiled. 'Scarlet stays hidden, SIS gets humiliated, Saul Northcliffe wins. Max Archer the man of principle sells his soul to British intelligence. I never thought I'd see the day.'

Max didn't say anything. He saw himself next to Scarlet in St James's Park. Once upon a time he'd believed that history was a random collision of different events. He studied counterfactuals, history branching off into hundreds of other formulations. Then he saw the handwritten card on his desk again and the first meeting in the Holland Park flat and wondered, deep down, if he'd known from the very beginning.

'Spying is never pure,' said Max, at last. 'Scarlet wanted absolution for her sins and for the world to know about Otto Spengler's role at Auschwitz. I wanted a new life. She found a way to achieve both.'

'If Hercules was all she cared about, why bother writing the rest?'

'Her daughter was dead. The rest of the memoir wasn't for the world. It was for me.' Max paused, fussing with his coffee cup. 'She really never told you?'

'She was a spy. She was pretty good at keeping secrets.'

'And Tel Aviv wanted you to work with her?'

'Yes.'

'Will they reveal the rest of the memoir?'

'Who's asking? Her grandson or MI5's newest NOC?'

'I'm asking.'

'Some secrets have more power if they stay secret. Scarlet King's life is one of them. That's presuming I have a copy.'

'You did the original scans. I bet Mossad has a file on a computer somewhere in Tel Aviv with all the sections saved for posterity.'

'Will you tell anyone else that you met me?'

'I could ask you the same question.'

Cleo spotted a look in his eye. She was curious. 'I'm good, Max, but not enough for Five to send you just on my account. What are you really doing here?'

There was no point delaying it further. Max reached down into his bag. He took out a small object and placed it on the table.

'This,' he said solemnly, looking at the small urn containing the ashes of Scarlet King. 'This is why I'm really here.'

59

The Jaguar XF scythed through the quiet village roads and stopped outside the tumbledown cottage with the bicycles outside. The protection officer performed the usual manoeuvre. The passenger door opening just before the vehicle was stationary.

Saul had seen the trick performed whenever the Prime Minister's motorcade arrived in Downing Street. He always marvelled at the fluency of it. He felt mildly embarrassed now at the flummery of his arrival home, like a minor royal. He got out and nodded to the member of Specialist Protection and then watched as the Jaguar pulled away. There was a uniformed member of Thames Valley Police who took over bodyguard duties when he was home, forced to endure the night with nothing more than a Glock 17 and Heckler & Koch G36C. Saul always offered him a cup of tea and force-fed him KitKats from his secret stash in the garage. The wrappers had been recently discovered by one of his daughters and both of them had endured an hour on the evils of sugar. Saul was still earning his redemption.

'Evening.'

'Evening.' Saul smiled. 'Thirsty? Hungry? In need of new reading material? Any or all of the above?'

'All good, boss. I'll knock if I need anything.'

'Made of sterner stuff than me. Have a good one. There's a key under the plant pot and ciggies in the bottom drawer on the left should the mood take you.'

'Cheers, boss.'

Saul entered the warmth of the cottage. He smelled the pungent aroma of something healthy and, probably, vegan. He shrugged off his coat and warmed his hands. He put on his at-home smile, so different from the bulldog scowl of Thames House. One daughter was out. Another was brewing the second batch of kale and avocado smoothies. Saul rolled out his usual jokes before sampling the concoction and forcing his way through a salad. Pudding consisted of berries and green tea.

He escaped to his home office half an hour later. He checked the door was locked, lit the small open fire and then found his favourite vinyl record – *Electric Ladyland* by Jimi Hendrix – and used the sonic overload as cover. He ate two Lion bars hidden in the bookcase and a packet of salt and vinegar crisps stashed in the desk drawer, before banishing the crumbs and pouring a finger of Scotch. He sat back in his armchair and closed his eyes to the solo from 'All Along the Watchtower'.

Eventually, Saul roused himself. He walked over to the safe hidden behind the painting on the far wall and typed in the passcode. Inside was a jiffy bag containing the various items from the flat on Île de la Cité near Notre-Dame: the notebook, the photograph album, the letter, the birth certificate and the Order of Lenin medal. Saul closed the safe and replaced the painting. He sipped at his Scotch as he read the letter again, still entranced by the orthographic style of the writing, with its curves and flow, each wisp of ink as delicate as a paintbrush.

At the top was the crest of 10 Downing Street. 'TOP SECRET' stamped beneath in faded red ink. Saul read on:

DRAFT MEMORANDUM 412A
SUBJECT: Operation SCARLET
DATE: 21 July 1940

With the imminent establishment of the Special Operations Executive – known under the cover names of the Joint Technical Board or Inter-Service Research Bureau – I am writing to faithfully record the details of the initial phase of Operation SCARLET for posterity. This note is strictly embargoed and must never be released publicly without my prior express permission.

Following the announcement of the Molotov-Ribbentrop Pact in 1939, a woman approached me through Frederick Lindemann and identified herself as Miss Scarlet King. Her papers were in order and she was soon to commence her studies at Lady Margaret Hall in Oxford. Her story was as follows: Miss King claimed that she was, in fact, a Russian national and that her name before she came to England was Miss Anastasia Chekova. She claimed to be working for the NKVD as a so-called 'illegal' operating within the British Empire. As evidence she offered a one-time pad and various other accoutrements of her secret life used

*to contact her handlers in Moscow. She said she was
herself Jewish and morally disturbed – indeed repulsed –
by the Soviet alliance with Herr Hitler and the Nazis.*

*As First Lord of the Admiralty at the time, I was
forced into a grave decision. The Molotov–Ribbentrop
Pact meant that the Soviets were, at that moment, our
mortal enemies. While the presence of an enemy agent in
Britain was usually cause for the harshest of
punishments, the possible military advantage of using
Miss Chekova as a double or, indeed, triple agent
impressed itself upon me and Lindemann. Miss Chekova
also had further worrying information regarding the
scale of Soviet penetration of our intelligence services,
informing me that Cambridge University had been used
as a recruiting ground in the thirties for Soviet agents
under the tutelage of a fellow Russian illegal called
Mr Theodore Maly.*

*Given this information, I decided that sharing Miss
Chekova's identity with either the Security Service or
the Secret Intelligence Service risked compromising the
agent and allowing the news of her defection to reach the
ears of Marshal Stalin and the NKVD. That, I realized,
would surely result in her eventual execution and render
her useless as an asset valuable to Great Britain and Her
Empire.*

*As First Lord of the Admiralty, my portfolio
encompassed Naval Intelligence. I therefore decided that
Operation SCARLET – my personal cryptonym; the
operation was too sensitive even to merit a cover name –
would be run personally by me with the assistance of
Rear-Admiral Godfrey, then, as now, the Director of
Naval Intelligence at the Admiralty who would be Miss
King's 'Control'.*

On subsequently leaving the Admiralty, I continued to run Operation SCARLET with Rear-Admiral Godfrey. Our mission was always clear and specific. By allowing Miss Chekova to retain her cover identity as 'Scarlet King' and to work, to all outside eyes, as a natural-born Briton within our intelligence services, we could use her as a vessel to feed disinformation to the Soviet side and harvest valuable intelligence regarding Marshal Stalin's plans and stratagems. That is, indeed, what we proceeded to do.

Many future historians may well question my judgement. Some may indeed demand that Miss Chekova should have been interned or executed along with other enemy agents on our shores. But the fact that she herself defected to our side in moral outrage at the Soviet collusion with Hitler demonstrated to me a moral temper and character which I then, as now, thought could be of considerable value. Indeed, the terms of our arrangement were not clouded by sentiment. In order to maintain her cover at all times, and retain the trust of her Soviet paymasters, it was agreed that Operation SCARLET would never be officially acknowledged by me or Rear-Admiral Godfrey and certainly never by His Majesty's Government. If she was caught, then she would face the consequences alone. Neither the Admiralty, Naval Intelligence nor 10 Downing Street would ever vouch for her existence.

To serve a foreign land on such terms does to me represent the highest and noblest form of courage imaginable. I write this brief missive out of guilt and conscience and in the hope of salvaging her reputation for the history books rather than to ameliorate any suffering – presently or in the future – in this her earthly life.

This is a true and factual account of all my dealings with Miss Anastasia Chekova and Operation SCARLET.

<u>**WSC**</u>

Prime Minister
10 Downing Street
London
SW1A 2AA

'WSC'. Winston S. Churchill.

Saul had many further questions. How had Scarlet obtained this? Was the memorandum ever sent? To whom would it be sent? Was it real or a very elaborate forgery by Department 2 of Directorate S? Had Churchill really run his own secret operation with the Head of Naval Intelligence and after an introduction from Frederick Lindemann, better known to history as Lord Cherwell, the first Viscount Cherwell or simply 'the Prof'?

Either way, it was irrelevant now. The past was past. The precise chronology was unknowable. Saul took another sip of Scotch and then walked over to the fireplace. He looked at the letter one last time and then began consigning it all to the flames. The notebook first, then the photograph album, then the birth certificate, finally the letter. The Order of Lenin medal would be kept as a souvenir. He finished his Scotch and texted Lucas Harper with the agreed codeword that all traces of Scarlet King had been expunged. Then he left his study and checked the door was locked behind him. He brewed a cup of tea and took a sugar-free oat biscuit from the tin. At last, he went to bed.

Saul Northcliffe closed his eyes and tried to forget all about the small bird-like lady with a story to tell. He dreamed of Nazis on the run and British agents on their tail. Scarlet King, Anastasia Chekova, Operation Scarlet, Christopher Sewell, Aunt Maria, Churchill and Stalin – in time, it would certainly be a tale to tell the grandkids.

But that was the problem of being a spy. The best stuff could never be told. He saw himself sitting at Scarlet's kitchen table and then rubbed the memory from his mind.

Operation Tempest was over.

60

They walked until they reached the centre of the city. The place hummed with the past. Max imagined these streets filling with Mozart, Beethoven, Brahms, Freud and Kafka. He saw spies watering here as they did in Istanbul, one of those liminal places where war was conducted in brush passes and signal sites and down alleyways with secret codenames and paroles.

They stopped, at last, and Max took the small urn from his jacket pocket. Cleo reached up and removed the lid. It was a calm night. There was no breeze to make this ugly. Max scoured the streets for police or officialdom. He saw no one.

'Ready?' said Cleo.

'Yes.'

This city was a fitting final resting place. Scarlet King was a woman of many names, after all. Scattering her ashes in London or Moscow would have been futile. She needed a spot where opposites met. This was a place that had no set allegiance, the neutral ground of spies rather than soldiers. Spooks were middlemen, fixers, the homeless souls, standing at the edge of life and refusing to join in. A tribe set apart from the rest.

Max sprinkled the ashes on the bare streets. He watched as the particles settled into the fabric of the city. That's all they were in the end, Max knew, flesh and blood turned into little urns of dust. No matter how big a life, death was the great leveller. That's all they'd ever be.

'What now?' said Cleo.

Max looked across the square. He saw her for a moment: a little snowy-haired lady skulking in the shadows and smiling through the gloom. He checked again, but the bird-like lady was gone. He thought of the professor from Moscow State University and the reason he was here in Vienna. He imagined Emma in California and Kessler tending his allotment and Saul Northcliffe tucked up in his Oxfordshire cottage. He thought of Oliver's last moments and Scarlet's final bequest.

The past was gone. History was finished. The future was now before him.

He took a deep breath and dried his palms against his trousers.

Showtime.

Acknowledgements

I am indebted to the work of numerous intelligence historians and non-fiction writers who I have consulted in the writing of *The Scarlet Papers*. A special mention must go to Dr Charlie Hall and his PhD thesis titled 'British Exploitation of German Science and Technology from War to Post-War, 1943–1948' from the University of Kent which was invaluable in furnishing crucial details about UK involvement in the hunt for Nazi scientists after the war.

Below are some of the other sources I've consulted during the research for this novel:

Books

Andrew, Christopher, *The Defence of the Realm: The Authorised History of MI5*, Allen Lane, 2009

Aldrich, Richard J., *GCHQ: The Uncensored History of Britain's Most Secret Intelligence Agency*, William Collins, 2019

Aldrich, Richard J. & Cormac, Rory, *The Black Door: Spies, Secret Intelligence and British Prime Ministers*, William Collins, 2016

Anonymous, *SOE Manual: How to be an Agent in Occupied Europe*, William Collins, 2014

Belton, Catherine, *Putin's People: How the KGB Took Back Russia and Then Took on the West*, William Collins, 2020

Burrow, John, *A History of Histories: Epics, Chronicles, Romances and Inquiries from Herodotus and Thucydides to the Twentieth Century*, Knopf, 2007

Blair, Tony, *A Journey*, Hutchinson, 2010

Blake, Heidi, *From Russia with Blood: Putin's Ruthless Killing Campaign and Secret War on the West*, William Collins, 2019

Corera, Gordon: *The Art of Betrayal: Life and Death in the British Secret Service*, Weidenfeld & Nicolson, 2011; *Intercept: The Secret History of Computers and Spies*, Weidenfeld & Nicolson, 2015; *Russians Among Us: Sleeper Cells, Ghost Stories and the Hunt for Putin's Agents*, HarperCollins, 2020; *The Illegal: The Hunt for a Russian Spy in Post-War London*, Amazon Publishing, 2018

Churchill, Winston S., *The Grand Alliance: The Second World War, Volume 3*, Cassell & Co., 1950

Carr, Edward Hallett, *What is History?*, University of Cambridge & Penguin Books, 1961

Connor, Ken, *Ghost Force: The Secret History of the SAS*, Weidenfeld & Nicolson, 1998

Dorril, Stephen, *MI6: Fifty Years of Special Operations*, Fourth Estate, 2001

Evans, Richard J., *In Defence of History*, Granta, 1997; *Altered Pasts: Counterfactuals in History*, Little, Brown, 2014

Evans, Harold, *My Paper Chase: True Stories of Vanished Times: An Autobiography*, Little, Brown, 2009

Feinstein, Andrew, *The Shadow World: Inside the Global Arms Trade*, Farrar, Straus and Giroux, 2011

Ferguson, Niall, (ed.), *Virtual History: Alternatives and Counterfactuals*, Penguin, 2011

Fox, Amaryllis, *Life Undercover: Coming of Age in the CIA*, Penguin Random House USA, 2019

Gilbert, Martin, *In Search of Churchill: A Historian's Journey*, Wiley, 1997

Gilbert, Martin, *'Never Despair'. Winston S. Churchill 1945–1965*, Cornerstone, 1988

Grey, Stephen, *The New Spymasters: Inside the Modern World of Espionage from the Cold War to Global Terror*, St Martin's Press, 2015

Harding, Luke, *Shadow State: Murder, Mayhem and Russia's Remaking of the West*, Guardian Faber Publishing, 2020

Hayes, Paddy, *Queen of Spies: Daphne Park, Britain's Cold War Spy Master*, Gerald Duckworth & Co. Ltd, 2015

Hastings, Max, *The Secret War: Spies, Codes and Guerrillas 1939–1945*, William Collins, 2015

Harris, Robert, *Selling Hitler: The Story of the Hitler Diaries*, Arrow, 1996

Higgins, Eliot, *We Are Bellingcat: An Intelligence Agency for the People*, Bloomsbury Publishing, 2021

Hodges, Andrew, *Alan Turing: The Enigma*, Vintage, 2014

Jacobson, Annie, *Operation Paperclip: The Secret Intelligence Program That Brought Nazi Scientists to America*, Little, Brown, 2014; *Surprise, Kill, Vanish: The Definitive History of Secret CIA Assassins, Armies and Operators*, Little, Brown, 2019

Kessler, Ronald, *The FBI*, Pocket Books, 1993

Kuper, Simon, *The Happy Traitor: Spies, Lies and Exile in Russia*, Profile Books, 2021

Macintyre, Ben, *Agent Sonya*, Penguin, 2021; *Agent Zigzag*, Bloomsbury Publishing, 2016; *Double Cross*, Bloomsbury Paperbacks, 2012; *Operation Mincemeat*, Bloomsbury Publishing, 2021; *A Spy Among Friends*, Bloomsbury Publishing, 2014; *The Spy and the Traitor*, Penguin, 2019

Marcus, Tom, *Soldier Spy*, Michael Joseph, 2016

Mitrokhin, Vasili and Andrew, Christopher, *The Miktrokhin Archive: The KGB in Europe and the West*, Allen Lane, 1999

Norton-Taylor, Richard, *The State of Secrecy: Spies and the Media in Britain*, Bloomsbury Publishing, 2020

Olson, James M., *To Catch a Spy: The Art of Counterintelligence*, Georgetown University Press, 2019

Preston, Diana, *Eight Days at Yalta: How Churchill, Roosevelt and Stalin Shaped the Post-War World*, Picador, 2019

Preston, John, *Fall: The Mystery of Robert Maxwell*, Penguin, 2021

Philby, Kim, *My Silent War*, Arrow, 2018

Philpott, Colin, *Secret Wartime Britain*, Pen & Sword Military, 2018

Pincher, Chapman, *A Web of Deception: The Spycatcher Affair*, Sidgwick & Jackson, 1987; *Their Trade is Treachery*, Sidgwick & Jackson, 1981

Reynolds, David, *In Command of History: Churchill Fighting and Writing the Second World War*, Penguin, 2005

Robert, Wallace, *Spycraft: Inside the CIA's Top Secret Spy Lab*, E.P. Dutton, 2009

Roberts, Andrew (ed.), *What Might Have Been*, Weidenfeld & Nicolson, 2004

Seldon, Anthony, *10 Downing Street: The Illustrated History*, HarperCollins Illustrated, 1999; *Blair Unbound*, Simon & Schuster UK, 2008

Sisman, Adam, *Hugh Trevor-Roper: The Biography*, Weidenfeld & Nicolson, 2010

Turnbull, Ron, *From the Flying Squad to Investigating War Crimes*, Pen & Sword, 2019

Trevor-Roper, Hugh, *The Last Days of Hitler*, Pan Macmillan, 2012; *The Wartime Journals*, I.B. Tauris, 2012

Urban, Mark, *UK Eyes Alpha*, Faber and Faber, 1997; *Task Force Black*, Abacus, 2011; *The Skripal Files*, Macmillan, 2018

Walters, Guy, *Hunting Evil*, Bantam, 2009; *Nazis, Spies and Fakes*, Lockhart Armstrong, 2013

West, Nigel: *At Her Majesty's Secret Service: The Chiefs of Britain's Intelligence Service MI6*, Greenhill Books, 2006; *Spycraft Secrets*, The History Press, 2016

Weiner, Tim, *Enemies: A History of the FBI*, Random House, 2013; *Legacy of Ashes: The History of the CIA*, Doubleday, 2007

The Scarlet Papers has been a monumental project. I couldn't have completed this project without the support of my family. Thank you to the team at Penguin too for getting this book out into the world, and to Conrad Williams at Blake Friedmann for all his support, advice and wisdom on the screen side.

And, finally, a particular thanks to Euan Thorney-croft of A.M. Heath. Euan was the one who saw the potential in my spy writing many moons ago, shepherded this project all the way and without whom this book would not exist. This book represents the end of a very long, but worthwhile, road – thank you, Euan.